C0001502S1

About the Author

Marjory Davidson has been a correspondent in New York, Washington, Moscow and the Far East, and a staff writer on the *Sunday Express*, *Daily Mail* and the *Sun*, which she left to write *In Love and Judgement*. Today she is the Royal Correspondent of the *Weekend Times* and combines reporting what she describes as 'the most fascinating running story of the late 20th century' with writing books she hopes people will not want to put down.

IN LOVE AND JUDGEMENT

Marjory Davidson

This first hardcover edition published in Great Britain 1995 by
SEVERN HOUSE PUBLISHERS LTD of
9–15 High Street, Sutton, Surrey SM1 1DF.
by arrangement with Pocket Books,
an imprint of Simon & Schuster Ltd.
First published in the USA 1995 by
SEVERN HOUSE PUBLISHERS INC of
425 Park Avenue, New York, NY 10022.

Copyright © 1994 by Marjory Davidson

All rights reserved. The rights of Marjory Davidson to be identified as
author of this work have been asserted by her in accordance with
section 77 and 78 of the Copyright Designs and Patents Act 1988.

British Library Cataloguing in Publication Data
Davidson, Marjory
  In Love and Judgement. - New ed
  I. Title
  823.914 [F]

  ISBN 0-7278-4720-1

All situations in this publication are fictitious and
any resemblance to living persons is purely coincidental.

Typeset by Hewer Text Composition Services, Edinburgh.
Printed and bound in Great Britain by
Hartnolls Ltd, Bodmin, Cornwall.

*For Edwin and another Marjory
whose happiness was dappled*

To JS

I loved you, so I drew these tides of men into my hands and wrote my will across the sky in stars

T. E. Lawrence

Of some things we feel that we know that we are certain: we know, and we know that we know. There is something that gives a click inside us, a bell that strikes twelve, when the hands of our mental clock have swept the dial and meet over the meridian hour.

William James

If we had a keen vision and a feeling of all ordinary life, it would be like hearing the grass grow and the squirrel's heart beat, and we should die of the roar that lies on the other side of silence.

George Eliot

Acknowledgements

Sue MacLelland read this book before anyone and when I had written it I had the good fortune to work at Simon & Schuster with Jo Frank and Lucy Ferguson, who both knew how to draw from me what the story still needed. In the final edit I worked closely with Kati Nicholl, whose encyclopaedic knowledge of the fabric of fiction added immeasurably to mine.

At an earlier stage Judy Paterson, the manager of the Stockbridge Bookshop in Edinburgh, read drafts and returned them promptly with her lively and pertinent comments.

Douglas Glauch, who recently retired as Sales Director of Richard Dunston (Hessle) Limited, took me clambering over a container ship in the course of construction at The Haven Shipyard, Hull, and checked the shipbuilding chapters for accuracy.

During her time as Press and Public Relations Officer for the Marie Stopes Clinic, June Macpherson briefed me on the original work of the Clinic, and her successor, Frances Perrow, later checked that section of the manuscript.

Katrina Potter and John Sloggie gave me the run of the fabulously refurbished Dryburgh Abbey Hotel, St Boswells, which became the model for Auchinvreck.

Martin Waghorn understood what I was doing and is the most perceptive banker I know.

And Barry Kernon, of Kernon & Co., my accountant for many years and good friend whose thoughtful counsel is always graced with such good humour, listened to me with patience for longer than either he or I realised it would take in the beginning.

Contents

PART ONE

1927–1931

Chapter One

Edinburgh and Glasgow – August, 1927

In a stuffy room on the top floor of the Queen Hotel in Edinburgh, 18-year-old Helen Randolph sat on the edge of a lumpy bed inspecting two summer dresses which hung limply against a tallboy. One, in green moygashel, a fashionable shift with a hip belt, had been bought at Lewis's in Glasgow. Its companion, a copy in yellow gingham, had been handsewn by her mother just before she died. They were the only frocks she possessed. Like everyone else, Helen had been taken by surprise by the heatwave which had the whole country in its thrall. She had not expected to wear dresses quite so often in Edinburgh and though she had brought a suit and two hand-knitted jumpers, the heat had forced her to live in her dresses these past six days – and the constant wear was beginning to show. The gingham one looked near collapse, so it would have to be the moygashel, which at least retained some of its pristine crispness. It would look even better if she ironed it. But she didn't have an iron and anyway she wasn't any good at ironing. Her mother had always ironed her things and laid them out neatly for her. Her teeth sank slowly into her lower lip and all the pain of recent days darkened her eyes. Then she remembered she had a hat – a really smart cloche – in exactly the same pale olive shade as her moygashel. That would cheer it up. She sprang from the bed, her long slender legs bearing her

3

across the room in fluid, graceful movements. She prized the wardrobe open and reached for the hat on the shelf above the hanging space. Then she walked, more slowly now, towards a rickety, heavily-scratched dressing-table and sat down.

She had never been able to bring herself to have her long golden hair cut in the fashionable shingle so many girls were wearing. Instead, she rolled it up so that she always looked cool and tidy when she went out but could still indulge in the sensuous pleasure of brushing it for hours. Now, getting it to stay inside the cloche was proving difficult. As her fingers pushed and struggled with her hair, wisps began to escape down the back of her neck.

'Go in and stay,' she ordered, noticing how flushed her face was becoming. No, she thought. I mustn't look like a beetroot. Not today.

She gave up the struggle and stared at her reflection as she waited for the colour to fade. Her face was a flawless oval and her skin so smooth and clear people said it could have sold Pear's soap. It made a perfect setting for her brilliant, jewel-green eyes with their slight enticing slant. People also said there was no mistaking that Helen Randolph had her mother's eyes. Resting her face in the palms of her hands as she watched the colour die away from her cheeks, Helen wondered if any of her features resembled her father.

Her mind drifted back to that dark hospital ward, the air pungent with disinfectant, her mother's face grey as ashes against starch-white pillows.

'How are you, Mummy?' she asked, her voice brittle with unshed tears.

'I'll be better in a little while. So much better. All the world will be better in a little while,' said Kirsty Randolph. The strength had gone from her voice, which was somewhere between a croak and a whisper, and

4

there was a quiet stillness and serenity about her mother which Helen had never seen before and it frightened her. It wasn't normal. It wasn't something that was part of her mother and she could share. She sensed it taking her mother away from her. She wanted her mother to be angry and shouting at her. Cross. *That* was normal.

'You mustn't leave me, Mother,' she blurted out, sensing now that she had to fight, *she* had to be angry and cross and shouting to save Kirsty. 'You mustn't leave me,' she cried. 'You mustn't die. Not now Aunt Cath's gone. I'll be all alone if you die.'

'No, no, you will not be alone . . .' Though her mother's smile was etiolated, a radiant ethereal light shone in her eyes. 'No. There is someone to whom you can go . . .'

'Who?' Helen was puzzled.

'Your father.'

'But − but my father's dead,' cried Helen, bewildered. Her mother must be delirious. 'You said he was killed by the Zulus in Natal before I was born.'

'No,' said Kirsty, shaking her head slowly, a glint of triumph in her eyes. 'Your father is not dead. Your father, Thomas Randolph, lives in Edinburgh in a fine big house in Moray Place. *Lord* Randolph,' Kirtsy's voice brimmed with tenderness despite being so hoarse. 'The Supreme Court judge.'

Now Helen knew that the fever had driven all sanity from Kirsty's soul. 'Mother, please.' Her shaking hands tightened around her mother's.

'It was in His Lordship's house that I worked, waiting at his table in Edinburgh and at his summer place in Rhu . . .'

A hint of colour had returned to Kirsty's cheeks and the pride of life to her voice, and Helen, transfixed, knew that her mother had not gone mad. Her fingers eased their grip and she sat stone-still, waiting. Her mind's eye recalled the picture her mother kept on the sideboard of the handsome officer she had believed was her father – Captain Thomas Randolph of the King's Own Highland Hussars, who had been a guest in the house of the 'distinguished iron master' (her mother's description of her employer) where her mother had been a table-maid and they had fallen in love at first sight. Her mother had told her the story of her brief romance, and marriage, and widowhood so often. And it had all been a lie.

'I was fourteen when I entered service in His Lordship's houses. His Lordship was such a handsome man.'

'You always said he was old,' said Helen laconically.

'No, not old. Older. Thomas will never be old.' Helen could not go on looking at her mother. She bowed her head, feeling slightly sick. 'And he had such wonderful eyes,' Kirsty continued. 'Soft and warm and brown – eyes a woman could swim in till she drowned. But he was unhappy. Her Ladyship was a shrew, a cold, hard woman and he had no children to bring him any happiness. I longed to comfort him, Helen. Oh, I think I loved him from the start. But it was two years before he noticed me.'

Kirsty's voice fell to a dreamy whisper as she remembered the summer afternoon in Rhu in 1906 when the sun had banished all the clouds from the sky and the roses were in full bloom, filling the air with their perfume. 'Her Ladyship had gone to Glasgow for the day and all the other servants had been given the afternoon off. I was sitting in the garden on a bench by the lily pond when he came and sat by me. I got up at once to leave. "No, stay by me a while, Kirsty," he said. It was the first time I had ever heard him say my name. And it sounded so beautiful – it made *me* feel beautiful and special . . .'

Listening to her, Helen felt she had lost her mother already as Kirsty retreated into her secret, alien past. 'For a while he just sat by me without saying a word. And I knew I would remember everything about that day. The bees – big fat bees with shiny black coats – humming in and out among the roses; a lawn mower somewhere and the scent of the new mown grass wafting in the air. I began to tremble inside, but I had been trained to control my feelings so they didn't show. Then one of His Lordship's hands reached into my lap and took one of mine. There was so much strength in his hand . . .' Kirsty took a deep, shuddering breath. 'All the strength a woman could ever need. I was happy and frightened and overpowered, all at the same time. Then I looked at His Lordship and all my fears were swept away. No one had ever looked at me the way Thomas did that day . . .' Kirsty's voice was fading to a whisper now and was all the more frightening for its intensity. 'I knew I could trust myself to him from that first day.'

'And what happened when you found out you were expecting me?' demanded Helen, stunned by her mother's revelations.

The colour was now fleeing from Kirsty's face faster than the light at winter sunset and her strength was fading with the effort of telling her story.

'Mother . . .' Helen leaned forward and stroked her mother's forehead, her voice softer now. 'What happened?'

'After I had begun to show, Her Ladyship summoned me to her sitting-room. She said – she called me . . . she called me a slut!' Kirsty swallowed the word and turned away from Helen, her voice strangled now. 'She said I was no longer fit to live in a decent house another day and she turned me on to the street there and then. That woman hated me, Helen. She cursed me . . . said my parents would not rest in their graves. That I and my child would be outcasts. Oh, Helen . . . Helen . . .'

Helen felt a sudden compassion for what her mother

had suffered. The tears were massing behind her eyes when she asked: 'And Lord . . . didn't my father come looking for you after you had left his house?'

'I never saw Thomas again . . .' There were tears now in Kirsty's dimming eyes. 'Two years later I read in the papers that Her Ladyship had died and eighteen months after that I read that . . . that Thomas had married again . . .'

'Married again!' whispered Helen, her heart wrenched by the callousness of it all. 'And that is all there was?'

'All? That was *everything*. For all time.' Kirsty's voice rose again and the colour flickered on her face anew. 'Everything and for all time. When you love a man like Thomas you can never love another man and I never wanted another man after him. In my heart I felt I was married to Thomas and I knew enough about the law to change my name by Deed Poll before you were born so that you would bear his name. One day, when you love someone, you will understand . . .' Kirsty's voice faded again. 'Now you must go to him and tell him who you are. He will love you, Helen. I was nobody, just a poor servant girl. But you are somebody. You are *his* daughter, a judge's daughter. Your father has no children by his second marriage, either. Go and claim your inheritance and your place with him in the bright world of society. It is where you belong.'

'But it's you I want, not a father I've never met,' Helen cried. 'And how can I prove I am his daughter?'

'And take the luckenbooth with you.' Helen knew her mother was talking about the silver heart-shaped brooch she kept in her tiny jewel box. In the early eighteenth century luckenbooths were exchanged between lovers on betrothal and later pinned on to the baby's shawl to protect the child from evil spirits. 'His Lordship gave it to me after our last time together. On the back of it

8

you will see the initials W and H. They stand for William and Helen, His Lordship's parents, and it was given by his father to his mother on their betrothal and pinned on your shawl when you were a baby. Thomas knew what was about to happen to me, though he could not say. But I know he wanted you to have it. I called you after your grandmother and he will recognise both your name and the luckenbooth . . .' Kirsty's voice lapsed into silence and she drifted in and out of consciousness until she died the next day.

Helen had sat very still, staring at her mother's body. Kirsty looked different now. Death wasn't white. It was grey, the colour of ashes . . .

The day after the funeral Helen asked permission to take a week off from her work as a clerkess with the Pier Shipping Line in Glasgow.

'I wish to visit my mother's only living relative in Edinburgh,' she told her employer, Harry Dunlop, when he stopped by her desk shortly after she had made her request to his secretary, Miss Austin.

'I'm sure that will be a great comfort to both of you at a time like this,' said Mr Dunlop.

'I hope so,' said Helen with a slight smile, responding to the unexpected warmth and kindness in his electric blue eyes. Though she had worked for the Pier Line for two years, this was only her third personal contact with Harry Dunlop and, in spite of his reputation for ruthlessness, she felt drawn to him in that split-second.

'If you feel you need any more time in Edinburgh, just let Miss Austin know,' Harry Dunlop said.

'Thank you.' Helen flushed. She was conscious of a dozen pairs of eyes intently watching her exchange with her employer and she didn't want to be singled out. In the days since her mother had died she had become acutely aware that she was now different from the other girls — she was illegitimate, a bastard — and she didn't want to be an outcast. Or different. They had all rallied round, especially Elizabeth. That Elizabeth Campbell, bright, wealthy and expensively educated, had chosen to be her friend still amazed her. She was the daughter of Mr Dunlop's lawyer and soon she would go to Glasgow University. Elizabeth came from a very different world, yet it was she who had come to stay with Helen in the flat in Partick until the funeral. But she would never stay again or be my friend if she knew I was illegitimate, thought Helen, meeting Elizabeth's questioning gaze across the room when Mr Dunlop had moved on.

The next day she took the train to Edinburgh, where she stayed at the Queen Hotel because it stood at one end of Forres Street, and Moray Place, where Lord Randolph lived, was at the other. It cost a lot more than a boarding house, but in the steaming heat it paid off, enabling her to spy out the land and be only a short walk from respite in the hotel before resuming surveillance of her quarry and his lair.

From behind a beech tree in the gardens of Moray Place, Helen observed Lord Randolph leaving his house at ten in the morning and four in the afternoon each day. She followed him around the grand, colonnaded plazas of the New Town down to the mean, working-class streets of Stockbridge; lingered in doorways watching him when he looked in shop windows; hovered when he cashed a cheque in a bank. As she shadowed him, Helen got a glimpse of another world. Gazing up at the elegant glass and black wrought iron gas lamps flanking the steps up to the great oak door of Lord Randolph's house in the twilight of a summer evening, she imagined herself descending them in a glamorous evening gown on her way to a grand ball, the lamplight catching the pearls and diamonds at her throat and her ears . . . returning from a shopping trip in an expensive limousine, a chauffeur bearing her hat boxes up the steps. She would be educated and go to University like Elizabeth Campbell. And young men who wanted to rise in the world would vie with each other for her hand in marriage. Because she was no longer the daughter of an unknown soldier but the daughter of a distinguished man of power and influence.

But she had still to tell him so, Helen reminded herself as the last wisps of hair finally obeyed and stayed tucked inside her hat. She had not meant to let so many days slide by and remain silent. But there had not been a right moment. At seventy-five, Lord Randolph still cut an intimidating figure who made people hold back from approaching him. But today was Helen's last chance. She had to be back at her desk at the Pier Line tomorrow. And if she did not speak to him today, all her hopes and dreams for the future would be lost forever.

Her fingers reached across the dressing-table for a crayon in a gilt case and she leaned closer to the mirror to colour her lips a vibrant claret red. But what if *he* didn't approve?

'Men have no respect for painted women,' her mother's words came back.

Her fingers hesitated around the crayon. Then, slowly, she withdrew the lipstick from the edge of her mouth and put the top back on its case.

Somewhere over the trees in Charlotte Square a church clock announced the time was a quarter-to-ten in clear, ringing tones. Helen checked it as she fastened her mother's dainty gold watch to her wrist. Then she pinned the luckenbooth on her dress and walked towards the cheval mirror where she studied her reflection. The moygashel no longer seemed well-worn and the world was bright with hope and pride. She swept out of

11

the room and down into the already breathless heat of the street.

It was cooler in the gardens of Moray Place, in the shade of stalwart oak and beech and sycamore.

A gardener sweeping a path looked up and bowed to her.

'Good morning,' she greeted him, smiling confidently. The gardens were private and he obviously thought that she already lived in Moray Place.

Her steps slowed as she neared the beech where she normally watched her father leave his house. As she gazed up at the portico, a knot began to form in her stomach. Be calm, she willed herself, her brow puckering as her eyes concentrated on that great door.

She heard the first stroke of ten ring out on the church clock, then the second. The door flew open and Lord Randolph descended the steps at the measured, dignified pace of a general inspecting a guard of honour. He had been a Brigadier on Earl Haig's staff in the Great War and he retained the straight spine, erect bearing and immaculate appearance of the high-ranking officer. His cavalry twills were plumbline-straight and his navy blazer, its brass buttons shining, looked as pristine as the day he bought it. Only his Homburg, worn at a jaunty angle over abundant white hair, had the air of having been in his possession long. He strode to the edge of the pavement, turned and looked up to the first floor window where his second, much younger wife, a dark beauty, was seated, smiling graciously. He raised his Homburg and bowed to her, then set off at a brisk pace.

Helen shot through the garden gates after him, down the hilly escarpment of Doune Terrace and a steep slum of a lane into Stockbridge, where Lord Randolph went into a newsagent's shop.

Helen stopped outside the shop, her pulse racing. The

12

shop was a long narrow ribbon of a place and the door was wide-open. Lord Randolph stood at the far end, his back to her, speaking to a man behind the counter. If she hung about by the door she could watch him and meet him face-to-face when he came out of the shop. It was perfect. Except she was now so nervous it didn't *feel* perfect.

As Lord Randolph lingered in the shop, the knot in Helen's stomach hardened. Her eyes glazed over the bright colours and cover lines of the magazines on a rack near the door as she clenched and unclenched her hands.

Then he turned and started to walk towards the door.

Helen's spine straightened. Her gaze hugged his face until his eyes met hers. His eyes were as her mother had said – soft, warm, brown 'eyes a woman could swim in till she drowned.' Vulnerable, gentle eyes which belied his public reputation for harsh judgements and excoriating sentences. A tentative smile crept over her face. But as he drew close, all the warmth and light seemed to flee from Lord Randolph's face. The air felt cold. Her mouth felt dry. His nearness was making her feel weak. He stepped from the shop and was at her side. She dug her nails into the palms of her hands and willed herself to speak to him.

'Good morning, Lord Randolph,' she said, mustering an over-bright smile.

He responded with a disdainful, stocktaking look that withered her confidence. Her nails dug deeper into her palms.

'So you know my name,' he spoke with the precise public school accent which had been branded into him at Edinburgh Academy.

'Yes . . . my Lord . . .'

A tramcar rattled and shuddered over the cobble-stones. Two keelies in pursuit of a ball skidded past, snarling abuse at each other. But Helen felt the time

13

had stopped as, eyes glued to Lord Randolph's, she waited.

'Am I right in thinking I have seen you walking the streets in this neighbourhood before today?' Helen thought he sounded friendly.

'Yes, my Lord.'

'It is an offence – '

'I am not a streetwalker, my Lord!' she cried, horrified.

'Then may I ask what is the nature of your business on these streets and with myself in particular?'

He sounded disdainful now, but Helen went bravely on: 'I wish to speak to you, my Lord.'

'My impression is that this is what you appear to be doing.'

She had never imagined it would be so difficult. She took a deep breath. 'My name is Helen Randolph . . .'

Lord Randolph was watching a tramcar shudder towards the bridge over the Water of Leith and did not appear to hear her.

'My Lord,' she said insistently, 'you are my father.' His eyes met hers in one rapid movement and in a naked moment Helen knew her mother's story was true. His eyes were soft and vulnerable again now. Lord Randolph *was* her father, and she had come home to him. Helen felt her heart overflowing with hope and love. Now she was no longer alone; she had a father who would love her and take care of her. And her only sadness was that her mother could not be with them and they could not all be a family together.

'My mother was Kirsty Stewart and I was born on April 2nd, 1909,' she added quickly, smiling confidently. But doubt was now clouding his eyes. Of course, he needed proof that she was who she claimed to be! 'Look, my Lord, you gave my mother this . . .' She tugged the luckenbooth

14

from her dress and held the reverse side up to him. 'See? The initials W. and H. William and Helen. Your parents and my grandparents. My mother worked in your houses and you gave her this brooch. You *are* my father.'

Lord Randolph peered disdainfully down his nose at the luckenbooth.

'When did your mother die?'

'Twelve days ago in Glasgow Infirmary'.

'What was the cause of her death?'

'A fever following a road accident. She told me you were my father on her deathbed and gave me this luckenbooth to show you because she did not want me to be alone. Lord Randolph, you are my only relative. I have no one else. With – without you, I am completely alone in the world.'

'No,' he said dismissively. 'I am *not* your father. That is merely the raving of some delirious woman in her death throes. Now I bid you good-day.' He raised his Homburg and started to walk away.

'No,' cried Helen, desperately grabbing his arm. It felt a lot more fragile than his appearance suggested and this helped to restore her sagging confidence. 'You cannot leave me!'

'If you wish any further words with me, you will let go of my arm immediately, young woman,' Lord Randolph told her icily. Reluctantly, Helen let her hands fall from his arm. 'Do you realise what you are saying by accusing me of being your father? You are accusing me of being an adulterer and a fornicator – '

'I am telling you I am your daughter and that my mother loved you till the day she died.' Helen protested. 'She worshipped you in her heart all her life and died believing that you still loved her. Was she right or wrong? Did she love you in vain?' demanded Helen, emboldened by her desperate plight.

15

Their eyes locked, but his expression was a stone wall, telling her nothing.

'Well?' Helen went on glaring at him.

Lord Randolph stepped closer to her.

'Do you see these two policemen coming this way on the bridge over the Water of Leith?' he asked, lowering his voice, his manner suddenly confidential.

'Yes,' she said warily.

'I am going to walk away from you. And if you make any attempt to follow me or repeat your allegations, I will summon them and you will be arrested on a charge of soliciting. Your punishment will be a term of imprisonment.'

'But you can't do that!'

'I can. And make no mistake, young woman, I will.'

Helen looked towards the two uniformed officers marching steadily towards them, then again at her father whose eyes were now hard as bullets. Lord Randolph meant what he said. Her mother had been right not to tell him about her birth. It would have made no difference to the way he felt about her and he had done nothing to save her mother from being thrown out of his house. How could she have gone on loving him after that?

'Goodbye,' said Lord Randolph, raising his Homburg once more.

Helen had never felt such pain. Coming so soon after the pain of her mother's death and the shock of discovering her illegitimacy, her father's rejection was like the worst pain of all. Until today she had had hope to keep her going: hope that there was someone in the world who would take care of her; hope that she would not be alone. Now that was gone. Extinguished with unmitigated cruelty by a man she wanted to love. She could almost feel the pain physically, paralysing her limbs as well as her will to run after the father who was walking away from her up the hill, his steps tired and heavy as if the encounter had been too much for him. How his figure was stooped, his assurance and erect military bearing gone, and he was leaning heavily on his walking stick. Her mother hadn't lied. Even though he had denied her, Lord Randolph *was* her father and he knew Helen was his daughter. My eyes, she realised. He recognised my eyes. I have my mother's eyes.

She knew now she should have written to her father first, sought an appointment to see him, pretended she a was a distant relative whose father had died, leaving her an orphan. Then she would have been respectable and perhaps she could have found her way into her father's life and gained his protection.

As she watched his figure vanish, a curtain rose up for Helen. She knew then that men could take what they wanted from women and leave the remains, and that love needed courage and had to be fought for.

Chapter Two

Glasgow – July, 1927 to March, 1928

The Broomielaw was the heart of the port of Glasgow. It was here the great liners which sailed the five oceans came to berth, with flags and bunting flying from their masts and yardarms and gleaming decks; where silvered trunks with polished brass locks waited to be loaded, and beautiful women draped in furs, came down the gangways on the arms of rich men. Here foreign statesmen and distinguished envoys were greeted by the Lord Provost and a red carpet in sunshine and in showers. The cargoes of the world came, too, to the great trading place of the Broomielaw. Fine silk from China and Siam, furniture moulded in cane and bamboo grown in the jungles of the East, tea from the plantations of Darjeeling stood beside coal and cast-iron bound from the Clyde for ports all across the Occident and Orient. The air was charged with the scent of foreign parts and men with swarthy skins and dark, flashing eyes who looked at Helen as if they could see her naked through her clothes, made her pink a little and lower the long eyelashes she darkened with a mascara brush each morning.

Helen knew by heart the colours of the flags and the funnels and even the hulls of all the great shipping lines. Cunard liners had red funnels with black tops and their flag was two long pennants – a blue and white saltire in the hoist flown over a narrower one in plain red. Ships

18

of the Canadian Pacific line had buff-coloured funnels, their flags were six red and white chequered squares and their hulls were black with a green waterline. The P and O fleet sailed under a flag quartered diagonally – blue in the hoist, red (fly), white (top) and yellow – and their black-topped white funnels were echoed in black hulls with a white riband. Pier Line ships sailed beneath a flag bearing a large letter – a yellow P set in dark green that matched dark green funnels with yellow tops and a yellow riband on the black hulls.

On the morning after her father's cruel rejection, Helen sat perched on some sacks of grain on the waterfront, watching one of the Pier Line ships packed with immigrants weigh anchor. A thunderstorm had cracked open at three in the morning, lighting the sky with sheets of fire and sending a monsoon down to quench them. The cannoning in the heavens had gone on for hours, exploding the humidity, lowering the temperature, sweeping the atmosphere clean. Eventually the cacophony, the fireworks and the deluge had ceased. Now the morning air was cool and fresh, but the sky, streaked violent crimson on pale aquamarine and spattered with a thousand fragments of red-rimmed grey clouds, still had a blotchy, tear-stained look. Helen raised her swollen eyes to the heavens, and then back to the ship and the relatives left standing on the quayside.

She watched the fluttering white handkerchiefs and tearful faces of the relatives who were being left behind. They were mostly old and they were saying goodbye to grown-up families and small grandchildren, who stood on the decks at their parents' feet; and the look in their rheumy eyes said they wondered if they would ever see their sons and daughters again. Parting was a kind of death and Helen didn't know if it was worse to lose someone who died or someone you would just never see again. Despite the ache in her heart, it reached out compassionately to the elderly relatives on the quay as the ship, coaxed and shepherded by tugs, cleared the dock and eased out into the river.

Perhaps that was what she should do; emigrate to New York. As an employee of the Pier Line, she could get a ticket at a reduced price. But it would only be in Steerage, the cheapest open berth accommodation in the bowels of the ship. She felt a lump come to her throat as she realised there would be no one to wave *her* away and no one to miss her and cry over her in Scotland. Perhaps Elizabeth Campbell and some of the girls from the office would see her off, but they wouldn't miss her, not really, afterwards. Swallowing, she lifted her eyes to the tearful sky and a crushing loneliness filled her soul. The docks and the city streets were full of people, but there was no one for her . . . no one to whom she belonged and could call her own any more.

Last night, in the middle of the storm, when lightning had streaked the sky and the cannon of thunder rent the heavens, she had tiptoed to the kitchen and remembered . . . Ever since she could remember she had come home to a fire burning brightly in the range and her mother, fingers flying with a sewing needle, sitting in a corner by it. Or else her mother would be standing by the kitchen window, rolling out pastry, and the warm scent of baking would be in the air. Her mother's Aunt Cath, whose home it had been until she died two years ago, would be sitting in the other corner by the fire, still in the black she had worn since her husband had been killed in the war with the Germans, her tongue ever-ready to scold or praise. On other days she would come home from school and a giant brass jam pan would be standing on the range and rows of gleaming jars would be waiting to be filled. Her mother would be flushed and harassed and Helen would know she must not speak or distract her. Making jam was high drama. So she would take her place silently by Aunt Cath and watch. Then, if she was good, she was allowed to put her little finger in the tasting pot where her mother kept samples of her jam. And it was warm and sweet and tasted even better than fresh strawberries and raspberries because her mother had made it with so much love. If she was quick, when her mother wasn't looking, she would put her finger in the tasting pot again. Then came the climax when once more she stood silently by Aunt Cath, watching anxiously as her mother counted the jars and pronounced whether she had got more or less pots of jam than she had done the previous year. And finally, when it was all over and her mother had wiped the sweat from her brow and Helen had helped her to tidy-up, they would all sit down and have some of last year's jam with their tea.

Last night, when the heavens were exploding she had sat by the cold, unlit range, clinging to that brass jam pan, her fingers stroking the smooth surface which her mother had so often touched, her life and sanity seeming to depend on this inanimate symbol of her mother's love. In the wildness and terror of the storm raging without and within her, it had become the thing which kept her spirit whole, her mind from fracturing. She had been loved at the beginning of her life – and she would not let the memory of that love go.

Now the day was fully morning-bright and a calmness filled Helen's soul. What she knew for sure now was that *her* life didn't have to be lived at the bottom of Society. There was a far, far better way to live. She had glimpsed it in Edinburgh as she followed her father around the streets of the New Town. A way which meant you lived in a fine house and people looked up to you and treated you with respect.

She was determined now to get on and rise up in the world. With the little money her mother had left she was going to take elocution lessons to get rid of her Glasgow accent and learn shorthand and typing at evening classes. There were lots of opportunities for girls who had shorthand and typing to become secretaries in commercial offices all over Glasgow. But Helen wanted to be more even than a secretary. She wanted to be a businesswoman who made decisions and ran her own company and had a secretary of her own. She knew she had the ability do it but an education and being able to speak properly were important qualifying assets. Then, all she needed was the chance.

As the immigrant ship slipped into the mainstream of the river she jumped down from the grain sacks and shook the chaff from her dress and started to walk slowly past the crates and boxes lining the wharves towards the Pier Line's offices in St Vincent Street.

The streets were getting busier by the minute as office workers like Helen hurried off the tramcars which shuttled up and down the city's hilly streets. Shipyard workers, on the dole because of the decline in orders placed with Clyde yards, were already starting to gather on the street corners where they had acquired golden suntans. It was too early, though, for the matrons, the wives of the prosperous Glasgow bourgeoisie who drank tea and gossiped in Miss Cranston's famous Tearooms, designed by Charles Rennie Mackintosh and the restaurants of the big department stores. But though out of sight now, they were not far away. There were no wide acres separating rich and poor in Glasgow. Vast and splendid wealth co-habited with direst poverty in the inner city into which over a million people were crowded. In the evenings women swathed in jewellery and furs and fine silk stockings rubbed shoulders with the ragged masses. Rich and poor knew each other well by sight in Glasgow.

As she crossed St Vincent Street to the blackened Victorian building across which the words PIER LINE were written in large brass letters placed between two brass rods, Helen hardly noticed the suntanned men, to whom she normally smiled. Her mind was fully occupied.

'Well, look who the East wind's blown in,' Elizabeth Campbell greeted Helen across the big cluttered office where the typists and clerks and clerkesses sat at dark wood tables piled with the stacks of paper it took to send ships around the world. It was a rather dingy, miserable room lined with cardboard drawer files and floored in dark brown linoleum. The only bright spots were the posters of Pier Line ships belching smoke from their funnels on the high seas. 'How are you?' Elizabeth added in a softer tone, concern filling her blue eyes as she drew closer. She was a slim, pale girl whose blonde hair was worn fashionably short and close to her head. She had a lot more money than the other girls in the office and the way she flaunted her expensive and extensive wardrobe – she scarcely seemed to wear the same outfit twice – had caused envy among some of the girls who could hardly wait for her to leave and go to University.

'I'm all right I expect,' said Helen carefully, determined to sound cheerful and in control. 'I'll know better when I've been here for a few hours,' she added, taking off her cloche and hanging it on a peg on a wooden coat rack near the table where she sat. 'What's been happening?'

Elizabeth looked cautiously around the room before she lowered her voice: 'Mr Dunlop and Miss Austin had a big row last week. Nobody knows what was said, but you could hear the sound of their voices right across the office and Miss Austin was all red in the face when she came out of Mr Dunlop's office.'

23

'Maybe he wants to give her the sack,' said Helen hopefully.

Miss Austin was Mr Dunlop's secretary, who ruled the office like a martinet, and was thought by some of the girls to be behind all the recent firings.

'I'll tell you all about it at lunch time,' said Elizabeth, dropping her tone still further as Miss Austin entered the room. 'Shall we have our sandwiches in George Square?'

'Yes, I've brought mine,' said Helen. Sitting down on the hard wood chair beside the table where she worked, she noticed that an order from the Irrewaddy Flotilla Company was at the top of the papers marked as needing urgent attention.

She had just started to write the Shipping Instruction when Miss Austin loomed over her: 'Mr Dunlop wants to see you.'

Helen's stomach knotted. Being summoned by Mr Dunlop meant only one thing: the sack. She looked at Miss Austin's portly figure and double chin. There was a look of triumph on that frosty face and Helen thought: it *is* her, not Mr Dunlop, who is behind the endless firings. She met the older woman's exultant stare with a cool, clear gaze. But there was no trace of insubordination in her voice when she asked, 'Did Mr Dunlop say what it was about?'

'Mr Dunlop did not inform me,' said Miss Austin, flushing at this questioning of her authority.

'I know the importance Mr Dunlop attaches to appearance,' Helen said carefully, her eyes not leaving the older woman. 'So if it is all right with you, I would just like to wash my hands and tidy my hair before I see Mr Dunlop.'

'Suit yourself, but be quick about it,' said Miss Austin, striding off. And Helen knew she had scored a tiny victory.

The thought helped her steady her nerve and her hands as she smoothed straying wisps of hair in the cloakroom. Then, shoulders well back and head held high and knowing that every eye was on her, she walked at a dignified pace across the big office and knocked on Mr Dunlop's door.

Miss Austin, back behind the rolltop desk where she sat guard on her employer, grinned maliciously.

'Come in.' Mr Dunlop sounded friendly.

Helen opened the door and, just as she had done in the gardens of Moray Place, stood on the threshold of another, better world: the sanctum of the great shipping magnate. Yew panelling with a rich patina, a winter green carpet in a deep luxurious pile, handsome portraits set in ornately-gilded frames and leather-bound volumes placed on shelves behind highly-polished glass all bore witness to wealth and power. A tantalus stood on a sideboard; there were gleaming silver inkwells and a quill pen and blotting pad in a soft leather case on Mr Dunlop's otherwise empty desk, and glass show cases containing models of ships built at the Dunlop Yard had been placed in corners of the room. Helen had never been inside Mr Dunlop's office before, but she knew at once it was the only place to be. This was where important decisions were made, the decisions that people outside had to lump and suffer, where it was decided who had jobs and who went on the dole. Her eyes sought Mr Dunlop, who was wearing a suit in the Prince of Wales check and standing with his back to the fireplace, which had been banked with bronze and yellow chrysanthemums.

Electric was the first word most people used to describe Harry Dunlop. Some swore they had seen sparks fly as he bustled about, generating so much energy he could give the impression of being in two places at once. His lean, wiry frame seemed to be controlled by a tight spring

25

coil forever on the point of snapping and, though he was fifty-four now, there was not a spare scrap of flesh on his body. He had a lot of dark, crinkly hair, his eyes were an extraordinary penetrating shade of cornflower blue. Harry Dunlop neither looked like nor was he in the classic mould of the great magnates who had made Glasgow the Second City of the Empire. He had never served on any Royal Commission or used his fabulous wealth to present pictures to Corporation Galleries (though he did subscribe to the Lord Provost's charitable funds) and he just wasn't dour enough. With expensively-tailored suits which somehow managed to appear slightly flashy on him, he still looked like the shipyard worker who had risen in the world because he had an eye for the main chance and had married the boss's daughter.

'Ah, Helen, do come in and sit down.' Keeping up the friendly tone, he raised a hand in the direction of a green leather chesterfield facing the fireplace.

Helen wondered exactly what was up. She had never heard of a girl being invited for a fireside chat. They were usually made to stand trembling whilst Mr Dunlop sat behind his massive desk snarling abuse and reciting a long list of sins and misdemeanours with which Miss Austin had provided him. Her eyes met his as she crossed the room and she could find no trace of anger or displeasure in them. Mr Dunlop appeared genuinely pleased to see her.

'Sit down,' he invited once more.

Without her eyes leaving his, Helen lowered herself on to the chesterfield in one fluent, graceful movement.

'How was Edinburgh?' asked Mr Dunlop, as he dropped easily on to the settee beside her. 'Some tea?'

Tea?

'Miss Austin brews an excellent cup. Or you can have coffee if you like. Some of my visitors prefer it.'

26

Visitors?

'I would like some tea, thank you very much, Mr Dunlop,' said Helen, thinking carefully about each word before she said it. She was finding the friendly Mr Dunlop a lot more intimidating than the man who reportedly snarled abuse at his staff.

He rose and walked quickly to the door Helen had left open.

'We'll have some tea, Kathleen,' he called to Miss Austin, then walked briskly back across the room and resumed his seat by Helen.

'Now then, how was Edinburgh?' he asked again.

'It was fine, thank you, Mr Dunlop.'

'Did you see your mother's relative?'

'Yes.'

'Your mother's cousin?'

'Second cousin.'

'How was he?'

'He was . . . very old . . .'

'Ah, yes, the years pass far too quickly for all of us,' Mr Dunlop said airily, leaning back in the chesterfield and laying an arm along the back of it in a way Helen found comforting. She noticed how the hands emerging from his beautifully crisp cuffs were long and slim and immaculately manicured and she became aware, too, of the scent of him – a male scent she had never been conscious of before. 'It must have cheered him up to see you,' he said.

Before Helen could answer a kefuffle at the door announced the entrance of Miss Austin, bearing a silver tray laid with fine white china and a plate of chocolate biscuits.

'I've got your favourite Carrs,' she fussed to Harry Dunlop, slightly flushed as she placed the tray on a low table in front of the chesterfield.

27

Helen's gaze was now riveted to Miss Austin, who was a different person in Mr Dunlop's sanctum. The outer office dragon was replaced by a skittish creature with nervous, darting eyes.

'I've told the boy who brings the biscuits that we want a good supply of Carrs,' Miss Austin trilled, stressing 'we', uncertainty squawking in every syllable. She laid the milk jug beside the sugar bowl, then moved it beside the teapot and back again, 'Will it be one spoon as usual, Mr Dunlop?' she asked in an arch voice, fingering the sugar bowl again, a too-bright gleam in her eyes.

'That's all right, Kathleen, we'll help ourselves,' said Mr Dunlop.

'Oh, it's no trouble – '

'I said we'll manage.'

The sugar bowl crashed on to the tray, breaking into three unequal fragments and littering the carpet with molehills of demerara.

'Oh! I've never done that before,' exclaimed Miss Austin, her cheeks crimson, the light gone from her eyes.

Helen would remember the looked that passed between Miss Austin and Mr Dunlop for the rest of her life. It would flash, rainbow-bright, in her memory and become a gauge by which she measured the ways things were between a man and a woman – if there was hope and a future or if it was all in the past. A deathly boredom seemed to glaze the furrows of Mr Dunlop's brow and his eyes become like blue marble. Fear, panic and then a terrible desolation teemed in Miss Austin's eyes and seemed to fill the air between them. Instinctively, Helen recognised it as the look of a woman who is losing a man. In a flash she realised that Mr Dunlop and Miss Austin had been lovers and now Miss Austin was terrified he would find some new young girl to take her place.

That was what lay behind the endless firings. Helen looked at Mr Dunlop, whose expression said that all he wanted from this woman now was that she would leave him alone. He had plans and a future and Miss Austin had only a past. A woman's power withered with age, but a man's did not and suddenly, violently, Helen knew she must get everything she wanted while she was young . . .

'You can leave us now, Miss Austin,' said Harry Dunlop coldly. She was no longer even Kathleen. 'And close the door behind you. I don't want to be disturbed.'

'As you wish,' Miss Austin faltered, shooting Helen a look that held more pain then venom.

Helen watched Miss Austin's heavy hips sway across the room. The girls often joked about her waddle. Now she was almost limping.

'I hope you don't take sugar.' Mr Dunlop lifted the teapot, smiling, as the door closed behind the abandoned, ageing spinster.

'No, no I don't, thank you.'

Seeing the way Miss Austin was with Mr Dunlop had made Helen even more aware of him as a man. She watched his hands holding the teapot, carefully pouring tea into the cups and replacing the pot on the tray before they reached for the milk jug and a fragment of the sugar bowl and ladled a large spoon of sugar into his cup. He really did have very nice hands . . . She saw now that his shirt was made of fine cream silk but most of all she was aware of his setting . . . the cushioned leather comfort, the portraits in their gilded frames, the trappings of a powerful man who could make all things possible . . .

'Why did you want to see me, Mr Dunlop?' she asked in a confident voice when he handed her a cup of tea.

'To find out how you are. To the best of my knowledge, apart from your relative in Edinburgh, you have no

29

family. As your employer, I believe I have a responsibility to be interested in your welfare.'

Helen knew he meant it. It was in those blue, blue eyes.

'Thank you,' she said, smiling, a sudden warmth coursing through her.

'Now, is there anything I can help you with?'

Helen looked at Mr Dunlop, at those blue, blue eyes, and saw a man who could help her on her way up in the world — if she told him that was where she wanted to go.

She placed her cup and saucer on the table and concentrated hard before she said: 'I think you know how very interested I am in my work, Mr Dunlop.' She paused and their eyes held as he nodded approvingly. 'Well, in the autumn I am going to go to night school to learn shorthand and typing. And I would like to think that when I have mastered these skills they will be of some help to me in my career as the Pier Line.'

'What a very enterprising young lady you are,' exclaimed Harry Dunlop, nodding approval again. 'Yes I'm quite sure that when you have acquired these skills we can put them to plenty of good use in the Pier Line.'

Helen was gaining confidence by the moment and, emboldened by approval, now told him: 'I like to think I am well organised and even while I am still learning shorthand and typing, if there is anything I can do to make the office run more smoothly, I will be very pleased to do so, in addition to my normal duties. I think that in these hard times, when so many people are on the dole, those of us who have jobs should work extra hard and learn to do as many new jobs as possible to help our employers.'

It was the first time she had ever flattered a man and, as she saw Mr Dunlop glow and preen and the look in his eyes turn to admiration, she felt a thrill of power which brought a hint of colour to her pale cheeks.

Mr Dunlop was smiling broadly now. 'You have quite a future with the Pier Line,' he said. 'Now, is there anything else you're worried about?'

Helen thought of the flat in Partick. 'Well, I'm not sure I'll have a roof over my head for much longer,' she said, frowning. 'I don't think the landlord will be willing to rent to me because I'm under twenty-one.'

Harry Dunlop looked thoughtful for a moment, then smiled.

'There's no need for you to worry about that. You are very welcome to stay in one of the Pier Line flats until we – you – can sort something out.'

Helen knew the Pier Line owned several fine properties in the West End in fashionable streets like Great Western Terrace, the most famous of Alexander 'Greek' Thomson's elegant terraces where they put up important foreign customers. She had often delivered papers and documents to them. 'But I would never be able to afford the rent!'

He shook his head. 'As an employee of the company, you would pay a nominal, concessionary rent. I was just looking over your employment record before you came in and you really are a very good worker. You've now been two years with the company and you're due for a rise. What we could do is to split the increase in your wages so that half of it goes on the rent of a company flat and the other half into your pay packet. How would that suit you?'

'It would suit me very well,' said Helen, hardly able to believe her luck.

'I'm not sure which properties are available at the moment, but take a look at the books and take the

31

keys when you're not too busy and go and have a look at them.'

Suddenly Helen knew she was about to take a step up in the world – and she was still glowing at the prospect when she left Mr Dunlop's office a few minutes later.

'So Miss Austin and Mr Dunlop were lovers!' Elizabeth Campbell's tongue lingered on the word, infusing it with excitement and naughtiness.

'Well, they might have been. I don't know for certain,' said Helen, wishing she had never said a word about her impressions of what she had seen in Mr Dunlop's office. But she had met a barrage of questioning looks when she emerged from his room, still on the payroll, and, though she had managed to fob off everyone else by telling them Mr Dunlop had simply wanted to know about her mother's death, it was not enough for Elizabeth Campbell.

Elizabeth, the youngest child and only girl in a family of four, had got her temporary job at the Pier Line while she waited to begin an arts degree course at Glasgow University simply because she was Mr Dunlop's lawyer's daughter.

'Well, *something*,' insisted Elizabeth, looking slightly disappointed.

'They may just have been special friends. I couldn't say for sure,' Helen prevaricated.

They were sitting on a wooden bench in the handsome Victorian plaza of George Square eating their sandwiches in the late summer sunshine.

'It must have been *so* romantic once upon a time,' said Elizabeth dreamily, gazing at the gleaming turrets of the City Chambers. 'I mean, when Mr Dunlop and Miss Austin were young.'

Elizabeth was a member of the Scottish National Players, the leading amateur dramatic company in Scotland, and liked to think of herself as an actress. She saw life in romantic, theatrical terms and was in love with what she called the great drama of it all, with everyone really just bit players' as she often told Helen.

Helen secretly thought Elizabeth had really no idea how harsh life could be. How could she? As the spoiled daughter of a wealthy Glasgow family, she had never wanted for anything. Her family had a huge house near Luss on Loch Lomond and a flat in town, in Kirklee Terrace, on the grand West End boulevard of Great Western Road. Like her brothers, she had been sent away to school and spoke with an accentless voice. Helen envied the utter security Elizabeth enjoyed – it was so easy for her to take such a romantic view of life when she had never been and was never likely to be up against its hardships.

But I think you're really quite snobby, thought Helen suddenly, watching her friend's profile against the skyline. If you knew I was illegitimate you would not want to be my friend, or, indeed, be anywhere near me – except if you found out my father's a judge, you might. Because you would think it was exciting and romantic, she decided, a wry smile coming over her face.

'What are you laughing at?' demanded Elizabeth.

'Have you ever met Mrs Dunlop?' asked Helen, ignoring the question. 'Has she ever been at any of your father's famous parties for his clients?'

'I may have done, but I wouldn't know her again,' said Elizabeth, polishing a rosy red apple with a white, lace-trimmed handkerchief. 'They're all old the people who go to my father's parties and they all look the same. And Mrs Dunlop is even older than Mr Dunlop – she's never been able to have any children,' Elizabeth added.

33

'People aren't boring just because they're old,' protested Helen.

'I never said they were,' replied Elizabeth defensively.

'But that's what your tone meant,' said Helen. 'At least old people have had a chance to live. My mother died before she'd had a real chance,' she added, feeling weepy all over again.

'Don't cry!' said Elizabeth, squeezing her hand. 'I didn't mean to be horrible.'

'You weren't, but I couldn't help thinking about her,' said Helen. 'Do you want to get married, Elizabeth?' she asked, changing the subject.

'I want to *love*,' said Elizabeth, opening up on her favourite theme. 'Love deeply. Love's more important than marriage. I want to love like Isadora Duncan, love and live fully.' She threw her head back dramatically.

'How would you feel about having a baby without being married?' asked Helen, greatly daring.

Elizabeth paused for a moment, looking thoughtful, then said: 'Well, I would need to live in London if I wanted to do that. It just wouldn't be possible in Glasgow.'

'What, not even in the free love set at the Scottish National Players.'

'Free love is different from having an illegitimate baby,' said Elizabeth repressively.

The word stung Helen. She didn't really believe in Elizabeth's talk of 'free love'. She was quite sure that for all her talk of 'flings' she had never really done anything with a man and would still be a virgin when she married because, beneath all her affections, she was really a conventional family girl who would do what her parents wanted.

Helen's heart suddenly felt heavy and, as they walked back to the office in the sunshine, she wished more than

34

anything she could have been born into a family such as Elizabeth's.

Over the next few weeks, whenever she had a spare moment or could find an excuse, Helen took the keys of the Pier Line's various empty properties and dutifully inspected them. She looked at all of them, but from the moment she crossed the threshold of the flat in Great Western Terrace she knew it was the only one for her. It was the grandest of all the terraces overlooking the leafy boulevard of Great Western Road with classical colonnades and elegant flights of steps up to its magnificent entrances. From the Pier Line's first floor flat she could see right over the northern part of the city to the distant uplands of the Campsie Fells. And when she stood by a drawing-room window, watching the smoke rise from the chimneys across the city, she experienced a strange and wonderful sensation, not just of stepping up in the world but of having come home to the place where she belonged.

She was also becoming increasingly interested and aware of Mr Dunlop – as a man. She watched the graceful way he moved quickly across the office, the way his suits, always in light colours, toned with his shirts – quite different from the dark suits and white shirts most men wore – and the way his fingernails were always perfectly manicured. She watched every word he ever said to Miss Austin in the big office and she wondered what was really going on between them. She wondered, too, about Mrs Dunlop. But no one seemed to know much about her and she never came near the office.

On the morning she decided to tell Mr Dunlop where she wanted to live, Helen approached Miss Austin's rolltop desk to request a meeting. But the older woman was not there. As she was turning away from the desk she heard the secretary's raised voice from behind the closed door of Mr Dunlop's office. Then she heard Mr Dunlop's, which was also raised.

Work stopped right across the office as every eye focused on the closed door. Helen wanted to linger, to try to hear what was being said, but knew better. She walked slowly back to her table. The shouting did not last long but it was some time before Miss Austin emerged from Mr Dunlop's office, looking disarrayed.

Helen decided it was not the best time to see Mr Dunlop. So she waited until the next morning before she told Miss Austin, with a meaningful look, 'Mr Dunlop asked me to report directly to him on an important matter.'

'Then you'd best go in,' said the older woman, her expression giving nothing away.

Helen knocked confidently on the door and opened it without waiting for Mr Dunlop to invite her in.

Henry Dunlop was sitting behind his desk and when he looked up and those intense blue eyes met hers she knew she could get whatever she wanted from him . . .

'Ah, Helen,' he said, getting up and walking towards the chesterfield by the fireplace. 'How's the flat-hunting going?'

'I know where I'd like to live,' she said, smiling as she reached his side by the settee.

'And where's that?' he asked as they sat down.

Helen looked carefully at Mr Dunlop, at his fine blue wool herring-bone suit and his toning shirt and contrasting cream silk tie.

'All the pain and bereavement and unhappiness I have suffered recently seemed to wash away as soon as I entered the flat where I would like to live,' she said carefully, watching every movement of Mr Dunlop's eyes. 'And when I looked out across the northern city to the Campsie Fells I felt I had come home. . .'

36

'You want to live in Great Western Terrace,' said Mr Dunlop 'An excellent choice.' Their eyes locked in mutual understanding and Helen realised how easy it was to play his game and win. 'I'll arrange it.'

'Mr Dunlop has *affairs*,' Elizabeth Campbell mangled the word between her lips and her teeth, and there was a storm warning in the eyes that met Helen's. 'Didn't you *know*?'

'With whom?'

'Women.'

'*Who*?'

'One of them was an actress with the Scottish National Players.' Elizabeth lowered her voice and looked around the Room de Luxe in Miss Cranston's Willow Tearooms. 'She was a lot younger than him and she lived with him in the flat in Great Western Terrace.' Elizabeth sat back in her chair, a slightly smug expression taking hold of her face.

'Really,' said Helen, adopting an indifferent tone, though Elizabeth's news was a bombshell. 'Who says so?'

'My mother,' said Elizabeth as if her mother was God's authority – which Helen reckoned she probably was on Glasgow gossip.

'One woman' said Helen.

'Oh, there were others.' Elizabeth leaned forward in her chair again and once more looked carefully around the room. The Room de Luxe, which was for ladies only, was the grandest of all the interiors Charles Rennie Mackintosh had designed for Miss Cranston's four Glasgow Tearooms – a boudoir of mirrored and leaded glass panels, exquisite silk and purple upholstery and silvered ladderback chairs, where the wives of the prosperous Glasgow bourgeosie gossiped over coffee and lunch and afternoon tea. 'A lawyer's wife in Milngavie. She and Mr Dunlop used to meet in London in hotels until her husband found out. He was going to divorce her, but Mr Dunlop agreed never to see her again. It was enormous scandal at the time, but it was hushed up.'

'That's still only two women,' said Helen in an even tone. But she didn't like to think of Mr Dunlop having affairs with different women and she felt quite upset.

'Three, if you count Miss Austin,' said Elizabeth, who was now a student at Glasgow University.

Helen looked at her friend with her blonde bob and blue eyes and scarlet smile and wondered why she was telling her all this. 'Have *you* had an affair?' she asked bluntly.

Elizabeth went scarlet. 'I have *flings*,' she murmured, flustered.

'I mean a *real* affair,' Helen pressed, fixing her friend's eyes with her own. 'All the way.'

'No!' Elizabeth gasped, going even deeper pink, her sophistication in retreat. 'Have – have you?'

'No,' said Helen coolly. 'And I don't intend to,' she added, remembering her mother. 'I'm going to be a virgin when I get married.'

'It really doesn't seem fair,' murmured Elizabeth.

'What doesn't?'

'That men can have affairs before they get married but girls can't,' said Elizabeth. 'Well, not if they want a man to marry them. He won't if you give in before you're married.'

'Yes,' said Helen glumly. 'Men just take what they want and leave the remains, like the bones of a chicken after a meal.'

'That sounds horrid,' said Elizabeth, pulling a face.

'Men *can* be pretty horrid,' said Helen, thinking about how her father abandoned her mother. She almost said

38

something about it to Elizabeth but managed to restrain her tongue in time. 'And I don't see why women should be forced to give up working when they get married,' she added, slightly changing the subject. 'We ought to be allowed to carry on.'

'Yes, woman's definitely got to get all she wants when she's young – a husband and babies – because nobody will want her when she's old,' said Elizabeth.' And that's not right either.

'Do *you* want to get married?' asked Helen.

'Well, a girl's got to, really. Otherwise she becomes an old spinster and nobody wants her. She's a joke.'

'It's not right,' said Helen.

'Do you want to get married?' asked Elixabeth.

'I don't know,' said Helen. 'I do want to have a great love affair that lasts all my life,' she added, suddenly brightening. 'Wouldn't that be *wonderful*?'

'Oh, it would be very romantic,' said Elizabeth, catching Helen's mood. 'But wouldn't you want to marry him.'

'I might not be able to,' said Helen, thinking of her mother. 'My mother wasn't able to marry the man she loved. She married someone else.'

'Why?'

'Because the man she loved was married to someone else and she had to forget him. Except she never did. She still loved him on the day she died.'

'And what about your father?'

'He died before I was born.' Helen felt a lump coming in her throat. For a moment she felt she had said too much. But it was a relief to talk at last about her parents' star-crossed love affair, even if only in a roundabout way.

'Oh, how romantic!' cried Elizabeth, quite carried away.

'It wasn't,' said Helen. 'It was very sad really. A waste of life. I feel my mother died before she had a proper chance to live.' Helen felt tears at her throat. 'I'm not going to be like my mother. I am going to live and live and if I meet a man I truly love I will fight for him.'

'And you will win him. I can see it all,' sighed Elizabeth as Helen signalled for the bill.

Two weeks later a couple of able-bodied young men with a Lunns' van packed up Helen's belongings in the Partick flat and a little while later decanted them in Great Western Terrace. They stored all her furniture in one boxroom and there was still room to spare.

It was the most enormous flat. A real mansion. The whole flat in Partick could have been fitted into the handsome drawing or dining-rooms. The bedrooms – there were four – were also huge and so were the kitchen and bathroom. Even the boxrooms were the size of proper rooms and when Helen hung her clothes in a vast wardrobe they seemed like doll's clothes. But the flat was hideously furnished with heavy Victorian furniture and plum-red flocked wallpaper and matching drapes which clashed with Turkish carpets in violent scarlet and blue patterns. Every chair and sofa was draped in dark grey linen antimacassars and every mirror caged in Gorgon brass frames. As she roamed through the flat, Helen decided it needed to be stripped and redecorated and furnished in the modern style.

Her thirst for knowledge and learning had been spurred on by her friendship with Elizabeth Campbell and she admired the Art Deco style in which Elizabeth's mother had decorated the family's Glasgow flat. She had started to read books on interior design and, when she lay down on the bed in the room she had chosen for herself, she closed her eyes and imagined the room all white the way

40

Syrie Maugham designed interiors – pure and gleaming and luminous with stylish modern lamps and glass sheathed in shining chrome. She pictured a bevilled Art Deco mirror in some amazing shape above the fireplace, a low settee in beige satin, bergere armchairs in cream and small enamelled tables displaying the glass objects Rene Lalique created in dazzling geometric shapes. All so modern and chic.

She opened her eyes slightly and peered at the ceiling rose through her lashes and her lovely face took on the look of perfectly-set marble. It would cost Mr Dunlop a lot to furnish this flat the way she wanted it. And even though he could easily afford to do so, it would take time and *lot* of persuasion, she knew that. Rich people and their money were never easily parted. That's how they stayed rich and got richer, her mother had said. But she would work on him. In the meantime, there was something else she wanted more urgently and thought she saw an opportunity. She knew she could not get Miss Austin's job until she had mastered shorthand and typing skills, but relations between Miss Austin and Mr Dunlop were becoming so turbulent that he might be open to a suggestion that he might appoint an assistant secretary to make sure the office ran smoothly.

She opened her eyes fully and her lips parted in a wide, conspiratorial smile which crept all over her face. Mr Dunlop would surely want to know that she was looking after his most prestigious flat properly.

It was then, gazing at the ceiling and wondering if Mr Dunlop had ever made love to the young actress in this room, that she decided to invite him to tea . . .

Autumn sunshine was lending a verdant glint to the southern slopes of the Campsie Fells and there was a

settled air right across the grey slate rooftops and blackened chimneys of the northern city; smoke, rising straight,
had a blueish tinge. In the heart of town shades of apple
red and peach staining the leaves were witness that the
fingers of autumn were now well wrapped around the
days – something quite forgotten in the lingering summer warmth of the afternoon as people lucky enough
to own motor cars streamed out along Great Western
Road towards Loch Lomond. From her drawing-room
window Helen stood watching migrating birds gather
in a sycamore whose branches were trembling beneath
the weight. She had been up till after midnight the night
before polishing brasses and mirrors and pictures and
every nook and cranny of ornate table and chair legs, and
placing freshly-laundered antimacassars on all the settees
and laying the fire and the china on a low table before
it. And in case the shops in the Byres Road didn't have
Mr Dunlop's favourite Melrose's Earl Grey and Carrs'
chocolate biscuits, she had raided the cupboard where
Miss Austin kept them, though she needn't have, and
she would put them back on Monday morning. And, to
make it all really special, she had baked a sponge cake
and filled it with jam just like her mother used to do.

Helen turned from the window and looked at her
reflection in one of the massive mirrors with the grotesque
frames. With money left by her mother, she had bought
several new outfits which, worked with a combination
of blouses, gave her a different one for each of the six
working days. A career girl on her way up needed to look
her best. And even though her new wardrobe came from
Lewis's, because she could not afford to shop at Dalys
where Elizabeth bought clothes on her mother's account,
Helen had chosen her clothes with care and was pleased
with them. This afternoon she was wearing a lemon crêpe
de chine dress and her long golden hair flowed loosely

about her shoulders. Mr Dunlop had never seen her with her hair down and she hoped he would like it. She smiled shakily. She had no experience of entertaining a man and she felt quite nervous now. More than anything, she wanted to please him Harry Dunlop . . . She heard a motor car hooting in the street and dashed back to the window.

But it wasn't a chauffeur at the wheel of Mr Dunlop's Daimler who was blaring his horn and waving wildly at a pedestrian who had got in his way. The driver at the wheel of a Mercedes coupé was a young man wearing a dark blazer and a boater at a jaunty angle and a huge bouquet of bronze and gold and yellow chrysanthemums lay on the passenger seat beside him.

Helen looked away towards the traffic making its way along the boulevard, then she heard the bell ring. Glancing down she could see no one in the street below. Mr Dunlop must have arrived on foot when she was watching the traffic and had let himself in at the entrance to the building.

There was a little knot in her stomach now and her hands were slightly trembling. She took several deep breaths to compose herself and walked slowly across the drawing-room and down the hall to the front door. She thought she was going to faint when she opened it.

The man in the dark blazer and jaunty boater was Mr Dunlop!

'For the house warming,' he said, thrusting the huge bouquet of chrysanthemums into her arms, dazzling her.

He looked so young! So dashing.

'Mr Dunlop . . .' was all she managed to say.

'Aren't you going to ask me in?' he asked, his eyes full of laughter. 'I had the impression I could get a cup of tea here.'

'Yes, yes. Of course. Please, come in.'

She opened the door wider and he stepped over the threshold and lightly tossed his boater on a peg of a coat stand in the hall. He didn't look *quite* so young without his hat. But he didn't look much older, either. Then Helen realised she was only used to seeing Mr Dunlop in business suits, not in the sports clothes worn by fashionable young men. She wondered if he kept a wardrobe in a concealed cupboard in the yew panelling in his office or if he had been driven home to Pollokshields to change after the office had closed at one o'clock. And if the Mercedes coupé was new. There was so much she didn't know about Harry Dunlop, who was becoming more fascinating with every passing moment.

'Let me put these lovely flowers in water and I'll make you some tea,' Helen said, growing excitement lending her confidence.

The flowers were beautifully fresh, their stems rigid with water and the leaves scented her fingers as she arranged them in a tall crystal vase, which she placed on a table beneath a pier glass in the drawing-room.

'Thank you, Mr Dunlop,' she said, standing back to admire them.

'You are something of a surprise away from the office with your hair like that Helen,' said Mr Dunlop, and she saw he was looking at her as a young man might . . . And it was nice.

'So are you, Mr Dunlop,' said Helen, admiration shining in her eyes.

It was true. Out of the Pier Line's dark Victorian offices, they were simply a man and a girl seeing each other for the first time and liking what they saw on a glorious afternoon . . .

Helen flew back to the kitchen and shortly afterwards, when she had poured him a fragrant cup of Earl grey and placed a Carrs' chocolate biscuit on his plate, she sat back in a big easy chair facing him and had no idea what to say except: 'Thank you for letting me stay in this lovely flat, Mr Dunlop.' There was so much she wanted to ask him and know about him but she didn't know where to begin and, for the moment, all she wanted was to be near him.

'I'm so glad you seem to be settling in here,' he said, taking a sip of his tea.

'Yes.'

The conversation came to a halt. But it was like a hay cart stopping in a country lane because it was a nice sunny day and there was no hurry to get any-where. There was no tension, no ill-ease in the tin-kle of china cup on saucer as they sat, eyes smiling at each other.

She poured him another cup of tea and one for herself and then she saw that he had cleaned his plate of the biscuit.

'Another biscuit?'

'I think I'd like a piece of cake. It looks very good to me. Did you bake it?'

'Yes,' said Helen, reaching for the cake knife. And that was nice, too, serving him the food she had prepared. It was so simple, really – giving him what he liked, pleasing his eye and his palate and feeling herself reflected in his pleasure.

'Mmm, tastes good,' he said when he had taken a bite of the cake. 'It's so good to be able to relax for half-an-hour and forget about the worries of running a shipyard and a shipping line.'

She quickly took her cue. 'I read as much as I can both about shipping and the problems of shipbuilding in the *Glasgow Herald*,' she said carefully, weighing each word before it passed her lips because she wanted to impress him with her *intelligent* interest. 'But I know there is a

45

lot I don't understand. Has shipbuilding got even worse problems than shipping?'

'It's chicken and egg,' said Mr Dunlop somewhat wearily. 'Shipping lines can't trade without ships, but when there's a massive fall in world trade, who needs new ships? And with the consequent fall in freight rates, no owner can afford to build new ships in any case.'

Helen puckered her brow. 'Can you tell me more?' she asked in that tone of sweetness and innocence and interest which is consummate flattery to the ego of a man.

'Well, the slowdown in world trade means there are far more ships competing to carry goods than there are goods to be carried,' said Mr Dunlop, easing back in his chair. Helen thought he looked older now, more like the boss she knew, and tired and in need of comforting. 'And it has driven the price of freight almost back to its 1913 level.

'It all stems from the war with the Germans, you see. During the war – and in the build-up to it – the demand for ships was insatiable. New yards opened up all over the place. The result is that British shipyards can now build 40 per cent more ships than they they could before the war. But there's no demand for them. Over half the yards in country are lying idle and it's costing £500,000 a year to maintain them doing nothing. Unemployment is twice as bad as it is in any other industry. It's 22 per cent at the moment – but that's 22 per cent too much. And there's nothing to stop it shooting up to 43 per cent, the way it was four years ago. There are very few orders, Helen, and we have to compete with foreign yards, who are subsidized by their Governments. We've asked the Government for subsidies, but they've set their face against us.'

'So what's going to happen?' asked Helen, concerned and fascinated.

'The shipyards are going to have to band together and

46

form some kind of co-operative for their own protection – and that goes against the whole spirit of shipbuilding. Shipbuilders are all highly individual entrepreneurial men. We don't believe in co-operatives or Socialism. But if we don't band together and decide among ourselves which yards to close down, the price cutting that is going on will drive us *all* out of business, because we'll be forced to sell ships for a lot less than it costs us to build them.'

'Do all shipbuilders feel as you do?'

He shrugged. 'In varying degrees. We all had a lot to say about it at a meeting of the co-ordinating committee last night.' Mr Dunlop took a sip of his tea and looked towards the window and the distant Campsie Fells. 'Shipbuilding is not like any other business. It's not just a trade or even a business. Building a ship is a work of art and science. And something more. There's a lot of love goes into building a ship. When they build a ship, men create something bigger and greater than themselves.' His voice rang with excitement and Helen, thrilling at every word, longed to know more simply for the sake of knowing.

'Miss Austin once said you were different to a lot of shipbuilders because you started your career working in a shipyard,' she encouraged.

'Ah, Kathleen was there from the start,' he said, a faraway look in his blue eyes, and Helen wondered just how much he and Miss Austin had meant to each other and for how long. 'When I left school at thirteen I started work, just like my father before me, as a joiner in the McKerron Yard. I learned to make the furniture that goes into ships. That's what joiners do in shipyards. The ship's carpenter does the heavy woodwork – the hatch covers, wood decking and stores shelving. He doesn't make the furniture. *He'd* be called a joiner if he worked on shore instead of a ship, he smiled. I loved making furniture,

47

carving beautiful things out of wood. You have so much power to create a beautiful world for other people to enjoy . . .' He placed his cup and saucer on the low table and raised his hands as if he was holding a piece of carved wood, and Helen thought suddenly that his slim hands with their long fingers were really the hands of an artist. And his eyes were shining. 'One man can make a piece of furniture, but it takes a team of men with different skills to build a ship. You need a whole team of designers, platers, riveters, plumbers, engineers, carpenters, joiners, electricians and painters.' He shook his head. 'I did quite well. I got promoted to be foreman in my department, then outfit manager, looking after the fitting-out, and then I became the yard manager, responsible for the ships from keel to truck. But it wasn't enough for me, Helen. I *loved* ships. I wanted to build whole ships myself. I wanted my own shipyard.' His voice rang with passion and Helen was now totally in his thrall, caught up by the sheer magnetism and willpower of him.

'And how did you get your shipyard?' she asked in a breathless whisper.

'The country was preparing for the war with the Germans. New shipyards were opening up all the time and orders were easy to get. But I had no money. And no banker would lend me any. But I always believed, right from my earliest days, that if you wanted something badly enough you could get it if you kept on trying. I was still getting the bankers' doors slammed in my face when my luck suddenly changed. The boss, Mr McKerron, decided I should marry his daughter—anyway, it was all a long time ago.' Mr Dunlop's tone changed abruptly and Helen realized instantly he did not wish to say any more about the past. 'I've got enough to worry about at present with the spectre of nationalisation,' he said.

Helen smartly took her cue. 'Nationalisation?'

Mr Dunlop drew a hand thoughtfully over his chin. 'If the shipbuilders don't do something about the number of redundant yards, the Government will move in and take over all shipyards.'

'But you own the Dunlop Yard. They couldn't do that! That would be *stealing*.'

He smiled glumly. 'It's not stealing if they pass an Act of Parliament empowering them to force us to sell our yards to them. And then *they* decide which yards are to be closed down.'

'Well, at least you would get *some* money,' said Helen, hoping she wasn't saying the wrong thing because she knew enough now about Mr Dunlop to know that money would never compensate him for the loss of his beloved shipyard. It would be licensed robbery if the Government took his shipyard away, even if they did pay him for it.

'We'd get what the Government felt like paying us, which would be a lot less than the yards are worth.' Mr Dunlop's face eased as he looked at her intent expression. 'But its not something you should be worrying your very pretty head about, Helen. What makes you so interested in shipbuilding? If you were a lad, I might understand it. But a lassie should be thinking of other things, surely!'

Helen knew she must choose her words carefully. Though it was supposed to be the age of the Emancipated Woman, most men did not take the idea of women working seriously.

'Well, I had no idea how interesting my job was going to be until I started doing all the paperwork which is involved in sending cargoes around the world and then going down to the docks and seeing them being loaded and unloaded. The names of some of the places sounded exciting and I tried to imagine what they were like. Then I started looking more closely on the maps on the office walls, following the journeys of the ships. The pieces of paper I was handling became journeys in themselves and I wanted to learn more and more about the business. Oh, and what you've told me this afternoon has made it even more alive and exciting!' She paused, lowering her eyes and letting her voice drop a little, hoping she was saying the right things. For though she was trying to choose her words carefully, they came as much from her heart as from her head. But she couldn't let it rest there. She had to remind him she wanted a career, not just an office job with Pier Line. 'I would work really hard to secure a *responsible* job in your company, Mr Dunlop,' she said, looking up and straight into those extraordinary blue eyes.

Mr Dunlop held her gaze for a moment before he said with a hint of regret in his voice, 'Oh, I've often wished I had a son who might have shown such as much interest. Helen have you ever seen a ship being built?'

'Only from a distance'.

'Would you like to see one close up?' he asked, smiling as she started eagerly.

'Yes, please!' She couldn't hide her enthusiasm.

'On Monday I have to go over to the yard to see how they are getting on with the *Papana Queen*. She's due to be launched in a few weeks. Care to come along?'

'Yes, please!' she said again. This was an undreamed of chance to learn more – and to develop her relationship with Mr Dunlop.

'Well', he laughed, 'just be sure to wear your thickest, flattest shoes. It can be rough-going underfoot.'

Long after Mr Dunlop had gone and the sun had set on the Campsie Fells, Helen sat in the darkened drawing-room. A new, unexpected element had entered her relationship with her boss, and it made her whole body ache. She *wanted* Mr Dunlop . . .

* * *

50

At first sight the Dunlop Shipyard looked like a scrapyard. Sheets of steel were strewn around an open yard along with piles of chains and cables. Tarpaulins the size of football pitches flapped and battered against scaffolding, making an eerie, desolate sound. A smell of grease hung in the air and it was greasy underfoot as well, where twisted, six-inch long rusty nails, lurked in the soggy soil ready to rip the flesh from any foot less than stoutly shod. Helen glanced down at her inelegant stout leather shoes ruefully, sincerely hoping she was making the right impression. Back from the river, beyond the open yard, stood two vast corrugated sheds; these were the plating and fabrication shops and they were as cold and damp and cheerless as the yard outside.

Towering above it all, defining it, lifting it above chaos and wasteland and attended by hundreds of men scrambling all over and around her, stood the *Papana Queen*. Like all great ocean liners built on the Clyde, she dominated the skyline, soaring above the mean tenement streets which backed on to the yards.

'Well, isn't she beautiful?' demanded Mr Dunlop, his eyes shining with pride and love.

'Yes,' Helen agreed, and her eyes were shining, too. Her heart had always lifted at the sight of the great liners. But to meet one in the making, when she was still a skeleton and powerless was a special thrill. Now she was glad she had worn her flattest, sturdiest shoes as she followed Mr Dunlop alongside the scaffolding, carefully minding her steps in the mud among the scrambles of wire and cabling and rusty chains and lengths of piping. As well as scaffolding and ladders, great logs were propped against the side of the ship and she felt the size of Thumbelina as she picked her way cautiously in its shadows. Then she had to clamber up two steep gangways placed at right angles to each other to reach the main deck of the ship.

The view was exhilarating. All around, the city lay like a tiny kingdom below, its spires and towers and steeples and hunks of solid Victorian architecture, soot-black and proud, mellowed by the gentle October sunshine. Yet, even on a clear day the air was hazy with the smoke belched out by the steel mills, the carpet and the textile factories, the railway engine and rolling-stock shops – all the industries which made Glasgow the Second City of the Empire. But here the air was better because you were above it all, thought Helen as a fresh wind blowing up river flushed her cheeks. While Mr Dunlop questioned a foreman, she stepped carefully to the edge of the deck and looked down at the tiny figures scurrying around in the wasteland on the ground. Being up here, above it all, she knew, with a huge exhilaration, that if you put your will to it, it was possible to climb out of the very greatest mess and get to the top.

'See here,' said Mr Dunlop, returning to her side, 'if you look down over here you can see right inside the ship.'

She followed him across the deck to where, like a surgeon who has made an incision into the abdomen, she could see right down into the bowels of the ship – from the first class staterooms on the top decks to right down to the open berth area where the steerage passengers, mostly immigrants, would travel. And it seemed a miracle that out of all the chaos this beautiful creature, perfectly carved and sculptured in steel, was coming into being.

'My job as a young man was to turn these steel-line spaces into elegant lounges and dining-rooms,' shouted Mr Dunlop above the racket of the riveters' hammers. 'Later on, when I was the outfitting manager, I had to see that every compartment and all the systems were finished in the correct sequences and the long programmes of tests leading up to the sea trials went ahead on schedule. I had to supervise teams of joiners and painters and pipeworkers and carpenters and joiners and French polishers and sparkies.'

'Sparkies?'

'The electricians,' said Mr Dunlop, raising a hand to greet a couple of them passing by.

Helen looked at them. They were both young men. And then she looked about the deck at the other men, all busy and earnest and dedicated to their jobs. But they could easily be out of work if the Dunlop Yard didn't get any more orders. And it wouldn't count for anything that they were good at their jobs. They'd be on the dole. Then she looked again at Mr Dunlop. There was pride in his gestures, in the way he spoke to the men, the way he was with them, as though he was one of them. Except he wasn't. *He* wouldn't be on the dole if there were no more orders and the yard closed. Because he was rich and owned the yard. For all the worry and responsibility, it was far better to own a shipyard than to work for one, Helen decided, and when Mr Dunlop said: 'Now, if you really want to know about shipbuilding, I'm going to take you back to the beginning,' her response was instant.

'Yes, please,' she said firmly.

She followed him down the gangways, across the muddy, greasy ground of the office where the naval architect – a bearded man who looked like the late Czar Nicholas – told her: 'To design a ship a naval architect has to think about everything on the scene in which it will operate. He's got to consider the likely loading conditions, and any limitations caused by locks and drafts caused by shoal or tidal conditions and air drafts by bridges. He must work out the capacity for cargo and fuel, machinery spaces, fresh water, passenger crew and accommodation and the space needed for the engine room.'

'That's a pretty tall order,' said Helen, concentrating hard.

'He's also got to think about the commercial, financial and practical needs of the intending purchaser,' the naval architect added, with a knowing smile to Mr Dunlop.

After that Mr Dunlop took Helen to the mould loft, where the ships' lines, prepared by the design office, were drawn out to full size on the scrieve board, and templates for steel plates were cut to size in thin wood before they were taken to the plating and fabrication shops to be marked on the plates before cutting.

Helen was fascinated by the lines drawn on the floor, showing the exact shape and size of the ship.

'In all the different views of the ship's hull, like the horizontal waterlines, vertical sections and the slices through the ship's fore and aft, which we call buttocks, the lines must be fair,' explained Mr Dunlop. 'If they're not, it would be impossible for the men to build the ship properly.'

When they reached the plating shop, in one of the vast, corrugated sheds, a small template taken from the mould lift was being checked over by several men, who looked just as tiny beneath its high roof as the men working outside in the shadow of the ship.

'Smalls units like Daily Service Tanks are built in the plating shop and much larger units, like parts of the superstructure, are riveted together in the fabrication shop,' explained Mr Dunlop.

The sun had come out when they stepped back out into the yard and was gleaming on the lusty black hull of the *Papana Queen*.

'Oh, I'd love to see her launched,' said Helen, feeling proprietorial.

'How good are you at waitressing?' asked Mr Dunlop, casting a penetrating glance over her. 'Because if you'd like to help with the tea and buns afterwards, you're welcome to come along. There's quite a lot protocol attached to the launching of a ship and Miss Austin is a great authority on it as she arranges them all. But if you'd like to know more, why don't you take a look at the newspaper cuttings in the attic in St Vincent Street?'

The next day Helen sought out Mr Robertson, who ran the post room and also kept the keys to the attic. The stairs to it were twisting and rickety and the dust on the banister looked as if had lain there for a long time, she thought as she followed him up to the musty attic, where the dust lay even thicker.

'I think it might be a good idea to open the window from time to time,' said Helen, looking round the room as Mr Robertson unlocked the glass cabinet where the albums with the newspapers cuttings were kept. The only other furniture was a chair and a table, oval and dark mahogany with a beautiful patina, which Helen uncovered when she flicked a finger over the dust. But there were pictures, a lot of them, in warm wood frames, of ships which had been build at the Dunlop Yard. Helen immediately had the idea that the attic could be developed into a small museum and opened to the public for a charge. It would promote the business, she thought excitedly. Sir Thomas Lipton, the multi-millionaire grocer who had been born in the Gorbals and became the friend of Royalty, had made his fortune by promoting his business. It suddenly seemed ridiculous to Helen that no one had ever thought of copying him.

'Nobody comes here much, Miss,' said Mr Robertson, producing a duster and taking it over the table and the chair in slow, methodical movements before he laid out the dark green leather album containing the newspaper cuttings. 'Now, Miss, I've got quite a lot to do today. So if you like to lock up once you've finished and bring the keys back to me . . .' he added, laying them on the table beside the albums.

'Yes,' said Helen.

The cuttings were neatly laid out – each one on a separate page – and began in chronological order with a report in the *Evening Times* of the founding of the firm in 1870. The founder, William McKerron, had been a highly distinctive entrepreneur and soon set the pace among smaller shipyards until he was able to buy out two neighbouring yards in 1890 when he got his first order for an ocean-going liner, the *Princess Wilhelmina*, for the Hanseatic Line of Hamburg. Since then the yard had built ships for Cunard and Ellermans and Union Castle and Canadian Pacific as well as the Bibby Line of Liverpool and the Scottish Lines of Donaldson and Anchor. Throughout its history it had remained flexible and versatile, taking orders for tugs and hoppers and paddle steamers as well as for the big ships.

An article in the *Evening Times* in 1895 explained the importance and significance of the launching ceremony: 'The launch day is one of the most important stages in the construction of a ship, the day when the Board of Directors of the shipbuilders and the company purchasing the ship celebrate their joint endeavour over cake and wine in the boardroom.

'Money changes hands on launch day, too, and the shipyard can look forward to getting a cheque for up to one third of the cost of the ship. This sometimes takes place on the launching platform once the ship had been named.

'Gifts, too, are exchanged on launch day; the most important one being a gift, often an expensive piece of jewellery, presented by the shipbuilders to the lady who has launched the ship.'

The lady who launched the ship, Helen gathered, was often the wife of the chairman of the company buying the ship or some other lady of importance associated with

56

the owner's trade, and she was the hostess at the party afterwards, though it was organised by the shipbuilder – in the Dunlop Yard's case, by Miss Austin.

Helen turned over the next few pages of the album, then stopped at a picture of a bridal couple. The date of the paper was July 12, 1897, and her eyes bore down on the caption: 'Miss Margaret McKerron and Mr Henry Dunlop pictured after their marriage in Glasgow Cathedral. Miss McKerron is the daughter of William McKerron, the Clyde shipbuilder and philantrophist, and the late Mrs McKerron. Mr Dunlop, a former ship's joiner and outfitting manager, recently joined the board of McKerron, which will become the McKerron Dunlop Yard from August 1.'

Helen peered closely at the picture. Mr Dunlop was still as slim as he had been as a young man – it was thirty years ago, she realised – but his face seemed flatter and a lot less interesting. Her gaze strayed to his bride, whose ample figure was corsetted in the S shape fashionable in the 1890's. Her veil was heavily edged in lace and she was pretty in a homely sort of way. But she really looked more like the big sister Mr Dunlop might be giving away rather than marrying.

And where did Miss Austin come into it? Helen was wondering when she locked the albums back in the cabinet and the door to the attic and came back down the twisting, rickety stair.

Miss Austin, red-faced and disarrayed, was rushing like a March gale out of the big office when Helen returned to her table.

'She's had another row with Mr Dunlop,' said the clerkess at the next table.

'Really?' said Helen, feigning disinterest.

Miss Austin had not returned to the office in the afternoon when Mr Dunlop sent for Helen: 'I'm afraid

Miss Austin is not feeling very well and has gone home and I'm not quite sure when she'll be coming back. But I've had a call from George Nicolaides, the chairman of the shipping line buying the *Papana Queen*. His wife has her guest list ready for the launching – '

'If you want me to help, I'd be delighted,' said Helen. 'I've just been reading the newspaper cuttings in the attic, as you suggested.'

Mr Dunlop looked relieved. 'Put a call into Claridges Hotel in London, where she's staying, and take the names and write them out for Miss Austin to type when she gets back.'

'I can type,' Helen said evenly.

'Since when?' asked Mr Dunlop.

'Since I started evening classes.'

Miss Austin did not return to work the next day and, in the afternoon, Mr Dunlop again sent for Helen.

'I'm still not sure when Miss Austin will be returning to the office,' he said wearily, 'so I think you should start making arrangements for the invitations to be printed. Go into Miss Austin's files and you'll see what the form is.'

Helen didn't need to be told twice. But the file she needed wasn't in the cardboard drawers where Miss Austin kept her files. Eventually she found it at the bottom of a pile of papers on Miss Austin's desk. The woman really wasn't very well organised – and neither was the office, thought Helen. They needed to replace these old cardboard drawer files with new, upright filing cabinets. But now wasn't the moment to tell Mr Dunlop. In a minute she found what she needed – a model for the invitation card, which was sent out in the name of the new owners of the ship. Guests were asked to RSVP Miss Kathleen Austin, Pier Line.

When she went to the printers that afternoon Helen told them: 'The RSVP is to Miss Helen Randolph.'

RSVP Miss Helen Randolph, Pier Line. The words drifted over Helen's mind as she fell asleep that night. Now she really was going up in the world.

She was still dreaming about them when she walked into the office the next morning.

'Miss Randolph!' The imperious voice of Miss Austin, who was standing at the other end of the room snapping a white card against the desk top, brought Helen up short. She instantly checked the wall clock and saw she was in plenty of time for work. Aware of the attention of the other early arrivals in the office, she took a deep breath and said in a cheery voice: 'Good morning, Miss Austin. How nice to see you back. I hope you are feeling much better.' She made her way to her desk and swallowed hard. The tension mounting in the office was almost a physical thing.

'Now that's a lie if ever I heard one!' Miss Austin's shrill voice was rising with the colour of her cheeks as she approached Helen's desk.

The starlings on the roof opposite could be heard through the closed windows. The office was deathly quiet.

Helen realised this was a showdown. Her hands were trembling as she laid down her bag on her desk. She steeled herself to remain in control. *She must remain calm.*

Miss Austin was now snap-snapping the card on Helen's desk.

'I am not lying, Miss Austin,' said Helen, turning to face the older woman. Suddenly she felt totally secure in her youth, in her command of herself and her smart, neat appearance. She almost felt a twinge of sympathy as she noticed Miss Austin's puffy red eyes and rumpled clothes. The woman's anger was making her chin wobble and she was making a spectacle of herself, thought Helen,

59

realising the least thing, a careless – or a carefully-timed word, would unleash all the uncontrollable rage in Miss Austin.

Her heart raced as she glanced at the clock, knowing that within the next two minutes Mr Dunlop would pop his head round the door and say good morning to his staff. *Now was her chance.*

'Of course we are all pleased to see you back, Miss Austin,' said Helen sweetly, standing her ground.

'So what's this then?' screeched Miss Austin, flinging the white card across Helen's desk.

'It's the invitation to the launch of the *Papana Queen*, Miss Austin,' said Helen, resisting the urge to pick up the card.

'I can see that!' Miss Austin thumped the desk and one of the girls stifled a giggle. 'Just what is your name doing on it?'

'It is there because Mr Dunlop asked me to take over the organisation for this launch, Miss Austin.' She raised her voice slightly in a tone of concern and included the rest of the staff in a sideways glance. 'We've all been concerned for you, Miss Austin, especially Mr Dunlop. He didn't know when you would be back.' She paused and shrugged her shoulders helplessly. 'And the launch had to be organised,' she continued reasonably. 'Any one of us would – '

'Ha!' snorted Miss Austin, coming round to Helen's side of the desk. 'You little bitch! You think just because you are young and pretty you can come in here and twist Mr Dunlop around your little finger – '

'Please, Miss Austin,' Helen stepped back under the onslaught, her hands fluttering to her shocked face. She was acting as though her life depended on it – and it was so easy to do it.

'You don't know the half of it.' Miss Austin stepped

60

even closer. 'Only *I* know Harry Dunlop. *You're* not interested in the company. We all know what you're interested in!'

Helen saw Mr Dunlop had now emerged from his office and heard every word of this latest blast from Miss Austin. Now she had to stop Miss Austin before it went too far and things were said which should never be said. Because that would damage her, too, in Mr Dunlop's eyes.

'Please, Miss Austin, this is unfair,' she protested.

'Unfair!' squawked Miss Austin, poking Helen in the chest. 'Unfair! I'll show you what unfair is. You'll be on the street before this day is out. On the street where you belong, you – '

A door slammed before the word was out. Its deafening sound echoed round the office as Helen sank on to her chair, buckling at the knees.

'Good morning, ladies.' Mr Dunlop's familiar greeting had a steel-rimmed edge to it. 'Miss Randolph, please bring me the proof of the invitations I asked you to organise. After that, I'd like to see you, Miss Austin, in my office. I see you are not really well enough to be back at work. We shall arrange some long term leave for you, I think.' He flicked a meaningful glance round the stunned faces of his staff. 'When you are ready, Miss Randolph. We have a ship to launch . . .'

A ship is born on the day she is launched. The long gestation period of planning and design and months of plates being shaped and riveted and cranes hoisting vast sheets of metal into place reach their climax on the day she is named and takes to the water. There was no concealing the excitement and the smiles on every face or mistaking the pride and love in the eyes beneath cloth caps on the mild November afternoon when the platform party mounted the scarlet and gold dias from which the *Papana Queen* would be launched.

The sunshine was exceptionally bright for the time of year as, stripped of the womb of scaffolding and ladders in which she had been nurtured, the great liner stood with her black hull gleaming and naked on the slipway. Though she was still only a shell, with no funnels or masts or engines, and her state rooms were only half done, she seemed as high as the skyscrapers Helen had seen in posters of the great liners arriving in New York. Her name was painted in huge gold letters on her prow, which everyone on the ground was now looking at. And in the shadow of her hull men were slithering in mud among 10-foot high piles of thick, rusty chains, removing the blocks of timbers along the length of the keel and attending to the triggers which, when released, would send her down into the water. Other men were scrambling around on her deck. One had thrown down the rope which would hold the launch bottle of champagne. The end of it had been decorated in the black and gold colours of the Athenian Line and, just before the platform party took their places, the yard manager climbed on to the dias and attached a bottle of champagne to the rope.

In their telephone conversations and correspondence about the launch, Helen had so impressed Mrs Nicolaides with her knowledge of shipbuilding and shipping that she had been invited to join the launch party.

'My dear, you sound as if you built the ship yourself!' Mrs Nicolaides had said more than once.

Now she stood at the back of the platform, craning her neck, as Mrs Nicolaides, a suntanned Mediterranean beauty, reached for the champagne bottle.

'I name this ship the *Papana Queen*. May God bless her and all who sail in her.' Her voice sounded tiny and faraway. But it echoed round the yard as she sent the bottle of champagne swinging, then crashing against the hull, spattering it with glass and spume. Then, as everyone held their breath, the great ship moved, gliding silently stern first towards the river. As she travelled down the 'ways' a gentle acceleration could be observed before she finally slipped into her natural surroundings in the water with a very slight dip of her bow, as though she was acknowledging the lady sponsor's blessings. This brought a great cheer from all the spectators. Then the piles of chains began to unravel, rumbling slowly at first before they went thundering after her to steady her and stop her from running away. Another great cheer rose all round the yard and the men threw their caps up into the air.

As the tension in the platform party now dissolved in smiles, Helen saw Mr Dunlop swallow several times. She knew what he was feeling because she had the same pride and love and she swallowed, too, to hold back tears which sprang from her heart . . .

Today the luxurious crimson carpet, with a pile deep as her index finger, and the dark mahogany furniture of mirror-bright patina in the directors' suite did not seem out of place beside the workaday desolation of the yard. Building ships generated wealth and power and an opulent setting was the only right one for the launch party, she decided. Watching Mrs Nicolaides dispensing charm and sipping Greek wine carefully chosen from the Pier Line cellars, Helen wondered if it would not just be easier to marry money than to make her own. Marriage certainly eased a woman's way in the world, but no, she wanted to have her own money, not to be dependent on a man for it, no matter how rich he was. . .

Helen had to wait another three months for the next big excitement, for the snowy February day in 1928 when the *Papana Queen*, her fitting-out completed, slipped out

63

into the river and headed downstream for her sea trials on the measured mile off Skelmorlie on the Firth of Clyde with Helen aboard, secretary now to the shipbuilder. Miss Austin had not returned from her enforced leave – and if ever a thought of her rose, Helen dismissed it instantly. She had done what she had to do . . .

While Harry bustled from the engine room to the bridge, making important supervisory noises, Helen roamed the First Class – fingering wood panelling and veneering, taking off her shoes to sink her toes into deep pile carpets, stretching sleekly as a cat on opulent velour settees, sitting daintily on rosewood bergere armchairs and boudoir chairs of lacquered wood and mother-of-pearl. This was the world where status demanded a traveller had at least twenty pieces of luggage in the hold and a gentleman needed to keep a trunk in the corridor outside his state-room for the four daily changes of clothes he needed on an eight- or nine- day voyage. A shiver of pleasure ran down Helen's spine as she imagined herself, swathed in white fox and satin, descending the grand marble staircase under an armature of hanging lamps. Then she roamed on through luxurious dining-rooms and pampered lounges to the Palm Court and the leather masculinity of the smoking room before she poked her nose into the staterooms, each one differently appointed in dazzling shades of textiles. The *Papana Queen* was a glorious work of art and science – and nearly half the men who had created her would be on the dole next week because there were not enough orders to keep them on.

Helen was angry when she returned to the promenade deck, where wealthy couples would foxtrot in the afternoon. The spectre of abandoned gantries stretched for miles on both banks of the river under the glowering winter sky.

'It's just not right that so many men should be out of work!' she protested when Mr Dunlop reappeared.

'Do you think I don't know that?' he flared. Helen had never seen him so angry. 'Do you think I enjoy putting men on the dole? It hurts me every time I have to give a man the sack. But if I haven't got the work for them, they have to go. I've always told every man who comes to the Yard: "Once a Dunlop man always a Dunlop man." And I'll take them back as soon as there is an upturn in business. They know that.'

Pride and defiance shone in those extraordinary blue eyes. Harry Dunlop sincerely cared for the men who worked for him and their suffering was his suffering, too, and all of a sudden Helen wanted to put her arms around him and comfort him and make it all right for him again.

'You really care about these men,' she said softly.

'Yes,' he said, his gaze meeting hers. 'I care very much.' They were silent for a moment, then a smile stole over his face. 'You're a very bright girl, Helen, but you're not asking me the next question.'

'What question?' Helen puzzled.

'You're not asking me *why* I care.'

'Because . . . they work for you . . . because you do . . .'

The smile took deeper possession of Mr Dunlop's face and Helen was flummoxed now.

'That's true,' he said, 'as far as it goes. Helen, I care about them because it is in my interest to care about them. If they work, I prosper. If I have no work for them, I go out of business. Never, Helen, ever care about anyone that it is not in your interest to care for. Call it ruthlessness, if you like. But it is the only valid caring there is. Any other kind of caring is hypocrisy. Only ever care about people who can enhance and promote your interests and everything will be possible for you.' He raised an eyebrow. 'Are you shocked?'

'No,' said Helen, her gaze meeting and holding those penetrating eyes. The more she learned about this extraordinary man, the more fascinated she was by him. She felt excited by him and, as she always did with every discovery she made about Harry Dunlop, she wanted to know more. And, as she'd known for months now, she wanted him physically – so much that it hurt. 'Would – would you like to come to tea on Saturday?' she asked.

'I would. Unfortunately, I can't. I'm leaving for Hamburg the day after tomorrow. I may be able to get an order from the Hanseatic line. But I can come to tea when I come back.'

Mr Dunlop was away for weeks and, in his absence, Helen realised how much she missed him. She was acutely conscious of being alone and exposed and, for the first time, the flat in Great Western Terrace seemed lonely. One Saturday she went out dancing to the Locarno with friends from the office, but all the young men who asked her to dance seemed crass and boring and had nothing to say.

Then she received a postcard from Hamburg. It said: 'The *Marguerite* (a Pier Line Ship) docked here this morning and the *Empress of the East* (built at the Dunlop Yard) arrives tomorrow. You'd feel at home here. Harry.'

Harry. It was the first time she had ever thought of Mr Dunlop as Harry. But that was his name. A nice name. She put the postcard, a picture of the port of Hamburg, on the drawing-room mantelpiece and read it before she went to work in the morning and when she came home every day until he was back in the office.

From the moment he crossed the big room, Helen was even more conscious of Harry Dunlop as a man. And now he was back the world felt normal again.

The next few days seemed the longest in her life, eased only by the joy of anticipating a few hours of uninterrupted time with him. She had bought a new afternoon dress in green wool, which matched her eyes, and she had brushed her hair till is shone like the summer sun, but there was a knot in her stomach as she waited for the bell to ring. And when she opened the door she had to make a huge effort to restrain her impulse to throw her arms around Harry Dunlop's neck.

'Hello,' she said, acutely conscious of him.

'Hello, Helen,' he said softly.

'Oh, Harry . . .' She said his Christian name for the first time and it sounded both natural and special on her tongue. 'I'm *so* glad you're back.'

'So am I,' he said, taking her in his arms and kissing her forehead as if it was the most natural thing in the world for him to do. And his arms felt so strong and protective she wanted to stay in them forever.

Then the moment passed and he let her go and his arms fell to his sides.

'I've got something for you,' he said. He took her hand and led her into the drawing-room, where he took a small black-and-white striped box tied with white satin ribbon from an inside pocket of his raincoat and handed it to her. When she opened it she found a model of the *Empress of the East* in a clear glass bottle.

'Oh, Harry, it's lovely! Thank you so much.' And now she did throw her arms around his neck and kiss him impetuously on the lips.

The now not-so-strange sensations started swirling wildly around her body. She had felt them before, in tiny waves. Now they surged in a great tidal movement. A powerful, overwhelming movement. And she knew Harry was feeling them, too. It was in his eyes, which were changing in a wild and beautiful way.

'Have you any idea what you do to me, Helen?' he demanded, drawing back from her.

67

'Yes.' She said the word with a new voice she had suddenly found within herself. And she recognised that, too – it was a woman's voice. 'Harry, I need you . . .' she said – and a sense of going home filled her.

Chapter Three

London and Glasgow – April, 1929

The overnight train from Glasgow Central to London Euston rumbled through the quiet country beyond Ecclefechan towards the Debateable Lands, the old lair of the Border reivers. Tossing beneath a single sheet, in her hot, stuffy first-class sleeper, Helen felt she was the only passenger interested in trying to sleep. Everyone else seemed to be trafficking up and down the corridor, shouting at the tops of their voices. She turned over on her stomach and hugged her pillow. She felt exhausted.

Oh, she hoped she wasn't pregnant. She was overdue by six days and worried sick. Ever since the start of her affair with Harry Dunlop she had been terrified of becoming pregnant . . . of being like her mother . . .

'What happens if I have a baby?' she once asked him.

'I'll see you're all right,' he answered gruffly, embarrassed.

'What does that mean?' she probed.

'What I say,' he said abruptly, and turned away.

And that had been the end of it. But she knew what would happen. She would lose her job and probably her home as well and all her bright hopes of rising in the world would be vanquished forever. She also knew it was her own fault. She should never have let him do it. Except she had wanted it, or thought she did, in the beginning. And now she couldn't stop him, except for certain times. He did it as of right, as if he owned her body. And it had destroyed every good and decent thing she had ever felt for him.

He nearly always hurt her. She often cried afterwards, but only after he had gone. Once he had seen her crying.

'You're very emotional tonight,' he said coldly, leaving in a hurry.

He had no idea what she felt and he didn't seem to care if he hurt her. Sometimes it seemed to her that all the violence and brutality and ugliness of the city were in what he did to her. Oh, she knew she wasn't alone. All over Glasgow men were doing to women what Harry Dunlop did to her – and all the women got out of it was babies, endless babies who robbed them of their beauty and their strength and eventually their lives. Sometimes she wanted to spit on the men standing on street corners. She knew what they did when they weren't sunning themselves on the streets – they were hurting their wives and giving them more babies.

Painfully she knew she had engineered the situation herself. She had been dazzled by Harry Dunlop and his aura of wealth and power and even admired his ruthlessness. Now, for the first time since she had stood her ground with Miss Austin, she felt empathy and sympathy for the ageing spinster abandoned in her declining years. And where had her manoeuvring got her? The truth was that she felt even lonelier than when her mother had died and her father had rejected her.

The worst times were when the office emptied and he would come through, asking her to check the cloakroom. It was his cue for her to remove her knickers. She would return to his office where he would have drawn the curtains and be waiting for her on the chesterfield. Each time she hoped it would be different, that he would find words of tenderness and love for her, arouse her gently and hold her close afterwards. But he never held her or kissed her properly. Instinctively, in the encircling darkness of his office, he would pull up her skirt and take her with the same business-like efficiency with which he performed all his tasks. Then he would go on to some business dinner or home to his wife in Pollokshields, leaving her to make her lonely way back to Great Western Terrace, sore and empty and heartsick.

Now she soaked her pillow with her tears. It was so humiliating. And every month she lived in terror till the magic flow came. She almost welcomed the pain because she would be safe for a week and he would leave her alone.

'You wouldn't like it now,' had become her coded expression and sometimes, but not too often, she cheated and told him he wouldn't like it when she knew he would.

Instinctively, deep down inside she knew that what happened between a man and a woman could be beautiful and tender – a perfect physical and emotional and spiritual union. She dreamed about it all the time now, dreamed about it when she was being humiliated on the chesterfield in Harry's office.

She hated him now, because of what he did to her, she felt cut off from her generation and her friends. Officially, she didn't have a boyfriend, and when she heard the girls talking and discussing their boyfriends she felt left out. She was too ashamed to admit to anyone, even Elizabeth Campbell, what Harry did and what had happened to her. So, because she could not confide in anyone, it was doubly hard to bear. And all the time, constantly, she was afraid of getting pregnant – like her mother – and being abandoned. Which was why, without telling Harry, she was on her way to London to the controversial Marie

Stopes clinic, the only place in the whole country where a woman could go for contraceptive advice and help – and then only if she was married, as Helen was going to pretend to be.

Why did she stay with Harry? Why didn't she give up her job and leave him? She had asked herself the question so many times, and now she asked it again as the train rumbled over the tracks. And the answer was always the same: she was afraid of losing her home if she refused to submit to Mr Dunlop. She was still only 20, one year below the legal adult age of 21, so it was unlikely she would be able to rent another flat and, after having enjoyed the freedom of a beautiful West End apartment, she didn't want go into lodgings. But she knew she couldn't go on as she was doing.

She sat up suddenly and switched on the light over her head. In one wide, sweeping movement she swung her legs on to the carpeted floor of the sleeper and reached into her black leather suitcase for the slim volume she read all the time now – Marie Stopes's bestseller, *Married Love*.

Helen had used a pencil to underline the passages in which she found most comfort and hope. And when she had taken the book from its place beneath the fine silk lingerie she would wear tomorrow, she lay back in her bed and opened it.

'. . . and there is nothing for which the innermost spirit of one and all so yearns as for a sense of union with another soul, and the perfecting of oneself which such a union brings . . .' The words brought the tears back to her eyes. There seemed to be no end to her tears any more. She had tears for everything. When she was in pain; when her heart lifted up as it did now to see her own feelings and beliefs, so beautifully expressed.

Her fingers fluttered through the pages to find her

favourite passages: '. . . Each heart knows instinctively that it is only a mate who can give full comprehension of all the potential greatness in the soul . . . To use a homely simile – one might compare two human beings in two bodies charged with electricity of different potentials. Isolated from each other the electric forces within them are invisible, but if they come into the right juxtaposition the force is transmuted, and a spark, a glow of burning light arises between them. Such is love . . . the complete act of union is a triple consummation. It symbolises, and at the same time actually enhances, the spiritual union; there are a myriad subtleties of soul-structure which are compounded in this alchemy . . .'

That was what it could be!

And then she came upon the passage which described what it was really like for her: '. . . When a woman is claimed at times when she takes no *natural* pleasure in union, and claimed in such a way that there is no *induced* romantic pleasure, the act reduces her vitality, and tends to kill her power of enjoying it when the love season returns . . . Trivialities are often the first indicators of something which takes its roots unseen in the profoundest depths. The girl may sob for hours over something so trifling that she cannot even put into words its nature . . . Then, so strange is the mystical interrelation between our bodies, our minds and our souls, that for crimes committed in ignorance of the dual functions to the married pair, and the laws which harmonise them, the punishments are reaped in planes quite diverse, till new and ever new misunderstandings appear to spring spontaneously from the soil of their mutual contact. *Gradually or swiftly each heart begins to hide a sense of boundless isolation.*'

That was how it had become with Harry. She felt utterly divorced and isolated from him and the times she

73

felt it most was when he performed his cruel caricature of lovemaking.

Burning, salty tears now fell on the page. Through them she read on: '. . . a woman's love is stirred *primarily* through her heart and mind . . .'

That was how it had been in the beginning. She had admired Harry Dunlop but he had killed her fine feelings for him by the insensitive way he invaded her body. He did the most intimate thing a man could do to a woman, he entered her body with his own, and he wouldn't even talk to her about it!

The book fell from her fingers and, as silence fell on the corridor and the night train thundered over the border into the north of England, she decided to do what had been in her mind for ages. *She would leave him.* She had managed to save quite a bit to add to the money she had been left by her mother; she would lie about her age to get another flat – and all she would ask from Harry Dunlop would be a testimonial for when she came to apply for another job. Whether she was pregnant or not, somehow she would survive. She wasn't going to be defeated like her mother had been.

A light April shower was starting to fall as the overnight train from Glasgow emerged from the long tunnel and approached the arc of platforms under the canopied glass roof of Euston Station. Helen's sleep had been fractured and though she looked fresh and smart in a fine black wool suit, she felt tired as she opened a compartment at the back of her handbag and took out the cheap plain gold band she had bought in Woolworths and slipped it on to the third finger of her left hand before she pulled on her gloves. She studied her immaculately made-up face beneath a white cloche which contrasted with her black suit.

74

She hoped she looked married. Then she turned from the mirror and made her way out into the corridor of the train . . .

After the harshness of the Glasgow climate, the air in London felt positively balmy; so soft it seemed to bathe her skin. It was also very noisy and as she stood by the stone portals of Euston watching the black London cabs and the red buses roaring by, Helen was filled with a sense of the excitement of London. Matching her memory of the A to Z securely tucked in her handbag with her surroundings, she crossed the road and turned right along the tops of Gower Street and Tottenham Court Road to reach Whitfield Street, a long narrow ribbon of Georgian houses in khaki brick. The doors with their fanlights and astragalled windows reminded Helen of the New Town in Edinburgh, though the houses were not nearly so grand or expensive and on an altogether much smaller scale.

Marie Stopes's house was at number 108 and she came upon it sooner than she expected.

Birth Control News, a billboard for Marie Stopes's newspaper, stood beside the railing outside the front door, which was painted white and had a large brass knocker. Helen walked past it, then crossed the road and looked at the house from the other side of it.

Between two ground-floor windows a large notice said: 'The Mothers' Clinic, Constructive Birth Control. Open Daily.' And the letters CBC, carved in panels the size of a window pane were stretched across the windows and above the board.

A look of calm settled on Helen's lovely face. She had come to the shrine of the knowledge she needed. When she came out of this house she would have the means to banish all risk of ever becoming pregnant. She would be in control of her life and her body again. A glint of triumph lit her emerald eyes. She briskly recrossed the road and banged the brass knocker against the door.

It was answered by a middle-aged woman in a dark grey suit.

'Good morning,' said the woman. Her blue eyes were kindly despite the severe way in which her grey hair was drawn back off her face into a bun. 'You will have come to see one our nurses.'

'A doctor?'

'No,' said the woman. 'There are no doctors here. Marie Stopes believes nurses are well qualified to look after women and give them the care they need. All our mothers are seen by nurses.'

As she stepped over the threshold, a layer of anxiety fell invisibly from Helen. She wasn't going to have to pit her wits or explain anything to a man. A woman would be kinder, more understanding, and her questions would not seem so intrusive.

'Please come this way,' said the woman, leading Helen down the hall to a small room at the back of the house furnished with a desk, two chairs and the kind of brand-new steel filing cabinet she wished to see at the Pier Line.

'Are you married?' asked the woman, taking a chair on one side of the desk and pointing to the other chair for Helen to take a seat.

'Yes,' said Helen, removing her gloves and seeing the woman notice her wedding ring.

'We do need your name and address,' said the woman, quickly adding. 'We will not be writing to you. The only circumstances in which we would write to you would be if you were to write to us, and our reply would be contained in a plain envelope. But we do like to know who our mothers are.'

She pushed a plain sheet of paper across the table and, when she had dipped the pen the woman gave her in an ink bottle, she wrote: Mrs Kirsty Stewart, Grange House, Rhu, Dumbartonshire. She was taking her mother's name and the address of her father's house, where she had been conceived.

'Thank you,' said the receptionist as Helen handed her back the sheet of paper. 'Now, if you will just follow me again.' She led Helen into the room which faced the street, where three other women were already waiting. 'If you care to take a seat, a nurse will see you shortly.'

The room was furnished by an assortment of high-backed and easy chairs, which had obviously seen better days, and a central oval table was stacked with copies of *Birth Control News*. There were also some old copies of *Good Housekeeping*. One lay open at an article on Breach of Promise, which had been published last year. 'Is compensation on this score an Anachronism in these days of Emancipated Women?' asked the writer, Helena Normanton, B.A. Helen looked around the room at the tired faces and ruined figures of the other women. Though they were older, they were not really old – probably only in their late twenties – but they *looked old* because they had been worn out by childbearing. Emancipated women were like the 'bright young things' – there were very few of them.

'Mrs Harvey?' a uniformed nurse put her head round the door and one of the women, a fair-haired woman with an anaemic pallor, rose and left the room.

Another nurse put her head round the door: 'Mrs Stewart?'

'Yes . . .' Helen got up and followed the nurse up a flight of stairs to a first-floor room overlooking the street.

It had a beautiful parquet floor and was furnished with a rolltop desk on which the nurse's papers were spread, a bed covered with a single sheet, a screen, a couple of chairs and a trolley with an assortment of basins and water jugs. A vase of fresh daffodils and irises stood on a table by one of the windows.

The nurse invited Helen to take one of the chairs by her desk.

'Do you have many children, Mrs Stewart?'

'Two. A boy and a girl,' Helen lied and immediately thought: I'm saying too much. I didn't need to tell her their sexes.

'And you don't want to have any more?'

'My doctor says my health might not stand up to having another baby.'

'Mrs Stopes is a great believer that a mother's good health and well being are essential to the happiness of her husband and children.'

'They are,' said Helen.

'Is there any particular aspect of your relations with your husband that troubles you?'

'He is very demanding,' said Helen, thinking quickly and wondering if the nurse was married. She wasn't wearing a wedding ring.

'A great many men are,' said the nurse sympathetically and Helen decided she *was* married.

'And not very understanding,' added Helen.

'Another very common problem,' said the nurse. 'Well, if there is nothing more you wish to ask, perhaps you would like to go behind the screen and undress.'

There *was* a lot Helen wanted to ask and talk about, but she was scared she might let something slip which could give away her unmarried state and she would never get what she had come for. She rose and went behind the screen and undressed and lay down on the bed, where the nurse fitted her with a contraceptive cap and instructed her on its use.

'How long is it since you had your last child, Mrs Stewart?' the nurse asked when Helen was dressed again.

78

'Three years. Angus is three,' said Helen.

'Remarkable,' said the nurse with a faint smile. 'You still have the body of a very young woman.'

'I'm really very lucky,' said Helen, blushing, realising the nurse knew she was not a mother.

She did not breathe easily again until she was back in the street and her precious cap and its instructions were secure inside her handbag. With joy she felt her period coming on as she walked quickly down the other side of Grafton Way until it opened on to Fitzroy Square where she stopped, amazed at its beauty.

Great plane trees rose in gardens in the centre of the square, spreading their high, bare branches like wings; glorious snatches of daffodils covered the rolling lawn in their shadow; and on the north side forsythia blazed bright as the summer sun.

She walked slowly round the square, her spirits soaring higher than the plane trees. For the first time in at least nine months she felt happy again. She would not be doomed like her mother. She was back in control of her life; she wasn't pregnant and now she had the means to ensure she would never again be in danger of becoming pregnant unless she was married and wanted to have children. And she would soon be free of Harry Dunlop.

As Helen fell into a deep contented sleep on the night train thundering north from Euston to Glasgow, Margaret Dunlop died of heart failure in her bed in her house in Pollokshields. She was sixty-one years old and the man to whom she had been married for nearly thirty-two years was, to his own amazement, overwhelmed with grief.

Harry knew his wife had not been particularly well in the last year. But she had not been very well for a number of years. If it wasn't her back, it was a migraine

79

or she was running a temperature or it was her chest. Apart from going to church on Sunday, to which she somehow always managed and insisted he accompany her, and the long summer hours spent in the garden, she had lived in her bed for years. And there had been such a lack of any sign of anything being worse than usual that Morag Macfarlane, Margaret's housekeeper-cum-companion, had been given the night off to visit an elderly aunt who was unwell. She would not be back till the morning. After the doctor had had a brandy with him and gone on his way, Harry found himself alone in the house.

He poured himself another brandy and stood twirling the glass in his fingers not knowing what to do. Normally, he would have telephoned Kathleen Austin. And then he would have sent the car for her and she would have come running over as she had done for years when there was an emergency. She had been the most discreet of women. In his wife's presence she had never given any word or sign that she had ever been anything to him other than his secretary. But now Kathleen was no longer a part of his life and Margaret was dead ... he was utterly alone.

Except ... there was Helen. Helen, so young and so eager to learn. She was a good listener – and he needed someone to listen. He took another gulp of his brandy and wondered how she had got on seeing her solicitor and going to her mother's grave. She did not often ask for a day off, but it had been important and he had been glad to let her have it. He looked at his wristwatch. It was exactly three o'clock in the morning. It wasn't really fair, but he would send the car for her. He knew now he needed Helen to do more than listen, knew what he needed to do to her desperately now ... Yes, under his own roof, with his wife's body not yet cold. But it was what he needed, more than anything.

He reached for the telephone and dialled her number. But there was no reply. He remembered the telephone was in the hall and she was probably fast asleep. He could ring his chauffeur and send him over to knock her up and bring her to him. But she might think it was some passing drunk. And if she got frightened she might ring the police. He could go over there himself – and leave Morag Macfarlane to find his wife's body in the morning? No! He would need to make it on his own through the night till morning came . . .

The rain had settled into a steady downpour as Harry Dunlop's Daimler turned up the broad gravel drive to his red sandstone mansion in Pollokshields. Seeing it loom, Helen, who cut a tiny figure in the cushioned leather comfort on the back, stopped wiggling her toes on the carpet and slipped them back into her black patent high heels.

It had been just after eight o'clock when she walked through the door at Great Western Terrace and the telephone was ringing in the hall.

'Did you oversleep or something?' Harry asked in the gruff tone Helen recognised as the one he used when feeling threatened to impinge on him. 'I've been ringing you since six and getting no reply.'

'Yes, I did oversleep, Harry. I had rather a tiring day yesterday,' said Helen, fully alert now. She had slept well on the train and felt refreshed.

'Mrs Dunlop died in the night. So I'm sending the car over. I'd like you to come here instead of going to the office.' For a moment the line fell silent. Helen had never met Mrs Dunlop, hadn't even spoken to the woman on the telephone. She felt it was a bit like being told the King was dead – someone she had heard of but with whom she had no contact, even though Harry went home to her at night after he had humiliated Helen on the sofa in his office. She really had no idea what to say.

'I'm sorry to hear Mrs Dunlop's dead,' she said eventually.

'Thanks.' The gruffness had gone from Harry's voice. He sounded choked, close to tears . . . as if he could no longer hold back his feelings.

'I'll come straight over when the car arrives,' she said softly.

The car had obviously already been on its way because it arrived five minutes later. But Helen made the chauffeur wait until she had washed and changed. *She* was not in mourning, so she hung up her black suit in the wardrobe and slipped into one of sombre clerical grey, which felt more appropriate.

As the Daimler made its way across the city and the river, Helen read the shipping news in the *Glasgow Herald*, mentally noting the progress of Pier Line Ships on the high seas. When it came to a halt on the broad gravel sweep outside the house in Pollokshields, Harry dashed out beneath a big blue and white golfing umbrella.

'Good to see you,' he said as Helen stepped from the limousine under the umbrella.

The gruffness was back in his voice, but Helen was shocked by his appearance. Overnight all the youthfulness had gone. The furrows around his mouth and on his brow were now real grooves and he looked haggard. He was an old man.

'I'm so sorry,' she said, proffering her hand, which he took. Gratefully, as if his life depended on it.

They walked briskly to the house.

His breath smelt of drink, which unlike him, especially so early in the morning. 'I'm expecting Morag

Macfarlane shortly. She was Mrs Dunlop's housekeeper and companion. I'll have to break the news to her . . .'

Watching the way he was nervously twisting his fingers as he stood back from her and turned towards the window, Helen had no idea what she felt for Harry Dunlop at this moment. But he was feeling something and she wondered what it was – guilt, regret, remorse?

The rain had eased off by the time Morag arrived and Helen decided to take a walk in the garden so that Harry could talk to Morag alone.

Margaret Dunlop had clearly taken a pride in her garden; rose bushes grew in circles in the centres of two lawns divided by a path and bordered by densely planted wallflowers. At the bottom of the garden the path split in opposite directions. One branch twisted way to a garden shed and a compost heap while the other led straight to a tiny summerhouse – a pretty, circular white-painted wooden structure with lots of windows. Helen picked her way carefully down the soggy path and gently pushed open the door. Inside, a rocking chair in light cane padded with striped Indian cotton cushions stood beside a cane table. This was obviously Margaret Dunlop's bower. Helen stepped inside and dropped on to the chair.

She sat for a while, dreamily enjoying the soothing rocking motion. Then she noticed the end of an old newspaper page sticking out of one of the drawers in the table. She leaned forward to push it back into the drawer and close it, but the paper refused to budge and the drawer would not shut. So she pulled it fully open and took the paper out. She was about to lay it flat on the bottom of the drawer when she recognised the photograph on the page. It was the bridal picture of Harry and Margaret Dunlop, the one she had seen in the album of newspaper cuttings in the Pier Line attic.

Then she noticed a notebook bound in stiff blue covers at the back of the drawer. Unable to resist, she picked it up and opened it.

The book contained dated entries, begun two months ago. Early in February Margaret Dunlop had written in a beautiful copperplate hand: 'I could no longer hold up my head if Harry left me . . .'

Helen quickly flicked through the pages, rapidly piecing the dead woman's story together: 'I knew Harry did not love me when we married. He had a girl, Kathleen. But he married me and I hoped that in time . . . Then after my father died he took Kathleen to work for him as his secretary . . . and I realised it was not to be. I think if I had been able to give him the son he longed for he would have loved me. But that was not to be either . . . we never had a family . . . so I settled for what there was. Harry was my husband and as long as he took his place by my side in church on Sunday I could hold up my head in the community . . .'

Yesterday, hours before she died, Margaret Dunlop made her last entry: 'Since Kathleen left him I have become afraid. My husband is not the man to go without what a man seems to need . . . And I know his new young secretary must be giving him what he needs or she would never have taken Kathleen's place . . . She is very young. She could give him the son he has always longed for. Then he would leave me and I could no longer hold up my head . . .'

The book fell from Helen's nerveless fingers. She had never given Margaret Dunlop a second thought. It was his secretary, Miss Austin's place, she had usurped in Harry's life, not that of the wife who had scarcely seemed to exist. But Margaret Dunlop had existed all right, right here in this place . . . silently suffering and hoping and waiting and feeling and eventually dying. Had she ever tried to speak to her husband and tell him how she felt? Helen suspected not. There was a resigned quality in that beautiful copperplate. And even if she had, she would have met a stone wall.

Suddenly Helen began to feel angry. What *had* he felt for the dead woman? Or for Miss Austin? And what did he feel for her? Helen's lips narrowed. Before she left him she was going to find out what he felt – and she would never have a better chance than she had today when he was obviously vulnerable.

She picked up the book and put it back in the drawer, which she managed to close. Then she took a comb from her bag, tidied a few stray hairs and applied some deep red lipstick from a gilt case.

Bright blue sky was making windows in the receding cloud, which was paler, creamier and more buoyant now, and a wind was getting up to chase the last of the rain away when Helen closed the door of the summerhouse behind her. She watched the clouds for a moment, then retraced her steps back up the path to the house, where Morag Macfarlane was laying a tea tray before Harry on a table by the drawing-room window.

When the housekeeper had gone, Harry poured Helen a cup and when he handed it to her she saw that tears were glittering at the corners of those extraordinary blue eyes.

'Margaret was a good woman,' he said, his Adam's apple bulging, his voice breaking. 'Better . . . better than I deserved . . .' Helen stared at him in stunned silence. 'I should never have married her, Helen. I never wanted to marry her. I had a girl. But I was young and ambitious. I wanted to build the most beautiful ships in the world. I wanted my own yard. I had risen as far as ability would take me. But that's only so far. After that you need money. Talent without money will achieve very little. There's no freedom for talent to develop fully or do anything much without money. But I was no one. And nobody was going to give Harry Dunlop the money to build the beautiful ships he dreamed about. Except Alfred McKerron.

'One day he called me into his office. "Look," he said, "you're a fine young man, Harry Dunlop. You've got a lot of talent and drive and you could go far. So I've got a proposition to put to you. Marry my daughter and inherit the yard."

'I had never met Mr KcKerron's daughter, though I knew she had kept house from him since his wife had died. By this time I also knew that life's big chances did not often come wrapped in fine boxes marked "Opportunity", that mostly it was a case of seeking them among the dust like gold and making them big. But here was one very big chance being presented to me on a plate. But somehow it didn't seem right. I intended to marry my girl. When I said nothing Mr McKerron said: "Well, at least meet her."

'I came for tea to this house the following Sunday. She was a nice soul, a homely body, and I liked her. But she wasn't the kind of woman to appeal to a man like myself. And she was thirty to my twenty-four. But after a few weeks and a few more teas Mr Mckerron sent for me again. "Well, what do you think?" he asked. I was in turmoil. I didn't know what to do about Kathleen. When I didn't say anything, he said: "I'd like to have you as a son-in-law. I've no son of my own and I'd like you to take over the yard. Marry my daughter and the yard will become the McKerron Dunlop on your marriage." My name would be on the yard, my dream could be reality. I asked him how Margaret felt about this arrangement he was proposing. "She's thirty and she can't bear the stigma of being single any longer. The only way she can hold her head up in society is by getting married." "But surely there are plenty of men who would marry her," I said. "There are plenty who would like to get their hands on her money but she hasn't a fancy for any of them. Nor have I. She likes you." He paused and his eyes narrowed and he looked at me knowingly. "It will be enough for her to be your wife. She won't stand in your way ..."

'So I could keep Kathleen. She could still be my girl. "Is that a deal then?" he asked, getting up from behind his desk and offering me his hand. I took it.' Harry gulped his tea. 'We were married six weeks later. I knew it wasn't right, that I ought to call it off. But Margaret was so happy and so looking forward to becoming my wife. I felt I would be letting her down. Besides, I knew I'd never get another chance like this.' An old gleam of ambition lit his eyes for a moment. 'I got what I wanted. I got my shipyard. After her father died I dropped his name so it was mine alone. But Margaret didn't get what she wanted. And now she's dead ...'

The tears which had been poised at the corners of Harry's eyes now rolled down his cheeks. Despite herself, Helen reached out across the table and took one of his hands between her own.

'Were you never able to talk about it?' she asked softly.

'Talk about what?'

'Your feelings for each other.'

He looked at her uncomprehendingly. 'There was nothing to talk about. People don't talk about their feelings. That's private.'

'But Harry, that's what you've just been doing, after your wife is dead and it's too late! You both needed to talk at the time,' Helen said, exasperated.

Harry withdrew his hand and stared at her across the table, a nonplussed expression on his face.

'Did you ever talk to Miss Austin about how you felt for *her*?' she asked. He averted his eyes from her and looked out towards the rose bushes of the lawn. 'What did *she* say when you told her you were marrying the boss's daughter?'

'I didn't tell her until after I was married.' He continued to stare out the window.

Helen stared at him open-mouthed. She knew she should not be surprised by this in a man so terrified of emotion but she couldn't help feeling shocked. After a long moment, while Harry went on looking out the window, she asked: 'What did Miss Austin say?'

'She left me for a bit,' said Harry, looking at Helen again. 'Then she came back to me and we carried on as if I had never got married. When Margaret's father died I was able to take her into the company. We were a pair, Kathleen and I.'

'Did you ever discuss your marriage with her?'

'No, we never talked about it,' he said, looking pained.

'How do you think she felt?'

'She knew how I felt about her,' he said, evading the question.

'How?' Helen insisted.

'She just knew.'

'How could she possibly know if you never talked and you never told her?' asked Helen, getting angry.

'Oh, Helen, people just don't talk about these things.'

'Well, they ought to! They *need* to. Did you never ask yourself what your wife felt, what Miss Austin felt? Have you ever asked yourself what *I* feel?' demanded Helen, her voice rising.

'Helen, keep your voice down,' pleaded Harry, looking anxiously towards the door. 'You don't want Morag to hear . . .'

'I want *you* to hear and listen,' said Helen firmly, fixing

88

her eyes on his. 'I want you to know how I feel when you perform your acts of coitus.' She had never said the word aloud before but using it seemed to express all her pent-up outrage and anger. She watched Harry blush from the roots of his silver hair to below the collar of his shirt. 'Yes, Harry, that's the word. Coitus.'

The word hung in the air. Coitus. Everything that happened between a man and a woman was in that word – joy and pain, intimacy and alienation, first encounters and last rites, everything most precious and most terrible, the life and death of all they shared. Coitus held them all.

'All you have ever done is hurt me,' she said, watching the colour fade from his cheeks. 'Hurt and humiliate me in your office when everyone else has gone till I *dread* seeing the last person go. You have destroyed all the admiration and respect I once held for you.' She felt tears beginning to clog her throat. 'I hate what you do to me – and it has destroyed every good and decent thing there ever was between us. And why do you always draw the curtains and do it in the dark, as if you were ashamed of what you are doing?'

His colour rose again and he bowed his head.

'I had no idea how you felt,' he said when he looked up at last, his eyes full of pain as they met hers.

She didn't hate him quite so much at that moment. It had been a release to tell him how she felt. There was also a release in death. Not just for the person who died. Somehow feelings carried silently by the people around them got released as well – perhaps because there was no longer any need or reason to keep silent about them.

But it was over between them now and all Helen wanted was to walk quietly away from him. Then he looked straight into her eyes and said: 'I'm not very good at finding the right words to say what I feel. If I hurt you as you say, probably no words of mine can ever put that right. But I would still like to say I'm sorry. The truth is that since the time you were orphaned and you came and had tea in my office, I've admired your spirit, Helen. You had nothing and no one, but your spirit remained bright and unbowed. I think I saw something of my younger self in you, a part, maybe, I had lost, and I've cared about you since that day. From now on I'll try to be different. I'll try to be considerate and show my feelings. I don't know if I'll be any good, but I want to try. And when a decent interval has passed I'd like you to be my wife. Will you marry me, Helen?'

She stared at him in disbelief, wondering if she had heard right. But she wasn't going to ask him to repeat it – in case he changed his mind. Suddenly, at a single stroke, the world had changed – and she wasn't going to let this glittering prospect slip through her fingers. Mrs Harry Dunlop, wife of the great shipping magnate . . . She would be rich and secure forever and move in the highest and best circles. All she had ever dreamed about of rising up in the world would be hers in one step . . .

Her eyes narrowed fractionally, holding his; 'Did you mean what you said about being considerate?'

He pinked again. 'Helen, I hate talking about this, but I give you my word from now things will be different . . . It won't be in my office . . . it will be where you want . . . and when . . . and only if you do . . .'

'You promise?'

'You have my word.' His colour was rising again. 'Now will you marry me?'

Glittering though the prospect before her was, she had no intention of making it easy for him. A man like Harry Dunlop needed a challenge and the more difficult it was, the better he liked it. He would enjoy the thrills and spills of courting her while she made him think she had to be convinced it was a good idea for her to marry him.

'I'll think about it,' she said, her gaze giving nothing away as it went on holding his.

Chapter Four

Glasgow – September, 1929 to May, 1930

The engagement of Harry Dunlop to Helen Cathleen Randolph, daughter of the late Mr and Mrs Thomas Randolph, was announced in the *Glasgow Herald* in September, 1929.

Almost immediately Helen was inundated with requests for interviews and photographs by the society reporters of the Scottish newspapers.

She took to the limelight like a film star, loved answering journalists' questions and, in the process, learned the skill of inventing an 'image' for herself as a caring young woman who had a deep sense of responsibility towards the community and the suffering on Clydeside.

'As an orphan I learned about the pain of loss very early in life,' she told the man from the *Bulletin*, mesmerising him with her fabulous jewel-green eyes.

In the five months since Harry had proposed and Helen had got control of their sex life, she had undergone a profound psychological change. She no longer felt she was a bastard or that she was being exploited and used – and she was quite clear about her motives for her marriage. She was marrying Harry Dunlop for his money and for the social position she would gain as the wife of a shipbuilder and shipping magnate. The great love affair she dreamed of would have to wait until after she was married – or he was dead.

Already he had given her a ring with a cluster of three diamonds which shone like stars on the third finger of her left hand and a brand-new Rolls Royce Silver Cloud, driven by a uniformed chauffeur, to take her shopping at Dalys and Coplands on accounts he had opened for her.

In the beginning after she had given up her job, she went shopping every day, buying everything that took her fancy. She once bought six hats simply for the pleasure of having a uniformed boy attendant lead her from the store carrying them in boxes all piled one on top of the other. She had been draped in sable that day and, as people in the shop and street turned to stare, she had felt as famous as Mary Pickford or Greta Garbo and acknowledged their homage with a smile. But after the first heady rush of being able to buy whatever she wanted, she quickly realised that department stores were really very clever businesses which ruthlessly exploited a woman's every whim and need. Once she had taken this in she haggled over prices, demanded discounts, made the staff run around getting exactly what she wanted, took back a lot of the things she had bought in the beginning and never paid a penny more than she had to.

This was consumer power and she revelled in it!

She also got Harry to agree to having the flat done up.

It was stripped from ceiling to floor and all the Victorian paraphernalia sent to the saleroom except for a few treasured pieces Harry wanted to keep, which were despatched to the house in Pollokshields.

Alexander 'Greek' Thomson's classical architecture didn't really lend itself to the Art Deco fashion of knocking portholes in interior doors. So apart from her own bedroom, which was all-white, and the palace

93

of mirrors and chrome and glass which she created in the bathroom, she compromised and used a blend of traditional and avante-garde decorative arts to achieve a style that was light and modern but remained in character with the building. A white and gold Empire scheme brought light to the drawing-room with its north face. Curtains, pale and hung in perfect flutes, were echoed in white painted columns placed by the windows; long low sofas, crisp chair covers in white and pale blue, pale Samarkand rugs and slim bevilled mirrors added the cool chic of the modern age. But the room of which she was most proud was Harry's bedroom – a bold masculine den in red and gold with lacquered black leather armchairs. The bright red carpet was echoed in the walls, the headboard, the valance and the trimming on the tailored golden canopy matching the pelmets and window curtains. A broad ribbon in two tones of red trimmed a satin bedspread, which was the same shade as the sturdy white bedside lamps on two black lacquered tables.

'It's a masterpiece,' said Harry when he was finally allowed to see it. 'But am I to sleep here alone?'

'I will visit my master in my seasons,' she replied provocatively. 'And I hope he will wish to visit me.'

'Does that mean we are starting our marriage as you intend to go on – with separate bedrooms?'

'Oh, Harry, you know it is best,' she said, smiling.

Their love life was very much better now and she had got him well trained to her 'seasons' – the times just before her period and in the middle of the month when her desire was at its height and she was happy to entertain him all night long. But privacy was vital to her peace of mind and happiness.

They married quietly early in May with only the Campbell

94

family as witnesses, and Harry decided to give a house-warming party at Great Western Terrace.

'In three weeks' time,' he said happily. 'I'll get a firm of caterers to organise it. I want to show you off,' he added and she knew it was important to him.

At least none of his friends and their wives could criticise her accent because she now spoke, thanks to all her elocution lessons, in a polished, educated voice. 'Fine,' she said.

'I'll draw up a guest list today and we can talk about it this evening,' he said.

His proposed guest list read like a Who's Who of shipping and shipbuilding. It included Sir James Lithgow, the chairman of the National Shipbuilders Security, which had recently been formed to reduce the risk of reckless price-cutting by closing down selected yards. Sir William Ellis of John Brown's, Sir Angus Macpherson of the Dalriada Line, Sir Ian Anderson of the Cowal Line and their wives were also among the intended guests. Running her eyes over the list, Helen was struck by the number of shipbuilders and ship owners who had been knighted. She looked across the dinner table at her husband and wondered if she would become Lady Dunlop . . .

'I'm sure they're all very charming people,' she said. 'and I look forward to meeting them.'

Before their marriage, they had accepted few social invitations, preferring to keep a fairly low profile but now that was decided, she was determined that her entrance into Society would be a success and the evening a memorable one.

It was only when she was satisfied she had the catering and decoration arrangements under control that Helen turned her attention to what she would wear and set off in the Silver Cloud for the department stores. The influence of Hollywood on women's fashion was only just beginning to be felt in Scotland but the moment Helen saw the white satin gown and white wrap, which would become its hallmark, she pounced. It was the first in Glasgow and had only just been draped on a mannequin in the Model Gown department of Dalys. And it clung to Helen's figure like a second skin, silhouetting her growing voluptuousness.

'It's the last time I'll think of white as virginal,' said Harry when she emerged from her bedroom in her gown and wrap and an aura of Chanel Number 5 shortly before the party was due to begin. Her hair was a golden crown from which ringlets fell and diamonds glittered at her throat and her ears. Tonight the mean streets of Partick seemed long ago and far away; tonight she would make her debut in the kind of society in which she would have grown up if she had been recognised by her father . . . She smiled at Harry as she slipped her arm into his. He was looking very dapper in evening dress. His hair was more white than silver now and those grooves on his brow were deeper than ever. The worry about the future of the shipyard was taking its toll, but they were happier now than they had ever been and though he was still hesitant and nervous and she knew it was difficult for him, he was now able to talk to her about his feelings and sometimes even ask what pleased her. He was, indeed, becoming a most tender lover.

'Before this very special evening begins I'd like to propose a toast,' said Harry, his eyes meeting hers over the rim of his glass. He paused, and as his eyes continued to hold hers, Helen saw there were tears in the corners of them. 'Thank you for all joy you have given me these past few months,' he said, a tremor in his voice. 'It seems strange so late in life . . .' his words trailed as he raised his glass.

'Think of it just as the prologue,' said Helen softly,

smiling, feeling a lump coming in her throat. Such moments of tenderness from Harry still took her by surprise and always moved her nearly to tears.

'Yes,' said Harry gruffly, swallowing to control his feelings. 'To us.'

'To us,' she murmured, linking her champagne flute to his.

They had only taken a few sips of their drinks when the doorbell rang.

'That will be James Lithgow,' said Harry. 'He's always very prompt.'

On looks alone Sir James Lithgow could easily have been His Majesty's Ambassador and Plenipotentiary to Berlin or Paris; his rich white hair and bronzed complexion and handsome build exactly fitted the popular conception of a distinguished elder statesman.

Most of the guests belonged to Harry's generation – people in their fifties and sixties – but Elizabeth Campbell and her three brothers, who all worked for their father's legal firm, and the young industrialist Russell Macpherson, who played rugby with the Campbell brothers and with whom Elizabeth was in love, added a sprinkling of youth to the gathering. So did Graeme Wilson, the young Trade Union Leader whom everyone seemed pleased to see. Harry had said he was the only Trade Union leader the bosses had any time for among all the agitators who had earned the shipyards the name of Red Clydeside and made it even harder to get orders. Graeme was a miner's son from Lanarkshire who had taken a degree at Glasgow University – one of an emerging new social class which wider education was creating and enabling to leave working-class districts for the leafier suburbs. Whilst he waited to stand as an Independent Labour Parliamentary candidate, he was liaison officer with the Unemployed Workers' Committee and did a lot

97

of useful work in the yards. He was standing by the log fire, a glass of Glenlivet in one hand, when Helen, momentarily without Harry by her side, noticed him quietly assessing her guests.

'I hope you're having as good a time as you appear to be doing,' she said, smiling.

'I certainly am. Thank you for inviting me,' he said. He was slim, looked about twenty-eight years old and his brown eyes were twinkling with laughter.

'My husband tells me you do a lot of good work helping people in the yards and their families.'

'I do what I can in a difficult situation,' he said in an even tone.

She wanted to ask him about what he did and what it was like in the yards from the men's point of view and how their families coped. But then Harry was back at her side and moving her on to meet more of his friends.

The buffet was served at ten o'clock and drew audible approval.

Helen was already confident in her success as a hostess when she announced her *pièce de résistance*. She had heard a young singer called Annabel Macmillan on the wireless and been struck by a haunting quality in girl's voice. When Harry announced he wanted to give a party, Helen had sought her out and, once they were all gathered back in the drawing-room, she introduced the young singer who was accompanying herself on the clarsach, a Celtic harp, to her guests.

A hush now fell as the singer, who had long black hair and eyes to match and was beautifully gowned in green silk, began with a ballad of the Yarrow Hills where she had been born. Her voice seemed to fill the room with haunting loneliness and Helen, sitting back from her by the white grand piano, let her gaze range over the guests, who, for the moment, had forgotten the problems and worries of shipbuilding and shipping and the whole tragic pageant of the Clyde. These were the men who with their fathers and grandfathers had made Glasgow the Second City of the Empire – powerful, ruthless, driven men – and now they and their wives were guests in her home. Her *friends*. A serene expression spread over Helen's lovely face as her soul filled with the sense she had 'arrived' in the world where she rightly belonged.

Enthusiastic applause greeted Annabel Macmillan's performance and there were cries for several encores. Helen's debut as a society hostess had been a triumph and the air was quite thick with congratulations when the time came for the guests to take their cloaks and say goodnight.

'You were wonderful tonight. I am so proud of you,' said Harry, taking her in his arms and kissing her forehead when everyone had gone.

'I enjoyed myself,' said Helen, heady with success.

'You seemed to get on very well with James Lithgow,' he said, letting her go and crossing the drawing-room to the drinks table, where he poured himself a nightcap of Glenlivet.

'He's very charming,' said Helen, dropping gracefully into a chair by the glowing embers of the log fire, feeling pleasantly tired from all the excitement.

'Nightcap?' Harry raised his glass inquiringly. Helen shook her head. 'James is the one everyone is going to have to keep on the right side of from now on,' said Harry, taking a seat across the fire from Helen. 'Make no mistake. The National Shipbuilders Security has got the backing of the Bank of England and it means business.'

'But what exactly will it do?' asked Helen, who didn't really feel like talking business now.

'The aim is to reduce cut-throat competition for orders

by reducing the shipbuilding capacity,' he said. 'The idea is also to improve co-operation between shipbuilders.'

'You all seemed friendly enough this evening.'

'Socially. But it's become a cut-throat business. If the Dunlop Yard ever runs out of orders and is forced to close down and go on to a care-and-maintenance basis then we will be vulnerable. Because it's when a yard has run out of orders that the National Shipbuilders Security can move in and buy it and close it down. "Sterilise" is the word that's being used. It means the yard can never re-open to build any ships in the future. I don't want that ever to happen to the Dunlop Yard.'

'How many orders have you got?'

'Enough for the next eighteen months. Beyond that, the outlook isn't good. And being one of the smaller yards makes us even more vulnerable.'

'With your energy and determination, I can't see that happening,' said Helen, trying to console him.

'There are no guarantees. Of anything. I'd like you to remember that, Helen.'

He took a gulp of his malt whisky and seemed satisfied he had said what was on his mind.

'Let's snuggle up in my bed,' she said, thinking how nice it would be to fall asleep in his arms tonight after their lovely party.

'Good idea,' he said, getting up.

Helen slipped her arm into his and they walked down the hall. Outside his room he stopped and took her in his arms. 'Thank you for this evening,' he said. 'I know it must have been quite an ordeal for you. Oh, Helen, I never thought I could be as happy as I have been with you. You are so young, with your whole life ahead of you, and yet you've chosen to spend it with me.

'And now that you have shown me what tenderness is

like, I realise how great the pain I inflicted on you in the days before I knew better must have been.'

'But that is the past,' said Helen soothingly. 'It was all a long time ago.'

'Oh, Helen you have made me happier than I deserve, than I ever knew I could be. You mean more to me than my own life now. I love you more than I knew I was capable of loving anyone.' Then his lips folded over hers in a kiss of incredible tenderness and passion.

When he stopped kissing her she took his face in her hands and held it for a moment, looking deeply into those extraordinary blue eyes. She had never felt closer to Harry than she did at this moment. That divine triple union of mind and heart and body might even be possible for them now, and her spirit soared in happiness at the prospect. This was how life was meant to be.

'Let's go to bed,' she urged, feeling her desire for him rise.

'In a minute. I'll just go to my room and get into my pyjamas.'

'Let me undress you,' she whispered into his ears.

'There are one or two things I want to see to in my room first.'

She smiled. He wasn't ready to be undressed by her, even in the dark!

She wandered down the hall to her room and stepped out of her beautiful white satin dress and, when she had hung it up in the wardrobe where she kept her best clothes, she slipped in between the cool cotton sheets. She was tired, too, after all the excitement of the party and she had to fight to keep her eyes open. But sleep crept over her and an hour had passed when she woke up. These was no sign of Harry and she knew he had fallen asleep in his room. She swung her legs on to the deep pile of the carpet and was about to reach into the wardrobe for a négligé when she caught sight of her naked body in a mirror. I'll shock him out of falling asleep on me, she decided, flying out of the room and across the hall into his room without a stitch.

Harry was sitting in an armchair by the fire. He's fallen asleep, she thought. I knew it. He'll think he's still dreaming when he wakes up and sees me!

She tiptoed across the carpet till she stood before him by the light of the fire.

'Harry.' She leaned towards him, running her fingers through his hair. 'Harry, wake up.' But he did not stir. 'Harry,' she placed her hands on his shoulders and shook him gently. 'Harry . . .' she said, feeling the warmth of the flames on her back and her limbs. Her hands reached for his face, which felt heavy with sleep. 'Come on, wake up.' She lifted his face towards her and it was only then she realised he was dead . . .

Harry Dunlop was buried three days later in the churchyard at Pollokshields where he had laid his wife to rest only thirteen months ago. The men and women who had so recently been guests in his West End home now stood at the graveside mourning their dead colleague. So did men, employed and on the dole, from the Dunlop Yard, who crowded among the tombstones in their cloth caps.

'"Then shall the dust return to the earth as it was: and the spirit shall return unto God who gave it."' The voice of the parish minister quoting Ecclesiastes rang out in the clear spring air.

As she watched the coffin being lowered into the grave from behind her veil, Helen uttered an uncontrollable sob and Elizabeth Campbell took her arm to steady her.

Harry had died from a massive stroke and she realised now that he had known he was going to die. That was why he had wanted to have their party at such short notice – he

102

had wanted her to know and be accepted by the people she needed to know. And that night, after the party, when had talked about the National Shipbuilders Security he had been trying to tell her what she needed to know and to warn her about not running out of orders. And when he had thanked her for his happiness and taken her into his arms and kissed her so passionately and tenderly, he had really been saying goodbye and he had wanted to go to his room to die quietly alone and not inflict pain on her by being in bed with her when he left.

They had been happy for so brief a time before it had been all snatched away – and now she knew that she had lost far more than a lover and husband. She had lost her best friend and the father-figure who had taken care of her and protected her against the cruelty of the world after her mother had died and her father had rejected her. Now he was gone and she was alone again . . .

Harry left everything to Helen, making her an extremely wealthy young widow. Now she owned the Dunlop Shipyard, the Pier Line, flats in Great Western Terrace and Kirklee Terrace, houses in Kensington Road and Kingsborough Gardens and Pollokshields as well as considerable sums of money and all the jewellery he had given her.

The jewellery alone was enough to keep her for the rest of her life, she realised the day after the funeral when she sat at her dressing-table reaching for the red leather case in which it was kept. But life went on and she had the staff at the Pier Line and the Dunlop Yard dependent on her for their livelihoods. She plucked two plain pearl drop earrings from the case and clipped them to her ear lobes and clasped a three strand pearl choker around her neck. They softened the severity of her mourning, she thought, placing a veiled pillbox on her head.

Everyone rose to their feet when she entered the big office at the Pier Line. Mr Robertson, who had once shown her the way to the albums in the attic, had been appointed spokesman.

He stepped forward now, 'Good morning, Mrs Dunlop. On behalf of everyone, I would like to say how sorry we are about Mr Dunlop and to offer you our condolences. We would like you to know that we will do all we can to help you.'

Helen shook the hand he offered. Touched by this unexpected display of loyalty and affection, she felt her throat closing and tears pressing at the back of her eyes. This is not good enough for the boss, she thought, swallowing hard.

'Thank you, George,' she said. 'And thank all of you. It is very comforting for me to know that I have your loyalty at a time like this. The best thing we can all do, what Mr Dunlop would want us all to do, is to get on with our work. And that's what I'm going to start doing right away. And I want you to do the same. Times are hard and we must all pull together as a team. Thank you.'

When she reached the yew-panelled office and closed the door behind her, she let the tears, hot and salty, tumble freely down her cheeks. Well, at least I didn't cry in front of them, she thought, so I haven't made too bad a start. When she had dried her eyes she walked slowly to the desk where Harry had sat for so long and dropped gracefully into his chair. She closed her eyes for a moment and pressed her fingers to her forehead. She had to get back in control. It was the only way to get through the day. In the past she had always started her working day by reading the shipping news in the *Glasgow Herald*. It was what she knew how to do. She reached for the copy which had been placed on the desk, opened it and started reading.

When she had been at her desk for half-an-hour the middle-aged woman who had taken her place as Harry's secretary put her head round the door and announced: 'Mr Ian Campbell is here to see you.'

'I wasn't aware he had an appointment,' said Helen, puzzled.

'He hasn't. He says he just thought you might like to see him.'

'I thought his father was Mr Dunlop's lawyer and I saw *him* yesterday afternoon after the funeral.'

'Will I tell him you're busy and get him to make an appointment?'

'No. No, you can show him in.' said Helen, resuming her reading of the *Glasgow Herald*.

'Hello, Helen,' Ian Campbell greeted her half-a-minute later.

She did not reply or look up immediately but made him wait before she raised her head slowly and said coolly: 'This is a surprise.'

'I thought you might like to see me,' he said affably.

'Why?'

'Well, my father's firm, Campbell and Aitken, have handled Mr Dunlop's affairs.'

'In the person of your father.'

'Mainly.'

'So what do you want to discuss with me that your father did not mention when I saw him yesterday afternoon?'

'May I sit down?'

'Pull up a chair,' Helen raised a hand in the direction of a pair of Chippendales standing against the wall.

'I'm sorry I didn't make an appointment,' he said when he sat down, plainly disconcerted by the coolness of his reception. 'My father thought you might prefer to deal with someone younger and nearer your own age and as I was passing your front door I thought I would look in and see how you were.'

But lawyers didn't make social calls, Helen knew that. Their time had to be paid for. Expensively. 'What particularly did your father want you to discuss with me that he may have overlooked to mention yesterday afternoon?'

'It only occurred to him after you had gone that he might not have made it plain that, despite all the problems on the Clyde, you will have no difficulty selling either the shipyard or the shipping line.'

So that was it! Harry wasn't yet cold in his grave and the people who had come to his house and enjoyed his food and drink only days ago were turning vulture and couldn't wait to get their hands on his property. She said: 'Your father didn't even mention it.'

Ian Campbell pulled a puzzled face. 'He thought he had.'

Shaking her head, she decided to lead him on. 'What basis do you have for believing this?'

'Campbell and Aitken have a number of shipbuilding contacts. Our ear is close to the ground.'

And you hope mine isn't, thought Helen. She said: 'You mean, surely, that you have a number of shipbuilding clients.'

He grinned. 'One or two.'

'Is the National Shipbuilders Security one of them?'

'I believe that, along with a number of other legal firms, we may have done some work for them.'

'I have no doubt there are plenty of shipbuilders who would like to buy the Dunlop Yard – if only to close it down so there is one less yard competing for orders,' said Helen, leaning back in Harry's chair and feeling close to him. 'However, as an employer, I have a responsibility to find work for my people and it is not my intention to sell either it or the Pier Line.'

'But it's a terrible responsibility for someone so young . . .' His glowering grey gaze met hers in a look of infinite hostility.

'One that I am both equal to and welcome,' she said severely.

The moment he had gone she summoned her secretary: 'Get me the shipyard manager on the telephone.' Four minutes later she told the manager: 'I'm coming over to the yard this afternoon. Move heaven and earth to find Graeme Wilson and ask him to be around. I want to talk to him.'

She needed an ally – and an intelligence agent. Fast.

Start as you mean to go on. Sitting in the back of the Silver Cloud taking her across the river to the Dunlop Yard, Helen was sure Harry had said that to her at some time. It had certainly been part of his philosophy and it was what she needed to do now. Show the world she meant business.

She was furious at the underhand fashion in which Alan Campbell had tried to rob her of the yard and the shipping line . . . sending his son round to make it seem as if he was actually doing her a favour. Because she was a woman and young, Alan Campbell had assumed she knew nothing and he could get away with daylight robbery. He would not have dared to suggest such a thing to a man. With orders on the books which would provide work for the next eighteen months, Alan Campbell would have congratulated a young man and wished him every success. Well, once her secretary had produced the figures on what Campbell and Aitken's services had cost for the past three years and she got herself thoroughly briefed by Graeme Wilson, Alan Campbell was going to have to explain himself satisfactorily if he wanted to keep her business. The determined expression on her lovely face took on the set of marble. There was no mercy, no kindness and you had no friends in business. You had to be hard and ruthless and constantly ahead of your competitors just to stay alive in these difficult times. In the year of her happiness she had almost forgotten just how difficult they were.

Rain clouds were gathering in the West as the Rolls wheeled through the great black iron gates of the Dunlop Yard. The clerical grey hull of the steamship *Lubeck*, which was being built for the Hanseatic Line, loomed in her berth. Helen's heart lifted at the sight of it and she rolled down the window to listen to the clash of hammer on hull, of steel on steel. This was the song of the Clyde, the song she intended the Dunlop Yard would sing forever. Some of the workers on their lunch break were playing football on a newly cemented area between two of the berths. When they saw the Rolls one of two of them drew back from the game, but she raised her hand to wave them on. If you worked hard you needed relaxation and they really should get a lot more of it.

The first person she saw in Harry's beautiful mahogany-panelled office was the shipyard manager, Robert Mackendrick, a small, dour, bald-headed man in his early fifties.

'Take a seat,' she pointed to the leather one on the other side of her desk.

'Thanks, Mrs.' But he remained standing, clutching the order book under one arm. 'You wanted to know about the order, Mrs.'

'When you are sitting comfortably,' Helen smiled encouragingly.

'It won't take long to tell you,' he said stiffly, unable to cope with a woman boss.

'I get the impression you don't intend to stay very long,' said Helen, 'and that's a pity. I was looking forward to having a chat with you and there is a lot I want to tell you.' Reluctantly, he sat down and placed the book before him on the desk. 'So what have we got?'

'There's an order for another steamship for the Hanseatic Line when the *Lubeck* is finished. And there are orders for three tugs and four hoppers and we've got quite a bit of repair work,' said Mr Mackendrick. 'Mr Dunlop was going for quite a bit of repair work lately.'

When he had finished going through the details of every item on the order book, Helen said: 'I'm going to have a cup of tea. Would you care for one?'

'I never had a cup of tea with Mr Dunlop,' said Mr Mackendrick, closing the book and looking ready to get out of his chair.

'Very sadly Mr Dunlop is no longer with us and I am now running this shipyard,' Helen glanced at the clock. 'I think it's quite likely that in view of the time I asked to see you, you were probably having your lunch break and doubtless a cup of tea. That's going to be cold when you get back to your office. So would you care to join me for a fresh cup?'

'Thank you, Mrs,' said Mr Mackendrick, smiling slightly at her thoughtfulness.

He seemed to relax when the tea arrived in a white china cup and he had taken a couple of draughts. How do I get through to men like Robert Mackendrick and let them see I mean business, wondered Helen. He was vital to the future and welfare of the yard and she had to convince him that it was in his interest to work for her just as he done for Harry.

When he had finished his tea she looked him straight in his eyes and told him: 'The motto of this yard has always been "Once a Dunlop man, always a Dunlop man." That is still the motto. If men are laid off because we haven't enough orders, they will be taken back as soon as we do. I want everyone to know that. I know that things could become dangerous if we run out of orders, but it will be my business to get those orders. And I will be working hard to get them. We must all work together as a team if we are to continue to be successful and I hope I can rely on you to start spreading this message.'

'Yes, Mrs,' he said, but Helen had no idea if he really believed her, or took her seriously.

'Now, did you manage to find Graeme Wilson?'

'Yes, Mrs.' Mr Mackendrick consulted the gold watch on a chain in a waistcoat pocket. 'I'm afraid he won't be here for another half-hour.'

'That's fine,' said Helen. 'And I'm glad we've been able to have this talk.'

Mr Mackendrick rose and she thought he looked a bit dazed when he left her office.

It was almost an hour before Graeme Wilson arrived. Harry had said he was a politician to his fingertips and had a politician's sense of timing and opportunity and knew when he could afford to keep someone waiting. 'Only care about people who can enhance and promote your interests.' Harry's words came back to her as she waited. It was in her interests to care about Graeme Wilson, so when her secretary ushered him into her office she rose from her desk and with the most cordial smile she could muster, graciously extended her hand towards him.

'Thank you for making the time to see me at such short notice,' she said. With his brown hair and soft brown eyes he didn't really look like the Red Revolutionary all Labour politicians were supposed to be, Helen decided when she sat facing him across her desk. His eyes were twinkling just like they had been at her party and she really wasn't quite sure how to handle him. She didn't feel she could charm him and flatter him the way old men could be charmed and flattered and she couldn't bully him or order him like an employee or someone she paid, like Ian Campbell. Graeme Wilson was her equal – young and powerful.

She tried a gentle approach to get him on her side. 'Though I am in a fortunate position of having worked for the Pier Line and having always been well-briefed by my late husband on the problems of getting orders for the shipyard in these difficult times, I do not know a lot about the problems of the most important people in the yard, the men who build the ships. And I would be grateful for whatever insights you can give me into those problems.'

Graeme Wilson's eyes stopped twinkling and he gave Helen a long hard look. 'Out of a long list of problems which beset the people with whom I work, the worst is not unemployment. The root grievance on the Clyde is housing.

'Out of the million people who live in Glasgow, 600,000 or nearly two-thirds of them live in accommodation that is below the minimum standard set by the Board of Health. 40,491 families live in one-room homes, 112,424 families in a room and a kitchen and over 13,000 in homes which have been condemned by the Medical Officer of Health. Out of all the condemned property in Glasgow only 32 one-roomed and 55 two-roomed apartments are standing empty. People live in them, if you can call it that, because there is nowhere else for them to go. It is very common for up to twelve families to share a single outside toilet facility. That is how people live in this great city of ours or, as one of my parliamentary colleagues puts it, "earth's nearest suburb to hell."' His eyes pinioned hers but she did not flinch. 'Do you wonder we are on the brink of revolution?' Helen shook her head. 'And have you any idea of how much money is needed to make Glasgow a city fit for human beings to live in?' Helen shook her head again and wondered what he must have thought when he came to her party. '£60 million.'

She realised she had to say something quickly to show she was on his side.

'Where do you think I came from Mr Wilson?' she asked. 'Why do you think I am interested in running this shipyard rather than selling it off to another shipbuilder or the National Shipbuilders Security?'

'Tell me,' he said, his eyes meeting her cool gaze.

'I come from a family like the ones you champion,' said Helen. 'That's why. My mother was widowed and I grew up knowing what hard work and wanting was like. I have *earned* this job, Mr Wilson. It is not an easy inheritance.' She watched his reappraisal of her in his eyes before she said another word. 'Could you get the money you need for housing from the government?' she asked, returning to the matter he had raised.

'This minority Labour Government under Ramsay MacDonald is nearly bankrupt. They only just hang on to power with the tacit support of the Liberals,' he sneered and Helen sensed division, weakness.

'You don't sound as if you approve of them very much,' she said.

'I don't. They're weak. Unemployment will soon be over two million and they refuse to do anything to boost the economy. All they are likely to do is to give in to Liberal demands for proportional representation just to stay in power,' he said. 'I'm a member of the Independent Labour Party,' he added.

'I'm sorry, I didn't know there was a difference,' said Helen.

'And I'm sorry I got up on my soapbox. I don't usually go round lecturing shipyard bosses. But you asked me,' he shrugged and the twinkle came back to his eyes, and Helen quietly registered his acknowledgement of her position as the shipyard boss.

'I'm glad you told me,' she said. He was obviously very ambitious and she wondered what he stood to get out of his caring. Fame, a seat in Parliament? He was endlessly interesting and she wanted to know a lot more about him.

When her secretary brought them tea, she got him to talk about *all* the yards on the Clyde – from Hendersons at Meadowside and Fairfields on the opposite bank, Stephen's of Linthouse, Connell, Inglis, Blythswood, John Brown at Clydebank, Beardmore's at Dalmuir, Simon's at Renfrew and all the others and way down past Dumbarton Rock to the Tail of the Bank and the open seas of the Firth. And when he had finished she not only knew all she needed to know but she had impressed him by her deep interest and made a friend.

Surer of her ground now, she telephoned Alan Campbell the next day and told him she wished to see him. But it was another ten days before he breezed in through the door of her office, offering his 'profuse apologies for the terrible misunderstanding which arose between my son and myself. And I have told the young rascal off for his quite appalling breach of good manners in barging in on you the way he did.'

Helen didn't believe him for a minute. She looked at his jowly face with its pale tan and hair as silver as his tongue and his expensive suit and decided she wasn't letting him off that lightly.

'It was an insult to my intelligence for either you or your son to think even for a moment that I was not aware of the situation on the Clyde and the National Shipbuilders Security,' she said, pinioning his blue-grey eyes with her own.

113

'Not many young women are so well-informed,' he came back at her with a smile.

But she refused to let him off the hook.

'I have been going through all our accounts,' she said. 'And I see that last year we paid your firm £10,000 in fees. I am not at all clear as to exactly what this was for. The invoices are rather sketchy and I have not been entirely satisfied with the explanation I have been given in the course of my internal enquiries. I would like a more detailed accounting . . .'

'As the Pier Line and the Dunlop Yard are now under new management and it is the sincere wish of Campbell and Aitken to retain their business, why don't I give you an immediate refund of ten per cent and save us both a lot of trouble?' he said smoothly.

'Cash?' Her eyes did not leave his.

'It will be in your office or paid straight into your bank this afternoon.'

'This office will be fine.'

'Done?'

'Done.'

'Now, if I may turn to more pleasant matters,' he said, smiling. 'Every year, during Clyde Yachting Fortnight, Campbell and Aitken give a party for their clients and friends aboard the firm's yacht, the *Monadhliath*, which was built at the Dunlop Yard. I wonder if this year we may look forward to the pleasure of your company.'

'When is it?' asked Helen, seeing a chance to weigh-up some of her rival shipbuilders.

'The eighth of July. We usually make a day of it, sailing from the Broomielaw around eleven right down to the Firth and the islands. We have lunch and tea on board and get back in time for a jolly dinner on shore for anyone who doesn't have to hurry off. Sir James Lithgow usually comes along. There would be ample opportunity for you

114

to talk to him if there was anything you felt you wanted to discuss . . .'

'There would indeed,' said Helen, writing the date on the blotter on her desk. 'The answer is yes, I will be very pleased to come to your party. I'll get my secretary to put it in my diary.'

'Good, I will look forward to that. In fact, we all will at Campbell and Aitken,' he said. 'Now, do we have any other business?'

'Not that I can think of for the moment,' Helen said evenly.

'In that case, I will take my leave. I *am* glad we have been able to clear up the misunderstanding,' he said, getting up and she took the hand he offered her.

As she watched him, Helen knew she had won his respect because she had shown strength. It was the only way to do business . . .

Chapter Five

The Clyde, Glasgow and Edinburgh – July to September 1930

Clyde Yachting Fortnight opened on a July day of brilliant sunshine, azure skies and majestic sails billowing over sparkling waters. Though the days when the Fortnight had rivalled Cowes Week, and Royalty and the great shipbuilding and shipowning and cotton-spinning families had brought their flotillas of graceful ships to the Firth, had long gone, it was still a great occasion. The rich still anchored their sleek, expensive vessels at the Royal Northern Yacht Club in Rothesay and partied every night. The Depression which had put half of Clydeside on the dole was a world away from the men in blazers and women in long dresses sipping champagne and nibbling smoked salmon delicacies on the deck of the ocean-going yacht, *Monadhliath*.

'Nothing looks quite so bad when the sun shines,' said Helen to Ian Campbell, pensively sipping her drink. It was her first trip down the river since she had accompanied Harry on the sea trials of the *Papana Queen* and her first day out since Harry's death. She had done nothing but work these past two months from early in the morning till late at night, re-acquainting herself with the Pier Line and taking every chance to learn all she could about the shipyard, getting to know the men and what each one did, trying to impress them with her commitment to the future of the yard. At times she sensed hostility, at others simply that the men were bemused by a woman trying to run a shipyard. She needed an order to stamp her authority on the yard. But there wasn't one in sight. She had thought of cancelling her day out at the Campbell and Aitken party – somehow it didn't seem right to be out enjoying herself when so many people were out of work – but Elizabeth Campbell had persuaded her otherwise, then steered her towards Dalys and the black and white striped silk dress that gracefully skirted her figure and the stylish white straw hat which had seemed to be waiting for her. Now, standing on the deck, watching the smiling faces, hearing the laughter borne by the breeze, she felt like a spectator. She wondered if she would ever love anyone again or if she would be alone forever now . . .

Across the sunlit deck her gaze fell on a beautiful, aristocratic-looking girl in a white muslin dress, whose gently billowing skirt gave her a dreamy, floating look as if she had stepped from a painting of an Edwardian beach scene. The girl's face was pale as ivory beneath her yellow straw hat, and her long black hair fell to a stunningly-slender waist. Though she seemed to have a lot to say to the two young men flanking her, Helen was struck by her stillness and lack of animation; beneath the cloud of muslin she held herself like a statue. Both men stood with slightly lowered heads, giving Helen the distinct impression they were bored.

One was below average height and had a thin, angular body. His features were angular, too, and a lock of lanky brown hair had fallen over his broad brow and was almost touching the large tortoiseshell glasses which framed the upper part of his face.

Then Helen noticed the other man was looking across the deck straight at her. His shoulders were broad, his hair black, his forehead wide and deep and his lower lip full and sensual; high cheekbones gave a slightly carved look to his face and his white shirt was open at the neck beneath a brass-buttoned navy blue blazer. But Helen was aware only of a pair of highly intelligent brown eyes speaking volumes to her.

'Who are they?' she asked Ian Campbell.

'Some of the *crème de la crème* of the Edinburgh legal élite,' he replied, a trace of envy in his voice. 'The girl is Grace Mitchell, the only daughter of Scotland's top judge, the Lord President. The man with the glasses is Henry Macrae – he also has a judge for a father and is himself an advocate. The other man is John Brodie, regarded by some as the most brilliant advocate of the younger generation.'

They will know my father! The thought suddenly blazed across Helen's mind, evoking memories she had put behind her. When she had accepted Alan Campbell's invitation, it had not entered her head she might meet lawyers from Edinburgh acquainted with Lord Randolph.

'Are there many lawyers from Edinburgh here today?' she asked Ian.

Ian wrinkled his brow thoughtfully. 'About eighteen or twenty. They're mostly the counsel my brothers hire for court work, but there are a few solicitors, too. Oh, I see John Brodie's decided to come over and say hello.'

The stunning realisation that there were people on the deck who must know her father had quite diverted Helen from the way John Brodie had been looking at her, but now she watched the breeze lifting his black hair and the nonchalant elegance of his figure as he crossed the deck.

'Ian Campbell . . . I see your brothers all the time in court but never you. Where do you hide yourself these days?' John Brodie's effusive greeting was spoken in the public school accent of Lord Randolph.

118

'I cover the waterfront, often in the company of Mrs Helen Dunlop, shipyard and shipping owner of this parish,' said Ian, smiling broadly and raising an arm in Helen's direction. 'Helen, may I introduce John Brodie, advocate from the eastern enclave of Edinburgh. John, the lovely Mrs Dunlop.'

'I am delighted,' said John Brodie, bowing low over the white gloved hand Helen extended to him. Then, as he raised his head, those articulate eyes challenged hers again, asking a thousand unspoken questions. She had the sensation they were standing on a lonely shore with no one else around and her spirit seemed to rise above its burden of bereavement.

'I'm very pleased to meet you,' she said socially, her eyes not leaving his.

'I should explain Helen's yard built this yacht, the ground beneath your feet,' volunteered Ian Campbell, breaking the spell.

'So why, if you built this beautiful ship, have I not had the pleasure of seeing you on the deck before?' John Brodie asked Helen.

'Because I didn't own the yard until recently,' she replied: 'My husband left it to me in his will.'

'Ah, now I know where I've seen you before,' he said, letting go of her hand as Ian Campbell murmured something about refilling his glass and vanished. 'I've seen your picture on the society pages of one the Glasgow papers. You married Harry Dunlop who died quite recently.'

'Eleven weeks ago. This is my first day out since . . .' She felt a lump coming in her throat and swallowed hard, blinking back unbidden tears.

'I'm sorry,' he said, sounding sympathetic.

Helen smiled and rallied. 'How does a busy lawyer from Edinburgh find time to read the Glasgow papers?' she asked.

119

'Because I spend a lot of time in the High Court in Glasgow, as a junior defence counsel in murder trials.'

She thought he would look distinguished with a gown on his shoulders and wig atop his jet-black hair. 'Have you saved many lives?' she asked.

'I would like to think I have made some contribution to preventing a number of innocent men from being sent to the gallows.'

His voice had a beautiful resonant timbre even when a summer breeze was carrying it away and she thought she'd like to hear him in court. 'It sounds fascinating,' she said.

'A lot of what goes on in court is very dreary,' he said.

'But it can't all be!' Helen protested. 'People queue up for seats at murder trials.'

He shook his head. 'One of the more unfortunate aspects of the judicial process is the atmosphere of the lynch mob which the death penalty encourages.'

'Are you against it?'

'I'm against the fact that if a man is later discovered to be innocent it is too late to put it right. I don't call that justice.'

He spoke with such passion and his brow came right down over his eyes, giving his face a dark, brooding look that made Helen think of a storm about to break. 'But it's the jury who decides isn't it?' she asked.

'You've got to convince them,' he said passionately. 'You have to win their hearts, engage their sympathy. They must believe in the rightness of your cause – and that *you* are a right and fair man.'

'But what if they don't believe you and find the person guilty? It must be especially hard if you believe a person is innocent and the jury disagrees with you.'

'Oh, you must believe in their innocence or you cannot defend them!'

He spoke with such conviction and he seemed so straight and honest for a lawyer, not like the Campbells whose main aim in life was evading responsibility if the advice they gave turned out to be all wrong. She wanted to know a lot more about John Brodie. 'What made you decide to become a lawyer?' she asked.

His face eased into a smile. 'The decision was as much my parents as mine. They were chauffeur and lady's maid to the Earl and Countess of Contin. But my father had the instincts of the entrepreneur. The age of the motor car was just dawning when they married in 1899 and my father saw an opportunity. So they came to Edinburgh and he built up a very successful business building and repairing motor vehicles. He started the first motor taxi service in Edinburgh and opened some of the first garages. He made a lot of money and we lived in a fine big house in Dick Place, looking out to the Pentland Hills.

'Unfortunately, my father's money could never buy my parents acceptance in the highest social circles in Edinburgh. Money alone never can in Edinburgh. You have to *belong*. Lawyers are the proprietors of Edinburgh and form the first circle. If you are not born into a legal family, then you need to know the people in the first circle from childhood by attending Edinburgh Academy, which was where my parents sent me. All the boys I got to know were the sons of advocates and judges. I was invited into their homes and I met their fathers and admired them. I became *fascinated* by the power of the law. By the time I left school I *wanted* to be a advocate and wield that power.'

Helen experienced a sense of *déjà vu*. The same thrust of ambition, the drive to power, the seeking after success she had seen in a pair of extraordinary blue eyes now burned in a pair that were molten brown.

'Your parents must be very proud of you,' she said.

A suddenly bleak smile crossed his face. 'I think I may have helped to make up for one or two of the things that hurt them . . .' Their eyes met and held. He was talking as he rarely talked to anyone – but this girl with the slightly-slanted green eyes and the golden hair tumbling from beneath her white straw hat on to her shoulders was different from anyone he had ever met. He felt he had known her forever. 'You'll meet my friends in a minute,' he said now. 'I'm really the odd man out.'

Helen sensed he felt he had said enough, perhaps more than he intended. So she asked no more, and they stood quietly looking out over the ever-widening waterway. The masts and sails of the racing yachts were now coming into view, their white sails billowing on the summer sea. The sun was high in the sky, blazing down on the sandy shores and red sandstone houses of the Clyde coast resorts and the islands washed by the waters of the Firth which would soon come into view – the sprawl of Bute, the modest Cumbraes, the craggy mountain garden of Arran shadowing Holy Island and, in the distance, the lone conical of Ailsa Craig. Clyde Yachting Fortnight didn't just belong to the rich with their yachts. It belonged, as well, to the city dwellers flocking 'doon the watter' in pleasure steamers to watch the sails sway and soar like wings on the shimmering seas, and the men thickly gathered on the shores armed with field glasses, arguing over the ships' manoeuvres.

'Ah, John there you are. Robert wants to take a picture of us all.' The shrill voice belonged to the girl whom John had been talking to earlier. She stood with one arm slipped though that of the young man with the tortoiseshell glasses.

'Ah, yes, Grace. Time for the picture of the Bar's annual boating outing,' said John, turning to Helen. 'Helen, may I introduce Grace Mitchell and Henry Macrae?' He smiled

122

at his friends. 'Grace, Henry, I'd like you to meet Helen Dunlop, whose late husband's company built this yacht on which we are all having such a splendid day out.'

'So pleased .,. .' Grace murmured perfunctorily, quickly slipping a possessive arm into John Brodie's.

Helen smiled at Henry Macrae, who took her hand and bowed low over it.

'Do come on! Robert needs us at once. He's been looking everywhere for you,' Grace chided John Brodie.

'Helen, you must come and have your picture taken with us,' said John, proffering her his free arm.

'Oh, but it's just for the Edinburgh Bar Group,' Grace said, irritated.

'And this year the Bar group is going to have the privilege of being photographed with the girl whose shipyard built the *Monadhliath*,' John insisted.

'What a splendid idea' exclaimed Henry, and Helen pretended not to notice the withering look she was getting from Grace as they made their way across the deck.

John's arm, bearing her along, felt strong to Helen and she wondered what Grace Mitchell meant to him. Then he smiled at her and their eyes met and held again and it seemed as if there was no Grace Mitchell or anyone else around.

On a corner of the deck a group of young men and women playing musical deck chairs were being photographed by a man whose black hair grew thick beneath a sailor's cap and matched a pair of bushy eyebrows. His eyes were black, too, with flecks of green, and one of them winked at Helen when John Brodie said: 'May I introduce Robert Warrender, King's Counsel and photographer extraordinary.'

'I plead guilty to what m'learned friend has said.' Robert Warrender shook Helen's hand warmly. 'I'm delighted to meet you and that goes for my wife, too,' he added, introducing the tall woman who appeared at his side in an elegant floral dress.

Then Helen was introduced to a whole crowd of mostly young people as Robert rearranged them for more photographs. He took the one with Helen first, seating her at the centre of the front row with John Brodie and Henry Macrae on either side of her and Grace Mitchell on the other side of John. When he had taken this picture Helen rose and went to stand beside him and Grace snatched her vacant place in the centre of the picture of the Bar group on its own.

Watching them laughing, joshing each other, all having so much fun together, belonging, Helen realised they would have been *her* friends, too, if her father had not rejected her and she had been allowed to grow up in his home. She would have belonged with them, instead of being an outsider, a guest allowed to appear in only one photograph. A pang of loneliness shot through her.

That night, when she laid her head on her pillow in Great Western Terrace, Helen remembered their happy laughing faces and their ease with each other and she felt more alone than ever. She thought about them a lot afterwards, particularly about John Brodie and how he looked at her and what Grace Mitchell meant to him. Three weeks later an envelope marked 'Personal' arrived at the Pier Line. Inside was a copy of her photograph with the Edinburgh Bar group and a note: 'I thought you might like a souvenir of a great day out. Hope to see you next year. John Brodie.' It was thoughtful of him to have sent her the photograph. But she felt a tinge of disappointment that his interest in her appeared to be so muted.

She had the picture framed, however, and kept it on her desk and she was looking at it wistfully one late September morning when her secretary put her head round the door and announced: 'Mr Wilson's here.'

Graeme Wilson was the one person who could drop in on Helen at short notice. He was proving to be an even more valuable source of intelligence, especially about the machinations and politicking of the inner élite among the shipbuilders, than she had hoped. And she found it extremely convenient that he chose to call on her far more at the Pier Line than he did at the shipyard, so people at the yard had no idea of how close her links with him really were. If his appointment was late enough in the day and she was not too busy, Helen sometimes offered him a glass of sherry and over a fireside chat listened to his ideas on the creation of a Socialist State with fair shares to everyone.

'It's good to see you, Mr Wilson,' she greeted him warmly. But the semi-permanent twinkle had gone completely from his brown eyes and she knew at once something was wrong.

'You look as if something is bothering you,' she said, getting quickly to the point.

'It is.' His eyes pinioned hers. 'And I need your help.'

She had always known it wasn't one-way traffic with Graeme, that one day he would seek a favour in return for all the information he gave her. She was quite happy about that. If it was within her power, she would grant his favour *so long as it was in her interests, too*.

Without a second's hesitation she said: 'Tell me what the problem is and I'll see what I can do.'

'My problem is a Dunlop man,' he said. 'Robbie McMenemy is in Barlinnie Jail charged with a murder I am certain he did not commit.'

'Oh, God!' said Helen, visibly shocked as her secretary came into the room bringing tea. 'Tell me what happened.'

Graeme Wilson waited until the woman had left the office again before he said: 'I think the police simply

125

picked Robbie out of a crowd and hope they can pin it on him.'

'What happened?' Helen asked.

'Robbie was with a group of men marching through the East End in support of the Independent Labour candidate in the last municipal elections when a gang of the Fascist candidate's supporters set on them. When the police arrived one of the Fascists, Alfred Wark, was dead. Now, after months of being hounded and harassed by the police, Robbie was arrested last night and charged with the murder.' Graeme took a sip of tea, leaned back in his chair and, pressing his palms and fingers together, pinioned Helen's eyes with his own. 'Robbie is not the first McMenemy to be a Dunlop man,' he said slowly, emphatically. 'His father was a riveter in the McKerron Dunlop Yard.'

'So what do you want me to do?' she asked.

'He needs a lawyer – a cracking good lawyer.'

'But I thought the Poor Law took care of it if you couldn't afford – '

'I hardly call it taking care,' Graeme interrupted. 'It's true that members of the Faculty of Advocates in Edinburgh do provide their services free for people who have no money to pay the lawyers to defend them, but it's a very rough-and-ready system. I know from experience that very often the first a counsel knows about a Poor Law case is when he arrives in court on the morning of the trial and a solicitor hands him a brief! Now, I believe that when a man's life is at stake he deserves the very best counsel and that counsel's fullest attention, whether or not he has the money to pay for it,' Graeme Wilson concluded passionately.

An arrow of sunshine seemed to shoot through the darkness. Helen glanced at the picture on her desk and saw her chance. In the absence of a new order, she

126

could stamp her authority on the yard if she paid for Robbie McMenemy's defence *and* she could develop her relationship with John Brodie at the same time. It was a gift from heaven!

'Robbie *will* get the very best counsel,' she said decisively, smiling and scarcely able to conceal her delight at taking Graeme Wilson's breath away. 'Give me a ring later in the day and I'll let you know what I've arranged. I'll also get my lawyers to liaise with you,' she added, rising and extending her hand to him. 'It's only right that a Dunlop man is supported to the hilt by the company in his hour of direst need.'

When Graeme Wilson had left her office, Helen rang Alan Campbell. 'I'd like to see one of your sons who deals in High Court work right away. A Dunlop man has been charged with murder and I'm going to defend him.'

'Oh, I don't think that's a very good idea, Mrs Dunlop,' Alan cautioned.

'I don't care what *you* think, Mr Campbell. I know what *I'm* going to do. Have someone over here within half-an-hour.'

Ronald Campbell – who arrived exactly thirty-one minutes later – was the eldest of Alan Campbell's four sons – a thin reed of a man whose hair was prematurely white at forty. He had the same cold grey eyes as his younger brother and, from the moment he stepped into her office, his condescending manner left Helen in no doubt that his purpose was to intimidate her.

When she briefly explained what details she knew of the case, Ronald Campbell drew a hand over his long chin and hesitated before he said: 'Whilst I consider that your concern for your employee is admirable, I, as your lawyer, question the wisdom of becoming involved in such a case.'

She drew herself up.

'I employ Campbell and Aitken to carry out my instructions, not to place obstacles in the way of their execution,' she reminded him sharply, eyeing him across the desk. 'I am not only instructing you to prepare Robbie McMenemy's defence, I am also telling you to engage Mr John Brodie for the task.'

'I am afraid it will be quite out of the question for Mr Brodie to take the brief.' Ronald Campbell's words had the triumphant ring of the last word and doubled Helen's determination to hire the lawyer of her choice.

'Why?' she demanded.

'Because he is not a King's Counsel,' said Ronald Campbell as if he was speaking to a tiresome child. 'It is the practice for a King's Counsel to defend a man on a capital charge.'

'I am not interested in any practice, Mr Campbell. I wish Mr Brodie to take the case.'

'But the Faculty of Advocates – '

'If Campbell and Aitken cannot persuade Mr Brodie to accept the brief, then I will be forced to find a firm of solicitors who can.'

'Very well, Mrs Dunlop,' he said coldly, certain that her threat was real.

'And when you have prepared the case and Mr Brodie has accepted the brief, I wish to go to Edinburgh to discuss it with him.'

'Yes, Mrs Dunlop'

When he had gone, Helen lifted the group photograph from its place on her desk and held it between her hands for several minutes. It reminded her of a school photograph and, though she screwed up her eyes, it was impossible to pick out the features of individual faces, but her gaze ran over her own face and the faces of John Brodie and Henry Macrae and Grace Mitchell again and again. She was going to know them all a lot better one day, she knew that now. And she was going to know John Brodie better than any of them.

It was over a month later and the autumn gales and frosts had made their mark, stripping and staining the trees russet and gold, when Helen and her solicitor boarded the Edinburgh train at Queen Street Station. She had not seen Ronald Campbell since he had called at her office and the case was being prepared by his younger brother, Stephen.

'Well, what do you think?' she asked when the train pulled out of the station. They had the first-class compartment to themselves, so were free to talk, 'Is Robbie McMenemy innocent?'

'There's no doubt about it in my mind,' said Stephen Campbell, honestly.

'But there's at least one witness who says he saw him kill Alfred Wark.'

'I wouldn't worry too much about that,' said Stephen Campbell. 'The precognitions are only a guide to what a witness's evidence might be. By the time a clever counsel like Mr Brodie has cross-examined them, the evidence might be completely different to what it looked like it was going to be.'

'I hope so,' said Helen, smiling. She liked Stephen Campbell, who had the same blue eyes and fair hair as his sister, Elizabeth, whom he closely resembled. He genuinely seemed to want to do his best to carry out her instructions; he had sent her copies of all the papers and precognitions and he had engaged John Brodie promptly.

Helen had wanted to know everything about the case and had even visited Robbie McMenemy in the grim fortress prison of Barlinnie. And though the laws of sub-judice placed strict limits on what could be said or written about the case, she had posted notices all over the Dunlop Yard telling the workers both that the accused man would be defended by a leading counsel at her expense and of her prison visit to him.

She felt excited at the prospect of seeing John Brodie again. It was three months since that summer day on the *Monadhliath* when he had talked to her about trying to save men from the gallows and believing in their innocence . . . and swaying juries . . . and his parents and how and why he had become an advocate. As the train plunged into the tunnel outside the station she caught sight of her reflection in the darkened window. She had chosen her black pony-skin suit with its silver fox collar and the emerald green toque that matched her eyes with great care, both to please *and* impress him.

'Would you care from some tea, Mrs Dunlop?' Stephen Campbell smiled at her brightly. He was so keen to please and his willingness did a lot to make up for the truculence and reluctance of other members of his family to do anything but what suited themselves.

'What a nice idea,' said Helen, smiling back.

'I'll go and see what I can arrange,' he said, getting up from the velour-cushioned comfort of his seat.

It was over three years since Helen had last gone on this journey – to find her father – and all came vividly back to her now. And when they reached Edinburgh and were hurtling down the cobbled escarpment of Howe Street in a taxi, the pain of his rejection felt as fresh and newly-inflicted as if it had only just happened . . .

There wasn't a soul about when the cab pulled up and Helen stepped on to the gloomy precinct of Northumberland Street. While Stephen Campbell paid off the driver she looked up and down its glowering walls.

'Right then,' said Stephen and they stepped towards the door whose gleaming black paint seemed positively cheerful amid the gloom. In the central panel a shining brass plate announced: Mr John A. Brodie Advocate. Beneath was another plate: Mr Henry M. Macrae Advocate.

Stephen pulled a circular brass bell beside the door, which gave a resounding clang. As the last strains of it died away, silence returned to the street, then the door was opened by a middle-aged woman with ferrety grey eyes and grey hair drawn into a bun at the back of her head.

She stared at Stephen Campbell blankly and then at Helen.

'My name is Stephen Campbell. I'm a solicitor and I have an appointment to see Mr Brodie,' said Stephen.

'Oh, yes, Mr Campbell. Mr Brodie's expecting you, sir.' She seemed to thaw a bit. 'If you'd like to come in and go straight upstairs. Mr Brodie's chambers are in the room facing you at the top.'

She opened the door wider and they stepped into the vestibule. In the hall, Helen was impressed. Though it was smaller and narrower and on an altogether more modest scale than the airy vastness of Great Western Terrace, it was beautifully appointed with architraves and cornices and wall panels and there was a lovely ceiling oval.

She looked towards the stairs, which were covered in a plain brown Wilton carpet. The balustrade, finely carved, had been painted white and sketches of New Town buildings, Register House and Princes Street and the broad avenue of George Street, studded the wall in delicate pale wood frames, creating a sense of infinite refinement. Helen's fingers fluttered over the banister. There was a landing half-way up and somewhere out of her sight beyond the next flight John Brodie was waiting for her. Her excitement mounted. But she was in no hurry, she wanted to savour every single one of those last delicious moments of anticipation. So she paused at the bottom of the stairs and glanced over her shoulder and her silver fox at her glamorous reflection in a gilded mirror. Then she took hold of the banister and began to ascend the stairs.

She did not see John Brodie immediately when she turned on the landing. Instead she was assailed by the delicious scent of woodsmoke warming the air. She stopped and breathed in deeply. Then she saw him, standing with his back to an open door – tall, broad-shouldered, his presence in a black pinstripe suit even more splendidly handsome and commanding than she had remembered.

For a moment time appeared to stand still as they looked at each other. It seemed both a long time and only yesterday since they had laughed and sipped champagne on the sunlit deck. Now they met in another season in another place . . . and the winds and wild colours of autumn had stolen the place of the sunshine and the shimmering seas. But he was looking at her in the same way as he had done on that summer day – and saying a thousand things with those intelligent brown eyes.

It was then she knew that she would love this man for as long as life was long, and there was no going back from what she knew or from this moment. And she had been brought safely to this day because he was her destiny . . .

When the timeless moment passed he stepped forward briskly to greet them.

'Stephen, it's good to see you,' he said, correctly addressing the solicitor first and shaking his hand.

'And you,' said Stephen Campbell. 'I believe you two know each other,' he added, smiling from Helen to John.

'Indeed,' said John Brodie, shaking Helen's hand in a professional manner. But his eyes were laughing, as if he was sublimely amused by the circumstances in which their acquaintance was being renewed. 'And may I say how delighted I am to have been given this brief, Mrs Dunlop? Now, if you both care to follow me. . .'

132

He led them into a charming sitting-room where a log fire was burning brightly, filling the air with its fragrance and warmth. Two comfortable, battered-looking red leather chairs and a companion settee formed a three-sided square around the fire, above which a delicately gilded mirror reflected the leather bound legal volumes lining one wall and the bright, warm scarlet of velvet curtains draped and swagged about the two windows over the street. Two desks in yew, with lamps and leather tops, faced each other by the bookcase and were strewn with parchment documents tied with narrow pink ribbon and a bowl of bronze and burgundy-red chrysanthemums had been placed on a small low table beneath a pier glass. This was John Brodie's lair and Helen concentrated hard wanting to imprint every tiny detail about this room on her brain.

As she dropped gracefully on to the settee beside Stephen Campbell, her silver fox fell slightly from her shoulders and her long legs in their fine black silk stockings lifted a little from the floor. It was intriguing meeting John Brodie in his professional capacity and the face she lifted to him held the cool, assessing gaze she gave to men the first time she met them in business.

It was her beauty which had impressed and drawn John Brodie on that summer's day all those months ago. Now he was impressed by her intelligence – and the sheer ruthlessness with which she went after what she wanted. Few could have broken down the barriers and established procedures of the Bar in cases of murder the way she had done.

'Mrs Dunlop wants Mr Brodie to lead the defence and she is going to tell all the newspapers if she can't get him,' Stephen Campbell had told the Dean of the Faculty of Advocates in John's presence when the older man had tried to insist that a KC be given the case. 'That could be very damaging to the profession, especially as she's *paying*.'

'Who is this woman?' asked the Dean wearily.

'The most remarkable I have ever met,' said John Brodie.

'My father and eldest brother are terrified of her,' added Stephen Campbell.

'All right, just this once,' said the Dean resignedly. 'But I tell you, if any more murdering Red Clydesiders go on the rampage and they happen to work for this Dunlop woman, the answer's no. I won't have it. A King's Counsel is going to be paid to do the job next time.'

Looking at her long black legs stretching before him and the slight hint of *déshabillé* in the way her silver fox had slipped from her shoulders, John Brodie wondered where her courage and determination came from. He said: 'I have now read all the papers and precognitions in Robbie McMenemy's case and I have come to the conclusion that any one of a dozen people could have been responsible for the death of Alfred Wark. What is most likely is that he was injured by blows from several people and died as a result of his multiple injuries.'

'Can you prove that?' asked Helen.

'I intend to cast so much doubt on the possibility that Robbie McMenemy alone was responsible for the death of Alfred Wark that it will be impossible for a jury to convict him.'

Then he led them through some of the lines of cross-examination he was considering, explaining that much would depend on what witnesses said in court when the Crown led their evidence.

'I have already seen Robbie twice in Barlinnie,' he said when he had finished, 'and it is my intention to visit him again next week with Stephen.'

'When do you expect the trial to begin?' asked Helen.

'Probably in November. It has to take place before Christmas or it will break the 110-day rule which says a prisoner must be tried within that time after his arrest or else walk away a free man. Will I see you in court?' he asked, his voice dropping to a softer tone.

'That is my intention,' she said, trying to sound businesslike. She had been even more impressed than she had expected by his command of the case and she was longing to see him in court.

'Good!'

'Well, Mrs Dunlop, is there anything more you would like to know from Mr Brodie?' asked Stephen Campbell.

'I don't think so,' said Helen, getting up from the settee.

'Then in that case, John, we'll take our leave of you,' said Stephen, rising to his feet.

'Can I get you a taxi?' asked John. 'There's a telephone downstairs and Mrs Weir can easily ring for one.'

'Thank you,' said Helen, 'but I feel like walking and getting some fresh air.'

John accompanied them downstairs and into the street where he shook hands with both of them and said good-bye.

He stood in street staring at the pavement on which she had walked, breathing the same air she had breathed long after she had disappeared from his view.

He had never run after a woman in his life. He had never needed to. He was rich and eligible and successful and women ran after him. But now he wanted to race after Helen Dunlop.

'Stop!' he wanted to cry.

But he couldn't and he wouldn't . . . He knew there could never be anything between them because of what

135

had happened on that terrible night in 1908 when he, barely eight years old, and his mother had stood expectantly in the drawing-room of their fine house in Dick Place, listening to his father's steps in the hall.

In a moment, John knew, when he had read the letter on the hall table, his father would be a taller, prouder man.

Instead, he burst into the room in a towering rage.

'The bastards have blackballed me!' he roared, his face purple, his body trembling. 'I am invited to put up for the Cockburn Club by one of their stalwarts, my own lawyer, George Donaldson. "Ah, James, times and the old ways are changing," he tells me. "This Edwardian era is not like the Victorian one. Men who have made their fortunes in trade are becoming peers of the realm. If the Court of King Edward can recognise a man's true worth, the Cockburn Club must surely follow. Believe me, James, a man who has done what you have done for Edinburgh will be welcome through its portals." So I apply and George and one of his henchmen support my applications. And what do I get but this . . . *humiliation*!

'It's because I've made my money in trade!' he shouted. 'It's because I didn't make it as a lawyer dressed up in a white bib and wig and a gown, prancing up and down Parliament Hall, profiteering out of people's misery!'

John dug his teeth into his lower lip to stop himself crying. Then his father grabbed his arm and propelled him across the hall into the dining-room.

'Now then, son, see this.' James Brodie got down on one knee so he was eye level with his son and laid an arm along the boy's shoulders. 'See it.' He pointed at the dining table.

'Yes, Papa.' John glanced quickly at the table, then anxiously at his father.

'Take a really good look, son. Not just at the table. I want you to remember everything in this room exactly as you see it now.'

The ominous note in his father's voice made John even more frightened. He thought he might be about to be punished for what unknown men had done to his father. He screwed up his eyes and peered at the elegantly appointed table laid with beautiful Herrend china, gleaming silver cutlery, sparkling Edinburgh crystal and graceful bowls of flowers. Succulent black grapes overflowed from an epergne and decanters of sherry, claret and port stood like faithful dogs at his father's end of the table and there was a bottle of Perrier where his mother sat. John concentrated hard, counting everything, in case his father asked how many there were of anything and became even angrier it he didn't know the answer. He looked at the gilded mirror and crystal chandeliers and white marble fireplace. William McTaggart's haunting sea-scape, *The Immigrants*, hung over the fireplace. People were being rowed to a tall ship anchored in a bay but others were left, frightened and abandoned, on a stormy shore. The picture had always filled him suspicion about the adult world. Why were some people chosen and special and others not good enough and left behind?

'Have you ever seen a finer dining-room than this?' James Brodie demanded.

'No, Papa,' John quickly reassured his father.

'Are you quite sure about that? With the sort of friends you're making at your fine school, you must go into some very fancy houses.'

'But they're not nearly as good as this,' John promised his father anxiously. 'This is the finest dining-room in Edinburgh!'

'But it's still not good enough for some people to

137

sup at.' John saw a strange terrifying gleam dawning in his father's eyes. 'And if it is not good enough for some people to sup at, then it must go. Watch this, son.'

James Brodie leapt from his son's side, bounded towards the table and seized the white damask cloth, sending the china and crystal skittering as if an earthquake had struck. As they bounced on the Aubusson carpet, he grabbed them sent them crashing towards mirrors and chandeliers, which splintered into a thousand pieces.

John started to run from the room.

'Stop!'

He froze at his father's command.

The commotion brought his mother and the servants scurrying.

'Oh, my poor boy!' cried Dorothy Brodie, seeing fragments of chandelier rain on her son's head.

'Don't let anyone dare cross this threshold!' bellowed James Brodie. 'Or I will not be responsible for my actions!' He slammed the door in their faces.

There was a terrible silence.

'John.'

He did not hear his father's voice. His teeth had begun to chatter and he wanted his mother.

'John, I want you to come here.'

John still did not move. Then he felt his father's hand take his and lead him through the broken china and glass to a chair by the window. His father seemed calm when he sat down, his voice normal when he said: 'It's all right, John. The storm's over. Now I want you to take another look at the room and remember this, too.'

A chandelier hung ragged and lopsided over the dining-table. A hundred arrow-straight cracks ran from the splintered centre of a gilded mirror. Fragments of china and glass were scattered like seashells on the carpet with roses and carnations strewn among them like flowers on a grave. The huge claret stains on the white damask tablecloth upset him most. They felt like his own spilt blood. He sank his teeth deep into his lower lip and willed his tears to stay away, but they still came.

He felt his father's hand squeezing his own, trying to reassure him everything was safe and normal again. But nothing could reassure him now. He knew the world could never be safe again. The peace and security he associated with his parents had been shattered and the psychic wound inflicted on him this day would remain open within him forever.

He looked up at *The Immigrants* through his tears. It had escaped damage; the little boat was still being rowed across the stormy waters to the great ship sitting in the bay. He wished with all his heart he and his parents could escape on it to a land far far away from the horrible men who hurt his father. And it was the fathers of his new school friends who had hurt *his* father. His pain felt unbearable.

'They're all horrible, the boys at my school, Papa!' he sobbed. 'I want to leave and never speak to any of them again!'

James Brodie shook his head. 'No, John. You must stay there. Become the friend of every boy you get to know. Find out their weaknesses and get them into your debt. Then, when you need to, exploit them. And never care who you hurt so long as it gets you to the top. Become a lawyer, John. Become the most powerful bastard lawyer who ever lived. Found a legal dynasty that can never be despised or looked down upon! And do it for *me*. Avenge what they have done to me and driven me to do this day!'

'Yes, Papa,' John promised fervently, climbing up on

to his father's knee and throwing his arms around his neck, wanting to comfort him more than anything. 'One day I will make them pay.'

'Yes, Papa ...' Unconsciously he mouthed the words again as he stood in the empty street.

He *had* made friends at school and had been invited into their homes, met their fathers and charmed them all just as his father wanted and he had vowed he would.

Since he had been called to the Bar he had made immaculate studied progress both through the Supreme Courts and, equally important, the drawing-rooms of the New Town. But the upper echelons of the Bar and Bench were only open to men with the right family connections. He, an outsider, did not possess them. To fulfil his father's ambitions he needed to marry a wife who did.

So he could *not* follow his heart and run after Helen Dunlop. Yet it was his life, not his father's, he thought bitterly as he turned indoors.

Helen said goodbye to Stephen Campbell in George Street and walked down Hanover Street towards Princes Street, where she stopped and looked to the great panoply of the spire and towers of the Old Town, glinting in the late morning sunlight. The ancient stone of New College and the Assembly Hall and the gnarled old tenements seemed like a fortress wall of a forbidden city. To the west the castle, disdainful upon its rock, appeared to hold the New Town at a distance across the green valley of the gardens ... But there was no time to linger. She quickly crossed the road and sped up the Mound, the old causeway created by the dumping of millions of tons of rubbish left over from the building of the New Town. When she reached the top and turned another corner she stopped again and looked diagonally across the junction where the old Royal Mile crossed the modern carriageway of George IV Bridge, towards the precinct of Parliament Square.

The square was dominated by the Supreme Courts and the lumpen mass of St Giles Cathedral, whose dour clerical grey walls looked even more forbidding than those of the court. Helen gazed up at the 15th century spire of the cathedral and the Ionic columns of the courthouse. The Calvinist spirit of thou-shalt-not seemed to be embodied in the sheer grimness of the buildings and she felt an almost oppressive sense of the utter greyness of Edinburgh. Spring, summer, autumn or winter, Edinburgh was a winter city. Not the winter of clear bright frosts and sparkling, snowy mornings; but the gnawing winter of raw damp days, hacking coughs and harsh, biting winds gusting in from the North Sea. Helen pursed her lips and her face took on a determined set few people ever saw because she was normally careful to cloak it in smiles. *She hadn't come this far to be put off now.* She stepped out quickly once more, her high heels clicking on the paved setts as she crossed the square and turned under the arched courtway towards the public entrance to the courts.

Beyond the swing doors a commissionaire sat at a large desk in a flagstoned reception area and on the wall behind him a notice-board gave the names of the judges and the courts they were presiding over.

'Yes, Miss?' said the commissionaire.

'I'm looking for Lord Randolph's court,' said Helen, scanning the board over the man's shoulder and not finding her father's name.

'His Lordship usually sits in the First Division. Through the doors,' he pointed to another set of swing doors, 'and first on your left.'

'But it says the Lord President sits in the First Division,' said Helen, wondering what on earth the First Division was.

'Ah, but the First Division is an Appeal Court and he's got two other judges to help him.'

So her father sat in the same court as Grace Mitchell's!

A mob of schoolchildren came charging through an entrance to Parliament Hall into the reception area.

'An educational visit,' explained the commissionaire. 'Like to take a look, Miss?' He raised a hand towards the entrance and, as the children scattered outside into the courtyard, Helen stepped on to the parquet floor of the ancient hall where the Scottish Parliament once sat.

Sunshine so bright it almost hurt her eyes was streaming through the great arched stained-glass window which dominated the south wall, depicting King James V and his nobles founding the College of Justice. Their magnificent robes, in jewel shades of scarlet and sapphire, lightened the dark soaring medieval splendour of the hammerbeam roof carved in stalwart Danish oak. There was heraldic stained glass too, in the more modest windows of the west wall, along which three massively-breasted chimney pieces were ranged. A fire was blazing in the middle one, which was the biggest, elaborately decorated by Madonna and Child caryatids, Ionic pilasters, a deep entablature of Jacobean reliefs, architectural panels and a bas-relief of Christ giving the keys to St Peter. Helen took a seat on one of the dark wooden benches placed around the walls and gazed up at the towering statues and massive portraits which looked down on the advocates in wigs and gowns walking in pairs up and down the hall, turning at each end in military two-step style, discussing their cases. She had thought she would never see her father again, but now she was about to step into his court. Nerving herself, she decided there wasn't another minute to waste. She got up smartly and left the hall and the uniformed attendant redirected her down the flagstoned corridor to the First Division, where she pushed through a set of double swing doors and came face to face with a large panel – the back of the public gallery.

It was quite dark and the panel towered way over her head and she couldn't see anyone or hear any voices. She straightened to keep her nerve.

Aisles ran down either side of the public gallery and Helen turned in the direction of the one on the north side of the court. When she got to the end of the panel and turned into the aisle she was nearly dazzled by the brightness. Beneath a ribbed ceiling tall, arched windows soared on all sides far above the pale wooden pews, making the figures of the four men in wigs in the front row and the three men in lounge suits seated behind them seem tiny. Apart from an attendant, the clerk who sat at an oval table covered in documents tied with pink ribbon, and the three judges, there was no one else around. She felt very conspicuous, positively exposed. She tiptoed up the steps into a pew in the gallery and was conscious of several pairs of eyes turned in her direction as she looked towards the bench where the judges sat in magnificent crimson robes.

Stone niches for stoves flanked the judges' seats and behind them were shelves lined with leather-bound legal volumes, just like the ones John Brodie had in his chambers. In the middle of the bookshelves, right behind the Lord President, the mace, the symbol of the power entrusted to the court by the Crown, had been placed in a bracket in a niche lit by a wall sconce and lined in material the same colour as the judges' robes.

One of the advocates was on his feet addressing the bench but Helen could not hear what he was saying. When she had settled down she raised her eyes towards the presiding judge, Lord President Mitchell, the father of Grace Mitchell. Beneath his wig his complexion was deep burgundy red and his brush of a moustache was the colour of pepper. Helen looked at him for a long moment, not really seeing him, her gaze lingering only until she could find the courage to look at the judge sitting on his right.

He was already looking at her with a fixed stare when their eyes met! Helen blushed to the roots of her hair and felt her cheeks burning. But her eyes didn't flinch and though they were more hooded now, *his* eyes still held the same hard, forbidding look they had done on the day he had rejected her.

Please, let us be friends, she wanted to say. I'm not poor any more. You wouldn't be ashamed of me. I own a shipyard and a shipping line and you don't need to tell anyone that I am your daughter. *I'll* not tell anyone. You could say I was your niece. Who I was would *be our secret*. And you needn't see me very often. Just now and again. When you are in Glasgow, you could come and have tea in my lovely flat – in Great Western Terrace. Oh, you wouldn't be ashamed of me! So please, please, let us be friends. All the longing she felt for him was brimming in her eyes – but her father's stare remained as hard and unyielding as granite. Then he looked away and she felt a light go out in her heart. But she didn't lose her courage. She sat there, watching him, wondering if he would look her way again and if he had recognised her, until the court rose for lunch at one. She stood up and pulled her fox about her as the judges rose and began to file out ceremoniously. It was then, just as he was getting up, that his eyes met hers again. It was a surreptitious look, and in that split-second she knew he had recognised her – and was rejecting her once again . . .

Chapter Six

Glasgow – November, 1930

The trial of Robbie McMenemy for the murder of Alfred Wark began in the High Court in Glasgow on a November morning when the city was enveloped by freezing fog. Helen pushed her nose protectively deep into the big black fox collar of her red wool coat as her Rolls Royce Silver Cloud groped its way among the trams and buses crawling along Great Western Road. The fog got thicker the nearer you got to the river, bringing shipping to a standstill, insinuating its way into office buildings, yellowing fine lingerie in the windows of the great department stores. Its murky pall had already permeated the marble pillared foyer of the High Court when the Rolls finally crept to a halt and Helen swept inside. After the historic dignity of Parliament Hall this place seemed a bit of a rough house with people milling everywhere. Advocates in wigs and gowns had their heads down, deep in conversation with solicitors in lounge suits. Clerks and macers, also in gowns, their arms laden with white documents tied with pink ribbon, were weaving in and out among a posse of policemen and members of the public were trudging up the steps on the way to the gallery upstairs.

'Mrs Dunlop,' Stephen Campbell breezed down the steps to greet Helen.

'Everyone's here and we've got permission for you and

Graeme Wilson to see the accused briefly before the trial begins.'

'Thank you,' said Helen. 'I very much want to do that.'

'I've arranged for you to meet Mr Brodie and myself downstairs,' said Stephen. 'You can come in with us and have a word before we have a chat with our client. Mr Wilson's standing over at the back with Robbie's family and I'll take you to him in a minute. But Mr Brodie would like a word with you first.' He took Helen's elbow and guided her up the steps and through the crowd and a set of doors into the corridor between the North and South courts, where John Brodie and his junior were standing with their hands clasped behind their backs.

John Brodie's face and manner was appropriately sombre as he introduced her to his junior. Though she had not seen him since they met in Edinburgh she had dreamt of him writing his opinions at his desk by the light of a table lamp and a flaming log fire. But today was utterly different from that calm morning in his chambers when she had been impressed by his quiet command of the case. Today the drama of the courtroom had already spilled over into the corridors even before the trial began. Today, in the presence of a judge and jury, before a packed, hushed courtroom, he would bring all his training and knowledge to the saving of a man's life. Today she sensed the fullness of his power – and she was struck with the thought that it was greater than the surgeon's knife or the power it took to build a ship.

'Have you any questions for Mr Brodie?' asked Stephen Campbell.

Helen shook her head as a sense of the awesomeness of the trial which was about to begin filled her.

'The judge is Henry Macrae's father, Lord Macrae,'

said John Brodie and she knew he was telling her to try to impress upon her that it was not a totally alien world, that his friend's father was a fair man. But the cosiness of it all behind the scenes seemed galling right now. Her father and Grace Mitchell's father sitting side-by-side on the same bench and now John Brodie appearing as defence counsel before his friend's father. Where did friendship end? Was justice really possible in such a cliqueish set? 'We have a very good case', he added.

'Well, if there is nothing you want to ask Mr Brodie, I'll take you to Mr Wilson,' said Stephen Campbell.

'Yes,' said Helen, looking again at John Brodie. 'Good luck,' she murmured. Then Stephen Campbell took her elbow and steered her out into the milling crowd to a corner where Graeme Wilson was standing with Robbie's wife, Meta, who was seven months pregnant, his mother and his mother-in-law.

Helen had been prepared to see fear in the eyes of the women whose hands she now shook — all huddled in their decent, dark wool coats. But what she saw was something much worse than fear — expressions which were flattened, faces from which all emotion had been driven out. And in the vacuum there was only numbness and a cowed quality. It took her breath away.

'I want you to know that Robbie has got the very best counsel in the land,' she said, latching her gaze on to Meta's dark, hollow eyes, but the girl, only seventeen and already brimming with the new life within her, had eyes as lifeless as the older women's and Helen was nearly overwhelmed by the sheer inadequacy of her words and her ability to comfort them in their ordeal. The money she was spending had no power to ease the anguish these women had endured.

Helen looked at Graeme Wilson whose eyes, full of compassion, said vividly that he understood.

147

'If you're ready now, Mr Wilson,' said a policeman who was standing nearby.

'Yes.' Graeme nodded and after a quick word to the women, shepherded Helen in the footsteps of the policeman.

At the bottom of the stairs they came to a dank underground passage, murky with fog. It was lined by twenty-one single cells where prisoners were held and deep, hollow tubercular coughs, sounding like the wind rattling through a scrapyard on a winter's night, seemed to rise from the very bowels of several imprisoned men. For a dark moment Helen thought death would be a blessed relief from this. Then she saw that John Brodie and Stephen Campbell, who had approached the passage by the lawyers' private stairs, were standing down at the end with two policemen outside the room where Robbie was being held.

'Right.' Stephen Campbell nodded to one of the officers on guard as Helen and Graeme Wilson joined them.

The man threw open the door of the room, which was lit by a single electric light bulb. Robbie, who was sitting under it behind a heavily graffitied rough wooden table, rose quickly to his feet.

Helen knew she must get the better of her own anguish fast and put some heart and hope into Robbie. She walked quickly towards him, extending her gloved hand across the table.

'Good morning, Robbie.' She spoke his name softly as he took her hand and bowed his head. Then he raised it slowly and his eyes, which were almost the same extraordinary shade of cornflower blue as Harry's had been, met hers. But Robbie's eyes were quite without the electric quality which had made Harry's eyes so brilliant and his incarceration and the monstrous threat hanging over him had given him a meek, cowed look. But his fair hair was neatly-combed and the blue serge suit he was wearing for his trial was obviously his 'Sunday best'. Grooming, she knew well, was the badge of rank among people who lived in single-ends in oppressed circumstances; often it was achieved by means of a single cold kitchen tap, but it enabled them to hold their heads high and keep their minds and souls from disintegrating. Robbie was clinging to that badge right now. Mightily. And her heart went out to him. Suddenly, all she had done for him seemed like nothing at all. Nothing could ever be enough when a man's life was at stake and she felt a huge, all-encompassing outrage that he should be subjected to this terrible ordeal. But she must stay in control. So, in a clear, firm voice, she said, 'I want you to know that you are in the thoughts of all the men at the Dunlop Yard, Robbie, and we are all looking forward to seeing you back there again when this is over.'

Robbie's eyes narrowed suspiciously. But her eyes did not flinch from his in a long moment.

Then he asked; 'Really?'

'Really.' She repeated the word in a clear tone. Then her courage flamed and she said it again in a louder, more powerful voice: 'Yes, *really*.' And the suspicion ebbed from Robbie's eyes and his hand lingered in hers long enough to tell her he believed her and that she had added to the precious store of whatever hope there was in his heart. When she took her hand away he almost smiled. 'Now I will leave you with Mr Brodie and Mr Campbell.'

Murder trials always drew the crowds, who were fascinated by the macabre spectacle of a man or woman in peril of being hanged. The core audience were middle-aged and elderly women, who came equipped with sandwiches and flasks of tea and coffee so they did not lose their seats when

149

the Court rose for lunch. The more sensational trials drew bigger crowds and often judges' wives attended the really big trials, which provided a stage for advocates to make names that could demand high fees in the civil courts.

Though Robbie's case was fairly undistinguished, it was still a murder trial and people had struggled through the fog to claim their seats in the public gallery. The fact that the defence was being led by a member of the junior bar had already caused a stir among the Press, where rumour was rife that he was being paid by Helen Dunlop, the young woman who had married Harry Dunlop and inherited his shipyard on his death.

The freshness of the air, unpolluted by the fog because the court had been air-conditioned when it was rebuilt in 1913, immediately struck Helen as she sat down. She was also struck by the clamour of the place. It was exactly like a theatre before the curtain went up and the gallery was packed. The judge's seat, carved in oak and cushioned in red leather just like a throne, stood at the centre of a stage flanked by white columns which soared to the ceiling. Light streamed in from tall, high, arched windows on to the yellow pine pews and the well of the court, which resembled an orchestra pit as lawyers gathered in it. It was filled by a huge oval table strewn with documents, books, notepads and several decanters of water topped with glasses. Helen leaned forward and peered over the edge of the gallery on to the hip-high cage which formed the dock, where the forlorn figure of Robbie was sitting, head bowed, between two policemen. The all-male jury, which had been sworn in earlier, now started filing on to their stand, which faced the Press Box over the well of the court.

Then John Brodie and Stephen Campbell entered the court, heads close together, deep in conversation as they approached the counsel table in the well of the court.

Helen's spirits lifted at the sight of John and suddenly she realised she was looking forward to the trial and immediately felt guilty and tried not to look at Robbie's womenfolk.

Then the cry of 'Court' went up and everyone rose to their feet as a small man wielding a mace led the judge on to the bench.

His robe was quite different from the gown Helen had seen her father wear. Lord Macrae was cloaked in the magnificent scarlet velvet and silver satin robes of criminal jurisdiction and its front panels were embellished with large red crosses. The trial of Robbie McMenemy for murder had begun.

'Mr Depute,' Lord Macrae addressed the Crown Counsel, who rose slowly and introduced the case and the counsel and explained the order in which he proposed to bring the evidence.

The first witness was Alastair Mackinnon. He was twenty-four years old, barely five feet tall with carrot-red hair, a deeply freckled face and beady green eyes. As he spoke only broad Glaswegian a policeman stood by the witness box ready to translate his answers. When he had taken the oath he told the court, with no visible emotion, how he had seen Robbie McMenemy beat Alfred Wark to death by striking him about the head and body with a club and a broken bottle.

'Robbie would *never* do that!' Meta groaned beside Helen, who squeezed her hand reassuringly.

'Just wait till you hear what Mr Brodie gets out of him,' she whispered.

'Mr Brodie?' Lord Macrae invited John to cross-examine the witness when the Advocate Depute had completed his examination-in-chief.

Helen sat forward in her seat as John Brodie rose and took measured steps towards the jury box. This was what she had come for, why she had hired him instead of a King's Counsel to defend Robbie McMenemy. This was what she had first pictured on the sunlit deck of a luxury yacht – the sight and sound, the power and thrust of John Brodie cross-examining a witness in Court.

Despite his youth, he already cut a distinguished figure in court. The wig enhanced his air of *gravitas*, adding authority to his years. Now, as he took a moment to arrange the papers in his hands, the packed, silent courtroom waited on his words. Then he placed an arm along a shelf in front of the jury box and, taking up a relaxed stand, asked the witness in a conversational manner, 'Can you see me, Mr Mackinnon?'

The witness grunted and the translating police officer said, 'Yes'.

'How *well* can you see me, Mr Mackinnon?'

The policeman translated the noise the witness made as 'quite well'.

John Brodie walked towards the counsel table. Half-way to the witness stand he stopped. 'Can you see me better when I stand here?'

'Yes,' the policeman translated.

John Brodie strode to the witness box, towering over the diminutive Mr Mackinnon. 'And when I stand here, what does that look like?'

The beady eyes squinted upwards and: 'Witness says he sees you best of all,' said the policeman.

'I see.' John Brodie looked thoughtfully at the ceiling, then walked briskly back to the jury stand. 'Well, Mr Mackinnon, how well can you see me now compared to when I stood beside you?'

'Witness says you're a bit blurred.'

'How blurred? What does my face look like?'

'Witness says your face is a complete blur. He can't make it out.'

'My Lord, I have a tape measure in court with me this morning . . .' John Brodie lifted the tape from the table. 'With your Lordship's permission, I would like to measure the distance between the witness box and my place by the jury stand.'

A smile flitted over the judge's wizened face. 'On the assumption that this measurement is relevant to your cross-examination, Mr Brodie, you may do so.'

'I can assure my Lord that it is. Thank you, my Lord.' John Brodie handed the tape to the macer who, together with a policeman, got down on his hands and knees to measure the distance.

A questioning murmur went round the gallery.

Then the macer and the policeman got up off their hands and knees and the macer wrote the measurement on a piece of paper he handed to John Brodie.

'The distance, my Lord, is well over twenty feet.'

The judge nodded. John Brodie replaced the tape on the counsel table and, adjusting his gown, walked back to the jury table.

He laid an arm along the shelf and placed a hand on his hip. 'Mr Mackinnon, you told my learned friend, the Advocate Depute, that you saw Mr McMenemy repeatedly beat Alfred Wark about the head and body with a club and broken bottle.'

'Witness says yes,' said the translating officer. 'He thought it was a terrible thing to do.'

'The court does not require to know the witness's opinion, only what he saw,' John Brodie said tersely. 'Mr Mackinnon, you also told my learned friend that you were standing some one hundred feet away at the time.'

'Witness says yes.'

'What was Mr McMenemy wearing at the time the beating you allege took place?'

'Witness says he didn't notice.'

153

'Was he wearing a tweed cap?'

'Witness says he doesn't remember.'

'How do you know it was Mr McMenemy?'

'Witness says he recognised him.'

John Brodie marched to the witness box, once more towering over the diminutive witness.

The beady eyes squinted up. The pit-pat of apparently even exchange had gone. High drama now filled the air.

'I put it to you, Mr Mackinnon, that your evidence is a pack of lies!' John Brodie's voice rang round the court. 'I put it to you that with your impaired vision you could not see anyone beating anyone else at a distance of one hundred feet – and you certainly could not identify him as Mr McMenemy.'

The court was completely hushed.

The witness looked at the judge, who was inspecting the length of his fingernails.

His wall eyes sought the public gallery.

He gaped up at John Brodie, who appeared to be riveted by something he had discovered on the ceiling.

He turned to the policeman, who was looking at his boots.

He grunted.

'Witness says he thought it was Mr McMenemy. But now he's not sure. He could have been mistaken.'

'No more questions.' John Brodie retreated rapidly to the counsel table and sat down.

The Advocate Depute declined the judge's invitation to re-examine the witness, who slunk from the stand.

'Mr Brodie's very good,' said Meta McMenemy, suddenly coming to life.

'Yes, *very* good,' said Helen breathlessly, her heart pounding. He had been everything she'd dreamed of and more. . .

For the next two days Helen watched as John Brodie undermined, destroyed and cast doubt on the evidence of witness after witness. People on oath to tell the whole truth and nothing but it, became confused, rattled, contradicted themselves – and it all added up to no one being sure who had murdered Alfred Wark. She was fascinated by the different approaches he adopted towards witnesses – at times beguilingly meek, trapping the unwary with his simple requests for their 'assistance' in helping him to understand what had happened; at others assuming a haughty mein, which could humble and intimidate the most arrogant and truculent of men. Sometimes he changed style in mid cross-examination, beginning gently until he had his quarry cornered when he became blunter, tougher, harsher, unrelenting in his demands for information.

'At its highest, advocacy is the sum total of all the things a man is,' said Alan Campbell, who joined Helen for lunch in the cafeteria on the third day. 'It requires not only all his intellectual abilities and skills but calls also upon his imagination and the qualities in his heart. To see a man bring all those skills and qualities to save the life of another can be a profoundly moving experience. It is also, in my opinion, the highest form of art.'

Helen agreed fervently. Watching John Brodie trying to save a man from the gallows *was* a profoundly moving experience. And though she was conscious of the other players in the unfolding drama – the judge, the prosecutor, the 15 men on the jury, the witnesses, Robbie himself – it was only in relation to John Brodie. She watched the angle of his head when he turned to speak to Stephen Campbell, who sat behind him, noticed his prompt responses when Robbie got a policeman to pass him a note from the dock. He would rise immediately and cross to the dock, where he would lean over and listen to his client, his expression full of sympathy and compassion. She watched his hands, too, as they turned the pages of the large notepad on which he took his notes of the evidence; beautifully manicured hands with long, elegant fingers. She noticed everything about John Brodie and committed it to memory. And she listened to his voice, powerful and resonant. Though she watched him like a hawk, sometimes she closed her eyes just to concentrate on listening to his voice because it was so beautiful and commanding. She thought she would do anything she was told to do by that voice . . .

On the fourth morning the trial collapsed when the Crown withdrew its case on the grounds of insufficient evidence and Robbie McMenemy walked from the dock a free man, straight into the arms of his tearful, pregnant wife, who was waiting for him in the foyer with Helen and Graeme Wilson and his mother and mother-in-law.

'Is it true you paid for Mr McMenemy's defence?' asked one of the reporters swarming round the group.

'And why hire Mr Brodie when the accused usually gets a King's Counsel in a murder trial?' demanded another, notebook poised at Helen's elbow.

'Can we have a picture of you and Mr McMenemy outside the court, please, Mrs Dunlop?' shouted a man at the back as the crowd draining from the public gallery milled everywhere.

In the uproar of voices Helen saw her chance to use the publicity to stamp her authority on the Dunlop Yard. She hoped the man from the *Bulletin* was there. It was the paper her mother and Aunt Cath had read and she knew most of the men at the yard did, too. They would be impressed if they saw her photographed with Robbie and his family in tomorrow's paper . . .

'If you'll just help Mr McMenemy and his family to get

out of here, I'm sure we'll be delighted to pose for pictures and I'll answer your questions,' she said, playing for time. 'You, too, Graeme. You must be in the pictures as well,' she added, as the reporters formed a posse around the party, elbowing their way out of the building.

The fog, which had blanketed the city for days, had lifted but it was a raw, miserable morning outside the court, where a barrage of photographers' light bulbs greeted Helen and her party on the steps of the building.

'Could you hold it there for a moment, please, Mrs Dunlop?' cried one as she stood between Robbie and his wife.

'Where are you from?' she asked.

'The *Evening Times*,' cried one man.

'And the rest of you?' she inquired, smiling and slipping her arms through those of both Robbie and his wife. As she heard the name of the *Bulletin* among the names reeled off in answer to her question, she turned to Graeme Wilson. 'Why don't you get on the other side of Robbie and take his arm?'

'I'm afraid I'll have to ask you to move on. You can't stay here,' said a policeman, because the volume of people trying to leave the court was building up.

'Then we'll go across the road to Glasgow Green and I'll answer your questions there,' Helen told the waiting Pressmen, who promptly stopped the traffic by forming a cordon across the Saltmarket to enable Helen and her party to get to the other side.

Inside the massive black iron gates which guarded the entrance to Glasgow Green, the reporters gathered closely around Helen, who was ready for them now. When the cameras had stopped clicking, she told them: 'My late husband had a saying "Once a Dunlop Man always a Dunlop Man." Since his death I have tried to carry on that policy. It means that the company's care for its employees is not limited to the time in which they are working. We believe in helping anyone who works for the company if they find themselves in serious trouble through no fault of their own. This is what I wanted to do for Robbie McMenemy. I wanted him to have justice – and he got it.' She paused and smiled at Graeme Wilson, who was standing a little back. 'I'd also like you to know that I am indebted to Mr Wilson for drawing my attention to Mr McMenemy's plight in the first place. It was as a result of Mr Wilson coming to see me that I decided the company should pay for Mr McMenemy's defence.'

'But why Mr Brodie?' asked the man from the *Citizen*. 'He's not a King's Counsel.'

Yet, Helen felt tempted to say. Instead, she smiled. 'A very good question,' she said. 'There are many fine King's Counsel – but they are all a lot older than Mr McMenemy.' She smiled at Robbie, who was looking dazed and disbelieving. 'I believed that a counsel nearer his own age might be able to strike a closer rapport with Mr McMenemy.'

'But why Mr Brodie?' The man from the *Bulletin* piped up.

Helen chose her words with even greater care. 'I happen to believe he is one of the finest legal brains of his generation – as do many of his fellow lawyers. He came highly recommended.' She smiled. 'Now, gentlemen, I hope I have answered your questions. As I am sure you will appreciate, Mr McMenemy and his family would now like to get home and I have a shipyard to go back to. I hope I have been able to help you on this very special day. And if you would like to give me your business cards or write your names on a sheet of paper in your notebooks and give them to me, I will let you know whenever I have some good news about the Dunlop Yard or the Pier Line,' she added, determined not to miss the chance of building on her newly-acquired Press contacts.

The reporters all saw Helen as a potential good contact among the normally elusive shipbuilding fraternity and, to a man, they produced their cards or names on scraps of paper.

When they dispersed and Robbie and his family, still dazed and disbelieving, had gone on their way, too, Helen smiled at Graeme Wilson. 'I told you I'd do my best for Robbie McMenemy,' she said proudly.

'And you were as good as your word – and better,' he replied.

Helen saw the admiration shining in his eyes and at that moment she knew that whatever happened to her or befell her, she had made a friend for life in Graeme Wilson and it filled her with a wonderful, glowing feeling.

They had started to walk back towards the gate when she saw John Brodie crossing the Saltmarket and coming towards them. Her heart missed a beat.

'I'm sure Mr Brodie has a lot to say to you, so I'll be off,' said Graeme. 'I'll see you soon. And thank you. For everything.'

He made his way briskly towards the gates where his path crossed with John Brodie's.

Helen's pulse was racing now. It was the first time she had seen John Brodie without Stephen Campbell being in attendance. But the case was over now and, apart from paying his bill, their professional association was at an end. So he was no longer required to have a solicitor at his side when he spoke to her.

'Mrs Dunlop . . .' The commanding court lawyer was hesitant now and looked at her slightly shyly as he reached her side.

And she, who had been so assured and articulate with the Press only minutes ago, was suddenly tongue-tied.

It was the first time they had been completely alone. Free at last from the people who had needed to be around them, suddenly they simply wanted to be near each other. Still and close and silent – and content. Bathing luxuriously in the moment.

As their eyes met and held, the biting wind gusting up the Clyde had no power to chill them.

It *will* be for us, she thought. I know it will. And, certain about life and all it held for them, she glanced at the dark obelisk of Nelson's monument in whose line they stood and said: 'We will not die facing the monument.'

His face broke into a smile and he understood her adapted reference to the days of public hanging when men found guilty of murder mounted the gallows outside Glasgow Green facing Nelson's monument. 'You will die facing the monument' had meant 'you will be hanged.'

He went on smiling at her for a long moment. Then he said: 'No, I think we will live. For a very long time.'

And then they were silent again. And it was enough just to be near each other.

'I had hoped very much to talk to you when the case was over,' he said eventually. 'I had even wondered if you might be free to dine with me this evening. But I have just had a call from the Crown Office. The Lord Advocate wishes to see me in Edinburgh this afternoon.' Disappointment touched her, but she knew there would be other times. 'I'll be in Glasgow again next Thursday. I'll telephone you, if I may.'

'I would like that,' she said. 'Very much . . .'

Now she took to the shops again, as she hadn't done for ages, making her way round the Model Gown and millinery and lingerie and shoe departments of the great city stores. 'How nice, to see you again, Moddom . . .' The words rang in her ears wherever she went. She had

160

money to spend in a Depression and so she was welcome everywhere. And the time to mourn was over – she needed a new wardrobe. Not just for her dinner date with John Brodie – he had rung her the morning after Robbie's acquittal and invited her to the Malmaison for half-past seven next Thursday – but for all the days and evenings she knew lay ahead of them.

She had been a work machine since Harry's death, slaving at the Pier Line and the shipyard from early morning till she nearly dropped late at night. Now she felt like a woman again, a very rich cossetted woman, and there was a new man coming into her life. She gave herself a little hug of pleasure. A set of last Friday's papers still lay in the back of the car. She had ordered twelve sets that day. Her picture with Robbie had appeared in all of them and most had used the interview she gave in full. Sir James Lithgow had sounded quite envious when he had telephoned to congratulate her and she wondered if John Brodie had seen all the papers. If not, she could let him have a set. The *Scotsman* had used an inset picture of him beside a large photograph of Helen and Robbie – he must have seen that.

When Thursday came she took the afternoon off and when she had had a bowl of soup, which Mrs Ramsay, her housekeeper, had prepared, she stepped into a warm scented bath.

Then her hair stylist arrived and took half the afternoon to arrange her hair in an elaborate chignon dressed with diamond studded combs; a manicurist came to paint her toe and fingernails the same brilliant shade of scarlet she intended to stain her lips. She had found her frock in the model Gown department at Coplands – a gorgeous black chiffon affair with a plunging *décolleté* that was filled like a bower with three white silk flowers. The dress had a black taffeta jacket with short, standaway sleeves which made a perfect frame for her slender arms as she swept into the restaurant.

'Helen . . .' As John Brodie raised the black velvet gloved hand she offered him to his lips, her Christian name slid off his tongue as easily as if they had been friends for years. 'Let me look at you before you sit down,' he said appreciatively and she stood before him for a moment, smiling. 'I must be the envy of every man in the room.'

Then the head waiter fussed her into her seat and laid white napkins on their knees and flourished menus as the wine waiter poured champagne into the glasses.

Helen felt slightly breathless as she settled at the table. Then she reached for her glass and her eyes held John's. I've missed you, she thought. So much.

'Your very good health,' he said, raising his glass to her and she joined him. 'Now tell me, are you quite settled back at the Pier Line and the shipyard?'

'Yes indeed,' she said.

'And Robbie?'

'He was back at the yard yesterday morning, though I haven't been over there to see him myself. I'm not sure that he should have been so soon after his terrible ordeal, but it was what he wanted to do.'

'Good,' said John smiling. She sensed there was something he wanted to tell her. 'I think I may have more to thank you for than merely the fee I earned.'

'Really?' Helen's eyes widened questioningly.

He nodded. 'Yes. The Lord Advocate was sufficiently impressed by the way I handled the case to have made me an Advocate Depute. My appointment was announced in the *Edinburgh Gazette* this evening.'

Helen remembered the judge had addressed the Crown prosecutor as 'Mr Depute.' 'Does that mean you'll be working for the Crown?'

'I will be one of a team of prosecutors working for the Lord Advocate. He is responsible for all criminal prosecutions in Scotland, but obviously he could never handle every single case himself, as he also has responsibilities to the Government and in Parliament,' said John. 'In the lower courts his work is done by full-time Procurators-fiscal. In the High Court he has a team of advocates called Deputes to whom cases are assigned and for which they are responsible. They are only appointed for a period of a few years and combine their work for the Crown with their civil practices.'

'How fascinating,' exclaimed Helen, smiling and raising her glass. 'Congratulations,' she added, longing to know more. 'Do you now have to do everything connected with a case for which you are responsible?'

'I am in charge,' said John. 'I have solicitors from the Crown Office and an assistant to help me with pulling all the evidence together. But I have to decide what it's worth and how a case is to be prosecuted – and if, indeed, it should be. If I do not think there is sufficient evidence to prove the case beyond reasonable doubt, it is up to me to tell the Lord Advocate so. In effect, I have to decide whether or not a prosecution should go ahead. And I have to be convinced that the Crown can win its case before I can recommend that it does.'

'It sounds quite a responsibility,' she said.

'There *is* a lot of responsibility,' he said. 'But it is also a privilege to be invited to join the Lord Advocate's team. It is an important step, even though it means I am debarred from being a Defence counsel for as long as I hold the post.'

'So I can't hire you again?'

'Not in the criminal courts, but if you want to sue anyone in the civil courts, I can still be your man,' he

163

said as a waiter hovered and he ordered plates of oysters for both of them.

'What happens if you lose your case? Do you get the sack?' she asked.

He grinned. 'It doesn't usually happen like that,' he said. 'There can be all sorts of reasons for losing which may not be your fault. As *I* did in Robbie's case, the Defence may simply be able to discredit your most important witness and you don't know for certain what anyone is going to say until you get them into the witness box. If things kept going badly wrong in a number of cases, your judgement could be called into question and you might be asked to handle less difficult cases. But things like that don't usually happen.'

'Have you started work on your first case?'

'Yes, I started today. And I want to win.'

She sensed he was probably not allowed to talk about it, so she said: 'The thing I would like to see you do, which was missing from Robbie's trial, is address the jury.'

'Then, you must come again,' he said, taking a sip of champagne. 'If you're appearing for the defence, the way to win a jury's heart is to have empathy with your client. Now I'm going to have to learn to empathise with victims of crime, not its alleged perpetrators.'

Then, wanting to know all of him, she encouraged him to talk about his childhood and his room in his parents' house in Edinburgh where he used to kneel by the window and say his prayers looking out to the Pentland Hills, about his early days at Edinburgh Academy and the 'cad fights' with local urchins on the way home from school; about his friendship with Henry Macrae and Robert Warrender's younger brother, Andrew, who had been killed in Von Ludendorf's offensive in the Marne in 1918 shortly after he joined up.

'So many of the boys I knew went straight from school

to be slaughtered on the battlefields. They were all so keen; couldn't wait to get to the war. At the beginning of the summer term in 1917 there wasn't a single boy of eighteen in the school,' he said sadly. Then he brightened and talked about his student days at Edinburgh University and later devilling for Robert Warrender before he was called to the Bar, working late in the Juridical library in Charlotte Square and saving up to buy the books he needed out of his legal fees. There was a lot of hard work but no money to be made at the Bar for a long time. But from what she had learned on the deck of the *Monadliath*, she knew there was a lively social life which he did not even mention.

So she probed: 'As you all have to work so hard without much money, I suppose none of you can afford to get married for a long time.'

'There is quite a bit of late marriage,' he said non-committally.

She had drawn a blank, so she tried another track.

'I had never been inside a court when I went to see you in Edinburgh with Stephen Campbell,' she said. 'And I felt I ought to before the trial. So after I left you that day I walked up to Parliament House and sat in the Lord President's court. It was the first one I came to.'

'How very enterprising of you,' said John approvingly. 'Were you impressed?'

'He seemed very able.'

'He has a first-class mind.'

'Does he have a son to follow in his footsteps like Lord Macrae?'

'Like Lord Uncle Tom Cobleigh-and-all,' sighed John. 'The Supreme Courts are full of dynasties but the Lord President's family is not of them.'

'He has no sons?'

'No.' John shook his head and took one of her hands

between his own and said: 'Oh, Helen Dunlop, I wonder why it is I can talk to you as I can talk to no other man or woman?'

So Grace Mitchell wasn't close to him! As their eyes held she had the curious sensation of being rooted in him already.

He was catching the late train from Queen Street Station and she took him there in her Silver Cloud.

'Can we do this again the next time I'm in Glasgow?' he asked before he got out.

'I would like that,' she replied happily, her eyes shining. 'Very much.'

'I'll give you a ring,' he said, taking one of her hands and raising it to his lips.

Then he got out. He stood and watched the Rolls pull out of the station and waved her off into the night.

But it was another two months before she heard from him again . . .

Chapter Seven

East Lothian – December, 1930

Grace Mitchell studied the figure she cut in a blue crêpe de chine dress in a gilded cheval mirror. As her eyes travelled from her dramatic looks of marble white skin set against long jet-black hair, she placed her hands around the slender waist that was the envy of every young woman in Edinburgh Society and took a deep breath. She knew that with her looks and the prospects she held out for a man's career because she was the Lord President's daughter she could have married anyone. But at twenty-four she had fallen in love with John Brodie and had seen her future in him – the dinner parties and receptions and soirées she would give as his wife, the guests she would invite *and* be able to guarantee their acceptance because of who she was. She would devote her life to his career, to getting him made King's Counsel, judge and finally, Lord President, just like her father.

Grace's parents encouraged the friendship, especially her father because he had no son and he wanted John Brodie to be his son-in-law and follow him on to the Bench. And Grace knew she could make it happen, because the upper echelons of the Bar and Bench were only open to men with the right connections, which John Brodie did not have; to fulfil his ambitions he *needed* her. Except he didn't seem to realise it . . .

She had now waited five years and the prospect of

still being single at thirty loomed like some high, incoming tide, relentlessly pushing its way closer to her with every passing day. She would be an old maid. Already she sensed her status in Society subtly diminishing. She detected pity in the eyes of girls without a fraction of her looks who had married years ago and young men who had once sought her favours were also married now and there were fewer would-be suitors. She was becoming ashamed of attending other people's weddings and being asked if she would be the next and she was starting to feel bitter and resentful towards John Brodie. All her mother's placatory words about a young man 'needing time to make his way at the Bar' could no longer lance or contain her impatience. The time had come to take matters into her own hands. She turned from the mirror and strolled towards the window. As she gazed out she was hardly conscious of the December day dying rapidly over the great plain of East Lothian or the low stone dykes and brown earth that stretched for endless miles towards the distant Lammermuir Hills. She was aware only that John Brodie's Austin Tourer was among the motor cars parked on the drive outside Lord Justice Clerk Dodds's magnificent Palladian mansion and that this night he would sleep under the same roof as she did.

She looked from the window around the room. Would it all still look the same afterwards? Would anything look the same afterwards? Or would the whole world be different after she had done what she had to do?

Handsome gilded wall mirrors made the ballroom of Lord Dodds's Palladian mansion seem twice as big as it really was and the gold and silver bells and garlands catching the light of the crystal chandeliers created an atmosphere of elegant celebration.

As dinner ended for the guests seated at the white-clothed tables around the dance floor, cigar smoke was beginning to waft upwards and the strains of *I can't give you anything but love*, *Baby*, played by a five-piece band, could be heard above the clatter of white-jacketed waiters clearing away the fine china.

Watching the dancers drifting towards the floor, John Brodie thought about how much his parents would have enjoyed a party like this – if only they had been considered fit people to invite. He would have to tell his mother all about it over Christmas and she would eat the names of the people who attended every bit as much as she would eat her dinner and look across the table at his father with eyes that said: we made it after all because they invite John. His eyes cast round the ballroom at the company . . . Lord President Mitchell, Lord Justice Clerk Dodds, whose party it was, the white and balding heads of all the judges and the greying ones of the Kings' Counsel and the younger faces of the Advocates Depute and their wives. While Lords Dodds invited everyone to his summer garden party, invitations to his pre-Christmas house party were limited to the cream of the élite – and this was the first time John had been invited. He had won his place at the high table. Now it was up to him to keep it.

His glance fell on Grace Mitchell, who was dancing with Henry Macrae. She was the wife his parents had seen for him in their dreams. With her by his side, his future would be assured, he would belong to the Establishment. It was all there for him tonight. All he had to do was take it. He had never seen Grace look more beautiful than she did this evening and he supposed he would have married her if he had not fallen in love with Helen Dunlop. But that had changed everything . . .

The music stopped and Henry and Grace returned to

their table and Grace said to John in a petulant voice: 'Aren't you going to ask me to dance?'

'If you'll give me a chance to do so,' he said, getting to his feet.

The band now struck up a Viennese waltz, which brought the older generation on to the dance floor.

Grace was light as air in his arms and such a good dancer. They remained on the floor for an energetic quickstep and then joined in an eightsome reel. And then Henry and Robert Warrender and one or two other lawyers asked Grace to dance before John could claim her back.

The music had slowed to waltz time once more when she seemed a little faint in his arms.

'Are you all right, Grace?' he asked, concerned.

'I think I need a little fresh air,' she said. 'It's rather hot in here.'

'Yes, it is rather,' he said, taking her arm and walking her out into the corridor, where she leaned heavily on his arm and breathed deeply.

'Better?' he asked.

'A bit – but I think I'll go to my room and sit down for a while.'

'I'll walk you.'

The room was softly lit, exactly as she had left it – by the two bedside lights and the pink standard lamp near the fire, whose rosy glow added to the atmosphere of warmth. But the bed had now been turned down and her nightdress and robe, filigrees of white muslin, arranged on the cover.

Grace leaned even more heavily on John's arm as he closed the door behind him and as they sat down on the settee she steeled herself for the performance of her life.

'Can I get you anything?' asked John. 'A glass of water?'

'No,' she said, shaking her head and leaning it against his chest and he ran his fingers through her hair. Then she pulled back from him and rested her face in her hand.

'Oh, John, I must go to bed. But I feel so weak, . . . I have hardly the strength to undress myself. Could you help me out of my dress,' she asked, getting up. She was terrified of what she was about to do but there was no going back. Not now. She steeled herself.

He looked at her uncertainly. He had never been more intimate with Grace than holding her in his arms when they danced. And now she was asking him to help her take her clothes off!

'Please . . .?'

As her dark eyes pleaded with his, he experienced an overwhelming sense of her need for him. She *wanted* him.

'Grace . . . are you sure?'

'Yes,' she gasped, reaching for the zip herself.

The next moment her dress fell on the floor and she was standing before him clad in nothing but her white silk stockings and suspenders and French knickers and her breasts were bigger and more beautiful than he had ever imagined and her luminous black eyes were saying she would die without him.

His desire was overwhelming now. He reached for her and her French knickers fell on top of her dress. And the most amazing thing was that she went on encouraging him even when he hurt her momentarily . . .

'Grace, I had no idea,' he said afterwards.

But she said nothing, just lay there looking up at him by the firelight with a smile in her luminous black eyes

171

bright as the moon on a frosty winter night. And she didn't bother at all with any filigree of muslin when he got into bed with her and they started to do it all over again . . .

Chapter Eight

Glasgow – January, 1931

Just after the New Year, on January 6th, a Pier Line ship, the *SS Ardvreck Castle*, was sunk in a storm in the South China Sea with the loss of all hands. The crew came from Port Glasgow and the story was front page headlines in the Scottish papers. Whilst Helen dealt with the shipping agents, the importers, the exporters and the press, Alan and Ian Campbell moved into the Pier Line offices to cope with the legal problems and Graeme Wilson, who knew the crew, at once volunteered to accompany her when she visited the families.

Snow blowing down from the northern mountains was falling thickly enough to lie on the tenement streets of Port Glasgow when they arrived the next day. There had been a time, at the very beginning when she first inherited the yard and the shipping line, when Helen had wondered if it was tactful to drive in the Rolls Royce when she had to meet poor and deprived people. But that didn't last long. The Rolls was a symbol of her power and she had quickly learned people respected that kind of show of power and felt almost a sense of magic when a beautiful young woman stepped from a fine limousine, her scented presence bringing words of comfort to the needy. It was how Royalty did business. So she had no compunction about pulling up in her Rolls among the mean tenements of Port Glasgow. The bereaved families, women with young frightened children gathered at their knees and many with another on the way, clustered round big black kitchen ranges just like the one at which her mother and Aunt Cath had sat. She had taken Graeme Wilson with her and now he smoothed her way as she sat stroking the heads of small children and listening to their mothers' needs.

'I am making £10 available to each family at once,' she told the women. 'And I am appointing an administrator to look after you immediately. She is a member of my staff who is also a young widow and it is her you should contact to discuss your needs until we can see what can be done.'

'No one should be left with absolutely nothing. It's inhuman,' said Graeme Wilson, sitting beside Helen in the back of the Rolls on the journey back to Glasgow. The snow was falling even more heavily now, piling up at the edges of the pavement and beginning to drift. 'It is extremely generous of you to make the provision you are doing, Mrs Dunlop, but by law there ought to be some floor below which people cannot fall.'

Helen, whose emotions had been stirred by the deprivation she had witnessed, felt moved. 'I agree, Mr Wilson, but how?'

'The State should make provision for everyone.'

'But that would be an enormous task! How on earth would they pay for it?'

'Everyone would be taxed to pay for it,' he said, looking her directly in the eyes. 'There would be a State levy on the wages and salaries throughout their working lives. So that when they were sick they would be paid, when they were ill they would be seen by a doctor without charge and there would be a State pension to take care of them in their old age. There would also be a State fund to which they could turn in time of disaster, a fund that would provide them with the kind of relief you are giving now to the bereaved families in Port Glasgow.' His eyes did not leave Helen's. 'You may think this is a pipe dream, Mrs Dunlop. But I am a Socialist and I will work to fulfil that dream.'

'No, Mr Wilson, it is not a dream . . . It is a vision.' Helen saw the passion in those eyes. It seemed to fill the Rolls and almost burn her skin. It was the stuff that kindled her soul. Men with visions and the ambition and drive to fulfil them changed the world and made it better. Men with visions of a better world had stopped slavery and public hangings and people sending children up chimneys. Even in these desperate times of Depression when half of Clydeside was out of work and disaster had struck in the South China Sea, there was hope. Because there were still men of vision, who dreamed of making a better world. Men like Graeme Wilson . . . She wondered how far he would travel, how high he would climb. As her eyes continued to hold his, she became aware of things about him she had not noticed before – how there was a tiny kink at the root of his hair before it straightened out on his head, that the beginnings of fine lines were already dawning on his forehead and that the scent of a peat fire lingered in his clothes. His lips seemed to quiver a little, his breath was warm and would made little vapour clouds in the outside air.

'You will make your visions come true, Mr Wilson,' she said in a low, husky voice, feeling that only the formality of his name provided a boundary between them at the moment.

'I will,' he said, turning his head away from her and looking straight in front of him towards the drifting snow.

The moment had passed. But it had confronted her with needs within herself she had all but shut away

175

because there had been no one to answer them – needs she reflected upon quietly as the Rolls pushed on steadily towards Glasgow and the safety of her office.

She had not seen or heard from John Brodie since they dined at Malmaison nearly two months ago, but she had thought and wondered about him a lot – especially over Christmas which she had spent at the Campbell family home at Luss on the shores of Loch Lomond and at the New Year when she joined their party at Gleneagles.

He had simply vanished from her life and she felt close to tears as she had often been in recent weeks, when the Rolls pulled up outside the Pier Line and she thanked and said goodbye to Graeme Wilson.

It was another week before her secretary put her head round the door and announced: 'Mr John Brodie is on the line.'

'Helen Dunlop.' Her tone was businesslike when she picked up the receiver. She wasn't sure what she felt about him at this minute.

'Helen, I was very sorry to hear about the *Ardvreck Castle* – and I'm sorry I've not been in touch, but things have been a bit hectic.' His voice was distant, formal, as if there had never been any closeness between them. But she supposed hers was, too. 'Look, I'll be in Glasgow next Tuesday and I wondered if you might be free to have dinner with me.'

'Why, don't you come to my place?' she said. She wanted to gage the situation and she reckoned she could do this better on her own ground in Great Western Terrace. 'I think my food beats any restaurant.'

'What a charming idea.' His tone sounded more relaxed.

She burst into tears the moment she replaced the receiver. She had missed him so.

*   *   *

176

John knew making love to Grace had been the biggest mistake of his life even before it was over.

Her mother, Lady Mitchell, had knocked on the bedroom as they embraced for the second time. 'Are you all right, darling?'

'Yes, Mummy, I'm fine,' Grace had cried as he quickly withdrew from her. 'I've just got a headache.' When her mother had gone, she told him, 'You had better go now. I won't tell anyone what you've done.'

'I thought you wanted it,' he said ruefully.

She said nothing but there was a triumphant look in her eyes as she leapt from the bed and covered herself in the muslin négligé which had fallen on the floor.

He hadn't touched her since, but that brief lovemaking had changed their relationship completely. Now, instead of writing him a polite note requesting the pleasure of his company, she telephoned him commanding his attendance at her soirées. And her arm slipped possessively into his the moment he crossed the threshold of her parent's home in Heriot Row.

We are a couple now – the message she was sending to the world was loud and clear.

He had compromised her, so he was going to have to marry her now. But she said nothing. He wondered if she was waiting for him to propose. But he said nothing.

He was uneasy – not just about Grace, but about his first case as an Advocate Depute. It was a very nasty double rape case which he desperately wanted to win and he longed to talk to Helen.

The next Tuesday felt like spring after a bitter winter to her. All Helen's pining and longing and missing of recent weeks were now the past. Today John Brodie would be hers again, and whoever he had been with he would soon

177

forget. Men were creatures of the moment and forgot, which was why they were unfaithful; only women lived in their memories.

'Forget her, forget her,' she whispered as she smiled at her reflection in her dressing-table mirror. Her golden hair fell gloriously loose this evening, a medley of curls cascading down on to her bare shoulders and the sliver of a strapless black velvet evening dress. 'Forget her, forget her,' she whispered again, like the voice of spring singing in the depths of winter. We are alive and everything, the whole of life, is ours and renegotiable.

And we're not even lovers yet, she thought, placing her arms around his neck and kissing him lightly on the cheek, when he rang the bell at twenty minutes to eight.

She had got Mrs Ramsay to prepare beef bourguignon and a sturdy claret was open and warming on the dining-table as the scent of woodsmoke filled the air.

She saw sadness in his eyes – but there was happiness now, too, that he was here. *Forget her, forget her.*

'I'm glad you could make it,' she said, slipping her arm into his as if she had done it a thousand times before and led him into the drawing-room where logs were crackling and flaming in the hearth. Then she poured them pale, dry sherry which they sipped across the fireside.

'I've missed you,' she said huskily, raising her glass and, over its rim, fixing his eyes in hers. Suddenly her heart felt very full. Why did people have to waste life playing games of hide and seek and not saying what they meant? And why did relationships get tangled? Because people could never say what was in their hearts for fear of compromising themselves and their relationships with others!

'I've missed you, too,' he said, holding her gaze.

I've missed you even more than I knew, he thought, watching her pouring them coffee by the fire. They had not spoken much over dinner. It had been enough just to be near one another. He felt as if he had come home to her this evening. And he'd never felt like that about a woman before.

It was then, swirling a cognac she had poured, that he decided to tell her about the case he was working on – because he needed her to understand. 'You're the only person in the world to whom I can talk the way I need to talk about what is on my mind,' he said.

'I'm not really supported to discuss my cases outside the Crown Office – apart from with the Defence when I need to liaise with them. This is my first case as a Depute and I want to win it. But it's very difficult.'

'Is it a case of murder?' she asked, remembering his reservations about the death penalty.

His look grew dark. 'There can be things worse than murder.' He placed his glass on the table and got up and stood with his back to the fire just as he had done when she met him in his chambers. 'Helen, I need your help. To sway the jury, I need to know how a woman feels.' Then he told her the story of how a woman called Kathleen McFadyen, who was twenty-two and the unmarried mother of a three-year-old daughter, had met two men in a pub in the Dumbarton Road in Glasgow.

'After a few drinks they went back to her two-roomed flat in Partick, which she shared with her alcoholic mother and child. It was late and her mother and daughter were asleep, though I doubt her mother would have cared much anyway. After a few drinks the young woman agreed to take one of the men into the alcove bed in the kitchen and asked the second man to leave . . .' He paused and looked towards the window and the blackness of the night.

'I think I know what's coming John,' said Helen trying to assist him. 'The other man refused to leave?'

'Indeed he didn't leave,' said John, a bitter edge to his

voice. 'There wasn't a thing those two men didn't do to that poor girl. The poor, stupid girl, too frightened to cry out, too hurt to defend herself. There wasn't one part of her that hadn't been invaded and brutalised. She was left so badly injured she needed surgery under a general anaesthetic. Her vagina was torn apart and she'll never be able to have any more children.' He picked up his glass and drained it. 'That's what I meant when I said there can be things worse than murder . . .'

Helen took his glass and refilled it and poured a cognac for herself. Listening to him had reminded her what it once been like for her with Harry, how she had felt humiliated and degraded. But what had been done to her was nothing beside the dreadful violation of this poor girl.

She gave him back his glass and they both sat down again.

He looked directly at her and asked: 'How do I get an all-male jury to understand enough to convict?'

'They've got to,' said Helen grimly. 'You've *got* to convince them. Because this is not an isolated case, John. Though mostly not as bad, things like it go on all the time and they are not even regarded as crimes,' she added bitterly. 'All over Glasgow women – wives and mothers – are raped and humiliated by their husbands every night. Rape within marriage is a licensed crime, John. One a man is entitled to commit under the Matrimonial Acts and there is nothing a woman can do about it. John, let me tell you about my friend's experience . . .' and, in the guise that she was telling him about a stranger, Helen described her thousand sufferings at Harry's hands, the humiliation and degradation and the pain. She came close to tears as she told her story but managed to stay in control. 'Then, one day it changed,' she said. 'My friend decided that she had had enough, that her life wasn't

180

worth living. So she stood up for herself and she was able to get her husband see how much he had hurt her. He began to talk about his feelings and understand hers. And eventually they grew to love each other. But that does not happen for many women.'

When she had finished he knew and understood how she had got her shipyard and her shipping line. But he also knew that she did not want to reveal the truth to him yet. One day, though, she would. He knew that and so did she. It had assuaged her pain to bring it up and talk about it. And she was glad she had told him because she wanted him to know what she was really like. She wanted them to be honest with each other and not play the game of 'let's pretend' so many couples did.

The rape trial opened in the High Court the next morning and by the afternoon it was making sensational banner headlines in the evening papers. One of them published a photograph of John, with a caption recalling that he had the unique distinction of having been hired by the shipbuilder Helen Dunlop to defend one of her employees on a murder charge – and achieved an acquittal. In the back of the Rolls as it nosed homewards in the evening traffic, Helen decided the picture must have been taken at least ten years ago – John looked little more than a boy and not nearly as attractive as he was now.

There was a lot of junketing attached to the High Court circuit; civil dignitaries and local sheriffs and prosecutors were expected to entertain the court, which meant John spent the evenings at official dinners and she did not see him. But he telephoned her every day and she had decided she was going to Court to hear him address the jury.

'I want to see you, listen to you in action, not just read about you in the papers,' she said softly down the line.

'I'd like that,' he said. 'Very much.'

Her arrival in the packed South Court on the fourth morning of the trial immediately caused speculation among the Press, though no reporter had the nerve to ask her about her interest in *this* case. John had arranged for her to have a front row gallery seat, to which she was escorted by a senior police officer. He was standing by the counsel table talking to his junior and Crown solicitors as she sat down and he bowed his head slightly in acknowledgement.

The South Court was identical to the North Court and there were the same crowds with their flasks and sandwiches, though the atmosphere was not as highly charged as it had been at the murder trial when a life was at stake.

Helen was still quietly taking stock of her surroundings when a macer crying 'Court' suddenly appeared, leading the judge on to the bench. A hush descended on the court.

'Mr Depute . . .' Lord Warrender addressed John, who had remained standing when every one else sat down.

'Thank you, my Lord,' said John, who then turned and took slow measured steps towards the jury stand.

Fifteen pairs of eyes focusing intently upon him now presented him with the biggest challenge of his career – to get an all-male jury to understand how a woman *feels*.

He paused – a well-timed, dramatic pause – leaned slightly on one heel, and, resting his thumbs inside the folds of his gown beneath his shoulders, began.

'Gentlemen of the jury . . .' His words rang out round the hushed court. 'My duty – that is, the duty of the Crown – is to prove the case beyond reasonable doubt. It does not have to be proved on the basis of mathematical truth; simply on the basis than when all things are weighed and considered, it has been proved beyond reasonable doubt. The burden of proof is on the Crown and, to stand up, the Crown's case must be corroborated. That does not necessarily mean it must be corroborated in words. It could be by a bloodstain or in the distressed state of mind the victim was found to be in by a doctor. The Defence Counsel may tell you a different version of things. But they don't have to prove anything. That is the burden of the Crown. That is *my* job.

'When he speaks to you, the judge will tell you what the law is. He will explain what the legal position is. That is *his* job.

'Only the jury decide the facts. That is *your* job.'

He paused and looked briefly into several pairs of eyes before he said: 'Now, gentlemen, I must explain the principle of acting in consort. The principle is that when people act together they are all responsible for all of it, whether or not they actually did it. For example, if four men rob a bank and are caught, all four are guilty. The man who drove the getaway car is equally as guilty as the man who actually took the money. If one man holds a woman down whilst the other rapes her, they are both guilty. They acted together.

'Gentlemen,' he paused and clasped his hands behind his back and looked into several more pairs of eyes. 'This is not a court of morals. Whatever you may think of Miss McFadyen, whatever she may have done in the past, whatever her reputation may be, she is still entitled not to consent. Though she may have been willing to do something with one of these men when she invited them back to her flat, that is not giving them both a blank cheque to do what they liked with her and abuse her in the horrifyingly brutal way they did.' He poured some water from a decanter into a glass and took a sip while he let the thought sink in.

'Gentlemen, you have to take Miss McFadyen with all her failings. Which one of us had not at some time failed and fallen short of what we would like to be . . .?' He stepped back, arms outstretched, palms upturned to the ceiling. Then he stepped in close, his voice ringing with command as he told them: 'Gentlemen, Miss McFadyen never had the chance to do anything *but* fail.

'You have heard her own testimony about the circumstances of her birth. How she was born illegitimate, with her mother not knowing who her father was; how, when she was only four years old, she was abandoned by the mother who now clings to her; how her childhood became a painful saga of journeys around orphanages and being fostered in the homes of strangers; and how, when she was only nine, she was seduced by a man she trusted, the only man who had ever shown her any of the affection she desperately needed. Gentlemen, Miss McFadyen was a fallen child before she was a fallen woman. She had never had the chance to be anything else. Every adult in her life had failed her miserably.'

Helen thrilled to his words. The court was in his thrall.

He took another sip of water. When he laid the glass down he pulled himself up to his full height before he said: 'Gentlemen, only the most unfortunate of men can ever experience anything akin to the degradation and suffering of a woman who is raped. When a man is brutally assaulted the bruises, the scars and the wounds can be seen by the world. When a woman is raped she is similarly brutally assaulted. But the wounds are inflicted deep inside her. And though no one can see them, she will carry these wounds and scars in her heart for the rest of her life. Rape is not a sexual assault. It is a crime against life itself. It is spiritual and emotional murder. The rape of one woman is a crime against all women . . . against *your* mothers and *your* wives, *your* sisters and *your* daughters. *All* women have been degraded by the rape of this one woman.'

184

The court sat in stunned silence.

In the afternoon the jury brought in verdicts of guilty and both men were sent to prison for fifteen years.

'I could never have done it without you,' said John to Helen. They were walking on Glasgow Green after the trial had ended. The afternoon was raw and damp with icy blasts gusting up from the Clyde and Helen, cossetted from head to calf in red fox, pulled her collar close. 'Everything you told me about what your friend had suffered became part of the case. By telling me her story, you heightened my perception and understanding of what a woman can suffer at the hands of a man. Her fears and terror became part of it. It was you and your story I was thinking about when I addressed the jury.'

Stopping, he laid an arm across her shoulders. It was the first time he had touched her, apart from raising her fingers to his lips. 'I drew my strength from you,' he said.

She looked up at him, her eyes meeting and holding his for an eternal moment. It was then, with the winter wind whirling round their faces and their strong young limbs, that what had been there suspended between them from the beginning, sprang to life, endowing them both with new life. And what was to be became . . . inevitable . . .

Chapter Nine

Glasgow, – January 1931

Their affair began that afternoon. The Irrewaddy Flotilla Company's demand for an immediate reply to its telegram, the urgent call to the international lawyers in London now involved in the aftermath of the *Ardvreck* disaster, the important letter to the Clydesdale Bank ... could all wait until another day. So could the last train to Edinburgh ... and those documents tied with pink string in a box in Parliament House. What had been urgent no longer was; previous priorities were dissolved by more pressing needs. Her fox coat and her stockings and her pretty things were strewn all over the flat like blossom scattered by a spring wind. The world seemed distant and unreal. The only real thing was the reflection ... they found of themselves in one another. It had never been quite the way it was for either of them with anyone before, so passionate and overwhelming that bathed in sweat that felt like dew they seemed to have been born into a new morning ... creatures of a different and more powerful race, in fuller possession of their faculties, more conscious of their being and of their strength, recreated, refashioned by their love. In their amazement afterwards they were almost shy with each other, stunned by the miracle the afternoon had wrought, at the nakedness and wonder of what had happened to them. Somewhere through the night they became a couple, new, confident and strong when they awoke in the morning and their tangled limbs greeted the new day.

Chapter Ten

Shores of the Moray Firth – April, 1931

Helen awoke to sunlight streaming through the cottage window on to the patchwork quilt on the bed.

She sat up slowly and stretched her arms wide above her head and lay back on the pillows.

'What's the time?' she asked John, who lay half dozing beside her.

'We came here to forget about time,' he murmured.

And other people, she thought, smiling and running her fingers through his tangled dark hair.

Outside seagulls dived and swooped over the incoming tide and tall grasses rustled in the breeze. The world beyond – where the Nazis were gaining a real foothold in Germany and unemployment soaring over two million in Britain had led Sir Oswald Mosley to leave the Labour Government and form the New Party – seemed faraway and uncertain.

The only certainty was this room, the scent of narcissi which filled the air, John's skin warm against her own, his body melting in hers. Now.

Though they had been lovers for only three months, it seemed as if he had always been in her life and she could not imagine being without him now. They had spent almost every weekend together since that first afternoon – at places like Gleneagles and The Ritz – and though they hardly left their suites, there were always other people, thousands of them, around just beyond the door. Which was why he had taken this cottage on the shores of the Moray Firth so they could be completely alone for a whole blissful long weekend and it was enough to be be, to love, to wring joy from each moment.

But today was the last morning they would wake up together in this room; after they eventually got up and had breakfast they would drive back south in his Austin Tourer to the hectic, crowded world of other people.

She knew that soon she would have to meet the other people in his life – his parents and friends. They couldn't stay alone, cocooned in a world of their own forever.

'Good morning, Mrs Dunlop . . .' John raised his head and looked at her and in a moment was making love to her.

'You're nice, very nice in the morning, John Brodie,' she said afterwards, wondering, as she often did, at his tenderness. One day she was going to ask him where he'd learned it. She smiled up at him. She belonged to this man in a way she had never belonged to anyone before . . .

'I've never loved anyone as much as I love you and I never will, whatever happens in this crazy world,' said John, looking down at her after they had made love again.

Sometimes he hardly recognised himself. Loving Helen he was feeling things he did not know he could feel, discovering things within himself he hadn't known were there, uncovering a depth in himself he had no idea he possessed . . . Until now his life had been a constant parade of going through the motions.

But it had seemed real until now. It had seemed to be what he wanted whenever he stood beneath the beautiful ceiling ovals and crystal chandeliers in the Lord President's house in Heriot Row. He had often looked across the room at the Lord President's beautiful daughter and imagined, the great judicial dynasty he would found with her. He would be the first of generations of Brodies who would sit in judgement on Scotland.

But none of it was that important any more. To live and love and be happy – that was what he wanted now.

Yet he had been apprehensive about his happiness all weekend, ever since he got a telephone call before he left his chambers on Friday afternoon, summoning him to meet the Lord President at the Cockburn Club on Monday evening . . .

Chapter Eleven

Edinburgh – April, 1931

'Lord Mitchell is in the library.' The Cockburn Club
secretary, a man in a dark suit who greeted John in the
foyer, gave the impression of being on sentry duty.

John nodded and mounted the marble stairs.

The stench of a thousand dead cigars assaulted him
as he entered the library where the erect figure of Lord
Mitchell stood with his back to a roaring fire and
his slush-coloured moustache seemed to be twitching
slightly. This was the highest and most powerful judge
in all the land, who had the last word on whether a
man lived or died or for how many years he languished
in prison. Apart from the monarch, there was no one
else to whom the convicted could turn for remission of
their punishments. His word was law among lawyers,
too. He prescribed the style of the Supreme Courts and
appointed the Kings' Counsel; with the Lord Advocate
he decided which men became judges, and no man
could become a Sheriff in the lower courts without his
approval. Though he had been schooled since childhood
to be confident and was equally at ease socially and
professionally with judges, alone and face-to-face with
Lord President Mitchell, John now experienced the most
appalling awe at this man's power to decide his future.
His status, earning power, the kind of cases in which he
was instructed, his whole career all lay in the hands of

this one man as much as the fate of any prisoner in the dock.

'Brodie,' Lord Mitchell's hands were clasped behind his back, 'you have put my daughter in the family way. What do you have to say for yourself?'

This was the worst John had anticipated and he had prepared for it as best he could.

'With respect, my Lord, this may not be the case,' he said carefully.

The Lord President gave him the measured, narrow-eyed look he normally reserved for men he was about to sentence. 'Do you deny that intimate relations took place between yourself and my daughter when you were both guests in the home of Lord Dodds?'

'No, my Lord, I do not.' John spoke confidently and looked the Lord President straight in the eyes.

'As a result my daughter is now expecting your child.'

'My Lord, may I ask what proof is there that as a result of this one isolated incident I am the father – '

'Do not impute the reputation and good character of my daughter,' the Lord President thundered. 'She was a virgin until then and has been near no man since. It is now just over three months since then, which is exactly the time she has been with child. What do you propose to do about it?'

John's desperate show of confidence was rapidly collapsing.

He cleared his throat: 'If, as a result of what happened between your daughter and myself, she has become pregnant, I will make generous provision both for your daughter and her child.'

'Brodie,' the Lord President said silkily, 'thoughtless as your conduct has been, you will not inflict the stigma of illegitimacy on my family. You will marry my daughter.'

'I am afraid I cannot marry your Lordship's daughter. I am about to become engaged to be married to Mrs Helen Dunlop.'

'You may have been. You are no longer.'

'My Lord, we are planning to marry in the summer!' John protested.

'Brodie, you seem to be having difficulty in understanding me. You will marry my daughter or you will cease to practise at the Scottish Bar. If you do not marry her, no solicitor will employ you and you will be asked to resign as an Advocate Depute. If you do not then leave Edinburgh, reason will be found to disbar you.' Lord Mitchell looked at his fob watch. 'You have thirty minutes to make up your mind. I will be in the bar downstairs. If your decision is to marry my daughter, you may join me. If you decide to abandon your career for a woman, you will leave this Club for the last time.'

The Lord President strode from the room.

Thirty minutes! It took years to build a career and a reputation — but it could all be lost in the brief time it took to make love.

He began to pace the room. Perhaps he could be called to the English Bar? Then he remembered how closely intermingled the English and Scottish legal professions were at the top. Two Scottish judges sat in the House of Lords, the highest Appeal Court in Britain, and two former Edinburgh Academy boys had been Lord Chancellor. He closed his eyes and gritted his teeth. The doors of the Inns of Court were closed before they had been opened.

'A man's career is always the most important thing. It defines who he is and where he is in the order of things and decides everything else that happens to him. Even if you do not think that now, you will one day.' Words

193

spoken by the first woman he had loved came back to him across the years.

She had been seventeen years older than he was, the wife of one of his law lecturers at Edinburgh University, and when he was eighteen she had expertly taken his virginity away. He had loved her madly and wanted to marry her. But she had only been amusing herself. When her husband was appointed Professor of International Law at Sydney University she had ditched John.

'But you don't love your husband,' he had protested. 'Surely our love is more important than his job.'

'It is a wife's duty to support her husband.' There had been a hard, triumphant look in those baby-blue eyes, which suddenly seemed old. He had known then that, in the running of the world, power was far more important than love and people were ruthless in their pursuit of it.

It was power Grace Mitchell wanted – the power being his wife would give her in Society.

He remembered when he first saw her on the terrace of Lord Justice Clerk Dodds's Palladian mansion in East Lothian in the summer of 1923. He had just been called to the Bar and it was the first time he had been invited to attend the annual garden party Lord Dodds first gave in 1919 to celebrate the return of members of the Bar who had fought in the Great War.

'Introduce me,' he had commanded Henry Macrae, who uncomplainingly led him across the terrace to where Grace was holding court among a circle of admiring young men.

A slightly irritated expression crossed her face at Henry's approach but she quickly swapped it for a radiant smile when her eyes met John's. She was exquisite – but there was an hauteur about her manner and his first thought was that a predatory nature lurked behind her smile.

'I am delighted,' she said as he bowed over her hand and raised it to her lips, but it was a couple of years before he had sufficiently made his mark at the Bar for Grace to wish to draw him into her close circle.

Before then Henry, who had known her since childhood, had frequently warned him: 'Grace Mitchell is a vicious bitch right to the very depths of her being. Everything she does is calculated. She's incapable of warmth and spontaneity.'

How right Henry had been, he thought now.

He remembered how Grace had lured him to her room that night in December. He remembered her smile – bright and luminous as the moon on a frosty night – and how amazed he had been at how desperately she wanted him. But it had all been deliberate and calculated. She had set out to get pregnant to force him to marry her.

Now he stood on the brink of a double-edged precipice. If he married Helen, his beautiful, brilliant career would be in ruins. If he married Grace, he would regret it for the rest of his life.

He looked at the books lining the walls and thought of the legal volumes, bound in fine red and cream leather and lettered gold, which lined half a wall in his chambers. Though his parents had made him financially independent at twenty-one, he had refused to buy his law books until he had earned the money in fees and he had used the Juridical Library in Charlotte Square in his early days at the Bar. Each book was a token of the success he had so carefully built. He loved the law, loved wielding it, honing its finer points to argue his cases. From the moment he received a brief a case became a great adventure, which called for all his resourcefulness and ingenuity and skill and imagination as well as his knowledge of the law. He loved the arena of the courtroom – the challenging, the duelling and, if he could achieve it, the winning. Though winning was not everything; *how* you won mattered just as much in the eyes of the solicitors who could put future work your way. Losing was no disgrace. In fact, the more your reputation grew the more likely you were to lose because you were instructed in more and more difficult cases. He loved it all . . . even cases which never got beyond the expression of his opinion; and he never forgot that cases which were small to him were big and important to the people involved, the law was a living thing, a reflection of how people lived and it could be used to help and shape their lives. The law was his life. He could not live without the law.

He looked up at the portrait of Lord Cockburn, the eighteenth-century judge after whom the club was called, and remembered how much his father had wanted him to have great judicial power.

'Become a lawyer, son. Become the most powerful bastard lawyer that ever lived. Found a legal dynasty that can never be despised or looked down upon. And do it for me, son. Avenge what they have done to me and driven me to do this day.' His father's words, spoken on that terrible night in his childhood, came back to haunt him.

He couldn't become the most powerful bastard lawyer if he married Helen. So had it not all really been decided by the unhappiness wrought in another generation? Had he ever had any real power over his own life?

He walked slowly from the room, down the marble stairs. The bar where Lord Mitchell awaited him lay to the left at the bottom of the stairs. Straight ahead the club's magnificent portals opened on to Princes Street.

He turned left . . .

Chapter Twelve

Glasgow – May, 1931

Over the rim of her wine glass Helen had watched John's eyes shifting nervously at their alcove table all evening. She wondered what was wrong, what he seemed afraid of telling her and why. She hadn't seen him for over three weeks – since the weekend they had spent at the cottage on the shores of the Moray Firth. Suddenly he had to go to Aberdeen and Inverness and Dumfries on High Court business and his parents had started making demands on his weekends and his voice was uneasy on the telephone. At first she had almost panicked. But then she got a grip of herself and knew she needed to see his eyes and watch the way his body moved before she said anything.

But he had been remote all evening. She could not get anywhere near him and her heart was bursting.

'John, what is wrong?' she asked, tears poised at the corners of her eyes. 'Whatever it is, we've got to talk.'

'Yes,' he nodded, 'but not here. Send your car and your chauffeur away and we'll go for a drive in my car and then I'll take you home.'

'We can talk at home as we usually do,' she said.

'Not tonight,' he said. 'I've got to see the Procurator-fiscal in Ayr early tomorrow so I need to get down there tonight. That's why I've brought the car.'

'But it's only down the road! You can drive there in the morning,' she protested.

'We'll talk in the car,' he said firmly, signalling for the bill.

Rain clouds were gathering in the west as he swung on to the Kelvin Way and into the park. The towering black edifice of Glasgow University stood in the heart of the park, shadowing the trees, and some students who had been working late were making their way home.

The first drops of rain were just beginning to fall when John pulled up. He leaned his elbow on the steering wheel and his chin on the palm of his hand and he was staring straight ahead into the rain when he said in a slow solemn voice: 'Helen, I'm not going to be able to see you after this evening.'

Stone-still, Helen stared at the grim outline of his profile against the darkening sky. 'What – what John?'

'Grace Mitchell and I are getting married on Saturday. Quietly, at the chapel on her father's estate on the Borders. I have no choice, Helen. She's pregnant.'

She thought she was imagining what her ears were learning. She was having a nightmare and she would wake up in a minute. Except she wasn't . . .

He turned his head slowly towards her, his eyes meeting and locking on hers in agony, 'Helen, I wish with all my heart and soul that it wasn't true. But it is.'

'When?' Her voice was bleak with unshed tears.

'Christmas . . . before I . . . before I found you . . . There's been nothing since . . .'

'Do you *have* to marry her? Can't she have the baby adopted?'

'Out of the question.'

'Why? Why do you have to marry her?'

'Because I do.' He closed his eyes and his face filled with undiluted pain. 'Because her father has threatened to ruin my career if I don't.'

Suddenly one of the things he had said on their last

weekend came back to her: 'I've never loved anyone as much as I love you and I never will, whatever happens in this crazy world.'

Whatever happens!

Suddenly she was angry.

'You knew!' she screamed. 'You knew – you knew on that weekend. Admit it!'

'I knew the Lord President wanted to see me. That was all, I promise you.'

'But you had a pretty good idea why! Oh, John! Why didn't you tell me? Why couldn't you have *shared* it with me?'

She stared at his profile, waiting for his answer, feeling she might kill him.

Then, when he looked at her again, she saw his eyes were bright with tears. 'I didn't want to lose you . . .'

He bowed his head and a violent sob rose from him.

And then she knew their happiness was over and she wanted to die . . .

Chapter Thirteen

The Scottish Borders – May, 1931

Sunlight streaming through stained-glass windows fell on tall urns of spring flowers whose perfume filled the air in the tiny chapel. The pews were almost full and, as the last of the guests were being ushered to their seats, the strains of a popular setting of the 23rd Psalm played on the tiny organ. A red carpet had been laid over the length of the flagstoned aisle and in front of the Communion table where the bridal party would stand. The bridegroom and his best man were already there. The bridegroom had had a lot to drink the previous evening and, though he was not hungover, he was experiencing a sensation of pleasant semi-numbness which he knew he needed to get through the ceremony. Then, above the organ music, he heard the cheers of the estate workers gathered outside the church and knew his bride must be arriving. Slowly his gaze travelled to the front pew, where his parents were sitting. He saw his mother's gentle, approving eyes, father's hard brown ones, shining with pride. And he thought, 'It is because of you I am here today . . .'

The organ thundering out the Wedding March announced the arrival of the bride on her father's arm. The bridegroom looked towards her but her face was hidden behind her veil. He looked at the erect, imposing figure of the man who was about to become his father-in-law. His place on the bench of the Scottish Supreme Court and his own legal

dynasty which would bear his name, were now assured
. . . just as his father had wished.

Then he looked up at the high, arched ceiling and he
felt he was giving up his life.

PART TWO

1934–1935

Chapter Fourteen

Glasgow – September and October, 1934

'Mrs Dunlop? Mrs Helen Dunlop?'

Helen looked round into a pair of brown eyes peering at her through enormous, slightly-steamed tortoiseshell glasses from under a huge umbrella. There was something vaguely familiar about the young man's thin, angular face and the way a lock of lanky brown hair was falling over his broad brow. As she turned to face him and quickly tried to recall where she had seen him before, he introduced himself: 'Henry Macrae. We met years ago on Alan Campbell's yacht.'

Of course! He had been the other man standing at Grace Mitchell's side on the sunlit deck the year before the yacht, chartered by an American lawyer, crashed on rocks in the wild seas off Cape Wrath with horrendous loss of life. She remembered, too, the second brass plate on the door of John Brodie's chambers in Edinburgh. And she recalled Henry Macrae was a judge's son. His father had presided over Robbie McMenemy's trial, and John had often spoken about him.

'Yes,' she said, smiling and taking the hand he proffered. As the Rolls had made its way through the rainswept streets, her mind had been full of the day ahead. She had to telephone Klaus Ruhe, the chairman of the Hanseatic Line in Hamburg about the ship he seemed about to order, talk to her lawyers about the Shanghai Port Authority's continued refusal to pay compensation for the damage inflicted on one of her cargo boats as it entered the harbour, attend an urgent meeting of the National Shipbuilders Security . . . Life was getting harder as the Depression deepened and unemployment continued to soar. Though the Cunard Liner *Queen Mary* had at last been launched after lying half-built in its berth for years, twenty-five percent of the Clyde shipyards had now been closed. The moment a yard ran out of orders the National Shipbuilders Security moved in on it. If they didn't shut it down for good, they took out at least one berth so that ships could never be built there again. They called it 'sterilising'. But for a moment, as she scanned Henry Macrae's earnest face and wondered if he might be her height when she wasn't wearing high heels, Helen forgot about her business worries.

It was over three years now since John Brodie had abandoned her to marry Grace Mitchell but hardly a day passed when she did not think of him. Since they parted she had withdrawn from social life and devoted herself entirely to her work, spending long hours at the Pier Line, getting home too tired to feel pain, too exhausted to do anything but sleep until another day dawned which she could fill with work.

'You don't understand what it is like for me,' John had said on that last evening when they sat in the park in the gathering storm. 'But how could you? How could you possibly know what it is like for me?'

His handsome face had been corroded by anguish, and her arms had reached out to comfort him. But he had jumped back and raised his hands to push her away. That was when her heart had broken, when all that had been beautiful shrivelled and withered and perished and became no more . . .

206

As she wept he reached for the ignition key and drove her home in the exploding storm.

When they reached Great Western Terrace he jumped out and ran around to her side of car and thrust the door open.

'Quick or you'll be soaked,' he urged, his voice cracking in the sheeting rain.

Helen swung her legs on to the pavement and stood up and he slammed the door behind her.

'I have to go,' he muttered, shooting back to the driver's side.

'No!' she cried, running after him. But one of her high heels caught on the pavement's edge and she almost fell over as her silk-stockinged foot plunged into a cold puddle. 'John, please!' She caught his sleeve as he reached for the car door.

'No.' He shook her off angrily and she lurched over on her shoeless foot. 'It's over. It has to be.'

Then he was in the car and starting up the engine and the beautiful green crêpe frock in which she had dressed so carefully to please him was spattered with mud as he shot off into the night. 'Come back, please come back,' she cried as he swung violently on to Great Western Road.

It was then, nearly blinded by the rain and her bitter tears, that her spirit rose in indignation. *It wasn't over. It would never be over with John Brodie.* Sinking her teeth into her lower lip until she tasted blood, she vowed that she would get him back. She had no idea how, only that somehow, some day, she would.

She often dreamed of meeting him again . . . of how it would happen and how she would look, what their lips and their eyes would say to each other . . . It was usually in a crowded salon of distinguished faces, but sometimes it was in the street. But she had never thought or dreamed

207

of meeting Henry Macrae outside the Pier Line offices in the rain.

'I wasn't quite sure of you for a moment,' said Henry, throwing the lock of hair back from his forehead with a toss of his head. 'But I didn't think any other beautiful young lady would be arriving in such style at the Pier Line,' he added, grinning. 'How are you?'

'I'm fine. Busy,' said Helen. 'And you?'

'Very busy. I'm on my way to the Sheriff Court.'

Helen wrinkled her brow. 'I thought advocates left appearing in the lower courts to solicitors.' That was the impression she had got from John.

'Mostly,' said Henry. 'But no crime or dispute is too petty to be unworthy of the advocate's attention.'

'Provided a client had the money to pay him?'

'Naturally,' he said, grinning broadly.

Helen had learned to spot and make the most of her chances years ago. She saw one clearly now. Henry Macrae was a new link to the two people she cared most about – her father with whom she still longed to be reconciled and the man she was determined to get back . . .

Then, as she was still thinking how to make the most of this chance, he said: 'I'd really like to know how you are, Mrs Dunlop, but I don't want to keep you standing in the rain. Might you be free to have a cup of tea with me this afternoon?'

'I can arrange to be,' she said quickly.

'Shall we say Miss Cranston's in Ingram Street?' He raised a hand to glance at his wristwatch. 'At four o'clock?'

'Yes,' said Helen, 'I'd like that.'

'Till then,' he said, grinning cheerfully once more.

'Till then,' she echoed.

Miss Cranston's in Ingram Street was only a short

distance from the Pier Line's offices in St Vincent Street and, as the rain had stopped by the time the hands on her wristwatch were pointing towards four o'clock, Helen decided to walk.

Before she left the office she doused herself in Mitsouko, carefully re-did her make-up to emphasise the sensuality of her lips and the way the jewel-green eyes shone and checked her appearance in a mirror concealed in a wall panel. The brilliant opportunity presented by meeting Henry Macrae required a major charm offensive.

The tearooms bore the same Charles Rennie Mackintosh hallmarks as the Willow Tearooms – the panelled walls and screens and ladderback chairs and dark wooden tables cloaked in snow-white cloths. As it was close to the Sheriff Court and the business quarter, its clientele was mostly businessmen and lawyers. It was fairly full with their earnest faces when Helen made her entrance just after five minutes past four and several bowed to her as she crossed the room, heightening Henry Macrae's awareness of her standing in the business community. He was sitting at an alcove table and rose as she approached.

'How was the Sheriff Court?' she asked, smiling and extending an elegantly gloved hand which he took and raised to his lips.

'My client won,' said Henry, looking pleased with himself.

'Congratulations,' said Helen as they sat down and a waitress appeared to take their order. 'And what are you up to in the higher courts?' she asked once they had decided on a pot of Earl Grey to accompany the afternoon tea selection of cakes and biscuits.

'I'm really busy,' he told her. 'I've been an Advocate Depute for the past couple of years, so I spend quite a bit of time on the High Court circuit.'

209

'How fascinating,' she sighed. She listened with a rapt expression as he talked about cases in which he had appeared at Dumfries and Perth and Dundee and Aberdeen – twice obtaining convictions for murder. 'But how does your wife feel about your being away from home so much?' she asked, putting a concerned expression into her eyes. 'Doesn't it get lonely for her?'

'I'm not married, said Henry, pinking slightly. 'Of course, landing up on a murder charge can often be a matter of luck or lack of it,' he said, quickly changing the subject. 'Prompt medical and hospital attention can make all the difference between a serious assault or a murder charge.'

As he launched into a recitation of cases he had handled of serious assault which were almost murder, Helen's heart took wing. For the first time in years she believed again in destiny, in things that were pre-ordained and meant to be.

Helen ached to know about John Brodie.

'Years ago,' she said, 'when I engaged John Brodie to defend one of my shipyard workers on a murder charge, the judge in the case was your father.'

He smiled. 'Yes. My family have been lawyers for four generations, though my father is the first to become a Supreme Court judge. My great-grandfather was a solicitor in Kelso and his elder son, a Sheriff Substitute, sent both my father and my uncle to be boarders at Edinburgh Academy. But my uncle was killed in the Boer War, so it was left to my father to take the family's name on to the bench of the Supreme Court.

'In the Borders you can meet Edinburgh New Town society in the country. As the Sheriff at Jedburgh my grandfather knew everyone and got invited everywhere – to the Warrenders at Auchinvreck and the Mitchells at Coldstream and the Duke of Roxburghe at Floors and

210

the Duke of Buccleuch at Bowhill and Thornhill. It's a very social place. Between the school and social life my grandfather engineered, my father grew up knowing everyone he needed to know, which was an enormous help to his career.'

'And your mother?' asked Helen, finding it easy to maintain her rapt expression.

'My mother is both the daughter and grand-daughter of Sheriffs,' he said with a slightly apologetic grin.

'Legal family on both sides!'

'Afraid so,' he said, grinning again. 'But it helps.'

'With your career?'

He nodded. 'It's almost essential.'

'What John Brodie called the vital connections,' she said, smiling.

'He should know. He married them,' said Henry, taking the bait.

'And how is he?'

'He's just become a father for the second time. His wife had a son two days ago.'

'Really?' Though her voice was calm, Helen was shaken by hearing this news.

'This time they were hoping for a boy. They've got a daughter, Vanessa, who's just had her second birthday. I'm her godfather.

'Two?' But she ought to be three, thought Helen.

'Yes.' Henry smiled. 'Delightful little girl. She's brought great joy to her parents. Grace lost her first baby in a late miscarriage shortly after John and she married. They'd been naughty, so they had to get married in rather a hurry – or so they thought, but not as it turned out. They went through quite a difficult time after the miscarriage, but Vanessa put things right between her parents when she came along.'

The news had stung Helen badly and she didn't even

stop to think why Henry was being so indiscreet and telling her . . .

That night she cried as she had not done for a long time. Not just in bitterness for the past. Henry's news had brought her face to face with what she had not been able to bring herself to think about before – that while she had wept alone, John had been making a new life with the woman he had married, making love to her, having children with her. And what did he feel when he made love to Grace? What he had felt for her? Was it the way it had been for them? Suddenly her wounds were open and raw again.

But when her tears dried she got up and switched on the light and sat staring at her reflection in the dressing-table mirror. Even though they were swollen, there was still a dazzling quality in her green eyes; her skin was smooth and her hair glorious as sunshine tumbling on to perfect shoulders and firm high breasts. John Brodie had loved to gaze at her naked body.

She rested her chin on her upturned palm and leaned closer to the mirror.

'Forget her, forget her,' she whispered. It was just after three in the morning and John would be in bed with the woman he had married, their limbs tangled in a mesh of sleeping and lovemaking. 'Forget her,' she whispered again.

Then she sat back and, with her hands clasped behind her head, lifted her great golden mane of hair up from her neck and shoulders the way John loved to watch her do naked. A wide, triumphant smile came slowly over her face. A sense of destiny, like a roll of drums, a call to arms, filled her soul once more. She knew now what she would do. She would marry Henry Macrae in order to become John Brodie's mistress. *That's* how she would get him back.

* * *

212

In the following weeks Helen regularly met Henry when he was in Glasgow preparing for the trial of George Johnston, a West of Scotland businessman who, with his mistress, Ruth Wardle, had been charged with the murder of his wealthy wife.

There had been quite a bit of publicity about the arrests in the papers and, realising it would be a *cause célèbre*, Helen arranged to give a late evening party during the trial with Henry as the guest of honour.

'Why don't you come along and see a bit of the trial?' he asked.

'Just try to stop me,' she said, smiling.

When Helen arrived on the opening morning of the Johnston-Wardle trial, the atmosphere in the court foyer was that of a first night. Expensively-perfumed women in jewels and furs mingled with foreign criminologists and lawyers in their wigs and gowns. Upstairs, in the public gallery, the distinguished guests had taken over all the best seats where, for the next three mornings, Helen beamed encouragement to Henry Macrae whenever their eyes met. She arranged her party for what turned out to be the late evening of the fourth day of the trial and had summoned her trusted Italian caterer, Luigi, to provide a midnight buffet.

The florists in the Byres Road had filled the flat with red and bronze and golden chrysanthemums and mugs had been lifted at one end of the drawing-room so couples could dance beside the grand white piano.

Helen dressed in a black satin frock that clung to her slim hips and flared below the knees with shoulder wings caught at the waist to which the back plunged provocatively.

The guests, who cut a broad swathe through the business community, started to arrive shortly after

213

ten o'clock and the talk on everyone's lips was of the sensational murder trial, which was expected to conclude with a guilty verdict the next day. The stars of the trial, Henry Macrae and Robert Warrender – who was leading George Johnston's defence – arrived just before eleven o'clock.

Voices dropped several octaves as Helen – a man on each arm – led them into the drawing-room. She thought Henry was looking extremely dapper in his dinner suit, though she hated that he was at least two inches shorter than she was in her high heels. Robert Warrender, whom Sir James Lithgow greeted like an old friend, was more handsome than she remembered him. Strands of silver were now through his thick dark hair and the bushy brows set over green-flecked eyes.

'You're looking very *soigné* tonight,' said Henry, raising his glass to her.

Watching both men look around the room, Helen knew they were impressed. Then Henry asked to dance and they foxtrotted to *The Way You Look Tonight*. In her arms he felt all bone, with no flesh anywhere to cushion or protect him. As they glided over the floor – he was a good dancer, guiding her expertly – she got a powerful impression of pain, and that every knock in his life had been on the bone.

The soprano and clarsach player Annabel Macmillan, whom Helen had first engaged for the party Harry gave the night he died, was now the best-known singer in Scotland, and it was to Annabel Helen had turned for the après-midnight buffet entertainment.

Seated by the grand piano, she began with modern songs of love to celebrate the engagement of Elizabeth Campbell and Russell Macpherson. Then she launched into the songs of Rabbie Burns.

'O, my Luv is like a red red rose
That's newly sprung in June,'

Her voice soared over her hushed audience and Elizabeth, glowing, squeezed Russell Macpherson's hand. Helen, who was sitting a short distance behind the singer on the piano stool, did not take her eyes off Henry Macrae as he watched Annabel Macmillan.

'O, my Luv is like the melody
That's sweetly played in tune . . .'

Sir James Lithgow looked at Robert Warrender, who was watching Helen intently.

'Till a' the streams rin dry, my dear,
And the rocks melt wi' the sun . . .'

Helen's eyes met Henry's over the singer's bare white shoulders and seeing the need and hunger in those eyes, she knew her plan to marry him was on course . . .

Chapter Fifteen

Glasgow – October, 1934

It was all going brilliantly well, thought Henry Macrae as he climbed into his bed in the Central Station Hotel in the early hours of the morning.

He had had a brilliant week and a brilliant evening and later today there would be the speeches to the jury, who would find George Johnston and Ruth Wardle guilty of murder, and they would be sentenced to death. The evidence was conclusive beyond a shadow of a doubt.

Resting his head on the hands clasped behind it on the pillow, Henry grinned at the ceiling in the darkness. He could see the golden road stretching ahead of him quite clearly now – more lucrative civil cases, being selected to partner top Silks in big commercial litigation, taking sure steps towards becoming a King's Counsel.

And next year he would marry Helen Dunlop.

Marriage to Helen Dunlop! What a triumph! What a *coup!* His grin deepened in the darkness. Two months ago the prosect was undreamed of – but now! Marriage to Helen Dunlop would be the devastating blow he had longed to strike John Brodie most of his life! He could see it now – John Brodie lusting after his beautiful wife in the New Town salons and not being able to touch!

Had he not always wanted it to be something like this? Right from his childhood when he had sought to become the friend of the seven-year-old stranger who sat next to him in the back row of his class at Edinburgh Academy, a glowing boy with bright brown eyes called John Brodie. One day he had taken John Brodie home and his father had taken at once to John. Making a friend of John Brodie had been the best thing he had ever done in his father's eyes and Henry had been happy to pay the price that became the basis of their friendship ... that John Brodie could take whatever was Henry's and keep it or, if he gave it back when he no longer wanted it, it was on the understanding he could take it again whenever he wished. That had been the way all through their lives at school and later at Edinburgh University and the Bar.

Yet Henry had never once uttered a word of protest or complaint. But the truth was that he hated John Brodie – the cuckoo who inspired affection in his father that his son never could. And when John had fallen in love with Helen Dunlop he had been nearly insane with jealousy.

Then he had found a lover of his own and that had taken a lot of the sting out of his pain. And when John had been forced to marry Grace Mitchell and lose the woman he loved, Henry had rejoiced ... 'Get married, Henry,' his lover had advised him, recently. 'It will make everything easier. We'll be able to spend a lot more time together once you're married. Marriage is an excellent cover for the likes of you and me.'

Now he laughed out loud in the darkness of his hotel bedroom. There could be no more brilliant cover for his outlawed relationships with men than to have the lovely Helen Dunlop as his wife!

But when his laughter died away there was a lump in his throat and he could feel tears behind his eyes. In the lonely silence of the night he knew that desire for revenge was not the whole truth ... that all his life

217

he had longed to be normal, to be like everyone else. In marrying Helen part of him was hoping beyond hope she would enable him to become normal. Like everyone else . . .

Chapter Sixteen

Edinburgh and Glasgow –
October, 1934 to September, 1935

From the night of her party there was a mutual, though unspoken, recognition by Helen and Henry that they were now a couple. Two weeks later she accompanied him to the annual dinner of the Glasgow Bar Association and the following week they attended the Society of Procurators dinner dance. And when Helen discovered he was a keen ballroom dancer they started making up foursomes with Elizabeth Campbell and Russell Macpherson – foxtrotting and tangoing the night away at the Plaza and Dennistoun Palais and Barrowland Ballroom. Some evenings they went jiving – banned everywhere else – at the Locarno. Helen felt she was catching up on a youth which had been weighed down in responsibility.

Shortly before Christmas, Henry took her to meet his parents in their beautiful New Town home in Drummond Place.

From the moment she crossed the threshold of the elegant first floor drawing-room overlooking gardens that were pretty even when the trees were bare, Helen sensed the high ambition which Edinburgh engendered. In Glasgow all they wanted was money and business success and their villas down the coast; in Edinburgh it was power. And there was an air of breeding and refinement about the Georgian interiors of Edinburgh which made the over-elaborate Victorian splendour of Glasgow seem vulgar and nouveau. For an instant she imagined herself presiding over a dinner table lit by candles and decorated with bowls of beautifully scented flowers and peopled by distinguished guests. She could almost hear the laughter, the tinkle of glasses and see the articulate eyes pregnant with meaningful looks. She pictured herself, beautifully gowned, the cynosure of every eye, promoting men's careers. Powerbroking. She felt she had come home.

Helen's engagement to Henry was announced just after Christmas and she immediately started looking for the right residence essential to her strategy and plans. She found it in Randolph Crescent – an airy, spacious double upper flat on the top floor of a corner, which made the panorama of the city and hills part of the interior design. The castle towered on its rock like a close neighbour; the Pentlands more distantly. Though it was in a fairly dilapidated state, Helen at once saw the possibilities of marrying light and space and landmark to Georgian elegance and the finest work of contemporary artists and she had to have it. Luckily, Henry was equally enthusiastic, and once the sale was completed Helen set about restoring the flat with the same efficiency as she ran her businesses. The result was that their new home was ready three months later.

Helen glowed with pride and happiness when she showed it to Henry whom she had banned from witnessing the refurbishing in progress: marble fireplaces which had been bricked-up for years were now restored and revealed in all their glory and to learn all she could about original New Town furnishing and decoration, Helen had made the Edinburgh lawyers who handled the purchase of the flat work overtime, digging out information from old wills and inventories and specifications and letter and drawings. She discovered the original interiors had been extensively and expensively gilded, especially in the public rooms, which had been furnished in mahogany, oak, satin and rosewood and curtained and upholstered in silk. Quickly understanding the climate of the eighteenth century salon, she had decorated accordingly. Then to Georgian elegance she added comfort. Central heating enhanced the warmth of log fires and in the vast kitchen there was a Aga cooker, a washing machine and – the latest hallmark of success – a refrigerator. She also added three bathrooms to replace a single dark Victorian lavatory. But her *pièce de résistance* was in the drawing-room. Towering above the white sculptured marble fireplace, catching the western and the southern sun, there was a scaled down version of the massive verre-eglomise mural Jean Dupas had designed and Charles Champigneulle had produced for the French liner *Normandie*, depicting the history of navigation in prodigious splendour, with Neptune riding on a sea serpent flanked by steeds and mermen and glittering galleons and a chorus of seagulls on a fantastically visualised ocean. Of all her acquisitions for Randolph Crescent, this had been the most difficult to obtain.

'I'd never have dared to put that into Great Western Terrace,' she said to Henry, who stood beside her, his gaze riveted to the eclectic panel. 'James Lithgow would have regarded it as an act of treachery and had me drummed out,' she added. 'The fact is the *Normandie* is a far more luxuriously appointed ship than the *Queen Mary*, but the French shipbuilders had the backing of their Government, which we on the Clyde did not,' she said, turning to him. 'Well, do you think you are going to enjoy living with me here?'

'I can't wait,' said Henry, taking her in his arms.

And they made love for the first time there and then before the blazing log fire and her adored verre-eglomise.

Giving up her career was the biggest sacrifice Helen

was having to make to get married – and the hardest thing to do.

'No wife of mine is going to work,' Henry had told her firmly. 'It simply isn't done for an advocate's wife to work. I'd be a laughing stock. If you want to work, the wedding's off.'

She knew he was in deadly earnest.

Parting with the Dunlop Yard was just about bearable. She had fought hard to keep it open in the toughest years of the Depression but she now only had orders for another six months. And there was none in sight.

Deep down, Helen knew that the great days of ship-building on the Clyde were over. Yet she still felt reluctant about accepting the inevitable. Though she had owned the Dunlop Yard for only a few brief years, she felt as if she had been born to it and run it all her life and she worried about the future of the men and their families almost as if they were her own family. She recalled what Harry had said about only caring about people if it was in your interests to do so. But then, more powerfully, she remembered what Graeme Wilson had said on the snowy day they had driven back from Port Glasgow and the wives and children who had been bereaved by the *Ardvreck* disaster. She remembered how he had looked at her and how close she had felt to him when he said that no one should have nothing and the State should provide for people in their old age. It was then she decided not to wait until closure was forced on the Dunlop Yard and, instead, to sell it directly to Sir James Lithgow to add to his portfolio shipyards.

'The money from the sale is going to set up a pension fund for the shipyard workers and another fund in case they need financial help before then,' she told him on the day they agreed the sale in Harry's wood-panelled office at the Pier Line.

'These are unique arrangements, but then, you were always unique among shipbuilders, Helen' said Sir James. 'We're all going to miss you.'

'And I'm going to miss you, too,' said Helen, suddenly feeling tears at the back of her eyes. It was then, looking at the warm affection in Sir James's eyes, that she decided to ask him to give her away.

'I'm very flattered,' he said and Helen knew he meant it. For a long time she had felt wary and on her guard with Sir James, but over the years she had grown to like and respect him and she didn't want to lose him from her life. So, as well as giving her away, Sir James became a trustee of the Dunlop Yard Pension Fund and the Dunlop Former Employee's Emergency Fund. The other directors were Helen, Graeme Wilson MP and his new wife, Alison.

'I'm not in a position to take care of the whole nation but I can at least look after my own people,' Helen said to Graeme. They were strolling on Glasgow Green the day after the funds had been set up. 'I've never forgotten what you said about it being wrong that people should have nothing.'

'Neither have I,' he said, his voice suddenly hoarse as his eyes met hers.

'I wanted to give you your dream,' she suddenly found herself saying, feeling all tearful again. It was then, holding his brown eyes in hers, she realised that though never a word had been spoken, Graeme Wilson had been in love with her for years. But the time had never been right because either she had been in mourning or falling in love or in mourning again. And she had just never seen the love that had been there for her if only she had reached out for it. Her thoughts flew to Alison, his wife, who had waited patiently for him and the pain she must have silently suffered. It was not until he had been elected to Parliament and removed from the

223

daily shipyard scene that Alison had got her chance and seized it.

'I'm so glad you asked Alison to be one of the trustees,' he said, swallowing. 'She'll do a lot of the work if you give her the chance. I'll be in London most weeks and you'll be in Edinburgh and we all know how busy Sir James is. But Alison will be here to keep an eye on things.'

'Yes,' said Helen. 'I'd like her to. I wanted both of you to be trustees. So we will be friends – all of us for life . . .'

Just as it had done on the snowy road home from Port Glasgow, the moment of impact, of truth, of reaching for each other was passing. And any more was best left as it had been in the beginning and had always between them, unspoken . . .

Without another word they turned towards the great black iron gate that guarded the Saltmarket entrance to Glasgow Green. Beyond it, on the other side of the road, stood the magnificent portico of the High Court. Helen had often done this walk down the main avenue with John Brodie when he had been appearing in the High Court and for a moment she had the sensation of the life she was leaving behind being rerun before her eyes . . .

The prospect of selling the Pier Line was quite a different matter to the Dunlop Yard. It was her first love and even harder to give up. In the end she decided to remain a director with a controlling 51 per cent interest and sold a 49 per cent stake to Russell Macpherson, who became the new managing director. It meant she could go on keeping an eye on her people. In a separate deal she sold off the properties the Pier Line owned in the West End but she kept the flat in Great Western Terrace for the personal use of herself and her husband when they were in Glasgow.

The wedding was to take place in Glasgow Cathedral

224

and the honeymooners would then sail from Southampton for New York on the *Queen Mary*. There were still weeks to go, but most people had now replied to the invitations.

'I'd like to see the list of who's coming to my wedding and their acceptances,' she told her secretary when she breezed into her office.

Sitting back in Harry's big revolving chair, Helen quickly scanned the list. Most of those invited would be able to attend – but the most prominent absentees as far as she was concerned would be Mr and Mrs John Brodie. Pinned to the back of their official regrets was a letter Grace had written separately to Lady Macrae explaining that she and her husband would be attending a legal conference in Canada when the wedding took place. Helen wasn't really surprised or disappointed. Her time with John Brodie was coming. Her eyes searched for the other name which concerned her and she saw that Lord Randolph had accepted . . .

Her father *would* be there to see her getting married . . . From the afternoon her secretary had hurried to the Post Office with the cards in their parchment envelopes, she had wondered and wondered. He *couldn't* have forgotten that hot summer day . . . he *must* know who she was, remember her face and her eyes, like her mother's eyes. She had the feeling the wheel was coming full circle . . .

The crowd which had gathered outside Glasgow Cathedral broke into cheers as Helen stepped from her black Daimler into the August sunshine.

'Could you look this way, please, Mrs Dunlop,' cried a photographer.

As the cameras started to roll, the women gasped in admiration at the exquisite sculpture of her figure in her dress of ivory satin, her golden loveliness beneath the delicacy of her veil and the way the lemon and white roses in her hair matched her cascading bouquet, laced with maidenhair fern.

The distinguished man on whose arm she stood, his face bronzed, his abundant hair snow-white, looked as proud as if she really was his daughter.

'... and now, please look at each other, Mrs Dunlop ... Sir James ...'

Inside the pale Gothic arches of the nave presented a scene of Presbyterian simplicity and the opaque peaked windows and bleached flagstone floor were spartan as the manger. The tumult of the crowd and the photographers died away and all things seemed bright and beautiful and tiny beneath the Gothic heights hung with the proud Colours of famous Scottish Regiments. The air felt cool and pure and hallowed and somewhere, faintly, she could hear the choir singing a hymn she had known since childhood.

'I'm so nervous,' she whispered to Elizabeth, who as matron-of-honour was adjusting her veil.

'So was I. It's just wedding day nerves. You'll be fine,' Elizabeth quickly reassured her before stepping back to take a last, scanning look. 'You look wonderful, Helen.'

'Right then, are we ready?' asked Sir James.

'Yes,' said Helen in a dry whisper, feeling as if she was going to choke on her emotions. She swallowed hard and leaned heavily on Sir James's arm as Elizabeth took up her position behind her.

'I think we can go,' Sir James told the minister, and the tiny bridal procession set off beneath the high pale Gothic arches.

Beyond the quire screen Presbyterian austerity yielded to near Roman Catholic opulence. The windows here were stained glass in brilliant jewel shades and the chancel carpeted in scarlet and gold. The Communion

Table, which bore a richly-carved tableau of the Last Supper and a foliate cornice of the Crown of Thorns, stood in the shadow of a magnificently-engraved Cross and, soaring high above, the lights of the Four Evangelists filled the Great East Window, with Royal coats-of-arms emblazoned at their feet.

The small, angular figure of her bridegroom was standing before the Communion Table in the towering, broad-shouldered shadow of the best man, Robert Warrender. But it was not the man she would marry Helen's eyes sought beneath her veil, but the figure of the man who was seated where she had arranged his place at the end of the second row of the bridegroom's guests. He was there! Her father, Lord Randolph, was there to see her be married.

She felt it was her parents who were being united at last on this day . . .

Helen had hired the City Hall for the wedding reception and the guests walked the short distance from the cathedral in the sunshine. She stood beside her new husband and in-laws receiving guests, smiling and taking their hands, her veil thrown-back and framing her lovely face.

'The Honourable Lord Warrender and Lady Warrender . . .'

Helen extended her hand to Robert Warrender's parents tremulously as she waited to hear her father's name announced.

'The Honourable Lord and Lady Randolph . . .'

Oh, Mother, I wish you were here, thought Helen, her heart pounding as she looked towards the figure of her father. She was shocked by how much he had aged. The distinguished man who had carried himself with erect, military bearing and walked with a sprightly step had been replaced by a stooped figure leaning heavily on his stick. And when she took his hand and looked into his eyes she saw they were much more hooded than they had been eight years ago. Her father was now an old man, but in that long moment when their eyes held she knew he recognised her – and needed her forgiveness.

But she had to wait until all the guests had arrived before she could seek him out on her own.

He was standing by himself beside a pillar waiting for her.

His eyes held hers intensely and a long time seemed to pass before he said: 'Tell me about your mother.'

Helen felt sudden tears clog her throat and did not know how she was going to control them or even speak, but she managed to say: 'She died still loving the man she had always loved.'

'She was never forgotten . . . by him . . .'

'Did he . . . did he know of me?'

'He knew there was going to be someone . . . But he heard no more. It was a terrible shock all those years later . . .' His voice shook and she felt an overwhelming compassion. He had been as much a prisoner of his class as she had been the innocent victim of it – and she could not find it in her heart to blame this fragile old man.

'I can understand,' she said, softly.

'Life can be quite difficult . . .'

'Yes . . . I've learned that . . .'

'But after that day on the city street . . . never forgotten . . . I think we've met in my prayers and I have kept myself informed about you. Had you been in trouble. . .' Helen could not stop the tears now and she wanted to throw her arms around her father, but knew she could not, for both their sakes. 'Have you ever told anyone who you are?'

'No one. Not even my husband . . .'

'Perhaps best . . .'

'Oh, there you are, Helen,' Henry called across the hall.

'Life is short,' said Lord Randolph. 'But I'm glad we've been able to talk at last. Grateful the Good Lord has let me live until this day. It has been a very long time for me as well . . .'

Helen could hardly see him through her tears and he was walking away from her back towards the centre of the hall when Henry reached her side.

'Helen, what on earth is the matter?'

'Something I can never say,' she cried through her tears.

She never saw her father again. He died two weeks later when she was still on her honeymoon in America and was buried in the Grange cemetery on a day of brilliant sunshine in the presence of leading members of the Bench and Bar.

Chapter Seventeen

Edinburgh – September, 1935

Mr and Mrs Henry Macrae's housewarming party took place on an evening late in September.

Helen was determined it would establish her as a hostess without peer in the younger generation and, as she made her preparations, she experienced the power of being a member of a prime family, for the first time in her life. It was a beautiful, delicious power which made all of life easier.

Now she no longer needed to negotiate and cajole her way into getting her will done. She no longer had to fight. People did what she said without question because of who she was. In her top floor study, with the city spread below and the distant backdrop of the hills, she planned her party with military precision. First she summoned Luigi from Glasgow – she would not trust an unknown caterer with the most important party she had ever given – and together they planned a running buffet of champagne and oysters, a warming coq au vin, brochettes of lamb skewered with onions and carrots on platters of wild rice and piles of exotic salads with peppers and endive and basil and cardamom and red cabbage and nuts and celery and lashings of green fruit. Several desserts – Macedoine of fruits Beaujolais, Pêches in Red Crozes-Hermitage and pear and red wine ice – would be bathed and drenched in wine; but others – honey ice cream with raspberry sauce and souffléd crêpe with almonds – would major more on eye appeal. And the wines would be vintage – 1921 Loire Savennières and 1929 Northern Rhône Hermitage.

For the decorations Helen chose a gold and silver theme which echoed the magnificent verre-eglomise. Twigs and branches gathered in the woods around the Macrae family home near Kelso were silvered and painted in gold leaf and placed in urns and vases, providing an elegant background to grand arrangements of chrysanthemums in the blood red and deep bronze shades of autumn. In the course of her research into the homes of the eighteenth century New Town residents, Helen had discovered that figures and ornaments had been popular accessories, so she placed silver and gold models of Neptune and his galleons and a chorus of sea serpents in niches and on stands under arches and alongside columns, sometimes overhanging them with silver and gold garlands of seabirds on the wing, creating a vivid tableau effect.

The soprano Annabel Macmillan now had her own troupe and she had married a leading tenor, Peter Macleod, with whom she sang duets. It was with great pleasure she accepted the invitation to provide the entertainment at Helen's soirée, even foregoing a more lucrative concert hall engagement in Glasgow.

'You thought I was worth engaging long before a lot of other people did and I don't forget,' she wrote warmly, accepting the engagement.

A feline smile which people rarely saw crossed Helen's face as she placed the letter on the desk in her study. Spinning round in Harry's big leather swivel chair which she had taken with her from the Pier Line, she gazed at the distant green prospect of the Pentland Hills, and felt a renewed sense of her own power. To the dazzling array of good food and wine and entertainment rendered in an elegant Georgian setting, Helen now added a potent new cocktail – knowledge of her new constituency. Once she had discovered her mother-in-law's encyclopaedic knowledge of Edinburgh lawyers, their wives and children (including those who had died), and family histories and which families were related by marriage, she milked it ruthlessly, to the older woman's delight, so that when the evening of her party arrived she had total confidence in her ability to attach a family history to a name and a face instantly.

Strolling from the hurly-burly of her vast kitchen to the composure of the dining-room, Helen was satisfied everything was under control. It was all quite perfect and just as she had ordered it, she rejoiced as she glided from the room into the hall where she caught sight of her reflection in an enormous gilded mirror. She was dressed in a blood red velvet frock that matched the flowers and plunged dramatically back and front over her pale golden skin to which it clung voluptuously before flaring below her knees. Her golden hair was worn in an elaborate chignon and diamonds sparked at her throat and her ears and in her hair. The reflection in the enormous gilded mirror told her this was all quite perfect, too. Turning, she wandered into the drawing-room and crossed towards a window. Outside it was a starry night and the lights of the city fanning out below and rising on Corstorphine Hill created the illusion she was cruising above it an airship or hot air balloon. And this was perfect, too.

'I've obviously married a born hostess.' Helen had not heard Henry enter the room. 'As well as a very beautiful one,' he added, unable to take his eyes off her.

He looked tiny, positively dwarfed beneath the towering verre-eglomise.

One of Luigi's waiters was hovering with a silver tray from which they both plucked glasses.

232

'To my beautiful wife on her entrance into Edinburgh society.' Henry raised his glass to her.

'Thank you,' she sighed, sipping her champagne and eyeing him over the rim of her glass. Henry had become so besotted with her physically he didn't want to let her out of his sight, and when he came home in the afternoon, he demanded to know how she had spent almost every minute of the day.

'I'll kill you if you ever do this with anyone else!' he had cried as he plunged deep within her last night.

Though she had no intention of letting him get in the way of becoming John's mistress, Henry's conduct was unsettling her. She had dreamed of this day for years, longed for it, ached for it, ever since John had abandoned her and driven off into the night to marry another woman four-and-half years ago. Now Henry was threatening to make a nuisance of himself and it was unnerving her.

The bell rang, announcing the arrival of their first guests.

'We're on stage,' she murmured, laying down her glass and crossing the room to slip her arm into her husband's.

'I'm so glad the waiting's over,' he said, pinioning her eyes with his own. 'So glad . . .' and he kissed her full on her blood red lips.

The Lord President and Lady Mitchell were among the first to arrive and they beamed amiability from the moment they crossed the threshold. He was Henry's godfather but, like his daughter and her husband, he had been unable to attend the wedding because he was attending the same legal conference in Canada as his son-in-law. Everyone took their cue from the Lord President and his goodwill was as essential to social as it was to professional success. In the midst of her own

233

drawing-room, a smile on her lips and her eyes, Helen for the first time felt the full force of the powers which had been ranged against the love she and John Brodie had known for each other and she knew absolutely that his career would have been blasted into oblivion if he had not married the Lord President's daughter once he had made her pregnant . . .

Then Barbara Warrender bore down on Helen. 'Oh, Helen, I've been meaning to ring you about the Bar Wives' Association,' she said in an almost confidential manner. She was a tall, rangily-built woman whose dark hair, worn loosely to her shoulders, was liberally streaked with grey. She had the same kind of broad frame as her husband and there was a masterful quality about her quick, agile movements. 'It's an association for the wives of advocates and we meet from time to time in the homes of different members. I'm the current chairman of the charity committee and we're meeting for coffee one morning next week. I wondered if you would care to come along and join us.'

'Most certainly,' said Helen. 'I'd like to very much – '

At that moment her eyes met those of John Brodie, who was standing at the entrance to the drawing-room. The years seemed to rise and roll away and she wanted to run straight into his arms.

She stepped towards him and held out both her hands and he took them in his and suddenly she knew the years *had* passed, wringing their changes. He had married the girl in the white muslin dress and had children with her and she had married the man who was his friend . . .

It was then the descent into darkness began and she realised that they belonged only in each other's

234

pasts. Just for a moment they had visited the dream they had once lived to say a silent goodbye and part forever . . .

PART THREE

1941–1945

All things have second birth;
The earthquake is not satisfied at once.
William Wordsworth

Chapter Eighteen

London – September, 1941

'I've opened the wine. What else can I do?' asked Henry, popping his head round the kitchen door.

'You could check there isn't a hole in the black-out in the dining-room for when it gets dark,' said Helen, pushing a wisp of hair back from her brow with a scarlet-tipped finger as she turned from rinsing lettuce in the sink. The blackout had been in force for two years now and, as an extra precaution against light showing outside, Henry had painted black edges round all the windows of the mews house near Marble Arch which had been their home since the start of the war. Even the slightest chink could lead to heavy fines and Helen constantly worried about getting into trouble. 'Well, then, don't just stand there,' she urged. 'Go and do it.'

'I can't take my eyes off you,' he said, stepping towards her. Her pre-war white silk dress was splashed with giant poppies and plunged to her waist at the back; her hair, sunset gold in the September evening light which bathed the room, was caught in an elegant chignon. 'You're enough to knock out the entire German Army,' he murmured, taking her in his arms. 'You make a man forget there's a war on.'

She looked at him. His face was thinner than ever and even more angular. Lines cut grooves in his forehead and the veins in his neck stood out like cords. It was those missions; the ones he never talked about behind enemy lines in Europe, which he and John Brodie undertook as part of an Intelligence Unit based in a country house in Hertfordshire under the command of Colonel Robert Warrender. All Henry ever said before he left was: 'I'll be away for a few days.' She guessed the rest. Then she would hear nothing until he rang her, usually at her desk at the Ministry of Information in Whitehall, and said, 'I'm back.' His message was always clipped, like the all-clear after an air raid. Life could be resumed.

'What do you do when I'm away?' he asked.

He was always asking that.

'Ask God to send you safely back to me.' She smiled up at him.

'And in the evening?'

'Work late. Or get dragooned into going for a drink with Hugh Cameron.' Hugh Cameron, a bald, jovial Scot with a beer gut, was head of Helen's department.

She knew Henry wondered if she ever saw John Brodie, though he never asked her; but when the three of them met occasionally she was conscious he watched her every eye movement. It was almost as if, without the strictures of Edinburgh society to maintain their orderly relationships, and with John being alone in London, Henry trusted neither of them, though John had been married for ten years and she and Henry for six and she seemed to have been smiling politely at John across crowded salons and dinner tables for so long it was hard to imagine their relationship had ever been any other way.

'Are you sure you don't mind John coming this evening?' he asked.

'It's your privilege to invite your friends into your home,' she said carefully, wondering what lurking insecurity still troubled him. And why he had suddenly decided last week to invite John to dinner for his birthday.

'Well, he hates going back to that dingy flat in Victoria on his own, and it's his birthday.' His arms stiffened around her. 'I want to make love to you,' he murmured, his lips brushing her hair, and she felt him hard and urgent against her.

'Your guest will be here in a minute,' she said.

'I don't care, Helen, I want you.'

'We can't – '

'You're my wife.' His fingers tugged at the straps of her dress.

'Henry, I've still got a thousand things to do,' she pleaded, pushing him away.

'A bomb might blow us to bits over dinner.'

'You mustn't think like that.'

'All anyone's got is the moment.'

The war had snatched all normal expectations about life. Helen had got used to seeing buildings which stood proud and tall one day reduced to rubble the next. People alive and well in the morning were blown to pieces in the night.

Helen placed a finger on Henry's lips. 'I'll make it up to you tonight.'

'Promise?'

'Promise . . .'

Once he had gone to check the blackout Helen scrutinised her preparations for meal. Food had been rationed since early in the war and she had used most of the weekly allowance to which she and Henry were entitled to produce the beef stroganoff for their dinner. But her exemplary kitchen garden enabled her to use fresh vegetables to create colourful salads like the one she had tossed in a garlic dressing to accompany the beef. She had made watercress soup for starters and a rhubarb fool to follow.

Satisfied with her preparations, she wandered into the

dining-room, where her gaze scanned the table. It was so long since she had entertained she almost felt she was giving her first dinner party. Snow-white bone china was laid with gleaming silver and crystal glasses in which the light danced, napkins set in mitres and bowls of delicately scented red and white roses. A frisson of happiness passed through her. In this room it was possible to forget there was a war on. She pressed her hands against the back of the chair on which she would sit, with a man on either side of her and imagined candlelight and firelight playing on dear faces.

She and Henry and John Brodie went back a long way and she wanted them to sit down as friends and be happy and grateful they were still alive. It was funny how life turned out, she thought, looking at the places which would soon be filled round the table . . .

She and Henry had their first row after the first party in Edinburgh that night after everyone had gone.

'I knew about you and John,' he said abruptly after he had closed the door behind the last of their guests.

'Knew?' Her voice was uncertain and she was glad her back was to him as she walked towards the drawing-room. She was emotionally shattered with the pain of knowing John could never be hers again, agonised by the triumphant possession she had seen in the eyes of the woman he had married. 'Knew what?'

'That you were lovers!'

She turned towards him, a pulse beating rapidly in her throat.

'Who told you that?' she asked evenly.

'He did.'

She felt all in. But she had enough control not to say anything.

'We shared chambers,' he said. 'John used to pace the

242

floor trying to make up his mind what to do. He was besotted with you. It nearly destroyed him having to choose between you and his career.'

'Why did you never mention this before now? Why are you telling me this now?' she asked in a low voice. But saw the answer in his triumphant eyes.

'You can't have him now,' he said, ignoring her question. 'John Brodie will let nothing get in the way of becoming a silk. He won't endanger his future by indulging in an affair, Helen.'

She looked at Henry and realised she knew nothing about him. Intent only on having what *she* wanted, she had married a stranger, and knew nothing of what *he* wanted.

'Why did you marry me?' she asked, genuinely interested in what he had to say for the first time.

He shook his head. 'The question, Mrs Macrae, is why did *you* marry *me*?' He turned on his heel and a few seconds later she heard the front door slam behind him.

She had walked over to a window. The moon was high in the sky over Corstorphine Hill and her teeth sank deep into her lower lip. After only two months her marriage was over . . .

Why did people do it, she asked herself, wrapping her arms around herself for comfort. All the pussyfooting that went on, all the pretence people got up to, the deceit they practised just to get married. Why? For what? Was it surprising there were so many unhappy people in the world? The way they manipulated each other, deceived each other. As she had done . . .

Henry had spent the night at his chambers and came back late the next afternoon.

She was in her sitting-room on the top floor of the flat, trying to soothe herself with petit point when he knocked on the door.

'Come in,' she said, looking up.

'Helen,' he said. 'We need to talk.'

He looked even smaller than usual, and pale and and tired.

'I agree,' she said calmly. 'Sit down.'

He dropped into a settee.

'Helen, I'm sorry, very sorry,' he said. 'I said things I never intended to say last night.'

'But they have been said, Henry, and we need to take our lives from there,' said Helen. 'If you want us to.'

He looked at her, his eyes bright. He had married her for his own reasons — and he had come, in his own way, to love her. 'Yes, Helen, I do want us to . . .'

It had been the start of them working out how they would live with each other. Henry, who had been adamant she must give up her career to be his wife, now agreed she could return to work at the Pier Line. Her energy and drive was too great for her to simply be a wife. Once they had children it would be different but somehow, though neither of them did anything to prevent it, the children hadn't materialised.

People in their circle seemed to accept that Henry Macrae's wife was an emancipated career woman who was never going to be a leading light in the Bar Wives' Association and she had carried on commuting daily to Glasgow until the outbreak of war when she sold all her interests in the Pier Line.

Admiring his fine brain and wit, she had grown fond of Henry, and the war had made him more precious to her than ever before. When he went out in the mornings she was painfully aware that she might never see him again . . .

The doorbell ringing brought her out of her reverie and then she heard Henry greeting John and ushering him into the drawing-room.

* * *

Henry eyed his friend's dark profile. Fear had haunted him for six years now; fear that John Brodie would take Helen back, that she was still in love with him, fear that they had shared a passion she could never share with him. Whenever they met for drinks, he watched them like a hawk. There was nothing he could *see*. Yet John Brodie's shadow hung over his marriage. In the dark of night when he made love to Helen he wondered if she was remembering John Brodie's lovemaking and on dangerous missions behind enemy lines, Henry fantasised about them being together in his bed. So he had invited John to dinner so he could study them closely, finally. Tonight he would *know*.

'You keep the finest cellar in war or peacetime London,' John raised his glass to Henry. 'Cheers.' His eyes fell on Helen. He remembered, long ago, slipping off the straps of a dress just like the one she was now wearing and kissing her breasts. He imagined them now, hard tipped in peach-soft flesh waiting for his lips beneath the drapes of silk on which candlelight flickered . . . 'At your table a man can forget there is such a thing as food rationing,' he sighed. '. . . or any other kind of restrictions on him,' he added under his breath.

'Thank you,' said Helen, smiling. 'Henry says I'm trying to make him a vegetarian with all the salads I feed him,' she added lightly, trying to draw her husband into the conversation. Henry had hardly spoken all evening and now pinioned her with a fixed stare.

'You could soon make one of me,' said John, reaching for her hand.

But she reached for the bowl of salad which had accompanied the beef stroganoff before he could touch her fingers. 'Here, have some of this,' she invited. 'What about you, Henry?'

'No, thank you,' growled Henry.

You work hard trying to love your husband, thought John, and you probably believe you do. But it's not love, Helen ... not the wild, heady stuff you and I know about.

'We're are going to need another bottle of wine,' said Helen anxiously.

'I know,' Henry rose from the table, a scarcely-concealed snarl in his voice.

He was hardly drinking, just grimly watching her and John drain the wine, with John taking the lion's share.

He rose and left the room, leaving the door ajar.

'He doesn't want to leave us alone,' said John. Helen laughed nervously. There was a strange tension in the room. 'Helen, if I had one wish ...' he fixed her with a blatantly sensual expression which darkened his eyes '... if I had only one wish left in this world, it would be to hold you again. Do you feel nothing for me any more, Helen?'

'It's over ten years, John. Life has moved on. You're married, I'm married.'

'Do you feel nothing for me?' he repeated the question.

She looked into his eyes and saw that they were heavy with sadness. There was a huge well of inner loneliness there and at that moment she did not know what she felt for him, only that she did not want her precious, hard-won harmony with Henry destroyed. Denied, she believed her passion for John Brodie had withered but now it seemed to be smouldering within him anew.

'The past was ours, John,' she said softly, 'but not the present or the future. Not any more.'

Henry closed the kitchen door noiselessly behind him. His palms sweated on the bottle of Châteaneuf-du-Pape.

There wasn't a sound in the dining-room.

He pushed the door open and saw that Helen sat alone, draining her wine.

'Where is he?' he demanded.

'Taking a stroll in the kitchen garden before it gets dark.'

He's determined to ruin the evening, she thought. They both are. And John's drinking too much.

Helen laid a tray with a coffee pot and cups on a table by the drawing-room fire.

The gramophone was playing *Whispering Grass*.

She looked anxiously at John. 'Where's Henry?'

'Gone to tell your neighbour opposite there's a hole in his black-out.' He eyed her. 'Dance with me.'

'This carpet doesn't take the Palais Glide,' she demurred, smiling nervously. Why did she feel she couldn't handle John Brodie? What was she afraid of? Why wasn't she in control the way she always used to be?

'We could jig on the spot,' he said.

'Henry would think we'd gone mad,' she laughed, retreating to the cabinet on top of which brandy and port stood in decanters.

He stepped quickly after her.

'Please dance with me, Helen. I want to hold you in my arms again.'

'That isn't wise!'

'Please.'

The gramophone started to play *Just One More Chance*.

'Just this once. Please.'

Her fingers slid down the brandy decanter and into his. It felt so right for her hand to be in his; so did his hand against the bare flesh of her back.

'I've wanted to hold you in my arms all evening,' he murmured into her hair.

247

She looked at him levelly. 'There's no going back, John, and there's no future.'

'There could be a present.'

'No.'

'Kiss me.'

Her lips lightly touched his forehead, and all she could think was that Henry would walk into the room in a moment.

'That's not a proper kiss.'

'It's a very proper kiss for a woman to give her husband's best friend.'

'But not for a woman to give the man she loves.'

'It's *over*, John. It was over long ago. This is an illusion.'

His lips bore down on hers, crushing them.

'Is *that* an illusion?' he demanded.

Her nipples were hard against the dark wool of his suit. Suddenly she ached for him to tear away the flimsy silk of her dress and gaze at her breasts and cup them with his hands and press them to his lips.

'No!' she cried.

'Why not?' She felt him hard and urgent against her. She did not hear the music stop or see the figure in the doorway. 'I love you.'

'It's over, John. It's over!'

'Your lips tell me one story. It's a lie. Your body tells me another. *That* is the truth. Deny you love me.'

'Let me go!'

'Admit it, Helen. It's not over. You still love me.'

She felt the silk being torn from her shoulders.

'Get your adulterous lips off my wife's breasts!' Henry commanded from the doorway, as if he had been practising the phrase for weeks.

*   *   *

248

We've got to talk, thought Helen, willing her emotions to calm.

She heard John's little Ford start up in the mews. Henry would be back in a minute. Suddenly the room felt cold. She had been so sure of Henry. Ever since they met, she had been the one who had loved less, who had needed the relationship less and therefore controlled it. But now she felt that she no longer did, that somehow, intangibly, she had lost him. She desperately wanted to feel close to him again, to wipe out this whole ghastly evening and pretend it hadn't happened. But it had and, even as she had resisted John Brodie, she had felt things she had never expected to feel again, things that she had never felt for Henry and that mocked the amiable compromise of her marriage. Their quiet happiness had seemed to be enough. But now she knew it wasn't enough, that it had never been enough. And at the same time she felt bitter towards Henry because he had deliberately set out to sabotage their happiness this evening. Why?

'John's had for too much to drink to be driving,' he said bluffy, swaggering into the room. There was an unnatural bravado about his movements and demeanour and Helen knew suddenly that he was in pain.

'We've got to talk,' she said, knowing she had to reach him quickly before his wounds froze and set.

'About what?' he pulled a puzzled face.

'This evening, Henry.'

'There's no more to be said. John's explanation that he was lonely and had too much to drink and got carried away is good enough for me.'

'You don't mean that, Henry Macrae!' she cried. 'You're hurt and it shows. We've got to *talk*. Henry, I'm not in love with John Brodie, if that's what you think. That's all in the past.'

'Who said anything about love?' he sneered. 'A bit of lust is natural enough in a healthy male.'

'That's not what you feel Henry Macrae, and you know it,' she cried. 'Have another brandy and talk to me.'

'I'd love to talk to you, Helen,' he said, looking at the gilded clock on the mantelpiece, 'but it's getting late and I've a bit of work to do. Why don't you go to bed and I'll see you in a little while.' His eyes mocked her behind his huge glasses. Then he turned to leave the room.

'No!' A chasm wide and deep as the Atlantic ocean had opened up between them and she knew if she let him go she had lost him. 'No, Henry, we've got to talk,' she insisted, running after him. 'Why did you do it, Henry? Why did you invite John here this evening?'

'Because it was his birthday.'

'But that wasn't your only reason,' she challenged.

'Tell me another.'

'You wanted to see John and I together. You set me up!' she cried. 'It was all over years ago. But that wasn't good enough for you. You had to dig up the past, see it re-enacted. Why?'

'The look in your eyes hardly spoke of the past!' he said bitterly.

They were eyeball to eyeball and she had nowhere to hide, no room to deny what they both knew was true.

Then he stood back from her.

'Good-night, Helen,' he said in a powerful, ringing tone.

He turned away from her and walked slowly from the room. Paralysed, she watched him cross the hall. His back seemed like a fortress wall she could never scale again. It was not good-night but goodbye that he had said. Goodbye to every decent thing that had been between them and bound them together. She had lost him . . .

*   *   *

250

'Your lips tell one story. It's a lie. Your body tells another. *That* is the truth.'

Henry had heard the truth on John Brodie's lips and seen it in his wife's dark eyes. Now it hammered on his brain and in his heart and reverberated all over his body, filling every cell with teeming undiluted pain. He hurled back the blackout of his study. He needed, at least, to see the coolness of the night to calm him. A full moon was casting long shadows over the graveyard of St George's Fields and for a moment he imagined a thousand wraiths were dancing there. A breeze shivered in the grass and rattled the window for a moment. He dug his hands deep into his pockets and tears he was powerless to stop burned his eyes.

Now there were no more doubts or questions in his mind. Now he knew what he had wanted to know for so long and suspected for so long and dreaded for so long — that it was *not* over between his wife and John Brodie, that it had never ended.

He stared at the moon and listened to the wind. He had got what he had always wanted with Helen. He had become so besotted with her physically that he had given up his lover shortly after he got married and had never looked at another man since. With Helen he had become normal, just like everyone else. Now he had ruined it, and there was no end to his tears . . .

Chapter Nineteen

London and Sussex – June to September, 1943

'Henry's dead! Admit it!' Helen challenged Colonel Robert Warrender.

'So far as we are concerned, he is simply overdue returning from his mission,' Robert Warrender replied in a steady, even tone.

'You mean missing, presumed dead,' she defied. 'And who's "we"?'

'I, personally, do not believe your husband is dead,' he said in the same even tone. Helen glared at him silently, steadying herself against the bar of the smoky pub in Victoria. It was full of soldiers in uniform and somewhere a gramophone was blaring Vera Lynn singing *We'll Meet Again*. Henry had been gone for two months, six weeks longer than on any of his previous missions. 'I have known Henry most of my life, Helen. If I thought he was dead, I would tell you,' Robert added, softening his tone slightly. 'False hope only makes the eventual pain greater. But Henry is tenacious. So long as he believes there is a chance, he holds on. Right now I believe he is in one helluva corner, but he *will* come through.'

Helen studied Robert Warrender's black eyes with their flecks of green. He was wearing a white military raincoat and, with his broad shoulders and the tapering moustache he had grown, he looked quite racy and Clark

Gable-esque. He also looked as if he meant what he said . . .

'I believe you,' she said eventually.

'I'm glad,' said Robert. 'The reason I wanted to see you was to reassure you. I will get in touch with you again the moment I have news, but I think it is much more likely you will hear first from Henry himself.' He looked at the large black hands on his wristwatch. 'I wish I could spend more time with you, Helen, but I have, unfortunately, to attend a tedious dinner with some Government officials before I catch a train to Edinburgh. However, I have instructed Major Brodie to look after you.'

'Thank you for being honest with me,' she said, smiling appreciatively as he drained the last of his Scotch.

'Thank *you*.' He bowed his head slightly and Helen watched him cut a swathe through the uniformed men as he left the crowded bar.

Then her eyes met those of John Brodie, who was also wearing a white military raincoat and looking slightly raffish. His skin seemed to have got coarser and he was smoking a Players' Navy Cut cigarette. He never used to smoke and Helen wondered if he was still drinking a lot. It was nearly two years since she had seen him, on the appalling night Henry had insisted on giving a dinner party for his birthday.

'Thanks,' she said as he passed her a large Scotch.

'Bob meant what he said. He'd really tell you if he thought it was any other way. He's absolutely straight,' said John.

'Yes,' said Helen. 'And I really do believe him.'

'And he was serious about my looking after you this evening,' he added. 'If you would like to have a few more drinks here or go for a meal or whatever, I am to do what is your pleasure and I will take you home and say goodnight on the doorstep.' He was looking at

253

her very solemnly. 'You have my word I will not make a pass at you, Helen.'

She scrutinised his face but all she could read in his eyes was a genuine desire to please and be amenable and she felt totally at ease with him. She seemed to have known John Brodie for so long now in different moods and in different seasons, in different circumstances and in different cities. He was really an old friend. And as he continued to look at her over the rim of his whisky glass, she felt she needed to talk to an old friend, perhaps even about the deadness she felt inside all the time now.

'I was going to have spaghetti. I made the bolognaise sauce before I went to the office mornng,' she said. 'You're very welcome to share it, John.'

'I'd like that,' he said. 'Very much.'

They finished their drinks and once outside John hailed a taxi. The June evening sunlight was flooding the city streets, softening the scars left by Hitler's bombing, which had reduced so many fine buildings to rubble. In Hyde Park people were walking their dogs and relaxing in deck chairs and couples were strolling hand-in-hand. London, the citadel of the free world, had become more cosmopolitan than ever as the war ravaged Europe and Helen's next-door-neighbours in the prettily paved mews where her terraced whitewashed cottage stood were Belgian and Australian. The Belgians were dining in the open air at a white wrought-iron table as she stepped from the taxi and they greeted her loudly in English.

'I think we'll stay indoors,' she half-whispered to John when she had returned their greeting.

Inside, she took his raincoat and hat and she settled him in the drawing-room with a glass of precious Glenfiddich. Then she made her way to the kitchen.

As she watched water begin to simmer and bubble in a pan she began to think how much she missed having a man around with whom to share her meals. This was really a special occasion.

'Come and open the wine,' she invited John from the door of the drawing-room.

He sprang to his feet and followed her into the dining-room where he uncorked the bottle and left it to stand on the table.

It was the season of long evening light so there was no need to worry about the black-out for hours yet. Helen was standing by the open French windows to her tiny garden and the white net curtains were billowing in the summer breeze.

'For all the years I have lived in London I can never get used to it being dark by ten o'clock at night on the longest days,' she said as he drew to her side. 'I still feel cheated of the eternal light of the Scottish summer.'

'Yes. I sometimes feel the same way myself,' he said as their eyes met and she was aware of an undulation in her emotions.

Over dinner, they seemed to spend a lot of time bridging the years with anecdotes and stories of the 'do you remember' kind till they found their way with each other again. He *was* drinking a lot and she wondered if he always drank as much or if he was simply nervous about being alone with her after all this time.

But Helen was completely at her ease now and she looked into his eyes and asked: 'How have things *really* been with you?'

'I tried to love my wife,' he said, a wan smile paying on his face.

'How did you do that?' she asked quietly.

He took a long draught of his wine, then he said: 'By dressing her in beautiful clothes, buying the house on which she had set her heart and filling it with the grand furnishings she wanted. I thought it would make her happy.'

'Did it?'

'For a bit,' he said, taking another gulp of his wine. 'It certainly established her position in society. But you've seen how she behaves. You must know what I mean.'

Helen was not going to fall into the trap of joining in any criticism of Grace. So she asked: 'And you? Are you happy?'

'My wife is very beautiful and has excellent taste. I admire the beauty of the home she created. But when I turn out the lights at night and I can't see the clothes or the fine furnishings and the people who come to our grand dinner parties have all gone home, there is nothing.' He lit a cigarette and drew on it thoughtfully and Helen found its fragrance oddly comforting. 'That has been the way for years now. There is simply nothing there, Helen.'

'Does Grace know how you feel?'

He drew on his cigarette again and looked towards the open French windows. 'Mostly I think she shuts out thinking about it,' he said. 'She's busy with the children and her social life and her charity work. But sometimes I wonder if she is as unhappy as I am . . .' He leaned his elbows on the table and laying his cigarette on an ashtray, pressed his fingers together and his eyes pinioned Helen's. 'There can be a terrible loneliness in marriage.'

Helen shook her head. She had learned all about the pain of married loneliness these past two years. Without a word Henry had simply walked away from her. He had insisted they had simply all had too much to drink the night of John Brodie's birthday and there was no more to be said and Helen knew it was not John's fault, that his clumsy pass had merely highlighted the fatal flaw which had been there since the beginning of their marriage. They hardly made love after that night. Then Henry began to

256

sleep in his study and eventually he had moved into his own room. But the saddest thing was not that they no longer made love, it was that they were now no longer even friends. Their relationship with each other was only of the most formal.

'Do you know that kind of loneliness, too, Helen?' asked John, who had not taken his eyes off her.

She nodded, swallowing to hold back her tears. 'Yes.'

'You, too,' he sighed. Then he was looking at her, studying her, but she could not decipher his look. Yet she felt at peace just being there with him.

'Let's get some fresh air,' he said and they rose. Helen grabbed a lemon duster coat off the coatstand in the hall and they strolled down the mews towards the old graveyard of St George's Fields. Some couples were playing tennis, lobbing balls over the nets of the three courts set surreally among the graves. Leaning on John's arm, Helen looked at the names of beloved wives and husbands, centuries dead, engraved on tall stones. Smaller stones commemorated the brief lives of children. Life was so fleeting, she thought sadly, and could be snatched at any time. Her fingers tightened around John's arm and he squeezed them, smiling down at her.

Beyond the graveyard German bombs had decimated the area all round and Helen and John unlinked their arms to pick their way carefully among the rubble.

She stopped for a moment by a huge post of masonry and looked across the road at Hyde Park, which was deserted now, the trees casting long shadows. Then she looked at John's profile, dark and sombre against the reds and golds of the sunset sky, and she was so filled with longing to live again that she felt her heart would burst.

'Can love be born again?' she demanded.

The world seemed to stand still and no bird sang in

the cool evening air as she waited for him to look at her. But when he did his back was to the pagan light of the dying sun and she could not see his face. She stepped quickly towards him.

'Oh, John, I can't live my life in the loveless way I've existed these past two years!' she cried, grabbing his shoulders and shaking them. 'Do you think there is something there for us? I don't mean trying to recapture the past – that's an illusion. We've changed, we're different people. But is there something there for the people we have become? Something living now?'

'Oh, God, Helen, I hope so,' he cried, seizing her in his arms so powerfully he nearly squeezed the breath out of her. 'I hope to God there is!'

She looked up at him and in the harrowed face in the wild light she saw the love that had been missing from her life for so long and hope surged through her . . .

Yet she needed time to mourn Henry. And so, she knew, did John, of whose life he had been a part since childhood. She hoped he had not been tortured or died alone, that there had been someone with him because no one should die alone. But somehow Henry, the only child, had always been so alone that perhaps that was how he wanted to leave the world.

As the days passed and there was no word from John or Robert Warrender, she wept for them both, Helen and Henry. She wept for their wounds and how they had been unable to help or heal each other; and she wept because she had loved him more after she had lost him than when his heart was hers, and now that he was dead she loved him most of all.

It was three weeks before John telephoned her at the office.

'Is there no word?' she asked cautiously in a small voice.

'No,' he replied in a hollow tone. 'And Robert holds out no hope now . . . it's nearly three months . . .'

'Will they ever know . . . what happened?'

'Word will come from the Resistance . . . eventually . . .'

'I see.'

There was a long pause before he said: 'How would the idea of a drink and a bit of supper appeal to you?'

'When?'

'This evening, if you're free.'

Yes, she was free. Quite free now. She had had a husband for nearly eight years but now she was no longer married. Now she was a widow . . .

'Yes,' she said, her voice breaking. 'I'm free.'

'Shall we say the American Bar at the Savoy at 6.30?'

'Yes. Yes, that would be fine.'

She stared at the black Bakelite telephone for ages after she had put it down. It seemed strange she would never pick it up and hear that terse, clipped voice say: 'I'm back.' And it felt as if she was looking at his grave . . .

The Savoy was milling with the American newsmen who had moved in for the war when Helen entered the mezzanine bar they had made their own. All at once her senses seemed to be assailed by a myriad of trivialities which sang of life's indifference to death. The glances of admiring men and the fragrant scent of newly-lit cigarette smoke were accompanied by the strains of *As Time Goes By* and Helen realised with a sudden sharp awareness that her life must go on.

John rose to greet her.

'You look sensational,' he said, admiring her pre-war silk blouse with its ruffle of white lace so glamorously worn with the silver foxtails thrown over her utility suit.

'You're giving the American Press a collective heart attack,' he said, taking her hand and kissing her forehead.

'It's called entertaining the troops,' she said, escaping into laughter. And her golden hair, which she had released from its chignon before she left the office, tumbled luxuriously about her silver foxtails as she sat down.

John ordered cocktails for them both and she found herself looking at his hands, still long-fingered and beautiful, and wondering if they still worked magic on a woman's body.

It had been so long – and as their eyes met and held it seemed like a miracle that they should both still be alive and together on this beautiful summer's evening. All of a sudden it did not matter if she was not to live beyond tomorrow, if the war took her life away in the morning, so long as she lived now – to share this night with this man.

'Say my name,' she whispered throatily.

'Helen,' he said it slowly, quietly, but still in that commanding timbre which had moved the hearts of juries to spare men from the gallows and send others to languish years of their lives in prison.

'Take me home,' she murmured.

She hardly saw the room or knew how her clothes fell away. She was only aware of his hands and his lips and his hair and his skin and all of him coming into her and bearing her away. She was alive again! She had reached up out of the pit of death and reclaimed her life. Dreams lost and long forgotten, hopes half-remembered and abandoned seemed to live again. She had died the day he left her, she knew that now. Ever since she had been as dead as those men and women beneath the gravestones in

St George's Fields. Now she was alive again. Gloriously. Love was *everything*. It was the beginning of life, which ended when it went away. All good things had their source in love. Bad and evil things began with the lack of love. The only time you were alive was when you loved and were loved in return. The rest of the time you were dead. Or in pain . . .

It was a sunny afternoon in August.

'Happy?' asked John, chewing a blade of grass and looking at her from beneath his yellow linen sunhat.

'Yes,' said Helen, smiling up at him.

They were sitting under the tamarisk trees on the Sussex shore near Rustington, cut off by coils of spiked barbed wire from the beach, which was spattered with mines. They often came here at weekends and the past two months had been her happiest for years. Living and loving only in the present, just for the day, kept life simple and uncomplicated. There was no need to talk about his distant wife or his children or the future when there might be no future.

A Spitfire buzzed low overhead, reminding her of the war.

Helen looked up at it. Then she looked again at John, still munching his grass under his sunhat.

She hoped the war would never end . . .

Helen reached for the black Bakelite telephone ringing on her desk.

'Information Department', she said.

'I'm back,' said Henry.

Chapter Twenty

London, Sussex and Normandy – September, 1943 to June, 1944

'What are we going to do? Henry will know! He'll guess!'

'Probably,' said John calmly. 'But he won't want to hear it from your lips, Helen. When he asks you if you're having an affair with me, he'll *want* you to deny it. It's what you would normally do. And it's what he needs and expects. He's been through a terrible time holed-up with the French Resistance. If he'd been captured he would have faced certain death, but he would probably have been tortured first and he's lived with that fear for five months. God knows what it will have done to him mentally. It is essential that he comes home and finds everything *normal*, just as he left it, including the fact that his wife denies she's having an affair with one of his best friends.'

Helen was in state of shock. Hugh Cameron had let her leave the office at once after Henry's call and she had raced home and thrown open all the doors and windows. Smells were the biggest giveaway. So she had hurled sheets into the washing machine, hung blankets out to air and cushions and pillows and chair covers – anything John had touched – had been spread out in the sunshine in the kitchen garden. She had scoured and bleached and packed John Brodie's clothes and papers into two suitcases ready to be taken back to his flat in Victoria. Fortunately, Henry's debriefing meant he had to stay overnight in Hertfordshire and would not be home until tomorrow. But she wasn't sure she would be able to handle it even then.

'I'm scared, John,' she said. 'Suddenly, he frightens me.'

John shook his head. 'Just don't hit him with your adultery and you'll be all right,' he said, placing his hands firmly on her shoulders.

'You mean *our* adultery,' she cried. 'I didn't do it all by myself!'

'Yes, yes, of course,' he said soothingly. 'When he asks you about me, say I've rung you regularly on Bob's orders and we've met a time or two for a drink. Bob will be able to confirm that and I'll back you up as well.'

'Has he asked *you* anything?'

'I've hardly spoken to him.'

'What does he look like?'

'Thinner about the face. Otherwise he's just the same.'

'What if he really starts probing and turns it into a cross-examination?'

'He won't. It's too risky, Helen. You might tell him the truth.'

'How can you be so sure he won't want to know it?'

'Psychology is part of my œuvre,' he grinned. 'Now, I must be going.'

He stepped briskly towards the hall, where he picked up a suitcase in each hand and carried them out to the mews and packed them into the boot of his little Ford. Helen followed him, feeling decidedly wobbly.

He pressed his lips lightly against her forehead, then stepped smartly into the driving seat. 'Bye,' he said, rolling down the window. 'I'll be in touch. Just remember to keep calm.'

263

It was only when the car had disappeared round the corner of the mews that Helen realised the rules had changed. The wartime snatch-the-moment, live-for-the-day rule had been replaced by the Edinburgh society kick-the-dirt-under-the-carpet, respectability-at-all-costs rule. And once again John Brodie had abandoned her and shot off in his car in swift obedience to that rule.

Henry was haggard and the crack in one lens of his glasses added to the haunted look in his eyes.

'You've come back,' said Helen, smiling with as much confidence as she could muster. She had spent a sleepless night pacing the drawing-room and the hall, rehearsing answers to every question she thought he might ask and about three o'clock she had started to get angry at the way she had simply been abandoned by John Brodie. But it wasn't the time to be angry and upset when she needed to concentrate and nerve herself for this vital performance.

'And you never thought I would come back,' Henry challenged, a strange look in his eyes.

'I never gave up hoping,' she said, placing her arms on his shoulders. There seemed to be no flesh left on him at all.

'Let me look at you. Let me touch you, let me know you are real,' he said, slowly running a skeletal finger over her forehead and her nose and her lips and her chin. His touch was as cold as if it belonged to a body risen from its tomb in St George's Fields. 'I dreamed of you all the time I was away,' he murmured, his hands straying through her hair.

'Well, it's time to stop dreaming,' she said in a voice that was as over-bright as her smile, 'and come and see that everything is just exactly as you left if and waiting for you to return home to.'

264

She stood back from him as he stepped into the hall. She had placed a large crystal bowl of chrysanthemums on the hall table and his eyes lighted on them at once.

'Ah, flowers,' he said slowly.

'To welcome you home. And there are more in the drawing-room,' she added, taking his hand and leading him into the drawing-room, where the fireplace was banked with flowers and a bottle of vintage champagne stood in a bucket of ice on a table before it.

'Yes, everything still looks exactly the same,' said Henry, looking round.

'Well, aren't you going to open the champagne,' she urged, seeing the way his narrowed eyes appeared to be searching for something odd or untoward.

'Of course,' he grinned, moving suspiciously across the room.

As she watched him take the bottle from its bucket of ice and remove the gold paper and the wire, she wondered just what he had suffered and how he had managed to survive. There must be a lot he wanted to do; because it was having things to do, lots of unfinished business in life, that enabled people to survive when they were up against it. Studying his stark profile against the light as he poured champagne into two tulip glasses, she sensed that however little she had really known this man before, he was now a total stranger to her.

He recrossed the room and handed her a glass.

'Welcome home,' she said, smiling and raising it to him.

'Thank you,' he said.

He headed towards a big fireside chair with its back to the light. And Helen, not wishing to face the scrutiny of his eyes facing the light, sank on to a settee at right angles to his chair.

265

'Are you able or do you want talk about anything?' she asked tentatively.

'Only to Bob Warrender, and I've already done that,' he said curtly. 'So, what did you do when you thought you were a widow?' he asked, changing the subject as his eyes pinned hers.

She had not expected the attack to be quite so soon or so direct and the cold determination in his eyes was making an onslaught on her confidence. The man she looked at now was not the man she had married or recently mourned. This man was a terrible, terrifying stranger.

'I didn't believe that I was,' she said, feeling her way into the part.

'But surely, after five months . . .' he teased the words out and his eyes did not leave hers and she knew that he knew.

'Robert Warrender never – '

'I know what Bob thought. I want to know what went on in *your* mind – and heart . . .'

'I believed in hope against hope,' she said with dignity, summoning up all her reserves of will and strength. If she concentrated hard on listening and on what she said, she wouldn't have time to let fear take hold. John had been right again – Henry didn't want to hear a confession from her lips. He wanted instead to torture her – by forcing her to lie, knowing that he knew she was lying and could challenge her lies at any second. She knew she must not lose her confidence or nerve – or she'd be finished.

'Did you see much of John?'

'Heard more than saw.' She spoke the well-rehearsed words carefully. 'He rang me once a week on Robert's orders to see if I was all right. And I had a drink with him on three occasions in the pub in Victoria.'

'How was he?'

'Fine. Haven't you seen him?'

'We've not talked,' he dismissed, then asked pointedly: 'How did he behave towards you?'

'Respectfully.'

His eyes mocked her. 'It sounds out of character,' he sneered.

'Well, it's the way it was,' she said, a bold hard look now lighting her eyes.

'I wondered about the two of you,' he said slowly. 'A lot . . .'

'Yes, you've always had a problem fantasising about John and I,' she said, seizing her chance. 'I am sorry if it added to whatever you may have suffered when you were away. But I am not responsible for that. The problem is of your own creation, Henry.'

'I used to be jealous of John,' he said, taking a long draught of his champagne and easing back in his chair as if he had not heard her. Helen felt her bold attempt to turn the conversation into his problem, not hers, was like the proverbial water off the duck's back. 'I used to think it was important that you did not love me as you had loved him . . .' She knew her best defence was to say nothing so she continued to look at him as if he was talking nonsense. 'Of course, I know John's not important to you any more or you would never have been able to behave quite so impeccably.' His voice was heavy with irony. 'Even if you were still in love with him that's not important either . . .' His words and his looks were crucifying her but she kept up the bland, bored face. 'You see, when I was holed-up in France and my life could have been taken at any minute, I learned that it is life, not love, that is important. Life going on is everything. It is *all* that matters . . .' he paused again and now she wondered what was coming and held her breath. 'Helen, I want us to have a child as soon as possible.'

She had not rehearsed for this! 'You mean?' But she regretted those two little words the moment they were out. Because they spoke of weakness, vulnerability.

'Yes, every night. And every day as well. After all, we have both been so deprived ... for so long ...' His words, opulent with irony, made her feel sick.

'But it was like that even before you went away ...'

'And it was wrong of me to deprive you for so long ...'

It was then, as his laughter rang round the room, she knew the reason he had survived and returned. It was to take his revenge on her ...

'I haven't seen you for six weeks. Even worse, I haven't made love to you,' complained John.

'You haven't had to live a lie,' said Helen bitterly.

They were having tea at the Ritz, surrounded by French and American officers with short, greased hair and shining epaulettes.

'I've had to live without you and pretend to Henry I hardly saw you,' said John peevishly. 'I'd call that a lie.'

'You haven't had to *live with him*.' Anger and bitterness at the way he had left her alone to fend for herself with Henry now compounded her feelings towards John Brodie.

'I thought it was best that we lie low for a bit,' he had excused when he telephoned her yesterday to suggest they met for tea.

She had wanted to tell him to go away – but she had needed to see him more than she had needed to tell him to go away.

I'm no longer in control, I'm having to play by someone else's rules all the time now and the excuse is always the war, she thought, looking at the dark outlines of his face. I hate it. And if it goes on much longer, I will hate John, too.

He signalled for the bill and paid it and they rose.

'Let's go.' He took her arm, propelling her along the carpeted corridor to the Piccadilly exit and into a taxi. 'Artillery Mansions,' he told the driver.

'My office is in Whitehall. I've got to get back!' she protested.

'Not this afternoon,' he murmured, running a hand through her hair.

As her eyes met his, she felt her protests weaken and melt. She had missed him so much, had ached for him to hold her and stroke her and undress her and make her his again. I am so weak, not strong like I used to be, she thought as his arms enfolded her and the black cab whizzed round Hyde Park Corner and sped down Grosvenor Place, past the back of Buckingham Palace, with its high walls shrouded in spiked barbed wire.

The roads were clear all the way to Victoria Street and the lugubrious blocks of Artillery Mansions, which lurked behind it. But Helen hardly noticed how dark the buildings were as she stepped from the cab and he led her into the lift and the gloomy enclave of his flat. She needed him too much, and it was only afterwards, hours later, when he had rummaged out a bottle of champagne and some caviar, which they fed each other with their fingers, that she felt calmer and much of her pent-up resentment at John had been assuaged. But she couldn't go on living the tortured lie she had done these past six weeks. Henry had to be told how things were between her and John. And she wasn't going to do so on her own; they must tell him together. She said: 'We can't go on like this.'

'I know,' he said. 'I've nearly gone crazy without you. But things are going to get better. Bob's rearranging the work schedules. It means Henry and I will be taking it in turns to spend a week plus a weekend out in Hertfordshire. The other week we will be in London and the weekend will be free. That means, if you like, we could go away some weekends.'

It was then she sensed that the moment was all she would ever have with John Brodie. The war didn't make any difference . . .

Towards the end of May, 1944, when the Allied invasion of Europe was imminent, the Channel Ports were choc-a-bloc with shipping and the roads in southern England were thronged with tanks and armoured vehicles massing towards their final assembly points along the coast.

On the first Friday in June John's little Ford weaved its way among the military traffic leaving London. Soon he was heading through the leafy lanes and rolling parkland of Sussex and over the Downs to Rustington. Helen watched his hands tense on the steering wheel, his face full of brooding as they drove in silence. It was strange how things had turned out. Just when she had felt she could no longer go on living a lie with Henry, the new working schedules had come in and, without a word, he had abandoned her. He now spent seven consecutive days and nights in Hertfordshire. On the week he was in London he left her alone and slept in his study. His weekend off was invariably spent doing overtime in Hertfordshire. So, for seven months now, she and John had been able to steal away to Sussex at weekends, but this would be their last until . . . but she didn't want to think about that. In the war there was only today; so you lived it and there was no time, no room for dark thoughts.

The tide was out when they reached Rustington, leaving the sand flat and damp. Hand-in-hand they strolled behind the spiked barbed wire to their spot

270

under the tamarisk trees and stood for ages looking out at the smooth sea, their thoughts too deep for words.

They went to bed early that night and stayed there, dozing and loving, till late on Sunday morning. In the afternoon they walked along the shore once more, gazing out across the sea to France. The sky was overcast, the only sound the relentless mowing of the tide towards the shore.

John was silent for a long time. At last he took one of her hands between his own and pressed it to his lips and looked at her.

'If I should die – '

'You won't!'

He swallowed. 'Well, if perhaps I should not see you for a long time . . . perhaps a very long time . . . perhaps not until we meet in another place far away from this war-torn world . . .' he swallowed again, '. . . I want you to know . . . to remember that you have meant more to me than any other human being . . . more than I knew it was possible for one human being to mean to another . . . yet I have probably caused you more pain than anyone – '

'That pain doesn't matter!' she burst in. 'It has all been worth it. My life would not have been anything if I had not loved you!'

He ran his fingers through her hair, which was shining like firegold. 'Helen, will you do something?'

'Yes.'

'Stay here tomorrow. And on Tuesday morning, early as you can, come to this spot. Pray for me. Pray for all of us. But for God's sake, *pray* – ' his voice broke. 'Wherever I am I will think of you here, alone in this place where we have been together, and I will know we *are* together, whatever happens . . .'

'Yes, John, I will stay here for both of us – and I will

know that wherever you are you will really be here,' she cried, throwing her arms around his neck and losing herself in his.

Then they stood still in silence for ages, holding hands, looking out to sea, unable any more to say what was in their hearts because what their hearts held was beyond both words and tears.

At last, they walked slowly back to the hotel, where they made love for hours. Quietly. Wordlessly.

John left her that evening. And she stood for ages looking up the lane long after his little Ford had disappeared.

It was quiet the next day. The armoured vehicles and lorries which had rumbled through the village for weeks had gone. Feeling strangely numb, Helen found her way back to their place under the tamarisk trees, behind the spiked barbed wire. The sea was calm now, like a gently lapping pond, and there seemed to be no movement in the air.

'Come back, John. Just live and please come back,' she mouthed the words silently. 'Just live, please just live.'

The tears, suspended all day, came at last and she hurried back to the hotel and locked the door of her room and let them come flooding.

That night the sky was filled with the roar of aircraft. Helen stood on the balcony of the room they had shared, watching wave after wave of planes soar out over the English Channel, blackening the sky at dawn on D-Day. The long-awaited invasion of Europe had begun . . .

She dressed quickly in the yellow gingham dress she had worn on Sunday and sped to the place under the tamarisk trees behind the spiked barbed wire.

The air was full of the scent of the sea and the pines and she felt it warm and gentle about her legs and her body, and the tamarisks, fine as maidenhair fern in a bridal bouquet, brush her bare shoulders. Two gulls were winging over the waves near the shore and daisies and marguerites and buttercups mingled with the greensward and the sun was struggling to find a window in the cloud. Somewhere, far beyond the beach huts and the barbed wire and the pebbles washed smooth and clean by a thousand tides, somewhere beyond where the sky met the sea, lay the shores of France, where all the men had gone, taking the hopes of the free world with them. Now the sky was empty and silent. And the only sound was the sea crashing on the shore as if the very heart of the ocean was breaking.

'Please, God, don't let John die!' she cried. 'Please God, keep him safe. If we have sinned, let me be the one to suffer and pay. I can suffer any pain if you let him live. But, please God, he is my life! So do not let him die!'

The sky was the colour it had been on the day he was born, a dull mid-grey. The colour it had been for most of his life, the eternal colour of Edinburgh. He could feel the pain, violent and brutal, assaulting his life. But it would be gone in a minute. And it was nothing to the pain he had suffered most of his life . . . the pain of not being loved . . .

But he knew he needed to be quick and use the last of his precious energy wisely for the essential tasks.

With a supreme effort he concentrated hard, focusing his eyes on John Brodie's.

'I knew . . . about you and Helen . . .'

'I couldn't help it,' muttered John, his face dark and heavy with pain.

'No, no, you don't understand . . . when you took her, it was different from anything you had ever taken before . . . I had already given her up . . . I had punished her enough . . . I no longer wanted her . . . You see, when I

273

married her I knew I could never make her happy ... I wanted to be normal ... More than anything I wanted to be normal ... I wanted to be like everyone else and I felt if I took what had been yours I would be.'

'No!' cried John.

'Yes ... that's what I did ... I was so proud of marrying Helen Dunlop ... I knew she wasn't mine, that she would never be mine ... but you couldn't get her back till I no longer wanted her.'

'Oh, God,' sobbed John and Henry saw tears wash the grime of war and gunfire down his face.

'Will you ask her to forgive me?'

'Yes.'

'I did love her, as best I knew or could, John. But it wasn't enough. Not what she needed ...'

'She did need you. And she'd want you to know that.'

'Did she?'

'Yes.'

'She always wanted to talk ... but I was afraid ... afraid I'd lose her if we talked.'

Another blast of enemy gunfire rent the air and John fell heavily on top of his friend.

At that moment Henry experienced the sensation of flying over his life and seeing what it could have been if he had been able to give and receive love without restraint or embarrassment. He felt strong and fit, not the emotional cripple he believed he had been all his life. And his soul seemed to rise up and come into its own ...

Chapter Twenty-One

London – November and December, 1944

'If I can get a divorce, will you marry me?'

The question filled the air in the drawing-room of the mews house, where Helen and John were sitting around a glowing coal fire, warming after-dinner glasses of cognac in their hands. Ever since he had returned to London at the beginning of September the spectre of the future had been suspended, unspoken, between them. Allied forces were now sweeping through Europe and people were beginning to make plans for the future, to think about the days after tomorrow.

'Is that really what you want?' she asked, unable to restrain her tears.

'Yes,' he said, 'it's what I've wanted ever since Henry died and I've thought about it long and hard. But I don't think we could live in Edinburgh, even though my father-in-law is now retired. Anyway, I've got used to living in London. And I like it. I think Edinburgh would seem very small and provincial now. So I've been making a few enquiries. This afternoon I saw Robin Rollinson. He's an English silk with chambers in Gray's Inn and if I want to practise at the English Bar he says there is a place for me there.'

Helen could hardly see him through her tears; her heart was so full she felt it would burst. It was what she had longed to hear.

'Look,' he said, getting up, 'why don't you get Hugh Cameron to give you a day off and we can go exploring the Temples and the Inns together.'

'Yes,' she said, smiling through her tears as he knelt by her and took her in his arms. 'Do you really think Grace is likely to agree to a divorce?'

'She's lived without me for five years now,' he said. 'I think she would find it an intrusion to have to live with me again.'

'A lot of wives have lived without their husbands during the war. That's very different from being divorced in peace time,' said Helen. 'And what about your children?'

'My children will always be the most important consideration,' he admitted. 'And it is about them I have had to think hardest and longest. I want them to be educated in Edinburgh, so they will stay with their mother, but I want them to spend their holidays with me. With us. And I want us to have a family, too.'

Helen now longed to have John's baby. She was thirty-five years old and she felt acutely conscious of time running out.

'Are you sure?' she asked, her eyes glowing in the firelight.

'I want us to have at least two children and I want them to become friends with the children I already have,' he said. 'There will of course be hurt feelings in the beginning but I hope that in time we can all become one big happy family.'

'I hope so,' she said. 'Oh, John, I hope so . . .'

They had this conversation many times over the next few weeks and each time they talked she grew more certain that what he said he wanted was what he *really* wanted. But she also had no doubts about the strength of the opposition he would face in Edinburgh.

All she was certain of as she waved him away on the overnight train out of Kings Cross to Edinburgh on a late December evening was that she would fight tooth and nail and skin and claw for them to be together . . .

Chapter Twenty-Two

Edinburgh – December, 1944

John's children clung to him like limpets from the moment he stepped off the train at Edinburgh Waverley, constantly taking his hands and pressing themselves against him and demanding to know where he was going whenever he tried to step out of their sight.

They were sitting round the fire on Christmas Day when Angus, who was ten and had laughing brown eyes and chubby cheeks, climbed on to his father's knee and asked: 'When the war is over, will you stay with us all the time, Daddy?'

'The whole idea of winning the war is that all Daddies can come home for good,' said John, running his fingers through his son's dark hair.

'So *will* you stay here?' persisted Angus, who had been asking this question several times a day ever since his father had arrived home.

'Of course I will,' John felt forced to say.

'I want you to stay at home always, Daddy,' said Angus, planting a soggy kiss on his father's cheek.

'So do I,' cried his sister, Vanessa, clambering on to her father's other knee and claiming a hug. At twelve, she was all bones and limbs.

For a moment both children snuggled up against John, who wondered just how much they had felt deprived by his absence at war.

'The children miss you,' said Grace giving him a hard look. 'It's only natural that they don't want you to go away again.'

He watched her closely for several minutes as she gathered up some discarded paper from the floor. Her facial features were now quite angular and there were lines around her eyes and her mouth and on her forehead, though her skin retained its lucid white marble texture. He decided she must now be dyeing her hair because all trace of the grey which had begun to grow in before the war had gone. He wondered what her price would be for agreeing to divorce him. But money wasn't going to be a problem, so they were unlikely to fall out over it. Then he saw the shining eyes of his children looking at him and he felt he could not bear to hurt them . . .

The day after Boxing Day John decided to go to court. It was a damp day and he wrapped up well, tucking a scarf inside his coat for the brisk walk up the hill to Princes Street. Unlike London, which had been pounded in The Blitz, Edinburgh had come through the war comparatively unscathed. The castle and the art galleries and the famous landmarks of the Old Town stretching down the Royal Mile still stood proud and intact. Surveying this, John was filled with a feeling of life returning to normal. It had been the same ever since he had arrived in Edinburgh. The beautiful streets of the New Town still stood as pristine and glorious as they had done before the war and their existence spoke of a deep security and permanence that was impossible in London. The nightmare of the inferno and the transient illusory relationships it spawned were far from here; this was what was real and enduring. And when he had climbed the Mound and stood on the corner of George IV Bridge and Parliament Square, gazing towards the Supreme Court buildings, it seemed almost as if there had been no war and he had never been away. His pace quickened as he cut diagonally across the Square and through the swing doors into the building.

Fires were blazing in the three big black hearths in Parliament Hall and the scent of woodsmoke filled the air. John paused at a doorway to watch several pairs of colleagues pacing the parquet floor, discussing their cases. Then his gaze scanned the portraits and statues of bygone judges lining the hall before sweeping upwards towards the great stained glass window depicting King James V and his nobles, which dominated the south wall and he was filled with an overwhelming sense that he had come home.

Across the hall Edward Hamilton KC, who had been called to the Bar on the same day as John, was standing with his back to one of the roaring fires. He raised a hand high in greeting and John crossed the parquet floor to join him.

'Everyone's escaping from too much family life over Christmas,' said Edward. Then he lowered his voice: 'Have you heard that Bob Warrender's joining the Bench as soon as the war is over?'

'As a matter of fact I haven't,' said John. 'But it doesn't entirely surprise me.'

As they newsed and gossiped with their backs to the fire, John recognised faces he had not seen since before the war. He had been thirty-nine and King's Counsel for only two years when it started. Now he was forty-four. Though he had lost five prime earning years and would have to compete for work with the new post-war silks, the chances were that most of them would be older than he was. He already had a stature and reputation which was envied in this place; and he had already done much and sacrificed much to achieve his status in this world. It is here I want to be, he thought, not the Inns of Court.

It wasn't just being back in Edinburgh or even the way his children had laid their claims to his heart. This was where he *belonged*, in the small intimate world of the Scottish Supreme Courts. And he would be tearing up the very root of himself and all that his life had been about if he gave it up to graft himself on to the English Bar. And though he was perfectly confident he would make a successful living, it would be the end of his career and his high ambitions. He would not become a judge in the English High Court or a leader in London society; he would never achieve the status that could be his in Scotland. And he knew that in time his love for Helen would be eroded by bitterness and regret at what he had sacrificed. They would *have* to make their lives here in Edinburgh – and that would be so much harder than what he had planned for them.

His thoughts stretched towards the peacetime years and decades ahead . . . to the 1950s and 1960s when he had hoped to sit on the Supreme Court bench in judgement on Scotland and after he left Edward Hamilton, he stole in through the public entrance to the First Division, where the Lord President and two of his fellow judges listened to appeals. As the Court was still on the Christmas vacation, it was quite deserted beneath the dark December sky.

This was the court where judges were installed and his mind's eye travelled to the bright day in the future when sunshine would stream through the high arched windows and cast an ethereal light on the pale oak pews . . . the spring morning when be became a judge . . . From this day forth other men must address him with a special kind of respect. They would no longer simply ask him for what they wanted . . . they would 'make submissions' in the hope of finding favour with him. They would stand on a lower level in simple black gowns when they addressed him while he sat on high, magnificently robed, looking down. He would no longer enter the court quietly by a side door. A macer would herald his entrance into the court and everyone would stand while he entered and no one would sit until he had done so. Convicted men would stand before him in fear and trembling awaiting his decisions on their punishments. From this day forth he would personify the majesty of the law and all the mighty apparatus of the State itself would lie ready to enforce his orders. From this day forth he was a man above and apart from other men.

'Become a lawyer, son. Become the most powerful bastard lawyer . . . And do it for me, son . . . Avenge what they have done to me . . .'

He had kept the promise and the faith.

His vision of the future faded, but certainty had taken its place: that proud, promised day when he became a judge would never dawn if he was divorced . . .

It was three days after Christmas in the evening. The children had gone to bed and John and Grace were sitting around a glowing log fire in the first-floor drawing-room in Heriot Row.

'The children are very excited about you coming home for good,' said Grace, smiling. 'Especially Angus. A boy needs his father around.'

He knew he had to speak to her tonight. The New Year of 1945 was only four days away. It was best to get it out into the open in the old year and her words seemed to be his cue.

'I certainly want to see a lot more of the children after the war,' he said, eyeing her steadily over his cognac glass. 'But I will not be able to see them quite perhaps in the way you think. Grace, I want a divorce.'

The words were suspended between them for only an instant before she demanded: 'Who is the bitch?'

282

The question rang out, stilling the air. He had expected
her to be shocked, speechless. Instead she had taken
command and her defiant eyes were fixed on his.

'Well, who is she?' Grace repeated the question.

'Grace, we need to talk about this in a civilised
fashion – '

'There is nothing civilised about divorce. Who is she?'

'Henry Macrae's widow'

'Not that whore!'

But John heard the change in her tone – from command
to pain and fear.

'Helen is not a whore,' he said quietly.

'How long has this been going on?' she demanded.

'Since after I got back to London following Henry's
death.'

'Four months? You should be ashamed of yourself,
John Brodie!'

He drew his breath for a moment, then decided to
reason with her.

'Look. Grace, you and I have not been happy. If we get
divorced, you will be free to find someone with whom
you *can* be happy.'

'You and I are not free to think about personal
happiness,' she said, her lips a thin, grim line, her jaw
set determinedly. 'We have two children to think about.
Can't you see how much they have missed you?'

'I would still see the children.'

'How would you do that?'

'They would stay with me at weekends and in the
holidays.'

Grace shook her head vehemently. 'The poor things
wouldn't know where their home was. I could never allow
that. Do you never think of anyone except yourself and
you own selfish needs?' cried Grace, her voice rising as she
got up and flung her needlepoint to the floor. 'Just how do

you think the children would be able to survive at school once the word got out that their father didn't care enough about them to stay with them?' she demanded, retreating towards the drinks table. 'Children like and need to be the same as other children. They don't want to be the odd ones out. Get it into your head, John Brodie, that I will never divorce,' she shouted, her fingers reaching for the decanter. 'Never! So you can forget about your whore – as you did once before.'

She plucked the crystal decanter from the drinks table and aimed it straight at his head.

Just in time he saw it hurtling towards him and dived behind a settee.

It splintered against the window, shattering the glass into a thousand pieces before it crashed on to the parquet floor.

John got up, staring at her wildly. 'You could have killed me.'

'I wanted to! I wanted to! You deserve to die! I have struggled on alone all through the war, coping with the children's schooling and illnesses and not bothering you with *anything* even when I have been desperately worried and wanted to talk to you,' she cried. 'Unlike most servicemen's wives, I could easily have rung up your Commanding Officer, Robert Warrender, at any time. But I felt it wasn't right. I have made no demands, even when I was very lonely, and I have tried to make your visits home as pleasant as I can and keep things as normal as possible despite the war. And the thanks I get for it is that you want to leave me and the children for the whore who lured Henry Macrae into marriage!'

Her fingers prized a second decanter from the drinks table and sent it whistling and spinning through the air.

John crashed back down on to the floor.

It smashed against a pier glass and bombed on to

the glass table below as Angus came running into the room screaming 'Mummy! Mummy! Have the Germans come?'

'Now see what you've done,' shouted Grace as she placed her arms around her son to comfort him.

'Did you do this, Daddy? Did you smash up this room?' demanded Angus, staring at the myriad pieces of broken glass and streams of brandy and whisky flowing like rivers all over the floor before he looked incredulously at his father.

'It was an accident, Angus. A terrible accident,' said Grace, who was kneeling now beside her son with her face against his cheek.

Angus pressed his face against his mother's shoulder, and his sobs, deep and wounded, wrenched his father's heart.

'Come on, Angus,' said Grace. 'It's all right now. Mummy will take you back to bed.'

She got up and, taking her son's hand, led him quietly from the room.

John drained his cognac and looked out on the utter blackness of the night over the gardens in Heriot Row.

Though Mrs Morrison, the resident housekeeper, and her husband, who doubled up as a handyman and general factotum, had quickly and silently cleaned up the broken glass, the room was still reeked of alcohol. Mr Morrison had boarded up the window panes, too. John looked at them and felt reminded of the London Blitz. People did not expect to find boarded up windows in Heriot Row in war or peace.

The house was silent now. Not a soul moved outside in the street and the world seemed to be at peace.

Till his last day he would see those glass missiles coming straight for his head, hear the shattering explosion of the

285

crystal, remember the hatred in his wife's wild stare and his son's frightened, accusing eyes. More than anything he would remember his wife's strength, how she had been able to turn from anger to soothing her son, protecting him from a far greater hurt than that which his eyes saw – that his parents' marriage was splitting asunder.

And she was protecting John, too. By refusing to divorce him, she was providing him with the excuse to do what he had wanted to do since he had stood in Parliament Hall and the First Division yesterday morning – abandon Helen and return to his career in Edinburgh.

Chapter Twenty-Three

Glasgow – December, 1944

'You're a marriage breaker, Helen Macrae! A dirty rotten marriage breaker! A husband stealer!' cried Elizabeth Macpherson.

'What brought this on?' asked Helen, amazed.

They were standing by a drawing-room window in the flat in Great Western Terrace. Helen had just got it back from the Government, who had requisitioned it to accommodate Polish officers during the war.

'Marriage is a sacred lifelong bond between a husband and wife and anyone who tries to break it is a sinner before God,' Elizabeth said piously.

'Is Russell having an affair?' asked Helen, getting to the point.

Elizabeth stared dumbfounded at her. 'How do you know? Did he tell you?'

Helen shook her head. 'No. But it's been obvious something was wrong between you two all over Christmas.'

'He wants a divorce,' sobbed Elizabeth, breaking down.

'And are you going to let him have one?'

'Never!'

'Why not?'

'Because . . .'

'Because you love him? Because you want him back? Or because you just want to punish him and hang on to the status of being married?' Helen asked.

'Because marriage is for life!'

Helen smiled. 'Everything in life is constantly renegotiable.'

'Oh, you would say that! A woman like you – '

'Don't say anything you don't really mean and might afterwards regret,' Helen warned. 'And don't judge me, because John and I will need this flat as our home. I don't need him to tell me his wife will never divorce him or that once he sees the courts in Edinburgh again that's where he'll want to be. I know it already. It might be difficult for us to live in Edinburgh, but here in Glasgow we can be together discreetly.'

'But that's immoral!'

Helen shrugged. 'Only by your standards. I happen to consider it's immoral for a woman to force a man to stay in a dead marriage.'

'But what if John's been unfaithful to you over Christmas with Grace?' said Elizabeth, desperately trying to score a point.

Helen shrugged again. 'I think it most unlikely, but it's not important.'

'How can you say that?' Elizabeth was dumbfounded again.

'Because it's true. Men are creatures of the moment and forget, which is why they are unfaithful; only women live in their memories.'

'I don't know what you're talking about,' said Elizabeth. 'But I've never understood, you,' she added enviously.

'I'm saying that men sometimes just get carried away at the moment and it doesn't have to be the end of the world or a marriage,' said Helen. 'Of course, some people marry the wrong people in the first place. Some marriages are a mistake.'

'That's not true!' screamed Elizabeth. 'Russell and I

288

were married in church. Before God. It wasn't a mistake. He has broken his marriage vows!'

'Oh, stop being such prig, Elizabeth,' cried Helen. 'Your trouble is that you have been so well protected from reality and the harshness of life you've no idea how hard it can be and what happens to people.'

'Your trouble is you're a whore as well!' Elizabeth screamed.

'You'll take that back, Elizabeth Macpherson, if you value our friendship.'

'I wouldn't want to be friends with a whore,' cried Elizabeth, bursting into tears.

She stormed from the room and Helen heard the front door slamming behind her.

The body of Elizabeth Macpherson was found several days later floating in the Clyde near Erskine.

Russell met Helen at the flat at Great Western Road that evening.

'Was it over between you and Elizabeth or was it just a wartime fling?'

Russell gave Helen a long hard look before he spoke. 'It was over before we got married, Helen.

'Elizabeth lived in a dream world of her own. I realised we weren't suited and I asked her release me from the engagement. But we'd been having an affair and there wasn't anything she didn't threaten to do to me if I didn't marry her.'

'Well,' said Helen. 'And she always swore she'd be a virgin when she got married because her mother said men didn't marry girls who did it before marriage.'

A wry grin crept his face. 'She "did it" because she thought you'd "done it" and she envied you. But she was terrified of her parents finding out.'

'And if you hadn't married her, what her mother said would have been right,' said Helen wearily.

'But I'm not the only man who's been checkmated or dragooned into a marriage after the affair is over,' said Russell. 'Why do women do it?'

'Because they think marriage will change a man and breathe new life into a dead relationship,' said Helen. 'And woman have no status in society if they are not married.' Helen shook her head sadly. 'Elizabeth was very good to me after my mother died, and we parted such bad friends. I had no idea what was in her mind and I am so sorry she's dead. So terribly sorry . . .'

Chapter Twenty-Four

London – January, 1945

'So I can never marry you, Helen,' John admitted in a low voice.

'I really didn't expect Grace would want to divorce you,' she said calmly.

They were sipping cocktails in the American Bar at the Savoy and the strains of *We'll Gather Lilacs* were drifting from a white grand piano.

'I'm sorry,' he said.

'Dearly as I love you, John, to be married to you is not the most important thing,' said Helen. 'Love is more important than marriage.'

'And I'm not going to be in London either. I want to resume practising at the Scottish Bar.'

'Great. I thought you'd want to do that,' said Helen. 'Well, I've got the decorators in at Great Western Terrace. It will be fit to move into again in a couple of weeks. It will be nice to live in Scotland again. I've seen enough of London.'

He stared at her hollow-eyed. 'You don't understand, Helen. I'm going back to my wife and children . . .'

It was then the world fell in.

'Going back to Grace?'

'Yes,' he nodded, reaching for his drink.

It had to be a mistake. It was impossible. It couldn't happen to her twice. Not *this* time.

'No, John, you can't go back to Grace,' she told him reasonably. 'Not this time. It's over with her and you know it.'

'Yes . . .' he said, taking a large gulp of his Scotch. 'But there are my children to think about. They've missed me. I hadn't realised how much. I – '

'But if we're living in Glasgow you'll be able to see plenty of your children. I'll be very pleased to have them to stay every weekend and in the holidays.'

'Helen, the war's over. I've got to go home,' he said angrily, desperately, in a much louder voice. Then he gulped the last of his drink and rose. 'In fact, I've got to go now. I'm catching a train to Edinburgh.'

It was as he strode from the bar that the curtains parted and the shades of war and peace became clear to her. This time she had merely been his wartime plaything. She felt as naïve as any simple village girl who had ever believed a man who said he loved her. She had no place in John Brodie's peacetime world.

And she would be as far from him as her mother had been from her father when, seven months from now, she had his baby . . .

292

PART FOUR

1945–1948

Chapter Twenty-Five

Sussex and London – May, 1945 to February, 1946

The triumphant Allied sweep across Europe towards Berlin and victory gathered momentum in the spring of 1945. In March the Allied armies crossed the Rhine; in April the Germans surrendered in Italy and Hitler blew his brains out in his bunker the day after he married his mistress, Eva Braun, whose body was found beside his. On May 7 General Alfred Jodl, the German Army Chief of Staff, surrendered unconditionally and guns and warheads which had battered a continent for six long, weary years fell silent.

Britain took to the streets to celebrate victory the following weekend. In London 50,000 people thronged the Mall and the King and Queen and the two Princesses made eight appearances on the balcony of Buckingham Palace in response to their cheers. In Whitehall the Prime Minister, Winston Churchill, dressed in the Homburg and siren suit he had worn throughout the war, gave his famous V-sign from the balcony of the Home Office and conducted a crowd singing *Land of Hope and Glory* before he broadcast to the nation at three o'clock.

The afternoon sunshine was warm as Helen, swaying gently in a rocking chair, listened to the broadcast on the first floor balcony of the summer house she had rented near Rustington. Its two storeys of sparkling granite beneath a red slate roof were lavishly furnished in cane and chintz and a wall at the bottom of the garden was fringed by tamarisk trees. A broad swathe of greensward shielded it from the spiked barbed wire and minefields on the seashore. She had taken it for six months at the beginning of April and hired a middle-aged couple to live-in and look after her, and she often sat on the balcony in the afternoon, watching and listening to the tide ebbing and rolling home and knitting for her baby.

As she reached to switch off the wireless when Churchill's broadcast ended, she felt a kick against the wall of her abdomen.

'Yes, Baby,' she said, smiling and looking down and patting her stomach. 'You are going to be born into a different and a better world,' she told him, 'a world of peace.'

She had watched her stomach grow slowly, imperceptibly day by day, for six months now; and although it would be another three months before her baby was born she felt it already had a life of its own. As soon as her son was born – she was convinced it was a boy – and she had recovered from the birth, she would return to Glasgow. Once she was back she would begin a paternity suit in the Scottish Courts against John Brodie. Not trusting Scottish lawyers, and knowing the incestuous relationship which existed among them, she had already engaged Charles Quinn, an English solicitor qualified to appear in Scotland. When the time was right, he would instruct a barrister with dual qualifications.

She could see the banner headlines now. The glittering ascent of John Brodie KC to the Supreme Court Bench would be over.

As she raised her face to the sea, her lips parted and her eyes narrowed in a triumphant smile. A woman could never get even with a man in love, because love was not that important to a man. Her only way was to destroy what *was* important to him – his reputation and career.

Thomas Randolph Macrae. Stillborn August 16, 1945.

A bitter wind gusted round the cemetery as Helen laid her bouquet of white flowers before the little gravestone. She had come here every day for four months now, ever since her son's body in its tiny white coffin had been lowered into its grave. She came here each afternoon and there was nowhere else she wanted to be except here, among the gravestones, close to her son. The flowers, white irises and lilies shipped expensively from the Channel Islands, had been piled high while summer lasted. But now they perished quickly in the winter winds or were blown away. Soon the snow would come, so she had started to take warm clothes she had knitted for him from the trunk in which she kept them and lay them on his grave. Today she had placed a white matinée jacket and leggings and a white bonnet tied with ribbon, and gloves among the flowers.

As she got up and drew her coat closer against the biting cold, she looked around the cemetery. There were no small children's gravestones here as there had been in St George's Fields, but this was a much younger burial ground and life was no longer as hazardous for children as it had been in Victorian times. She hoped Baby was not lonely here . . .

'I'll see you tomorrow, Baby' she whispered through her tears, looking at his little stone. 'It won't be long.'

It was just after three and the light was already beginning to go. It would soon be Christmas, Baby's first Christmas. Though he had been given her father's name of Thomas, so that there was a name to put on his grave, Helen had never used his name. Because Thomas had never lived. Only his body had reached the world.

But Baby had lived within her and it was Baby to whom she brought the white flowers each day.

Her step was always slower going home, because she never wanted to leave Baby. She decided to walk the last part along flat damp sand on the deserted shore and when she reached the house she stood before the greensward looking out across the sea to France.

Dark bloated rain clouds were massing over the English Channel in the twilight and the tide was romping powerfully home.

Within weeks a new year, 1946, would be born. But it would hold nothing for her. Nothing that could bring joy or happiness would ever happen to her again. Now she had lost everything ... and everyone. Her lover and her baby son. Even her husband's family were gone, too. Lord Macrae had suffered a fatal stroke in June and his wife had died a few weeks later. Helen, who had been heavily pregnant, had not attended either funeral. And she couldn't even take revenge on the man she hated most. Somewhere in the depths of her mind the Calvinism which insinuated its creed of thou-shalt-not into every soul that spent its early years in Scotland rose up and condemned her: she was a sinner who deserved to be punished. The last flicker of light, which each soul needed to endure it afflictions, perished.

'Thomas ...' As the light died within her she spoke the name she had given to her son for the first time. Thomas was dead. So there was no reason for her to live. There was nothing she could do to stop herself walking towards the incoming sea ...

'George, quick. It's Mrs Macrae. She'll be drowned in a minute!' The housekeeper Helen had hired to look after her began running as she shouted to her husband. 'Quick,

quick, George! Give me a hand to get her out of the water. Oh, I hope we've got her in time. Then we'll need to ring for an ambulance!'

Helen was taken by ambulance to hospital in Worthing and her lawyer notified by the housekeeper.

'Mrs Macrae has not been right since she lost the baby,' the woman told Charles Quinn. 'She's been trying to go walking in the sea these past few weeks as it's been getting dark. I know her time, so I've been able to keep an eye out for her but I nearly didn't make it today.'

Helen stayed in the Worthing hospital for ten days before Charles Quinn had her transferred to the London Wimpole Clinic where she was put under the care of Edward Carson, a Harley Street psychiatrist who had worked for British Intelligence during the war.

'Mrs Macrae has suffered a nervous breakdown,' Dr Carson told Charles Quinn. 'She has withdrawn completely from the real world. Emotionally she has lost everything and very nearly the will to live. For the time being she has even lost the will to speak.'

Early in January, on a day when snowflakes were drifting from an icy sky towards the Sussex Downs, Dr Carson had Helen installed at Havering Manor, a country house set amid fine lawns and stately trees near Arundel. This was where he kept his wealthiest patients and he visited Helen twice a week, on Tuesday and Thursday afternoons.

For weeks she sat in her pretty sitting-room, staring out across the snowy landscape towards the Downs — occasionally smiling at the doctor but never speaking to him or to any of the staff.

She did not rise until ten each morning and when she had bathed and breakfasted she sat at her dressing-table for ages, brushing her hair. It was often lunch-time before she dressed and finished her toilette. In the afternoons, on better days, she walked in the gardens on the arm of a nurse, taking a stick to shake snow from bushes and the branches of tall trees, smiling but never saying a word. The days were short in January and, as the light faded, she turned her footsteps back to the house, whose sunny ochre bricks glowed like a beacon in the blanched landscape. Once indoors, when she had drunk her tea, she reached for the basket with her knitting. She had made masses of baby clothes ... matinée jackets, boottees and pretty blue coats and leggings and hats which would suit a boy. When she had finished each item she pressed it carefully and held it up, smiling, for a nurse to admire. Then she put it in a cupboard to join those she had already knitted ... till the cupboard was so bulging with baby clothes they fell out when it was opened.

In the middle of February she read a newspaper report that blizzards had stopped all shipping in the English Channel. A frown puckered her brow and she began to pace her sitting-room, clasping and unclasping her hands.

She was so agitated that when she saw the taxi bringing Dr Carson from Arundel Station nosing up the snowy drive, she ran down the hall to greet him.

'If there are snowstorms at sea, I will never find my baby!' she cried.

It was the first time she had spoken since she came to Havering Manor.

The doctor's fingers paused on the top button of his great-coat.

'Of course we'll find him,' he assured her, not letting his eyes leave hers as he hung up his coat on a brass peg. 'But first you had better tell me exactly where he is.' He took her arm, feeling the animation coursing through a body which had been too still for too long.

Half-way down the hall she stopped, her expression completly serious as she looked up at the doctor. 'You won't be angry with him, will you?'

'Of course I won't be angry,' said Dr Carson. 'The important thing is to find him.'

A young nurse in a blue uniform, who was laying a tea tray on a low table by a roaring fire in Helen's sitting-room, beamed an admiring smile at Dr Carson as he and Helen entered the room and sat down.

'Would you like me to pour the tea, Mrs Macrae?' the girl asked.

'Thank you . . .' Helen nodded agitatedly, not seeing the look which doctor and nurse exchanged as she launched into the story of how her baby son had walked into the sea at Rustington just before Christmas. 'But I have not been an idle Mummy while he's been away. Look!' She rose and ran towards the cupboard with the baby clothes. Matinée jackets, leggings and bonnets all in blue tumbled on to the floor as she prized the door open. 'Look! See all the clothes I have made for my baby!'

Dr Carson rose and walked towards the cupboard.

'Yes, Mrs Macrae, you *have* been very busy,' he said. 'You are a very good mother indeed.'

'No, I'm not! I'm a terrible mother! My baby is never coming home! I have lost my baby! He's dead!' cried Helen, snatching clothes from the cupboard and hurling them at Dr Carson and the nurse.

'I believe Mrs Macrae has taken the first steps on the road to recovery,' Dr Carson told Lord Warrender on the telephone that evening from his consulting rooms in Harley Street. 'It will be a long one. But she's begun to talk.'

'That's the best news I've heard for long time,' said Robert. 'I'll trust you to keep me informed about when it is best to get in touch with her . . .'

Chapter Twenty-Six

Sussex and London – April to July, 1946

My dear Helen,
When I shook the dust of southern England off my
shoes at the end of the war I did not expect to see it
again on a regular basis for a very long time. But my
masters in Government have decided otherwise.

When I returned to Edinburgh I had the good fortune
to be appointed to the bench of the Scottish Supreme
Court and the Secretary of State has now decided
to second me to run a Commission of Inquiry into
Scottish Affairs. At present this involves me in taking
evidence from Scottish Members of Parliament and
various Government Departments, which means that
for the next few months my time during the week will
be spent in London. As I have seen no sign and heard
no word that you have returned to your lovely home
in Randolph Crescent, I write this assuming that you
are still living in London. If this is the case, it would
give me very great pleasure if you might be free to dine
with me one evening. With my sincere best wishes that
this finds you well.
Robert Warrender.'

The letter, which had been sent to the mews house and
forwarded by Charles Quinn, who was looking after
Helen's affairs in London, fluttered in her fingers.

'It would be nice to see Robert Warrender again,' she said, lifting her clear eyes to Edward Carson. Long hours spent reliving the anguish of her baby's death were restoring her mental and emotional health and she knew she would soon be ready to start thinking about the future.

'Why don't you invite him to tea,' suggested Dr Carson. 'I'm quite sure he could easily give his Commission of Inquiry an afternoon off from taking evidence.'

'Yes,' said Helen thoughtfully. 'Yes, I could do that.'

The lawns of Havering Manor were colour-washed by banks and mounds of daffodils and tulips in the April afternoon sunshine as Helen watched the Honourable Lord Warrender park his Rolls Royce Silver Wraith. It was over two weeks since she replied to his letter and invited him to tea.

As the day had approached her feelings had become a strange cocktail of excitement and nervousness. Would he wonder what she was doing here and why? All that she had said in her letter was that she had been unwell and was convalescent.

'It's none of his business,' Dr Carson had assured her. 'All you need to indicate, if you wish, is that while you could carry on bravely despite your husband's death so long as the war was on, it all became too much afterwards.'

'I've just lost all my confidence with people,' said Helen, smiling wanly. She seemed to have lived at Havering Manor and not seen anyon e apart from Dr Carson and the nurses for so long now she had become unused to people.

'Your confidence with people will return once you start seeing them again,' said Dr Carson. 'That's why it's been such a good idea for you to invite Lord Warrender to tea.'

That had been yesterday. But Dr Carson wasn't there to reassure her as Lord Warrender stepped from his Rolls and, closing the door on the driver's side, paused and looked towards the house. Helen glanced in the mirror. She was wearing a wool dress that hugged her figure and was the colour of the narcissi which bloomed in such profusion on the lawns, and her halo of golden hair was shining and healthy. She smiled at her reflection. Hanging back wasn't going to do anything to improve her confidence. So, throwing her shoulders back, she stepped smartly from the room into the hall and out beyond the front door on to the wide gravel sweep, where Lord Warrender was already walking towards the house.

From the first day she had met him on the deck of the *Monadliath*, Helen had thought Robert Warrender a handsome man, that there were hidden depths in those roguish black eyes flecked with green. She noticed at once that his wartime moustache had gone and the peacetime judge looked altogether a more respectable character than the rather racy-looking wartime colonel in a white military raincoat had seemed.

'My very dear Helen,' he said, extending a hand towards her. 'It has been far too long.'

'Yes,' sighed Helen. As she took his hand she experienced a sensation akin to suddenly breathing a long forgotten scent which in an instant brings back a world that has flown with the years. This man seemed to evoke all the men she had loved and lost and a world she had known long ago ... the world of her father and her late husband and the lover who betrayed her twice ... Whatever he thought and whatever he wondered, she was glad she had had the courage to invite Robert Warrender to tea.

'And now you must come and tell me about your exciting new job,' she said, letting go of his hand and leading him towards the house. 'Oh, what perfect timing,' she declared as they entered her sitting-room and found the pretty young nurse who admired Dr Carson was laying a tea tray on a low table before the fire.

'There you are, Mrs Macrae,' said the nurse, looking from Helen to Lord Warrender.

'Thank you,' said Helen, smiling.

Helen and Robert dropped easily on to the fireside chairs and when she poured the tea and handed him a cup, her eyes met his in a sympathetic look as she asked: 'And how are you and the boys getting along on your own? They must be quite grown-up now.' His wife, whom she had known slightly, had died shortly before Henry.

'The boys are fine,' he said. 'They are both out of the Army and law students at Edinburgh University. They've bought a flat in Great King Street with money left to them by their mother and left their old father to fend for himself.' He smiled and took a sip of his tea. 'I think you might approve of what I've done, Helen. Since they moved out for good, I've had the place painted and added a few new bits and pieces. Not, of course, that my efforts can compare with the fine home you created, to which I trust you will be coming back in the fullness of time.'

'I don't know,' said Helen, frowning. She was so unused to people that she had got out of the habit of thinking quickly. She was wondering if and what Robert Warrender knew about her affair with John Brodie. 'I may go back to Glasgow. I still have a home there, too,' she added. 'Are you you able to say much about the job you're doing in London?' she asked, changing the subject

'Since we last met I've been cut down in my prime from doing what I am good at – defending men in trouble with the law – and been shunted on to the bench of the Scottish Supreme Courts, where I can now only watch other men do my job less well than I did it,' he sighed, stretching expansively back in his chair. 'Don't misunderstand me, Helen. It is a very great honour to be chosen for a seat on the Scottish Supreme Court bench. Such an honour has run in my family for generations and I would have felt a failure if it had not been offered to me. But after the hurly-burly of the Bar, with all its skirmishes and challenges, the Bench is very dull. I've found it difficult to settle and have let everyone know I was bored so that the Secretary of State for Scotland put me in charge of this Commission of Inquiry into what needs to be done in post-war Scotland.'

'But why do you need to be in London to do that?' asked Helen, looking puzzled.

'Because so much of what affects Scotland is decided in London,' he said. 'And the Scottish Secretary has given me a rather interesting room in which to do my work,' he added with a puckish grin. 'It's at the back of his Whitehall Office in Dover House and it is the room where Lady Caroline Lamb conducted most of her affair with Byron. A procession of Members of Parliament, civil servants, industrialists and Trade Union leaders now climb the very stairs he did in order to see me and my Commission. And we enjoy a truly magnificent view across Horseguards to St James's Park.'

'I'm very impressed,' said Helen, smiling. 'Tell me more,' she encouraged.

Helen was so fascinated by his exposition of the problems Scotland faced that she invited him to stay to dinner, which they ate at a table overlooking the terrace.

It was only as the sun was setting and he was draining the last of the pre-war cognac, which had been miraculously produced, that Robert Warrender asked in a concerned voice: 'How much longer do you expect to be here, Helen?'

She shook her head. 'Until I'm better.' For the first time since he arrived she felt vulnerable and exposed. 'Henry's death affected me more than I realised at the time,' she added quickly. 'I wasn't very well after the war ended. But I honestly think I feel better because you've come to see me today,' she said candidly. 'I need to start seeing people again, getting out and about.'

'Well, if company's the cure now, would you care to let me return your hospitality? What are your plans for the Saturday after next? Would you care to have dinner with me?'

'I would like that very much,' said Helen, feeling a sudden glow. She had really enjoyed this man's company and though he had known both Henry Macrae and John Brodie since childhood and worked with them closely during the war, he had not even mentioned their names. She felt safe with Robert Warrender, she would enjoy seeing him again ... Much later, it seemed to her that it was on this day she had really started to get well ...

That was how it began and as the spring stretched towards the early summer of 1946 they found themselves sharing almost every weekend. Watching cricket on sunny afternoons in the shadow of Arundel Castle, buying ice-cream on the seafront at Bognor, writing postcards on the promenade at Worthing, discovering sleepy inns along the Sussex lanes. Helen was gradually being drawn back into the outside world. Sometimes she talked about Henry, but she never mentioned John Brodie's name and neither did Robert Warrender.

Then, on a glorious Sunday in June, he took her to lunch in the medieval dining-room of his hotel, which nestled under the pines on the seashore. Looking out across the sea towards France and breathing the scent of the pines through the open window, Helen was filled with a deep longing to return to Rustington and see her son's grave.

'I'd like to go to Rustington this afternoon,' she said, looking at him over her coffee cup.

'Why not,' he said affably. 'It's only a few miles down the road.'

He signalled for the bill and when he had paid it, he drove along the coast in the Silver Wraith.

'Where to?' he asked as they approached Littlehampton. 'The seashore?'

'The cemetery.' Her voice was hollow as she directed him to the Horsham Road.

'Will you come with me?' she asked

'Certainly.' He got out quickly and opened the passenger door for her.

She was quite unconscious of slipping her arm into his as they passed through the cemetery gates . . .

They walked slowly until they came to a little white stone before which a circle of white flowers lay on neatly cut grass. Charles Quinn had carried out her instructions for fresh flowers to be laid each day and the previous day's removed and given to an old people's home.

Thomas Randolph Macrae. Stillborn August 16, 1945.
He would be ten months old if he had lived . . .

As unconsciously as she had slipped her arm in Robert's, she now took it away as uncontrollable tears clogged her eyes.

'Oh, Baby, you were all and everything to me,' she sobbed, 'and I could not bear to live without you.'

'But he is happy now in the place where he has gone.' Robert's voice – clear, calm, certain, commanding – cut through the air.

She blinked her tears away and stared at him.

'How do you know that?' she demanded.

'Because his little soul was never corrupted by the world.'

She swallowed and went on staring at those black

eyes flecked with green, which seemed to be so full of understanding. At that moment she sensed that he held all the strength she needed, the strength which came from having someone with whom to share life.

Then she looked again at the little white gravestone and the white flowers.

'Happy in the place where he has gone,' she repeated Robert's words. They seemed to make sense, enough to still her heart. 'Goodbye, Baby,' she whispered. 'Good-bye.' And when she lifted up her eyes again she knew that at last she was well.

'Did you know about John and I?' asked Helen.

'I did,' said Robert.

They were seated around the fire in her sitting-room at Havering Manor, where they had driven when they left the cemetery.

'When he believed he had lost you, your husband took me into his confidence.'

Robert said no more. His discretion was total. He guarded secrets behind a fortress wall, and she sensed that whatever pain or sorrow Henry had confided to him, he would take to his grave.

They sat in silence for a while watching the dappled sunshine playing on the lawn.

'You must be a very good judge,' Helen said eventually.

A smile spread over his face. 'I am flattered that you should think so, but I would make no such claim,' he said. 'What I hope I do is to bring some humility to my tasks. Humility is the most lovely of the spiritual graces and from it so many good things spring. Judges have a great need of humility, but it is a rare thing to find among them. They are all so full of the pride of life and temporal power.'

'And you are not?'

'Of course I am! I believe in a man's right to rise and make of himself in the world. But even the strongest and most powerful among us is weak. And there is in all of us a need to surrender. I believe we forget that at out peril.'

'*Woman's love is stirred primarily in her heart and mind*' . . . Marie Stopes's words rose from deep in her memory.

It was then their eyes met and held in the summer evening light that was playing on the flowers and the lawn — and what had seemed remote and unlikely and unthought of a moment ago became real and urgent and necessary.

'Don't go back to London tonight,' she whispered. 'Stay with me. Make love to me.'

'I think you ought to marry me,' said Robert Warrender.

They had been lovers for two weeks now and were breakfasting on the terrace of a hotel in the New Forest where they had gone for the weekend.

'You sound very convinced it's the right thing,' said Helen, smiling.

'Yes,' he nodded, pouring fresh coffee for them both. 'Marriage is a most excellent institution, a great shield for human weakness.'

'I hadn't quite thought about it like that.'

'Look,' he said, leaning across the table. 'Time is short and I hope you will make a reasonably quick decision. My work in London will be finished in a few weeks and I'll be going back to Scotland for good. I want to take you back with me as my bride.'

Though she had known him a long time, there was still so little she *really* knew about Robert Warrender, but she could not bear to live without him now. And she knew he would not wait for her. He wanted them to get on with

311

their lives ... and since that Sunday at her son's grave she had longed to have another baby.

'I *have* made up my mind,' she said. 'The answer's yes. Is that a quick enough decision for you?'

'Quick enough for me to get the banns posted tomorrow!'

Chapter Twenty-Seven

The Scottish Borders and Edinburgh –
July to November, 1946

Auchinvreck, the Warrenders' ancestral home in the Scottish Borders, stood on a sheltered bend on the River Tweed, guarded by trees as old as history. Magnificent Atlantic cedars, cedars of Lebanon and Deodar trees soared to the sky and spread their branches protectively around it. In their shadow, beech and copper beech, sycamore, lime and silver birch circled the lawns surrounding the house. Beyond the lawns and the trees the land rose steeply, creating the impression of a distant fortress wall around the property. The original house was a handsome pink sandstone mansion built in the early nineteenth century; a wing with a darker, rosier hue and a stepped, towered roof had been added in Victorian times. It was approached by an avenue of lime trees up a drive which then curved and widened until it opened out into the broad sweep of tarmacadam that lay between the house and the front lawn.

Helen saw the house, glinting in the sunlight through the trees.

'It feels like home already,' she said. Everything had happened so fast that just to come to rest felt like bliss.

'That's the general idea,' he said.

As he parked the Rolls by the front lawn, two black labradors came bounding out of the house.

313

'The dogs can't wait to meet you,' he said, squeezing her hand.

Helen knelt and placed an arm around each animal, and they began to lick her face and neck furiously.

'Right then, Rannoch, Flora, that's enough,' said Robert, calling them to order. They obediently let Helen go and their soft brown eyes focused on their master.

'Well then, Lady Warrender, this is your new home,' said Robert, looking first towards the house and then at Helen.

She hadn't really thought of herself as Lady Warrender. But of course, that's who she was now. The name gave her a whole new identity and picture of herself. It was . . . intriguing.

'Want to take a walk before we go in?' asked Robert.

'Yes,' said Helen, anxious to get her bearings.

As they walked back towards the curve in the drive where it widened, she became aware of the scent of cedar, pungent and refreshing, and a chorus of bird-song in rich, musical harmony. Standing back, she realised the house was chiefly guarded by a great Atlantic cedar which rose to the sky above every other tree for miles around and spread its great lower arms protectively across the drive and the lawns. Its bark was hoary and grey as stone and it carried the miniature silver birch and lime trees which had taken root in its upper branches as lightly as if they were birds. It was a tree which said come and sit beneath me and I will shade you from the heat of the sun and shelter you from the terror of the wind and the rain from heaven . . .

It was only when her gaze fell from the mighty cedar that, through other trees beyond a low wall, she noticed the rose pink ruins of an ancient abbey. It was then, too, she took in the stillness of the place, the deep spiritual peace of sanctuary which pervaded the air.

314

'Let's take a look at the river. Then we'll go in,' said Robert. He took her arm back along the drive and the dogs, who had been lazing in the sun, got on to their legs and shook themselves and tailed along.

Beyond the broad sweep in front of the house a gravel path led between the lawns the river bank, which was partially fenced off from the garden. A fisherman in waders was standing midstream. Powerful currents were swirling on the surface around him and the play of light and shadow was creating patterns of dark murky water mingled with clear shimmering waves in which the sunshine danced. But the surface friction did not deflect the river or alter its purpose and course. She looked back to the house and the abbey and great cedar trees. She had come to a place of history and substance and permanence, a place where no mere surface vicissitude altered the course or purpose of things. And then she looked at her new husband, who owned the land beneath his feet and all the eye could see. He was that kind of man – a man of substance, steadfast in his course and purpose.

'Shall we go in?' he asked.

'Yes,' she said, smiling and taking his arm. And they walked towards the house with the dogs at their heels.

Robert had bought a new camera, the very latest, which took colour photographs. And he insisted in taking a picture of Helen standing with the dogs outside the door of her new home before they went in.

Just as he finished taking her photograph the door opened and a middle-aged couple – the woman petite, slim, dark-eyed, her husband tall, broad-shouldered, with a slight paunch – stood at the entrance.

'Ah, Janet, George . . .'

Robert Warrender greeted them, striding towards the

315

house. 'Helen, I'd like to present Janet and Sandy Anderson, who do a splendid job looking after Auchinvreck. Janet and Sandy, Lady Warrender.'

Helen extended a hand first to Janet, who took it and bowed without smiling, and then to her husband, who also bowed solemnly.

'Would you be ready for some tea?' Janet Anderson asked respectfully. She had only learned of the new Lady Warrender's existence when his Lordship telephoned from Harrogate last night.

'Thank you. That would be a splendid idea,' said Robert and they all went inside.

Auchinvreck had been the Warrender family home since Robert's great-grandfather, the Supreme Court judge and founder of the judicial dynasty, had married. Since then three generations of Warrender men had made it a bastion of masculinity. Swords, flintlock holster pistols, sporting guns, bayonet blades, spears, stags' heads and antlers, all proud symbols of male prowess at hunting and shooting, lined the entrance hall.

While the tea was being prepared, Robert took Helen on a quick tour of the house, which was somewhat rundown. Though a carpet sweeper had been carefully worked over threadbare carpets, dusters taken to dark heavy furniture, and cushions of faded chintz battered into looking plump, the musty smell of Wellington boots and rain-sodden tweeds left to dry where they had been discarded, clung to the air. In the drawing-room, where they finally came to rest, the springs had gone from the chair in which Helen sat down. Looking around the room, she felt no woman had held sway in this house for generations. The dark red velvet curtains had a distinctly Victorian air, the Regency striped wallpaper was peeling, several gas lamps were cracked and the gilt in the overmantel was chipped in a score of places.

She looked at Robert, who was sitting across the fireside. This man, now carefully buttering his scone was an almost unknown quantity to her . . . yet she was his wife. And this was their home where they would make their future and lives. And in Edinburgh as well. But she wasn't ready to think about Edinburgh yet . . .

Robert Warrender watched his new wife replenishing their cups and wondered how they would get along.

'Thank you,' he said as she handed him back his cup. If she left him alone to go his own way, he was sure they would be fine. 'I expect you'll want to make one or two changes,' he added, noticing the way she had been taking stock of the room.

'Only with your approval,' she said, smiling, and he liked her tact.

He smiled. 'I admired what you did in Randolph Crescent. So long as you leave the outside walls and billiards room standing, you can have *carte blanche*.'

'Really!' Her face was bathed in a radiant smile and he felt confident he could manage her.

She moved heaven and earth and an army of men and the work went on day and night, taking advantage of the long summer light, and the weekends as well, and she and Robert took refuge in the mews house over the stables.

The result of this ruthless dedication was that towards the end of September the renovation of Lord Warrender's ancestral home was complete – and now it was Helen who conducted the guided tour.

From the outset she had wanted to combine the warmth of the building's pink sandstone fabric with classic country house elegance. So she had decided on a range of coral shades from pale salmon to russet and toned them with soft, pale grey.

317

Light from both the southern and western sun streamed across the abbey and the river through the big bay windows of the principal drawing-room on to doors and shutters and deep skirting boards of pale oak. A gilded mirror overmantel set above a fireplace of grey sculptured marble reflected the deep coral wall panels which blended with the upholstery and the curtains elegantly swagged beneath ceiling roses and intricate cornices. In the smaller drawing-room next door she had lowered the ceiling to create a more intimate family atmosphere and in the dining-room, the panels, which graced every room, became mirrors set in gilded frames. But her *pièce de résistance* was the ballroom, which had its own romantic stairway to the west lawn.

'I want us to give a ball for our daughter's twenty-first birthday here,' said Helen. She was longing to have another baby now and this time she wanted a girl whom she could indulge with the privileged life she herself had been denied.

'I'm sure your wish will be granted,' said Robert, his black eyes full of promise.

'You've done a wonderful job, Helen,' he said, 'and I like what you've done.' He looked at her in an assessing way as their eyes met. 'We married as strangers and I think we are going to enjoy each other as we get to know one another. At least, that is what I hope.'

It was what she, too, hoped for – with all her heart.

Towards the end of September, when Helen and Robert were back at his New Town house in Moray Place for the start of the new legal year, a gynaecologist in Heriot Row confirmed that she would have a baby in May next year.

'You mean that despite being virtually homeless through

318

the summer while you tore Auchinvreck apart and put it together again, we actually managed to start a baby!' exclaimed Robert when she broke her delighted news to him.

'We did indeed,' she said, remembering their nights of love-making, passionate and tender on a hard bed in a cramped room over the stables.

'Congratulations, Lady Warrender,' he said, raising his glass. 'To us both.'

'To us both,' she echoed. She was thrilled he seemed as genuinely delighted as she was. They were really still on their honeymoon, still finding their way with each other, but she was sure their baby would bring them close together. In the hours since she had been given the news she had experienced a strange sense of forgiveness – that whatever had gone wrong in the past, she was now being given a chance to start all over again with the new life she now carried within her.

She relaxed back in her chair. Robert normally took the decanter of port to the library after dinner to work on his judgments and tonight she felt the time they spent lingering at the table made the evening special.

'I think it's about time we gave a dinner party,' he said. 'I haven't really entertained as I should have done since I was elevated to the bench. Do you feel up to taking this kind of thing on in what I suppose we must now call "your condition"?'

'Of course I do!' she cried, feeling her heart give a leap. 'In "my condition" I feel I could do anything. I feel so strong again.' Her hands reached out to him across the table. 'Oh, Robert, I want to be the wife you need.'

'Oh, Helen, I think you are,' he said, taking her hands in his and raising them to his lips.

They had never talked of love. His proposal had been so practical – 'Marriage is a most excellent institution, a

319

great shield for human weakness' – and he hadn't given her time to make up her mind. All she had known was that she couldn't bear to live without him, that she needed to hang on to him just to stay alive. But now, looking into those green-flecked black eyes, she wondered if love might yet be possible for them . . .

Six weeks later Helen was presiding over one end of her dinner table with her husband seeming a corridor's length away at the other. Around the table sat twelve of the most important power brokers in Scottish political-legal circles and their wives. They included Lord President Carlyle, who was sitting on Helen's right, and the Lord Advocate, Charles Hamilton KC, on her left. The Lord Justice Clerk, Lord Farquharson, was also among the guests and, standing in for the Secretary of State for Scotland, whose presence had been suddenly demanded at Westminster by the Prime Minster, was the Minister of State at the Scottish Office – Graeme Wilson MP.

Helen had been delighted when her housekeeper put her head round the door of the room she used as a study and announced: 'Mr Graeme Wilson has telephoned to say he will be coming in place of the Secretary of State, my Lady. He said he was particularly pleased to be coming and to tell you he was sorry he did not have the pleasure of speaking to you himself.'

'We'll make up for that when he gets here,' said Helen, smiling. And she did when she and her husband received Graeme and his pretty wife, Alison, at the entrance to their drawing-room. With his twinkling brown eyes and his flat brown hair, Graeme hardly looked a day older than he had done fifteen years ago on Clydeside.

'Carpentry. Making things with his hands in one of the finest things a man can do,' Lord President Carlyle was now saying into Helen's right ear. Robert had told her he was really a rather shy bachelor who hated social occasions and making small talk and would far rather be at home working on his carpentry. 'Jesus was a carpenter.'

'Yes,' said Helen, nodding, her lips carefully parted like a model girl pretending to smile. But she hardly heard a word he was saying. All she saw was the dark, brooding features of the man sitting half-way down the table, his beautiful hands breaking a bread roll as he appeared to be listening to what a woman was saying into his left ear. His head was held high and still and strands of silver in his once jet-black hair made John Brodie KC look as distinguished as the reputation he was building in the courts. He was now Dean of the Faculty of Advocates and the talk was that he would soon be a judge.

She had been so sure she could handle John and Grace Brodie.

'I did it when I was married to Henry. I can do it again,' she had bravely assured Robert when he had offered to find a way of not inviting the Dean.

But that had been before she had lived with him in London, before she had his baby. And it was the pain of her dead baby which was hurting her more than anything and had done from the moment John Brodie, with his appallingly impeccable manners and mask of a smile, had arrived this evening.

She watched him now sitting at her table, eating her food and drinking her wine as if nothing had ever happened. As if Thomas had never been born! Then she remembered John Brodie knew nothing about their child.

She could not go on looking at him. Her eyes sought the long white corridor of the table and she swallowed hard to contain her tears. Fruit overflowing from an epergne seemed to take on softer, darker, richer colours in the candlelight. Everything seemed to merge and blend into one, then divide sharply again as her eyes traversed the table.

If she had sinned she had paid for it. And she had suffered more, far more, than she deserved.

Slowly she raised her eyes and fixed him with them.

At last his eyes met hers – and it was then she decided to destroy him.

John Brodie's gaze was riveted to the perfect oval of Helen's face. He had never seen her look more beautiful – in bold sculptured black silk satin which formed a ravine from her shoulders to the white valley between her breasts. Tonight, too, there was a calmness, a serenity, in her loveliness that had not been there when he had walked away from her in the American Bar of the Savoy on that evening early last year.

The day before he was appointed Dean of the Faculty of Advocates he had got news of her marriage to Robert Warrender and he had still not recovered from the shock. Robert was his only real rival for the Lord Presidency when Lord Carlyle retired in a few years – and from the moment he had arrived this evening he had longed to reach out and touch the flawlessly-soft, smooth skin of Helen's neck and shoulders, to press his lips down that white valley between her breasts and then to lose himself somewhere deep within her.

'It's all over with Helen,' he had assured Grace on the frosty morning he had arrived home in Heriot Row last year.

'For how long this time?' she demanded.

'For good. I will simply never see her again,' he said. 'As it is your wish for us to remain married, I would like to think it is possible for us to put the past behind us and try to find some common ground, something we can agree on as a starting point. Whatever may have gone wrong between us, we have two lovely children. For their sakes, if for no other reason, I think we should try to make a fresh start.'

'That has been my view for a very long time,' she said icily. 'I'm glad you're coming to your senses at last.'

'But *we* have to find something for ourselves,' he said. 'Our children will not benefit if **we** live in a state of conflict. We have to find some common ground on which to live harmoniously. We ought at least to try.'

Try they did. As the summer of 1945 passed, they were on their best behaviour with each other. Then he was appointed Sheriff Principal of Perth, Argyll, Lochaber and Strathspey, which meant he needed a house out of Edinburgh in his Sheriffdom where he could entertain the local gentry – even though it was only a part-time job. And Grace had found Craigendhu, a small estate which a nineteenth-century English industrialist had planted with native Scots pine and larch on a considerable scale. The principal residence, a grey stone Victorian mansion, had been refurbished and elegantly furnished in the late 1930s, when a guest wing had been added. There was also a dower house, several cottages, a disused church and some arable land where ripening corn swayed in the shadow of the pines at the approach of harvest time. The pre-war furniture, furnishings and carpets were of a quality difficult to obtain in austerity-bound post-war Britain. So the Brodies bought the lot, right down to the mat on the porch.

John's ancestors had come from this part of the country and when he stood in the hall on a day when the wind was whistling through the pines and the snow lay thick and deep on the Cairngorms, he experienced an overwhelming sense that he had come home. He owned the land beneath his feet and its possession added immeasurably to his conviction about his identity and place in the world.

'This is our new ground,' he said to Grace. 'We have not been here before. We can make our life here what we want it to be and it could be very good.'

'Yes,' she said, 'we can.' And there was a light in her eyes he had not seen for years.

But it had already been too late as he found out when he went out walking in the woods later that day with Angus. He wanted Craigendhu to see a new start with his children. All the warmth and spontaneity seemed to have gone from their relationship since he came home from the war. They no longer clung to him as they had done the previous Christmas. Vanessa positively avoided him and was sullen when he spoke to her and there was a reserve in Angus's manner despite the eternal smile that played around the boy's mouth.

'You were away for six years. The children need time to get used to your being around again,' Grace had told him when he questioned her.

'Do you like this house, Daddy?' Angus had asked when they walked in the woods.

'Yes, I like this house.'

'Do you like it a lot?'

'Oh, yes. Very much.'

'Do you like the garden?'

'Yes.'

'And this wood?'

'Yes, even when some of the trees haven't got any leaves.' He saw the smile had gone from his son's face. 'Why are you asking me all these questions, Angus?' he inquired gently.

He saw Angus swallow before he asked: 'Daddy, do you like everything enough to stay with us?'

Vanessa's sullenness. He made the connection at once.

What had Grace said to his children? What betrayal had taken place behind his back, when he was far away and powerless to defend himself?

'I like this house and the garden and the wood and everything about it very much,' he reassured his son in an even tone. 'But I'm not staying here or at our house in Edinburgh just because I like *them*. I'm staying because I'm your father and I want to be with *you*.' He knelt so that he was eye-level with the boy. 'I couldn't help being away from you during the war, but the war's over now and my home is with you. Always.'

'I just wanted to be sure, Daddy . . .' Angus said with dignity, but John heard the tears in his voice as he retreated behind his happy mask.

'What have you been telling my children?' John demanded the moment lunch was over and Angus and Vanessa had left the table.

'About what?' Grace, facing him, tensed.

'About whether or not I would live with them after the war,' he said grimly, his eyes pinioning hers. 'Now don't prevaricate, Grace. I want the truth.'

He watched her swallow and her fingers clutch the edges of the table before she said in an icy voice: 'After you asked me for a divorce I warned them you might be leaving us. It – '

'But you knew we weren't going to be divorced! You had *refused* to divorce me.'

'That couldn't stop you leaving us!'

'Once you had refused to divorce me that was the end of the matter. You *knew* I wasn't leaving.'

'I knew you were perfectly capable of changing your mind. We had no guarantee that you would be coming back to Edinburgh when the war was over.'

He drew his breath and saw cold fury in her defiant black eyes. The past was still the present for Grace.

Nothing had changed. There could never be a new beginning for them. In an even tone he asked her: 'Didn't you even for a moment stop to think of the hurt you would inflict on the children by telling them such a thing?'

'They had a right to know where they stood with you,' she said, her stare unflinching.

'What exactly did you tell them?' he asked.

'That you were thinking of staying in London because you wanted to work at the English Bar,' she replied icily.

'Is that all?'

'Yes.'

'I don't believe you,' he said, rising from the table. 'I believe that because I had asked you for a divorce you deliberately set out to turn my children against me.'

He strode from the room, knowing it was over between them and their last chance of happiness had gone for ever.

And now he could not take his eyes from Helen. And the longer he looked at her, the more terrible his mistake seemed in leaving her. And he knew it was his own selfishness which had been his undoing. He had often dreamed about her and thought about her and remembered what they had shared, but he had closed his mind to her fate, preferring to think of her remaining alone, waiting for him to return some day.

Grace Brodie swallowed hard to suppress her tears. The way her husband was looking at that whore felt like an arrow shot straight through her. Then a malicious glint dawned in her eyes. She thought: but you can never have that bitch now. She is married to a judge and you would not dare to touch her. I know you, John Brodie, you will always do what is best for your career. You cannot touch her ever again. But the thought did nothing to assuage the bitterness in her heart . . .

She remembered how the children had found her sobbing in the drawing-room in Heriot Row the night after he had asked her for a divorce and gone back to London.

Vanessa had been in her pink flannelette nightdress and Angus in his blue pyjamas and they had looked so small and helpless and frightened as they stood at her knee.

'What's the matter, Mummy? Why are you crying?' asked Vanessa, her face creased in pain as Angus looked on sorrowfully.

'I'm crying because Daddy doesn't love us any more and wants to leave us for good. He wants to stay in London.'

'Why doesn't he love us any more?' wailed Vanessa and Grace saw tears tumbling down the faces of both her children.

'Because he loves other people in London better and he doesn't want us any more,' said Grace, seeing her own pain reflected in her children's faces.

But he had come back and she had not been able to offer them a satisfactory explanation for what she had told them that terrible night when she wanted to destroy him.

'He changed his mind. Thought the better of what he was doing,' she said when they asked her why he had come back.

'But he could still love other people in London better,' said Vanessa.

'And if he doesn't like staying with us he could change his mind and go back to London,' said Angus.

'Now, look, your daddy's very sorry about it,' said Grace. 'But you must never ask him about it because he will get very upset and he might decide to leave us all

327

over again. Now, do I have you promise you will never ask him about it?'

'I promise,' said Vanessa.

'Angus?'

'Yes.'

'Do you promise?'

'I promise.'

'Right, that's enough. We will never talk about it again.'

She hoped that was the end of the matter. Neither child mentioned it again, but their doubts had lived on in their hearts. And then one fatal day John had found out enough to know what she had done . . .

At the far end of the table Lord Warrender was watching his wife intently and wondering if he had done the right thing in marrying her.

As an extremely eligible widower, he could easily have found another wife in Edinburgh or the Borders . . . but that would have meant reneging on his promise . . .

The guttering candles, the bobbing heads, the animated faces, seemed to recede from his vision . . . Instead he saw endless acres of ugly spiked barbed wire, a stretch of shore implanted with mines and obscene cement blocks, and an endless grey sea and a sky impervious to the sun . . .

Silhouetted against the barbed wire and the grey sea stood the slim figure of a man he had loved so well and deeply in his youth in an affair that had begun on another shore on a summer day in Scotland long ago . . . a young man who had eventually grown away from him because of a woman and then, in his deep unhappiness, had turned to him again . . . and loved him again . . . a young man who had meant more to him than any other human being . . .

'If anything happens to me you must marry Helen.' Henry Macrae's voice had been firm.

'Don't be such a pessimist, Henry. Nothing's going to happen to you,' Robert said gruffly. 'You're a survivor, as we all know.'

'I said "if." These matters have to be faced and prepared for,' said Henry sternly.

'Allowing for the "if," it is possible that your widow might have other plans. I would have thought she would want to marry John Brodie if she could.'

'But John won't marry her. I know him of old. His career and ambition come before everything with John. He'll make her think he's going to marry her, and she will believe him – he may even believe it himself. But when it comes to the bit, he won't. Not ever. I *know* him.'

'Well, in that case wouldn't Helen be better to make a fresh start somewhere else with some other man?'

'No!' Henry barked the word. 'I want *you* to marry her and take care of her. If I have meant anything to you at all, you must do it for my sake. I was happy with Helen for a while, until I realised that she was still in love with John Brodie. It is like an illness with her, a malaria which goes away for a while, then comes back and attacks again. I think she will never be free of him and so I want you to take care of her, protect her as best you can!'

'But what of my own happiness?'

'Your first marriage never got in the way of it. You even said it was very convenient being married because it put you above suspicion,' Henry reminded him sharply. 'Your wife never understood what there was between us – and I doubt if even a woman as sophisticated as my wife would ever suspect. Women have no idea about these matters, of how things can be with men. Now, do you promise me that you will marry Helen?' He held out his hand to Robert, who saw the unhappiness in that dear pale face.

He took Henry's hand.

'I promise,' he said, clasping the beloved man to him, never believing for a moment that one day he would have to fulfil his promise.

The scene faded. He looked back down the white corridor of the table towards his wife, who was now in animated conversation with the Lord Advocate.

Years ago he had hated Helen Dunlop more than he had ever hated anyone. Hated her for seducing the man he loved and taking him away. Henry, so desperately in need of a father's love, had been *his* boy. They had been happy until Helen Randolph had persuaded Henry he needed to marry, not expecting marriage to end her relationship. Except he knew that wasn't the whole truth; his beloved Henry had always longed to be 'normal . . .' But then the imposter Brodie had snatched Helen back and Henry had returned to him and they had been happy again until death had taken Henry away for good. In any event, he had kept his promise to Henry and the truth now was that Helen fascinated him. She had a good mind and, having worked in the world of men, she understood men and knew how to talk to a man in a dispassionate, intelligent way. Looking at her now, smiling at Lord President Carlyle, he hoped sincerely that the baby they were expecting would make her really happy and help her forget the son she had lost. He knew she wanted a daughter this time and so did he.

Fractionally narrowing his eyes, he fixed his gaze on John Brodie, whom he had despised ever since the little upstart first came to his house with his late younger brother, Andrew, as a boy of seven. He had been a calculating, manipulative little imposter even then, forever smarming up to the parents and trying to impress them.

Now he was a Sheriff Principal in the shires. But

330

the truth was that despite the way he usurped and assumed other people's roles and mantles, John Brodie simply did not belong and never would belong to the legal aristocracy. Like his father, he was an outsider. And just as the previous Lord Warrender had been instrumental in keeping the upstart James Brodie out of the Cockburn Club, it was Robert's secretly avowed intention to keep John Brodie out of ever gaining any real power or authority in the legal Establishment. In his wartime role in British Intelligence Robert had made it his business to collect enough information to ensure that the publicly charismatic John Brodie never sat on the bench of the Scottish Supreme Court, and when he was conducting his Commission of Inquiry in London he had paid a visit on his own to the cemetery in Rustington and taken a picture of the grave of Thomas Randolph Macrae for inclusion in the file. The question uppermost in his mind, as plates of pears and fresh ginger in spiced red wine were being laid before his guests, was whether *he* would need to destroy John Brodie – or whether his new wife now hated the imposter sufficiently to do it for him.

Chapter Twenty-Eight

Edinburgh – February, 1947

Britain was in the grip of a cruel winter. Heavy snow-storms combined with sub-zero temperatures had blocked roads and railway lines, disrupting travel and transport and bringing down power lines that left four million workers idle and the nation's homes without electricity during the day. Non-stop blizzards had stopped all shipping in the English Channel, creating a new threat to food supplies only weeks after the Government had cut the meat ration. Throughout the country troops had been called in to clear snowdrifts, sometimes twenty feet high, and Buckingham Palace and Whitehall civil servants had joined shop and office staff in working by candlelight.

Seated by a blazing log fire in her drawing-room in Moray Place, Helen watched the branches of the trees in the gardens sagging under the weight of snow. She had not ventured out since the storms had come in case she slipped on the icy streets and hurt the baby who had been growing within her for six months now. Ever since her pregnancy had been confirmed she had been acutely conscious of the need to take special care of herself in mind as well as in body. Not only did she supplement the extra meat and milk and other allowances made to expectant mothers with lots of fresh fruit and vegetables from the nursery and market garden at Auchinvreck, but she had placed herself once again under the care of Dr Edward Carson in case her worries and anxieties about the baby affected its well-being. He had visited her four times since November, putting her mind at rest as he listened to her talk about the fears which had suddenly started to crowd in on her, and skilfully allowing her to voice her deepest feelings and come to terms with them and reach an understanding that everything about this baby was different and there was no reason to believe it would be stillborn.

'I dump all my rubbish on you,' she said on his last visit before the storms came. 'I get it all out so it stops building up inside me.'

'It's what I'm here for,' said Edward Carson. 'I'm really a dustman who collects emotional garbage and takes it away!'

But she remained cautious about making preparations for her new baby. This time she did no knitting and nappies, clothes and the pram and cot remained in the shops, and the second floor nursery suite would not be prepared until after the baby was born.

Somewhere over the trees a church clock announced the hour of three. In another twenty minutes Mary Douglas, the housekeeper, would bring tea. And then Robert would come home. Though the court did not rise officially until four, cases often ended well before then. And it was nice when he got home early in time for tea – it meant they had more time together in the day before he had to adjourn to the library in the evening after dinner to work on his judgments.

'How was your day?' she asked when he had entered the drawing-room and stood warming his hands over the fire.

'I've been sitting in the First Division today, but I feel my day's work has hardly begun. There's a big commercial case starting tomorrow and I've still got quite a bit of reading up to do on it. I'll be working very late tonight.'

'You're always working very late,' said Helen, slightly disappointed that he was going to bury himself in the library for a fourth consecutive evening. 'You haven't come to bed for the last two nights.'

'I've been so late I haven't wanted to disturb you,' he said. 'You and the baby need all the rest you can get,' he added, smiling.

'Is Donald MacLeish in this case?' asked Helen. Robert shook his head. 'Then why has he called to see you these past two nights when you've been working late? I'd hardly call ten o'clock a normal social visiting hour.'

'Because he's been passing the door on his way home from the Juridical Library,' said Robert, taking draught of his tea and dropping on to the chair facing Helen across the fire.

'But you don't encourage every young advocate who happens to be passing your front door at ten o'clock at night to ring the bell!' she protested.

'That's true,' he admitted with a grin. 'But I have an interest in Donald. It may be difficult for you to understand how hard it is for a talented young man with no connections to make his way in the legal world. Donald is a truly gifted advocate but he has no family connections with the Bar. He needs someone who will help to pave the way for him. I would like to feel I have a hand in fostering so great a talent.'

Helen had disliked Donald MacLeish almost on sight. Robert had invited him to dine with them in Moray Place on two occasions – once in late November in company with several members of the Junior Bar and again just before he left to spend Christmas on his parents' croft in the West Highlands. Though his soft brown eyes reminded her of the labradors at Auchinvreck, she saw avarice and something else which made her uneasy but she could not quite put her finger on beneath his excessively

334

deferential manner. He stood barely five feet four inches tall, a small neat figure with shiny swept-back black hair and a slightly rounded face. Despite her husband's faith in his ability, Donald MacLeish did not strike Helen as a great advocate. In her eyes, he quite simply lacked the presence to cut the masterful figure in court which an advocate needed to be.

Helen went to bed just after half-past ten and awoke at two o'clock to find she was still alone though he had promised her he would come to bed tonight. This late night working is becoming ridiculous, she thought, swinging her legs out of bed. She threw a white satin robe over her nightdress and glided down the magnificent stairs.

At the bottom she heard voices coming from the library. One of them belonged to Donald MacLeish. At this hour! And he must have arrived *after* she had gone to bed at half-past ten. His visits were getting later and later.

Her fingers reached for the door handle, then she realised that Robert would probably be affronted if she burst in in her state of *déshabillé* and demanded his presence in her bed when he was entertaining a junior member of the Bar. But this was no way for a newish husband to behave. They hadn't had one single row in the seven months since they married, but as she and retreated back upstairs she could feel the first one coming on.

She knew if she went back to bed she would fall asleep, so she sat down on the button-back chair and left the bedroom door slightly ajar.

She realised she had fallen into a light sleep when she looked up and saw the hands of the mantelpiece clock were at three-fifteen. Robert had still not come to bed!

Then she heard voices coming from the hall.

She tiptoed from the room down the stairs. On the

first floor landing she knelt down and peered through the balustrade.

Robert was standing in the hall in a maroon velvet dressing-gown, locked in a passionate embrace with Donald MacLeish!

Helen's fingers froze around the balustrade. She could feel the blood drain from her face and her body become still and cold as stone.

Men were sent to prison for what they were doing! There was a *law* against it. And they were the highest practitioners of the law . . .

The men parted and moved towards the vestibule and the front door without a backward glance.

'I'll see you tomorrow, Donald,' she heard her husband say in the soft, caressing after-love voice she thought he used to her alone. She felt her stomach retch and churn and quickly closed her hand over her mouth.

Then she heard the door shut and a great rattling of chains as Robert locked up. Helen rose silently. She was shaking now and her fingers reached for the banister to steady herself. She raised her eyes to the stairway to the bedroom floor. She could tiptoe up there and pretend she had not seen anything; She could live a lie . . . let her pain seep and leak out in mute, unspoken ways. But she knew that was wrong and from long, bitter experience she knew that failure to speak up about what hurt you and what you were afraid of in a relationship in an effort to avoid pain only led to greater pain. When she was young she had had the courage to speak out to Harry about what had hurt her and love had grown. But with John Brodie and Henry Macrae she had shied away and not spoken when she should have done. And it had led to greater pain. No, this wasn't going to happen with Robert Warrender! Her agony was too great, and the chasm which had opened up between them far too deep and wide for her to pretend it wasn't there.

She swallowed hard and her fingers tightened around the banister. She began to descend. Halfway down the stairs her eyes met those of her husband, who was emerging from the vestibule.

'I've just been seeing Donald off,' he said affably.

His voice sounded so normal. So was his appearance. For a split-second she almost thought she had dreamed or imagined what she had seen. At that moment she realised he had no idea he had been seen and it was still possible for her to draw back – to save their marriage, to live a lie. But . . .

'I know,' she said, her eyes not leaving his as she reached the bottom of the stairs.

Till her last breath Helen would remember the shock and disbelief and horror that crowded her husband's eyes. *But only for an instant.* The speed with which Robert Warrender regained his aplomb was almost more terrifying than her discovery of his passionate relationship with Donald MacLeish. Faster than lightning, those eyes were now saying, so you know, what is there to get upset about? So you have discovered some minor flaw, some peccadillo of which you do not approve, so what? This was the acme of personal power, supreme unshakeable self-confidence, magnificent self-possession which had been bred into this man as much by his ancestry and the position of his family in society as by his education. The naked strength at the root of this man was total self-belief. Helen had never encountered such conviction before and its effect was devastating. She almost felt she was in the wrong.

'We need to talk,' she managed to say. But even to her own ears her voice sounded feeble.

He strode ahead of her into the library, marching straight to the drinks table.

'I need a drink,' he said, 'I expect you could use one as well.'

'I'll have a brandy,' she said, sinking into one of the big black leather fireside chairs and surveying the disarray of a room she had rarely entered because her husband had made it very plain this was his private domain right from the start of their marriage.

Robert's green leather-topped desk, which stood in one corner, was littered and unkempt with documents and pink string, and legal books, gilded and bound in leather, were everywhere – strewn by the fire and the drinks table and the chesterfield which matched the fireside chairs – as well as lining the walls. But the room, with ash spilling from the grate on to the hearth and the air impregnated with the stench of stale cigars, was nauseating. Then she noticed the door to the ante-room, where Robert sometimes slept when he worked late, was ajar. Through the gap she saw the sheets on the bed were rumpled and she felt sick.

'There you are,' said Robert, handing her a bowl of a glass containing a large measure of brandy. Then he dropped on to the big leather chair facing Helen, picked up a half-smoked cigar from an ashtray, and started chopping the end off it.

Helen felt she was seeing the Honourable Lord Warrender for the first time as he really was . . . Supreme Court judge, landowner, lawbreaker who was completely above the law. For there was even a law to protect him in his lawbreaking, a law which made it an offence to utter a word against a judge in Scotland. 'Murmuring a judge,' as the offence was called, could be punished with a prison sentence. All the tools she had, womanly and worldly, all she had ever learned about men as partners and men in business, all she knew about not getting upset in a confrontation, seemed like child's

338

toys arrayed against the nuclear arsenal of her husband.

She saw those black eyes flecked with green challenging her to master her raw, wounded emotions and prove he had done anything wrong. She looked down. She could not handle this man! She swirled her brandy glass in her fingers and took a sip of the drink. Then she raised her eyes to him once again and all her pain and shock and horror filled her anguished cry: 'Why?'

'Why what?' The consummate lawyer came back at her quickly.

'Why did you marry me if . . . if . . . that is what you wanted?'

'Relations between men and women are not necessarily mutually exclusive,' he said. 'I married you because I gave my word to Henry Macrae that I would do so.'

She stared at him, thinking her ears were playing tricks. 'Why was that?' she gasped.

'Because I loved him.'

Now the whole world started to unravel and spin around her.

'Marriage is most excellent institution, a great shield for human weakness . . .' Robert's words when he had asked her to marry him burned in her brain.

There were wheels within wheels, subterranean channels and secret canals which bound Edinburgh lawyers to each other in a freemasonry so powerful it made a mockery of marriage and a dupe of a wife.

'Henry had been mine for a long time before he met you,' said Robert. 'He came back to me when he knew you had resumed your affair with John Brodie. He had a premonition he would be killed in Normandy and he did not believe John would marry you. For a time he had been very happy with you, indeed, he still loved you, in a way, and he wished to protect you — '

339

'No!' Helen uttered a strangled cry as her eyes fell on her husband's hands. She had always thought Robert had beautiful hands. But now she knew that they had fondled Henry and Donald MacLeish as well as her they seemed horrible, repulsive things. She would never let them touch her again or get near the baby growing within her. She must protect her baby at all costs, get her away from the depraved, corrupt monster who had fathered her. 'No, I do not want to hear another word. Our marriage is over. I will not stay another night in this house!'

She got up and fled from the room.

Chapter Twenty-Nine

Edinburgh – February, 1947

Robert Warrender took a long draft of cognac.

He had never wanted her to know.

He had been so sure she would never find out.

He had been so sure she would be asleep . . .

He had wanted to be the paternal husband who took care of her and provided for her and gave her the child or children she wanted . . . and never let her see he was fragile and had his weaknesses, too.

He felt he had let Henry down, ratted on their bargain.

He had been getting quite fond of her . . . and more than anything he regretted the loss of a woman who was becoming his good friend and ally, and the loss of the child he had been so happy to father . . .

Chapter Thirty

Glasgow, Edinburgh, Lothian and the Scottish Borders – May, 1947 to June 1948

Roseanna Randolph Warrender was born in a nursing home in the West End of Glasgow on a sunny morning in May, 1947. She had the lightest covering of fair hair and dimpled cheeks and a lusty cry and Helen loved her with a love she did not know she had to give until the moment her daughter was placed in her arms and took her first suck from her breast. This tiny bawling creature had changed everything forever.

'She's a miracle,' said Helen, looking down at her daughter's tiny, perfectly-shaped fingernails. 'A perfect miniature. And there is nothing wrong with her despite all I've been through.'

She had not seen Robert since the terrible winter night she had fled from the library in Moray Place. Though he had made no attempt to follow her, she could not bear to spend the rest of the night in the bed they shared and had locked herself in one of the spare rooms and sobbed for hours. As soon as she had heard him leave for court the next morning she had packed several suitcases and taken the train to Glasgow. By the end of the day she was installed back in the flat in Great Western Terrace and had hired a middle-aged couple who were distantly related to her trusted old caterer, Luigi, to move in and look after her. She had also sent for Dr Carson who had been stepping off the overnight train from Euston to counsel her every week for three months now.

'What men do to each other is so horrible,' she cried. 'Why do they do it?'

'Well, opinions differ on the roots and causes of homosexuality and bisexuality,' said Dr Carson. 'I myself believe that it is the lack of love, not the need for sex, which lies at the root of most human problems, even those which appear to be of a sexual nature. And it usually stems from lack of love in childhood.'

There was a lot Helen did not understand about what Dr Carson told her; his ideas often sounded so removed from what people accepted as normal in marriage and family life. And there was even more she could not quite grasp in some of the books he loaned her. But as the weeks passed she recalled the insight she had gained into the reasons for her involvement with Harry Dunlop, which had been motivated by her need for a father figure. The idea that any daughter of hers – she was sure it was a girl this time – should ever enter into such a relationship and suffer what she had done in the early days was utterly repugnant to her. More than anything she wanted this baby to have the normal life she had been denied.

'But if you remain separated from your husband your circumstances will not be so different from those of your mother's, except you will be better off materially,' said Edward Carson.

'My circumstances will be completely different,' Helen argued fiercely. 'I am married, so my daughter will be legitimate and as soon as she is old enough to understand she will be told who her father is.'

'But Helen, she needs to develop a relationship with him to be normal.'

'But he's queer! How can he help my daughter to be normal?'

'He has a bisexual element in his personality, which is a completely different thing,' corrected Dr Carson. 'And with whose voice are you speaking loudest – that of a mother concerned for her child or a woman who feels painfully wronged?'

The question, like so many Doctor Carson posed, made Helen draw her breath and fall silent.

'I sometimes wonder whose side you're on,' she said eventually.

She had a lot more arguments with him in the weeks approaching her daughter's birth. Round and round over the same ground, never reaching a decision or knowing what to do for the best. The gap between her own repulsion for her husband and the need to do the best for her baby seemed impossible to bridge and reconcile.

Roseanna's birth changed everything. Looking down at the day-old baby at her breast, Helen knew that whatever her differences with her husband, they both owed it to their daughter to do their best for her. If it meant reaching an amicable agreement to live separate lives under the same roof, she was prepared to do so – so long as Doanld MacLeish or any other 'boyfriend' of her husband's never crossed the threshold. She wanted Roseanna to have a normal life and to grow up enjoying all the privileges she had been denied. And to achieve that she needed to be living, officially at least, with her husband. She smiled at her baby and her imagination raced ahead seventeen, eighteen, twenty years . . . picturing the beautiful grown-up Roseanna making her entrance to the ballroom at Auchinvreck. I designed that ballroom especially for you, she thought, as she laid her daughter against her shoulder and began gently to pat her back.

'It was for you I built the stairway to the gardens and

344

the stars,' she whispered into the baby's ear as Roseanna gave an enormous burp.

After she had handed her precious daughter back to a nurse, who laid Roseanna in a cot beside her mother's bed, Helen reached into the drawer of the bedside table for her writing paper. Since she left Robert she had only communicated with him through her London solicitor, Charles Quinn. But now, in her own hand, she wrote; 'My dear Robert, Your beautiful daughter made her début yesterday. Both she had her mother would welcome a visit from you. Helen.'

There was a lump in her throat as she sealed the envelope. She looked down at Roseanna, who was now asleep in her cot. 'I could never have done this without you,' she whispered.

Two days later two enormous bouquets of red and white roses, each wrapped in cellophane and tied with white satin ribbon, arrived in Helen's room. The inscription on the accompanying cards said 'To My Darling Wife' and 'To My Darling Daughter.' Both were signed 'Robert.' In the afternoon the matron informed Helen she had received a telephone call from Lord Warrender saying he would be coming to the nursing home to visit his wife the following day at two o'clock.

Helen felt nervous from the moment she woke up that morning and almost immediately started wondering if she had done the wrong thing in inviting her husband to see his daughter when she was still so young and defenceless. He can look but he *cannot touch*, she decided.

By one o'clock Helen had fed and dressed Roseanna in a long white muslin dress with a prettily smocked front. It was the very first time she had experienced the pleasure of getting a little girl dressed-up, and it was delicious. As she tied the last button at the back of her baby's neck and looked at the delightful bathed and sweet and scented creature in her arms, she caught a tantalising glimpse of the future – and all the joy that would be hers in the years ahead getting this little girl dressed-up and sharing her life.

Checking her own appearance in a hand mirror, she could not help noticing the new radiance in her eyes. Giving birth and life to another human being had endowed her with a new sense of completeness.

Her room was on the first floor of the nursing home and looked out over gardens filled with trees that were bursting with fresh spring green. Over and beyond them Helen could see the spires of several churches and the clock on Dowanhill Church was just striking two o'clock when the matron opened the door and ushered in the Honourable Lord Warrender to see his wife and new baby daughter.

'Hello, Helen,' said Robert from the end of the bed.

She was powerless to stop the tears which gushed as the matron closed the door, leaving them alone.

'There are tears in my heart, too,' he said. 'Tears of joy that I should be alive this day to see you again with your baby.'

Everything was different when there was a man with whom a woman could share a baby, a father who wanted the child. Now she seemed to be crying for her mother, who had been so alone, and her little fatherless son who died, as well as with happiness over Roseanna. It was Robert who had healed her heart and given her Roseanna and now she saw he wanted to find a way back.

'Do you have a name for your baby?' he asked softly.

'Roseanna. I want to call her Roseanna Randolph Warrender,' she said. 'But won't you sit down.'

'Thanks,' he said, stepping from the end of the bed and settling into the Lloyd Loom at the bedside.

She looked at him. Both his hair and his bushy eyebrows seemed more silvery than she remembered them. She sensed that he had missed her. And it was then she realised just how much she had missed him, too.

'Would you like to hold her?' she asked tentatively.

'If I may.' His reply was tentative, too, as his eyes sought hers in a long, tender look.

Helen gently placed her hands under her baby's arms and her eyes remained locked in that look of tenderness as she gave their daughter to him.

Helen studied them, eagle-eyed, as Roseanna's tiny hand clasped her father's little finger and he marvelled at her. Then she saw the love streaming from him to the tiny creature in his arms. It lit his eyes and his whole face, endowing every gesture and movement as he held her. And a wave of gratitude surged through Helen's heart.

'We've got to do our best for Roseanna,' she said, feeling the tears surging again. 'What's happened to us doesn't matter. *We* don't matter. But she does. We've got to give her the life she deserves.'

'With the two of us?'

'Yes,' she whispered. 'With the two of us.'

When Roseanna was four weeks old Helen returned to live in her husband's house.

In the days following his first visit to the nursing home they had talked at length about the future. Robert had assured her that apart from his appearance in court, he had not seen Donald MacLeish and had not sought a relationship with any other man or woman and his life was now devoted entirely to his work.

They agreed to live as friends under the same roof, maintaining a public face as a couple for the sake of their daughter, and the second floor rooms designated as the nursery suite were quickly prepared and furnished in white and pastel pinks and blues. At the same time Robert had his library and study redecorated along with the vestibule and hall so that when his wife and new daughter came through the front door there was an air of freshness about the place; and the door of the library, which had always been kept closed, was left wide open like the doors to all the other rooms.

The baby's suite was at the back of the house and looked out over the grey stone tenements and green parks and suburban villas of the northern city to the Firth of Forth and the shores of the Kingdom of Fife — 'the view from heaven' as Helen's mother had called it.

A contented smile lit Helen's face when she laid her daughter to sleep in the long June evening light on the day she returned to Edinburgh. This is yours, all yours, my darling daughter, she thought, looking around the pretty bedroom and beyond to the sunlight playing on the waters of the Firth of Forth. It all belonged to Roseanna. Even the view, which *did* look heavenly. Nothing, but nothing is ever going to spoil things for you, Roseanna, she silently promised. That is why I have come back here, so that you can enjoy what is yours. She walked to the window and pulled down the blind, shutting out the light. Then she walked back to the cot. She bent to kiss her sleeping daughter on the lips, then stood and looked down at the child. Nothing, I promise you, nothing . . .

When Roseanna was a year old Helen gave a birthday party for her. For two hours twenty toddlers aged from one to three wrecked havoc in a brightly painted basement playroom in Moray Place while the little girl whose party it was spent most of the time in her mother's arms, gurgling her protests only when a doll was torn from her hands and three boys climbed on to her rocking-horse all at once.

For the past year Helen had lived only for Roseanna and the little girl, who daily grew in strength and good looks, had made it had the happiest in her mother's life. It was impossible now to imagine life without Roseanna and even hard to remember quite what it was like before she was born. As she laid her precious daughter in her cot on the evening after her first birthday party it seemed as if Roseanna had always been there somewhere in her heart even before she was born.

'May I join the ladies?'

Helen looked up and over her shoulder and saw her husband standing at the door of the room.

'You may indeed. The ladies would be delighted,' she said, smiling.

Robert had delayed the start of a fraud trial in Dumfries so that he could put in an appearance at his daughter's first birthday party. Knowing only too well the precedence a man's career took over his private family life, Helen was overwhelmed by this gesture – particularly in view of his active ambitions to become Lord President now.

'I've just laid Roseanna down, but she's nowhere near sleeping. It's going to take time for the excitement of her party to wear off.' She looked down at her daughter, who was gazing up at her with smiling eyes. 'Come and say good night to daddy,' she said, leaning over the cot and gently lifting up her daughter.

Roseanna beamed at her father as she was handed into his arms.

'She's positively flirting with you,' said Helen, delighted by her daughter's early show of femininity.

'She's a woman of good taste,' replied Robert, whose black eyes were shining with pride.

Roseanna grabbed the red rose in his lapel and several petals came away in her hand. She looked puzzled for a moment, not understanding what had happened. Then she looked questioningly at her father.

'Oh, dear,' said Robert softly. 'It's not a very strong flower if it falls to pieces so easily, eh?' Reassured all was well, Roseanna grabbed the flower again and more petals came away in her hand. 'Oh, what a useless flower. Daddy will have to get a better flower than that.'

Roseanna laughed and let the petals fall from her tiny hand over the sleeve of her father's jacket on to the floor.

Watching the tender exchange between father and daughter, Helen smiled. With every passing day she knew she had been right to return to live with her husband for Roseanna's sake because of the interest he took in her. If he was not home early enough to spend some play time with her, he always looked in to say goodnight and wanted to know how she had spent her day; and when he returned from an out-of-town sitting of the High Court he always brought a present appropriate to her current needs.

It was about the same time the next evening, and shortly after Robert had telephoned from Dumfries to ask his wife about his daughter's day, that the housekeeper, Mary Douglas, entered Roseanna's bedroom and told Helen: 'Mr John Brodie's downstairs. I explained his Lordship was away in Dumfries, but he says he would like to have a word with your Ladyship.'

'Did he give you any indication of what it is about?' asked Helen.

'No, my Lady. And I simply said I would see if your Ladyship was available.'

It seemed a lifetime ago since Helen had even thought about John Brodie. John's name seemed to belong in the life of the person she had once been long ago. She looked at the clock. It was nearly seven. John Brodie must be on his way home to dinner.

'Show Mr Brodie into the drawing-room and tell him I will join him shortly,' she instructed Mary Douglas.

When the housekeeper had gone she leaned over the cot and tucked a small white Teddy Bear into her daughter's tiny arms.

'There, it's bedtime for Teddy too,' she whispered.

Roseanna cuddled the toy close. Sleep was already stealing into those jewel-green eyes as Helen drew her fingers through her daughter's pale golden hair.

'Good night, sweetheart,' she whispered. Then she stole from the room.

But she did not go straight downstairs to see John Brodie.

Instead she walked into her bedroom and she sat down at her dressing-table gazing at her reflection in the mirror. She was now thirty-nine-years old and she had been having relationships with men since she was eighteen. She had had a lover and three husbands in over twenty years, which was a lot more than most women, who only ever went to bed with their one and only husband. But for over a year now, since months before her daughter's birth, she had been quite celibate. Without love there was no point in being anything but celibate. Sex alone had never meant much to her. And since Roseanna's birth she simply had not wanted a man. She had her daughter and the supporting framework of what had become a wonderfully amiable marriage, and that was enough. She and Robert were enormously respectful of each other and each other's needs. United in their love for their daughter, they led separate lives in an atmosphere of mutual regard. When they dined alone, as they often did, Helen enjoyed the intellectual stimulation of her husband's brilliant legal brain. She sensed that he talked to her as he would do to another man, as an equal, and she felt enormously flattered because most lawyers – and most men – did not talk to their wives, whom they considered their intellectual inferiors. As the months had passed she sensed, too, that she had almost become his confidante in professional matters, and over the Easter holiday at Auchinvreck he had actually told her that his ambition was now to crown the Warrender judicial dynasty by becoming the first Lord President in the family when the current incumbent, Lord Carlyle, retired in four or five years time. He would need her help socially and diplomatically and she would give it gladly. But that was still ahead. For the moment her sense of completeness, of being on an emotional island with her daughter, pervaded the whole of her life. At present she had no wish to be anyone else, to play any other role, but Roseanna's mother. Of course she knew this would change; that her little girl would grow up and away from her and develop needs she could not satisfy. But until that happened, and for as long as she was the centre of her daughter's world and able to answer the child's every need, there was nothing else she wanted to do with her life.

Drawing a finger across her face to push back some stray hairs which had escaped from her chignon, she smiled at her reflection; there still wasn't a single line around her eyes or on her forehead or anywhere on her face or neck. Years of careful creaming and looking after her skin had brought their reward and she felt she had good reason to be pleased. She applied some fresh lipstick and sprayed the back of her ears and her wrists with Mitsouko. She really looked more like twenty-nine than nearly forty, she thought, secretly delighted as she descended the stairs.

John Brodie was standing by a window looking out over the gardens and his dark profile was lit by the evening

352

sunshine teeming through the astragalled panes as Helen swept into the drawing-room.

'I gather Mrs Douglas told you Robert's in Dumfries,' she said as her gaze met his in a wide-eyed, questioning look. It was the first time she had been alone with John Brodie since that fatal January evening over three years ago when he told her he was going back to his wife.

'I was aware that Robert was away on the circuit,' he said, taking slow, measured steps in the direction of the fireplace, which was banked with summer flowers. 'It is not him I called to see. It's you.'

Suddenly Helen was struck by the sheer bloody arrogance of this man, who had barged into her home unannounced when he knew her husband was away and made no apology for doing so. She resented his unapologetic self-possession. Mightily. And it was triggering the welter of emotions which were suddenly beginning to surge through her.

What if she had told him, three years ago, that she was expecting his child? What would he have done? He would still have abandoned her – and he would have wanted her to have a back-street abortion into the bargain, she felt sure. As the memory of her stillborn son reared up from the depths, the desire to avenge his death and destroy John Brodie's career surfaced anew in her heart and mind.

'Would you like a drink?' she asked in an even tone – and immediately wished she hadn't. She didn't want to drink with this man – she wanted him out of her house fast.

'Thanks,' he said, looking relieved.

'Whisky or sherry?'

'Whisky, please.'

She toppled a large measure into a sturdy tumbler and handed it to John Brodie.

'Won't you sit down?' she invited, raising a hand to

indicate the fireside chair facing the window so that she could position herself facing him with her back to the light and study every line and angle of his face.

'Cheers,' he sighed, raising his glass as he sank into the chair.

'Why did you want to see me?' she asked briskly, taking her own seat.

'Oh, Helen, I've missed you so,' he said miserably. 'I made the biggest mistake of my life when I let you go the second time.'

For a split second some spark of the old feeling shot through her heart, but it was instantly extinguished by the crushing pain of the reality she had suffered. She took a sip of her sherry to steady herself and with a supreme effort of will she managed to say with great dignity: 'The time was just never right for us.'

'It was at the end of the war, but I sacrificed it,' he admitted bitterly.

Helen felt a lump coming in her throat. This talk of the past was dangerous and threatening to undermine her completely. Despite the happiness Roseanna's birth had brought her, the time of which he spoke was still far too close to yesterday and the suffering she had so recently endured. She knew she must change the subject, move the conversation forward. She took another sip of her sherry and asked in a low voice: 'What is happening to you now, John?'

'My marriage is over in everything but name,' he said sulkily, taking a huge gulp of his drink. 'There's been nothing between Grace and I for years.'

'But you have two children,' said Helen. 'Surely you have some common ground there.'

'My wife has turned my children completely against me,' he complained.

'I'm sorry to hear that,' said Helen, glad she and

Robert had settled their differences so that Roseanna did not suffer.

'Oh, Helen, I can't go on like this, seeing you across a room or a dinner table!' He leaned forward towards her in his chair. 'Can't we be friends? Can't we meet . . . from time to time . . . and talk?'

So he wanted her back!

She drew her breath and swallowed and took a sip of her sherry. 'Where on earth could we possibly meet?' she managed to ask in a calm, even tone.

'I have a cottage in the Lammermuirs,' he said. 'It's all my own. My retreat. Grace never comes there. It's near Garvald and is quite isolated. I often go there at weekends.'

'Not to Craigendhu?'

'Rarely. My wife has built a most satisfactory social life for herself in the shires. Except when my presence is required in my official capacity, I do not go there. Though we must remain married, our lives are quite separate.'

'How long have you had this cottage?' she asked curiously.

'Just over a year. It was a ruin, but I have restored it. I live there like a monk. No one would ever know if we met there.'

Now she felt bitterly reminded of how he had always wanted their relationship to be cloaked in secrecy right from the start . . .

'There has to be a way for us Helen' he said. 'There just has to be.'

She looked at him, his face full of brooding as he looked down into his empty glass.

How could he even think of such a thing? Every good and decent thing that had ever been between them had perished with her son's stillbirth.

Once more she felt her heart would burst.

She swallowed to restrain her tears. 'No,' she said, getting up to ring the bell for Mary Douglas to show him out. 'There is *no* way for us. Everything we ever had died . . .'

'I had a visitor when you were away,' said Helen.

'Male or female?' asked Robert, taking a draught of his claret.

They were facing each other across the table in the ground-floor dining-room and the evening sunlight was playing on the white and pink and purple summer stocks banking the fireplace and filling the air with their sweet scent.

'Male.'

'Name of?'

'John Brodie.'

'And the nature of his business?'

'He wants us to be friends.'

'You and he?'

'Yes.'

Robert's matter-of-fact manner was taking Helen's breath away and rapidly diffusing the ammunition she thought she had in this piece of news.

'Can't say it really surprises me or the way he seems to have gone about approaching you in my absence,' he said equably, cutting a piece of Stilton.

'Why not?' demanded Helen.

'My dear, lovely wife,' said Robert patiently. 'It is well known among his colleagues at the College of Justice that John Brodie is among its more miserably married members. But unlike most of those similarly placed, Brodie has not made any casual or permanent arrangement with any other woman and is not known to visit our local house of ill-repute. So in my view it has only been a matter of time before he approached

356

you about making some kind of clandestine arrangement.'

Helen was shocked and disappointed at her husband's indifference. And her pride was hurt, too. She had expected Robert to be outraged and to chalk up John Brodie's approach to her somewhere at the back of his mind as a score to be settled with a man she had sensed increasingly that he disliked.

'He has a house, a cottage near Garvald, and he wants me to meet him there,' she said, desperately trying to stoke flames of fury in her husband.

'Oh, that pile of stones he's been restoring. His hovel in the hills as he calls it. I might have known what it was about. There's always some ulterior motive to whatever Brodie does.'

'How do you feel about it?'

'It's not my friendship he's seeking,' said Robert.

'But you're my husband . . . at least in name . . .' Helen faltered, nearly choking at his indifference and feeling pain at the sham of her marriage.

'Yes, my dear, and very proud and happy to be, and proud, too, of the daughter you have given me,' said Robert. 'But you are a young woman, Helen, and I have accepted ever since you returned to live under my roof with me that one day you might want to take a friend . . . or a lover. I understand.'

'You mean you don't mind . . .' Helen's words trailed away and there was a lump in her throat.

'Helen, I have no right to mind,' said Robert. 'Though I must confess I'll be a bit surprised it you have much truck with Brodie in light of his past conduct towards you. But be warned. Don't get any fancy ideas about him leaving his wife this time. Whatever their private differences, Brodie and his wife are very much a couple so far as his career is concerned. And they both pursue it socially

357

extremely actively in the shires even more than they do in Edinburgh. Members of Parliament and Lords Lieutenant and any members of the aristocracy with the slightest scrap of influence are regularly and lavishly entertained at Craigendhu.'

'But he says he hardly every goes there and it's mainly Grace who entertains.'

'In light of what he would appear to have in mind with you, it's only natural that's what he'd tell you. But he's there most weekends. And so's his wife,' said Robert, quaffing his claret. 'What he's after is a safe seat in Parliament so that he can become Lord Advocate and make it straight to the top from there by getting the Secretary of State for Scotland's blessing to appoint himself Lord President.'

'But you want to be Lord President.'

'Oh, I can stand a bit of competition. Makes life more interesting,' said Robert, reaching for the decanter and replenishing his glass.

For the second time in her life Robert Warrender's implacable self-possession was undoing her – coupled with his indifference. She had hoped for outrage and fury at John Brodie's arrogance. At the very least she had expected him to disapprove and save her from falling into John Brodie's arms a third time. But the way he was cheerfully leaving her to make up her own mind about whether or not to tangle with John again, while mildly warning her of the dangers like a kindly uncle, pained her to the marrow. She felt alone again as she had not done for a long time.

Which was exactly what Robert Warrender wanted her to feel . . .

The clouds had parted, seeming to promise settled days ahead and smoke was rising blue and straight as arrows from the scattered houses as Helen drove her little pre-war Austin 7 furiously into the Lammermuir Hills towards the pink sandstone village of Garvald.

Her heart was still wounded at Robert's indifference as to whether or not she resumed her affair with John Brodie. How could he love their daughter, Roseanna, so much and be so utterly unaffected by her? The opposite of love wasn't hate; it was indifference. She was driving into the hills to make love to John Brodie as an act of revenge on the husband who cared so little for her. Then she would go home and tell him what she had done!

She was nearly choking over everything . . . over men's supreme indifference to women . . . over the way men were bonded from childhood into an all-powerful brotherhood which ensured their first loyalty was always to each other . . . over how they covered up for each other. Men only wanted women to bear and rear their children and clean up after them. Men were all pigs, who simply dumped the jobs they didn't want to do on women and treated them as unpaid servants.

Her emotions had been in a turmoil ever since John Brodie had come marauding just over a week ago, stirring up painful old memories, destroying the peace of mind and heart she had enjoyed this past year. He had forced her to face up to the sham of her marriage and she hated him for that. She thought of turning back, standing him up. But now that she was nearly there she decided she might as well press on and see what his 'hovel in the hills' was really like.

She looked at her watch. It was twenty-past two. She was already twenty minutes late. John would be waiting for her anxiously. Good, she thought.

In no time she reached Garvald. She pulled up outside the one hotel to check the directions John had given her on the telephone about getting to his cottage and she was puzzling over her notes when she saw a man in an old brown tweed jacket and plus-fours and tweed cap pulled down on his head emerge from the hotel.

'Excuse me,' she said, rolling down the window, 'I wonder . . .'

'Yes,' he said, smiling broadly. 'I know the way. I thought you might find it a bit confusing so I decided to hang about the hotel and keep a lookout for you. Will I get in?'

'Yes,' said Helen, opening the passenger door. But a chill descended on her heart as he slid on to the seat beside her. Studying his profile, she saw a ruthlessness in the carved angular structure of his bones and a determination in the jut of his jaw that she had never noticed before. This man cared for no one but himself. It was there before her eyes. All her desire to avenge her husband's indifference vanished and she sincerely wished she had not come.

'Ah, you've brought Roseanna,' he said, noticing the carry-cot.

'I thought the hill air might do her good,' said Helen in an even tone.

'Yes,' he said. 'I'm sure it will. It was a good idea to bring her.'

He guided her out of the village and at last they pulled up outside a whitewashed cottage with a red pantiled roof. Smoke was rising from a chimney.

'This is it,' said John with a proprietorial air, opening the passenger door.

The view from the high roof of Lammermuir over the vast floor of the Plain of Lothian and the great sweep with which the Firth of Forth embraced the North Sea was landscape on the grand scale. Half of Scotland could be seen towering away to the north in a magnificent spectacle of blue and purple mountains.

She looked at John surveying the scene. When a man owned the land over which he could tramp for miles it affected the way he held himself when he stood on it, giving him a proprietorial air, endowing his gestures with an assured pride, imbueing him with a powerful grace. She had seen it in Robert at Auchinvreck and in the late Lord Macrae when he tramped his Border acres; but Harry Dunlop had not possessed it, and nor had John Brodie until now. Watching his dark profile she cynically wondered where ownership of the land came in his priorities. Obviously it would come after his precious career. But was it more or less important than his brilliant social life? And was it fifty or was it sixty places ahead of the importance he attached to love? It was then she realised how deeply she loathed this man . . .

The desire to destroy him, to bring his brilliant career tumbling to the dust had lurked somewhere in the depths of her heart and mind ever since she had returned to Edinburgh. But now it rose like a brilliant, bright arrow within her. If it was the last thing she did, if she made no other achievements with the rest of her life, she would destroy the brilliant career of this arrogant man who had fathered and then been responsible for the death of her firstborn child.

'Shall we go in?' he asked turning to look at her.

'Yes,' she said without smiling.

'Let me give you a hand with the cot,' he said. 'It's just like she's *our* child,' he added, smiling at the sleeping Roseanna as they each took a handle of the cot and walked towards the house.

Helen looked at him and felt sick. Her sense of repugnancy for this man was increasing by the minute.

John led the way into the sitting-room where a coal fire glowed and they gently laid the cot on a plump beige moquette sofa. Two matching armchairs sat on either side of the fire and an oak dining-table and four chairs stood at the bow window curtained in white net.

'Like to see the rest?' he asked.

Helen nodded and they crossed the hall to where two bedrooms had been furnished simply yet comfortably.

'Some tea to refresh you from your journey?' he asked back in the hall.

Helen now felt she had cheapened herself by phoning him and coming here. She had only done it to spite her husband and now all she wanted was to get away. But Roseanna would probably wake up in a minute and it would be easier to change her here than it would in the car.

'Yes, I'll have a cup of tea,' she said. 'I'll just get Roseanna's things from the car whilst you're making it.'

Left alone, John returned to the sitting-room and looked down at the sleeping Roseanna.

The child was lying on her tummy, her white Teddy just beyond the reach of her tiny outstretched hand.

He knelt beside the cot and gazed at her, marvelling at her perfection. For a moment he imagined Roseanna was *his* child, *their* child. He had wanted them to have a family. He had had big plans for them and they had talked about it. But then he had come back to Edinburgh . . . Still, if Helen had been pregnant, if it had happened 'accidentally' as it did to a lot of people, he would not have left her. They would have made a life together, a life he now needed more with every passing day.

He saw Roseanna was stirring in her carry-cot and, getting up, he bent over and picked her up. She felt soft, round, just like a little doll in his arms. But the movement had disturbed her sleep. Her eyes flew open and, finding herself in the arms of a stranger, she uttered a piercing cry.

'Shush . . . Mummy will be here in a minute,' he murmured. He began to pace the room, cuddling her close.

Roseanna was bawling at the top of her voice when Helen came back into the cottage. At the door of the sitting-room she saw John was pacing the floor with Roseanna in his arms.

The sight ripped her deepest, rawest wounds wide open and she was powerless to stop the way her face creased in anguish. This was what could have been, *should* have been! John Brodie should have been around to carry their son the way he was carrying her daughter.

'There, there, Roseanna, Mummy's back,' said John, crossing the room towards Helen.

Helen snatched her daughter.

'She woke up,' he said sheepishly.

'I can see that,' said Helen roughly. All she wanted to do was to get herself and her child far, far away from here.

'What is it, Helen?' he asked, looking puzzled.

'We can't stay. It was a mistake coming here,' she said tersely.

'But what is it? Everything seemed all right a moment ago,' he said. Her eyes met his in a moment of blinding clarity and truth. It was then she knew that even if she told him now about their son, all that would concern him would be whether Robert knew and how it might affect his chances of becoming Lord President. 'There has to be a way for us, Helen.'

'No, no! Never,' she shouted, her voice shrill.

'Why not? We found the love that people dream of all their lives. We found the grand, enduring thing – '

'And a fat lot you have ever cared about it, John Brodie!' she blazed. 'You've never had the guts to stand up and fight for it. All you have ever cared about is your career. Every time you have had to choose between our love

363

and your career, you have always sacrificed our love. It has always only ever been second or third or umpteenth best to you. You loved me once, but you married Grace Mitchell for the sake of your career. You loved me a second time, but you went back to her for the sake of your career. You have ruined my life twice. You will not do it for a third time – and you will certainly not do it to my daughter's!'

'But there is no need for anyone's life to be ruined, Helen. We can meet here secretly. No one will ever know. I've *made* this place for us.'

'So you can have some hole-in-the-corner affair with me, John Brodie? Do you really think that's what I want? You don't know *anything* about love, John Brodie. All you want is someone you can pick up when it suits you, when it's not going to damage your precious career. Well, you can't have it. You can't have it. Not any more.'

'Please, Helen – '

'Tell me something, John Brodie. After you abandoned me in London, did you ever ask yourself what happened to me? Did you ever give me even one tiny thought?'

'A day never passed when you were not in my thoughts,' he said. 'I thought about you all the time.'

'And you hoped I'd be sitting around waiting for you to pick me up again when the fancy took you? Well, it's not on, John Brodie. Not now. And not ever again.'

She shot past him, gathered up the carry-cot and fled.

The depth of Helen's bitterness and grief had shaken John Brodie to the core and he realised he had been very selfish in thinking only of himself.

Her pain must have been far greater than his when he married Lord President Mitchell's daughter, but he had at least had the compensation of children and family life while Helen had no one. He had simply closed his heart and mind to her pain, telling himself she was young and rich and beautiful and would get over him and meet someone else. Yet he had been incandescent with jealousy and rage when Henry Macrae had announced his engagement to her and for once he could not take back what Henry had at will when he wanted it. Then death gave him a second chance of happiness and again he had walked away from her.

At forty-eight, John Brodie KC, Dean of the Faculty of Advocates, was poised to climb the highest wires of his profession. He was automatically every solicitor's first choice for the most glamorous *causes célèbres* – the crimes of passion, the most scandalous divorces and the big commercial cases. His assiduous cultivation of his political contacts had now put a seat in Parliament within his grasp and it was likely to be his at the next general election. From there his appointment as Lord Advocate would be a matter of course and, by tradition, he would then step into the top job of Lord President of the Court of Session and Lord Justice-General of Scotland when the present holder of that combined office and dual title, Lord Carlyle, retired. And his childhood promise to his father to become 'the most powerful bastard lawyer' in Scotland would be fulfilled.

Yet for all his professional success and glittering prospects there was a hollowness in his heart . . .

'*After you abandoned me in London, did you ever ask yourself what happened to me? Did you ever give me even one tiny thought?*'

Helen's question ran around in his mind again. And there had been a look he could not fathom in her eyes as she asked it. It was true a day had never passed when he had not thought of her. But it had only been in relation to himself and almost in an abstract way; he had wondered if she missed him as he had missed her – but he had never

never thought about what she might be suffering, never allowed his mind or imagination to picture her.

Now he knew her grief must have been very great and he had been shocked by the depth of the bitterness in her heart towards him.

Yet there had to be a way for them, another chance somehow, he thought, his face dark as he watched the storm clouds gathering over the moor.

Helen drove for miles and hours – mindlessly criss-crossing the moor, not knowing where she was going except she wasn't going home to her indifferent, uncaring husband.

Half-way through the afternoon she found herself in the whitewashed village of Gifford, which nestled at the base of the hills. She had a cup of tea at the Tweeddale Arms Hotel and gave Roseanna her bottle.

Afterwards she strolled along the green that had once been a sheep pound towards the Gifford Water, carrying Roseanna in her arms and the sky was completely clouded over and the hills lost in mist as she got back into the Baby Austin and drove towards Haddington. She was in the mood to stretch her legs again and wander among the small shops clustered around the old Town House and its surrounding streets, but it meant carrying Roseanna again and the little girl was becoming restive at the number of times she was being lifted up and down.

'All right, we won't get out here,' said Helen, seeing her daughter's slightly flushed face. She was going to have to find somewhere to feed and change Roseanna.

From Haddington she took the road across country and though harvest time was still almost two months away, golden ears of corn were already beginning to cut a glorious swathe across the plain, taking on a weird, slightly haunted look in the strange light of the darkening sky. The rain already shrouding the hills would soon strike the plain.

The shops were still open when she reached North Berwick. She bought an ice-cream wafer from a café in the High Street before she drove along the sea front, where she parked the car and sat for ages slowly licking ice-cream and staring out to sea, her emotions tossing as restlessly as the incoming tide.

She remembered coming here with Henry and his parents on Sunday afternoons . . . how after lunch at the Marine Hotel she and Henry would wander hand-in-hand by the sea, looking out to the islets of Fidra and the Lamb and Craigleith and the bizarre cliffs of the Bass Rock. Now it seemed both yesterday and long ago, and a wave of nostalgia washed over her.

Just after six o'clock she booked into the Marine Hotel, giving her name as Mrs Warrender as the Identity Card, which everyone had carried since 1939, did not give the prefix 'Lady', and her address as Great Western Terrace, Glasgow.

Roseanna needed to be fed and changed and when she had done that and got her daughter off to sleep, Helen slipped downstairs into the dining-room. A waiter led her to a table by a window and placed a menu before her but her stomach was knotted and churning with tension and she didn't feel much like eating, so she ordered a simple salmon salad.

But she only picked at it before she left the restaurant and retired to her room.

Roseanna was sleeping soundly now. Looking down at her daughter, Helen decided that for her sake she had better go home. She had no more fresh nappies and it really wasn't right to deprive her.

But she wouldn't leave until it was dark. That would at least give her husband the fright he deserved.

It was shortly after eleven o'clock when she paid her bill, checked out of the hotel and set off towards Edinburgh.

The rain was now coming down in sheets and blowing in from the sea and the little car skidded all over the oily surface of the road. She could only drive at tortoise pace and she was nearly blown off the road as she swung round Gosford Bay. To escape the coastal gales she turned inland and it was well after midnight before she came within the lights of Edinburgh.

A clock somewhere over and beyond Charlotte Square was booming out one in the morning as Helen tiptoed up the steps and put her key quietly in the front door.

'And just what time of the night do you think this is to come home?' bellowed Robert, who was standing in the hall, his face flushed.

'Count yourself lucky I've come home at all because I nearly didn't!' cried Helen, startled to find him waiting for her.

'You're a grown woman, Helen. If you want to stay out half the night, that's up to you. But you're not keeping my daughter out at all hours.'

'Roseanna is sleeping,' said Helen in a more reasonable tone. 'So if you will keep your voice down and excuse me I will take her upstairs to her bedroom.'

'Mrs Douglas can do that,' said Robert, taking a firm grip of his wife's arm as Mary Douglas emerged from the top of the basement stairs. 'Mary, take my daughter's cot from Lady Warrender. You and I are going to have a talk,' he told Helen, marching her into the library and closing the door. 'Just where have you been?' he demanded, letting go of her arm.

'Out,' she said. There was an air of menace about Robert's manner, which was frightening her and she

368

was starting to shake. 'I've had a terrible journey. I need a drink.'

'Once I've got a few answers.'

His eyes locked on hers and their relationship at that moment was exactly that of interrogator and witness. She was deeply thankful she had not made love to John Brodie but had been repelled by him – because there was not the slightest shadow of a doubt that the Honourable Lord Warrender, King's Counsel, Supreme Court Judge and Senator of the College of Justice had the will and means and wherewithal to get the truth, the whole truth and nothing but the truth out of her.

'I went to visit John Brodie at his cottage in the Lammermuir Hills,' she said in a calm voice.

Silence.

'Pray continue,' he said in the kind of voice he would use in court.

'I didn't stay very long.' Her voice began to wobble as her jagged, churned emotions produced a lump in her throat. 'It wasn't that I felt guilty or felt I shouldn't have gone when I got there.' She swallowed to stop the tears. 'It was that I simply didn't want to be there. I didn't want to be anywhere near John Brodie or have anything to do with him. I felt repelled by him and everything about him. We had a terrible row and I fled.'

'What was your row about?'

'The way he thought he could pick me up and drop me when he felt like it.'

'Did you tell him about your son?'

'No . . . I didn't want him to know. I felt I might have done if I stayed any longer. That was why I left in a hurry,' she said as her tears broke. 'I was very, very upset when I left there, but I didn't want to come home. I drove for miles and miles around the moors and then I drove around the plain and eventually I found myself in North

Berwick. I wasn't going to come home at all. I booked into the Marine Hotel as Mrs Warrender and gave my Glasgow address. But Roseanna needed to come home. So for her sake . . .' She dabbed her eyes before she burst out: 'And do you know what drove me to go and see John Brodie and why I didn't want to come home? It was your indifference, the fact you simply didn't care whether I made love to John Brodie or not, whether I lived or died,' she cried. 'I know our marriage is no longer a real one, but you *are* my friend. At least, that's how I think of you, and you could have supported me when I needed a friend.'

A different kind of silence now lent its sweetness to the air, like the sweetness of the scented earth after the rain. And they stood beholding each other, far apart.

'It has been a stormy evening,' he said eventually in an entirely different tone. 'Would you care for a brandy?'

'Yes, I need one,' she said, sensing the storm was over between them, too.

Robert handed her the glass of brandy. 'That will help to calm you down,' he said. He took the seat facing her across the fire. 'I'm glad you're safely back. Helen. I was worried almost out of my mind. I nearly called the police.'

'The police?' She wrinkled her brow.

'Yes. My heart, my world, my life would have been shattered if I had lost you and our daughter in some terrible accident in the storm,' he said. 'I care for you very deeply, Helen, as deeply as it is possible for a man of my inclinations to care for a woman. If it had been possible for me to love a woman, it would have been you.'

She saw the tender light in his eyes and it was then she realised that this strange, complex, fascinating man was the protector she and Roseanna both needed, and she felt they had truly come home to him tonight . . .

* * *

370

When she had gone, Robert poured a large cognac into a balloon glass, sank into his comfortable leather fireside chair and lit his first cigar of the night. He had been too deeply concerned about his wife and child to settle to write the judgment he had needed to write all evening. Now they were safely back under his roof he would begin work in a minute. But as he watched the fragrant smoke rise over the mantelpiece the question uppermost in his mind was whether his wife now hated John Brodie enough to act as the vital accomplice he would need when the time came . . .

PART FIVE

1952 to 1972

Chapter Thirty-One

Edinburgh – October, 1952

In October, 1952 Lord President Carlyle collapsed and died on the golf course at Muirfield. By tradition, his job went to the Lord Advocate.

So it is now yours, thought Grace Brodie triumphantly, gazing down her dinner table past the glances of her guests towards her husband.

At last all her hard work and years of sacrifice, all her entertaining and cultivating of the 'right' people would be rewarded.

Already the jockeying for position had begun and she could see the anxious eyes of the wives. She returned their glances with a gracious smile, which took on a gloating quality when it met the emerald eyes of the whore who had seduced both Henry Macrae and Robert Warrender into marrying her.

'Do you mean John automatically gets the job just because he's the Lord Advocate?' Helen asked Robert.

They were sipping cognacs by the fire in the library.

'He's not forced to take it,' said Robert. 'By tradition it is offered to him. He can turn it down. But no Lord Advocate ever has.'

'There's always a first time,' said Helen. Her loathing for John and her desire to destroy him had been carefully and subtly nurtured by her husband over the past few years and now he was delighted by her outrage that Brodie seemed to be getting away with everything unscathed. 'He's such a hypocrite, the way he stood for Labour just to get a safe seat in Parliament so that he could become Lord Advocate!'

'Be fair, Helen,' Robert cautioned, deliberately trying to seem reasonable. 'He was approached by them and offered the job and the seat because they had no one when their last man died.'

'Well, Graeme Wilson's not going to like it.'

'As Secretary of State for Scotland, Graeme's going to have to work with him, whether or not he likes it.'

'Graeme has never liked John. Couldn't he stop it?'

'Oh, technically the job is in his gift and that of the Prime Minister,' said Robert, taking a draught of his cognac. 'He would have to find some very good reason why John Brodie should not be appointed Lord President.'

'Perhaps he will . . .' said Helen, laying down her glass and getting up. '*You* should be Lord President,' she added, kissing her husband on the forehead. 'Good-night.'

'Good-night, my dear.'

He watched her leave the room and close the door behind her. Then he refilled his glass and lit a fresh Monte Cristo No 4.

A serene smile lit his eyes as he sat back in his chair and watched the fragrant smoke rise. He felt confident he had brought his lovely wife's hatred of her former lover to fruition at just the right moment . . .

The Edinburgh skyline from the Calton Hill in the east to the Pentlands in the West was clear in the midday October light as Helen and Graeme Wilson walked beneath trees stripped bare and ready for winter.

'. . . and to this day white flowers are laid every day

on my little son's grave,' Helen concluded her story, tears filling her eyes.

'Oh, Helen, why didn't you tell me at the time?' said Graeme reproachfully, placing his hands on her shoulders. 'You didn't need to be alone. I'd have come to see you. I would have wanted to be there for you. And Alison would as well.'

'I didn't want anyone to know. I was so ashamed. I was just like . . .' but she stopped herself in time before she betrayed her mother's secret.

'The Prime Minister will be most concerned and I'm glad I know now. If the newspapers ever got hold of this and John was Lord President there would be a terrible scandal which would bring the whole system into disrepute,' said Graeme. 'Of course, John will have to be told the reason why he can't get the job . . .' His eyes pinioned hers.

'I think it's about time he knew.'

The day after the funeral and burial of Lord Carlyle, the appointment of Robert Robertson Warrender as Lord President of the Court of Session and Lord Justice-General of Scotland was announced in the *Edinburgh Gazette* . . .

Chapter Thirty-Two

Edinburgh and Sussex – October and November, 1952

John Brodie's expression was haggard as he stood with his back to the blazing log fire in Helen's drawing-room waiting for her to join him.

He was still in a state of shock from the events of the past few days and the pain and humiliation he had suffered in the Secretary of State for Scotland's office in St Andrew's House.

'Dram?' Graeme had asked as he entered the room.

'Not yet,' said John, smiling and deciding he would leave the celebration drink with the Scottish Secretary until after he had seen the Prime Minister and his appointment as Lord President had been announced in the *Edinburgh Gazette*.

As Graeme took a call, John crossed the room and sat down by the window. Glancing around the beautifully furnished office, he felt glad he not chosen the precarious political route to high office. Graeme could be robbed of the trappings of power at the next general election – whereas the Lord President kept his job until he either died or retired. At last, real power was about to be his. He would be able to initiate changes in the law, appoint the Queens' Counsel, set the whole style of the Supreme Courts as well as preside over the Appeal Courts and he would have his own senior and junior counsel to do his legal legwork. At that moment, as Graeme replaced the telephone and crossed the room to join him by the window he felt replete and all his sacrifice seemed worthwhile.

'Ah, John, the Prime Minister has asked me to have a word with you . . .' said Graeme, dropping easily into the chair beside him. And John knew instantly that something had gone wrong. All his faculties keened. 'He wants you to know how much he appreciates the splendid job you've been doing as Lord Advocate and if he felt he could offer you the appointment of Lord President purely on professional ability, he would do so. But the PM has to take a wider view – '

'What Establishment figure wants to steal my clothes?' John demanded, unable to rein his tongue in the face of a sudden possible fatal blow to his dearest, most cherished hopes. It was a cry from the root of him as all his old childhood feelings about being an outsider and not belonging rose from the depths of him.

'No one,' said Graeme. 'That's not the problem.'

They stared at each other in silence for a moment.

'Then what is?' he asked in a more reasonable tone.

'The Prime Minister is afraid, and I have to say I agree with him, that if the Press ever found out about the son Lady Warrender bore you at the end of the war – '

'S-son? *What* son?'

Their eyes met.

'*Your* son, John, who was stillborn on August 16, 1945 in Rustington and given the name of Thomas Randolph Macrae.'

A lump that felt the size of a rock filled John Brodie's throat. She had let him walk away from her and never told him! And she had never told him since! The memory of how she had snatched Roseanna from his arms and fled from his cottage in Lammermuir flashed across his brain. He had known then that she hated him, but she had never said a word! Instead she had nursed her hatred and waited until now – and when he thought he held the whole world in his hand she had snatched it from him. He had the sensation of the world opening up beneath his feet and of falling into a deep, bottomless chasm.

'What proof do you have?' he asked, bleakly.

'The word of both Lady Warrender and Lord Warrender, who accompanied his wife on a visit to your son's grave shortly before they were married.'

So all along Robert Warrender had known. Both of them had been able to laugh at all his wife's manoeuvrings and his own power plays, knowing they could bring him down and put an end to all his hopes and dreams and plans whenever they chose. How they must have laughed when he became a Labour MP so he could become Lord Advocate!

John knew he was beaten. He also knew the same utter humiliation his father had known the night he was blackballed by the Cockburn Club. Just like his father, when he reached for the pinnacle, confident it was within his grasp, it had been snatched from him – and he had hit the ground face first without a parachute. What he had feared ever since that night – that he, too, would not be good enough for that society to which he aspired to belong – had now come to pass. He knew now he didn't belong any more than his father had done. And the son Helen had borne him had simply been used as an excuse to exclude him.

He looked around the room at the Secretary of State's fine desk and furniture and all the trappings of high office which he had given his life to achieve and suddenly none of it mattered any more.

All that did was finding his son's grave.

He rose and walked from the room.

The next day he resigned as Lord Advocate and told

the Prime Minister he wished to give up his seat in Westminster and apply for the Chiltern Hundreds . . .

Helen had dressed with very special care in a full-skirted taffeta afternoon dress for her meeting with John Brodie. The delicious sweetness of revenge had flooded her soul for days – ever since she had heard her husband's appointment as Lord President announced on the one o'clock news on the wireless. She had promised herself a day like this ever since John Brodie had walked out on her at the Savoy coming up eight years ago – a day when they would sit down and talk about the son she had borne him. And she would be the victor and he the vanquished.

Now, as she swept into her drawing-room and saw his haggard face and how he had aged almost overnight, she could almost taste the full bouquet of vengeance. And it was finer and better than the very best champagne. The years she had had to wait for this moment now seemed worth waiting.

'Tea will be in a minute,' she announced, extending a hand to him before she dropped gracefully into a chair with her back to the light so she could see every wrinkle of agony on his face. 'Do sit down,' she invited as Mary Douglas entered the room and laid a tray with tea and biscuits on a low table before them.

But he remained standing and waited until the housekeeper had departed and closed the door behind her before he demanded: 'Why didn't you tell me you were going to have my baby? Why did you wait until now?'

'Because you wouldn't have wanted to know,' she said, seeing the pain in his haggard eyes. 'You deserve to suffer – even more than you are doing right now.'

'I had a right to know,' he said.

'Would it have made any difference to your plans?

381

Would it have stopped you returning to your wife? Would you have stayed with us?'

'Whatever I did I would have stayed in touch with you. And I would have made provision for you and your . . . our . . . child.'

'I don't believe you. If you're not lying you're certainly deceiving yourself,' she said, getting up. 'Because I know what you would have done. Your first thought would have been for yourself and how an illegitimate child might affect your career. You would have wanted me to have a backstreet abortion, John Brodie, that's what you'd have wanted.' She felt her anger rising now, the pent-up rage of years surging from the depths, not just for her son but for their lost happiness, the years of joy they had lost because he had sacrificed them and thrown them away. 'Was it really worth it, John?' she cried. 'Throwing away what we had? Not once, but twice.'

'Why didn't you tell me about our son before now?'

'Because you nearly destroyed me. And, after he died, I vowed that one day I would use his death to destroy you. That's why I've waited until now,' she cried triumphantly, seeing the agony in his eyes. 'What you are suffering now is nothing to what I suffered when I lost our baby!'

'You said "our".' He repeated the word as if he was drawing some comfort from it.

Helen stared at him for a long moment.

'You nearly told me about Thomas once, when you came to my cottage in Lammermuir. It was when you found me carrying Roseanna in my arms. It reminded you of what could have been. *That's* why you fled.'

'Why did you do it, John? Twice?' Her voice was softer now.

'Helen, I no longer know. I thought it was right at the time. It was what my father wanted.'

'Your father?' She was bewildered.

382

'Yes. But it doesn't matter now.'

'But it does! What did *he* have to do with it?'

'Oh, a long time ago, when I was a little boy, I promised him I would become the most powerful lawyer in Scotland. But I don't want to talk about it now.'

She remembered what he had said the day they met all those years ago on the sunlit deck of the *Monadhliath*. '. . . my father's money could never buy my parents acceptance in the highest social circles in Edinburgh. Money alone never can in Edinburgh. You have to *belong*. Lawyers are the proprietors of Edinburgh and form the first circle . . .'

She remembered how handsome and full of promise he had seemed that day. And she looked at him now, and all the promise was in the past . . .

'Oh, John,' she cried, 'if we cannot trust our hearts, if we cannot trust what we know to be true, we are nothing at all and our lives are doomed to be lived out in misery and pain.' A terrible sense of loss was beginning to fill her.

'I want to see my son's grave,' said John as if he hadn't heard her.

She looked at the anguish etched in the lines around his eyes and his mouth. And then she looked beyond the window at the gardens and the trees and the birds soaring high above. Then her gaze returned to the crumpled figure of John Brodie. It was then she knew she no longer had any quarrel with this man, that all pain and sorrow had been drained and washed away, her anger and hate and desire for revenge were all spent. She was almost free at last of the painful legacy of their love – but not quite . . . And now what she needed more than anything was to go with him back to Rustington so they could mourn their lost son together . . .

John was waiting in the shadow of a tall pine, when the

limousine which had brought Helen from London pulled up outside the cemetery gates.

'Helen . . .' He bowed as she stepped on to the pavement.

She returned his bow without speaking or smiling and he followed her through the gates.

She led the way along the paths and then she saw them . . . the fresh white flowers which had been laid earlier in the day on the beautifully-tended grave of Thomas Randolph Macrae. Charles Quinn continued to be totally reliable in seeing that her instructions were carried out.

She stepped forward quickly and stood alone before her son's grave, the sunlight playing on her golden hair, her heart reaching out and wanting to call him up and tell him she had brought someone to see him. His father.

But he was no longer there, and his little grave was only a memory.

'But he is happy now in the place where he has gone . . .' Robert's words, spoken on the day she had let her son go at last, came back to her. And her heart filled with tears of happiness for Thomas. He had brought her joy as well as grief — joy in the days when he lived within her and kicked her stomach wall and she had spoken to him.

She turned and looked at John through her tears. 'Come,' she said, raising a hand to beckon him to her side. He stepped forward and took his place by her. 'This is his place,' she whispered.

She watched John look at the inscription on the stone: Thomas Randolph Macrae. Stillborn August 16, 1945.

He bowed his head and in a moment she saw tears washing down his face.

It was then she knew there could be no revenge in love . . . that they had both lost when they lost Thomas Randolph Macrae . . . Perhaps that was why he had been stillborn . . . perhaps he knew they did not have enough love to allow him to live, that neither of them had really deserved him.

John looked at her and reached for her hands.

'I'd like ... I'd like ... if I may,' he said, 'to come back on my own ... from time to time to see him ... Would that be all right?'

'Yes,' she whispered. 'Yes, yes, of course. He was your son, too. Our son.'

It was then she knew that, while her grief was over, John Brodie's was only just beginning ...

Afterwards they walked along the shore and sat under the tamarisk trees just as they used to do. The tide was now romping home and small children and their parents were building sand-castles.

'I nearly died,' she said. 'Four months after Thomas died I nearly died, too. I had no wish to live. They found me one afternoon after I had been to his grave lying in sand with the tide rolling in. I was ill for a very long time afterwards. And it was when I was convalescent that Robert found me.'

'Oh, Helen', he cried, reaching for her hands. 'What have we done with our lives? How did we lose our way?'

'We lost because, for you, your career was the greatest force in your life and you never had the courage love needs. Instead, you were driven by fear. So you threw away all that was best in our lives.'

She was emotionally exhausted now, as she looked his profile dark and brooding against the light. But she was glad she had come here with him this day. Because she had needed to. And now her heart was purged of all the bitterness it had held for him for so long. They were at peace with each other – and she was free at last of her burden of pain.

* * *

385

He watched her car drive up Sea Lane till it was lost from sight.

A strange feeling filled his soul. He wasn't quite sure what it was, except that it was different to anything he had known.

His life, the life he had constructed for himself through all these years had seemed to end at his son's grave, his brilliant career come to dust where his own flesh lay. Whatever it was, he was glad he had lived this day and Helen had come back with with him to where they had once been so happy.

In some strange way he did not quite understand, he felt everything would get better from now on.

Chapter Thirty-Three

Sussex, Scotland and London – 1952 to 1967

John remained in Rustington for several days visiting his son's grave; taking his own flowers to lie beside those ordered by Helen, retracing walks he had shared with her, reliving all he had so carelessly thrown away.

He had no idea what he would do with the rest of his life. He was only fifty-two and he was still the most dazzling and charismatic Queen's Counsel of his generation, and when he got back to Edinburgh he was inundated with approaches which kept him busy all throughout the winter.

The following year, shortly after her Coronation in Westminster Abbey in June, the new Queen Elizabeth paid a State visit to Scotland and John was caught up in the round of parties and balls that went on for a week. But for the first time in his life he had no cause, no purpose to which to devote himself and so his spirits often were heavy.

In the summer evenings he liked to work in the ground-floor dining-room where he could enjoy the light playing on the garden. Catching up on his required reading, he picked up a copy of Hansard for July 1, when Members of Parliament had thrown out the Bill to suspend the death penalty for five years.

'That is so wrong,' he muttered to himself. 'The death

penalty should be abolished.'

As he closed the report his heart gave a sudden leap and his spirits suddenly lifted. All at once he knew what he wanted to do with the rest of his life. Now he would make good the life of his stillborn son by saving the lives of grown men. *That* would be his atonement.

For the next twelve years the abolition of hanging became John Brodie's *raison d'être* as he campaigned and lobbied, addressed public meetings, wrote pamphlets and spoke regularly on radio and television on the subject. But the road to reform was long and hard. In February 1955, Members of Parliament voted to keep the death penalty but two months later there was a public outcry when Ruth Ellis, a one-time model, was hanged for the murder of her faithless lover, and the following February the Commons voted in favour of abolition. But the Bill was defeated in the House of Lords, who voted overwhelmingly against it.

Yet times were changing. The Homicide Act of 1957 abolished the death penalty except for murder of policemen and murder accompanied by armed robbery and finally in the more liberal climate of the 1960s, both Houses of Parliament approved the abolition of the death penalty and on November 8th, 1965, it became law.

In recognition of his work in achieving it, John was made a Life Peer in the New Year's Honours of 1966, taking the title Baron Brodie of Craigendhu in the County of Inverness-shire.

His sponsors on the April day he took his seat in the House of Lords were the Life Baron Warrender of Auchinvreck and Viscount Grampian of Auchentony whose estate bordered on Craigendhu.

Helen watched the ceremony from the gallery accompanied by her daughter, Roseanna, who was now nearly nineteen years old, and James Brodie. James was now a very sick man and close to death but he had been determined to make the journey to London and see his son installed as a Peer of the Realm.

'Ah, John, you kept the faith and didn't let the bastards get you down,' he whispered afterwards to his son. A week later he died a proud man and was buried in The Grange Cemetery in Edinburgh, near his home in Dick Place.

Six weeks later John was pouring over his papers in the dining-room in Heriot Row when Grace, on one of her rare visits from Craigendhu, entered the room.

She was now sixty-five years old, a slim figure who still held herself well. She was wearing a powder blue silk dress and her hair, still jet black, was obviously newly done. She walked precisely across the room, seated herself carefully on a chair facing her husband, folded her hands neatly on her lap and announced: 'I want a divorce.'

Arthur Charles Lomax Buchanan-Scott, third Baronet and second Viscount Grampian, soldier, diplomat and Scottish Representative Peer, had returned to live on his Speyside Estate when the British Mandate in Palestine ended in 1948. Within two years he had become a Deputy Lord Lieutenant. His wife was the eldest daughter of the seventh Duke of Stirling and Clackmannan and from the moment their feet touched the moors on their 25,000-acre estate, Viscount and Viscountess Grampian were at the top of Grace Brodie's list of lunch, dinner and party guests at Craigendhu. Though the peer and his wife amply returned her hospitality, Grace both sneered at and envied Camilla Grampian's indifference to impressing people and lack of attention to detail as a hostess.

Lady Grampian died of cancer in 1965, leaving a husband who was still very much in his prime at the age of sixty-three. He was of medium height with a lean, athletic frame and a round face housing grey eyes which were constantly lit by laughter, a slightly pug nose and a surprisingly determined chin. On his Speyside estate, where he lived in plus-fours or the kilt, he was as much part of the scenery as the buzzard or the deer. And even when he wore an expensive Savile Row suit on the river terrace at the House of Lords, he brought an air of the hills to the city. He was a gregarious, witty man, who got on even better with women than he did with men.

'You've made me believe in life and the future again,' he said to Grace six months after his wife died. They were sitting on the terrace at Craigendhu, where the light was making the brilliant jewel blue Cairngorm mountains seem just at the bottom of the garden and the first shades of autumn were colouring the silver birches swishing in a light breeze. 'Because you've invited me to so many splendid parties you've forced me to get out and keep moving and stopped me staying at home and sinking into a slough of despond and despair,' he said. 'And even when you weren't giving a party I always knew I could drop by and have a chat with you. And that has meant a very great deal to me.'

His clear grey eyes met hers in a look that for a moment she was not quite sure how to handle. Though she was very social and manipulative, Grace had never really been at ease with men.

'It's what we're here for,' she said briskly.

It made such a difference when one's efforts were appreciated. Of course she knew she was a much better hostess than Viscountess Grampian had been. But she'd had to work at it to help her husband's career, unlike the aristocratic Camilla Grampian, who had done nothing with her life. Quite what a man as charming as Arthur had ever seen in Camilla, Grace had never understood.

That Christmas Viscount Grampian and his three

grown-up sons were house guests at Craigendhu and Arthur stayed on for the New Year as well.

'What you need, Arthur, is a new wife,' Grace informed him on the afternoon of New Year's day.

The snow had come on Boxing Day and the bright white mountain wilderness which now invaded every room seemed all the more beautiful when you could toast toes by a blazing log fire, as Grace and Arthur were doing in a cosy, chintzy sitting-room.

'You're right,' he said in an even tone, his eyes meeting hers in a direct look. 'But, unfortunately, there is a problem.'

'You mean you've met someone?' Grace's voice was shrill and a hollow feeling filled her heart. She thought she knew all about the women in Arthur Grampian's life – at least, that there weren't any except his sister in Canada. He had talked so much about his wife and how lonely he was. There had even been times she had thought he was drawn to her, though she had never encouraged anything like that. Now her lips settled into a familiar thin red line. Men! Even the nicest of them cheated.

'Oh, very much,' he said. 'You look upon a man who has fallen deeply in love.'

How dare he tell her such a thing! She had listened long enough to him talking about his wife . . . she didn't want to hear about some other woman. She felt such a fool. Yet . . .

'And what is the problem?' she asked frostily.

'The lady with whom I am in love and wish to marry is not free.'

'You mean she is married to someone else?'

'I do.'

That's disgraceful. The words were on the tip of her tongue. Why did men always want other men's wives when the world was full of single women who would

391

be only too delighted to marry them? The tea in her half-empty cup was already cold, but she reached for it and took a sip before she said: 'Well, Arthur, all I can say is that I am sorry.'

'For whom? Me or the lady?'

'For all of you,' she said primly, replacing her cup on the table. 'Her husband as well.'

'Don't waste your time feeling sorry for him,' said Viscount Grampian with feeling, leaning forward in his chair. 'He's got this wonderful, absolutely splendid wife and he hasn't given a damn about her for years. She has been unhappy for as long as it has been my privilege to know her but she is so loyal to him. I have never heard her once complain.'

'Do I know this paragon?' she asked sharply.

'Oh, Grace, don't sound so hard,' he said, reaching for her hand before she could snatch it away. 'Don't be so ready to condemn. People cannot always help where their hearts take them, even if it may be to some unsuitable places. I know you have had a very hard and difficult time, though you have never complained. But don't let it make you bitter. It is you with whom I have fallen so deeply in love and it is my dearest wish to make you my wife.'

She blushed to the roots of her hair and her ears and her neck. She was totally overcome and she had no idea what to say or do. Her soul was being stripped naked by this man, her pretences and pretensions being shown up for the rags they were, but suddenly she didn't mind. In fact, she felt glad that at last someone understood what she had suffered.

That was the day she began to change. To find the warm wind of affection and admiration blowing across her life at the age of sixty-five after thirty-six years of loveless marriage was a heady experience. And, as the spring came and snow began to melt on the high Cairngorms and the golden eagle and osprey soared above them, the perma-frost which had encased her heart began to thaw, too – ridding her of old inhibitions. And when Arthur Grampian became her lover, she decided to ask her husband for a divorce.

'Arthur is a good man. I hope you will be very happy,' said John still hardly able to believe what his wife had told him.

'I am,' she said.

The lines around her eyes and at the corners of her mouth seemed softer, her lips fuller and a gentleness seemed to have replaced the normal gauntness of her appearance. Even her voice was softer and her movements more fluid.

'I'll need to think about a divorce,' he said. 'This has all come as a bit of a shock.'

'I'm serious, John. I wish to divorce you on the grounds of your adultery with an unknown woman. That is the most decent, respectable way I can think of doing it. We have to be divorced because I am not going to live in sin.'

'Of course you're not,' he said. 'But I think you should leave it to me to work out the best way of doing it.'

He had had no idea of his wife's attachment to Arthur Grampian, though in retrospect it seemed natural enough. She had made a life of her own at Craigendhu and he had been grateful for it. Now, quite suddenly, the painful journey of his marriage was nearly over and he was going to be free.

He pressed the fingers of both hands together and studied her silhouette against the evening light playing on the gardens. Had they really been bound to each other for thirty-six years? And why had she waited so long?

'Something like this could have happened to you over twenty years ago, if you had given yourself the chance,' he said.

Grace shook her head. 'Twenty years ago I had nowhere to go. I never had until now.'

Something in the way she said it pierced his heart. They had wasted each other's lives.

Grace had never been on a grouse moor, but Arthur had got her interested in forestry and hill-walking and, as his Land Rover bumped over the high moor on August 12th, 1967, she felt full of pleasant anticipation about watching her first shoot from the butts.

There was an Arctic chill in the wind where the Land Rover halted and Grace swung open the passenger door and plonked her feet on the peaty ground. Winter never left the high moors where the air blew pure and clean and fresh as the streams tumbling down them. She inhaled it deeply and looked back down the maze of lower hills through which they had climbed. The trees, far below now, were just beginning to be bright with the apple reds and sungold of autumn; a flawless sky was reflected in a loch of dazzling azure. The woman Grace Brodie had been for most of her life would immediately have thought that all this land belonged to the man she was going to marry and therefore it would belong to her. But the woman she had become these past few months didn't think about who owned the land. She experienced the world through her senses, tingling and bright, as she had never done before.

She saw the sunlight sparkling on granite mountains and a land coloured lilac and purple unfolding to the north and the south and the east and the west, sensed the wind willing her into its embrace and felt at one and at peace with the world and everything in it. I have never

394

been happier than I am today . . . the realisation floated up from her heart and over her mind. I didn't know it was possible to be so happy.

She looked at the man who had made it all happen, standing yards away in his green tweed plus-four suit, peering down the barrel of his gun. He clicked his gun shut and looked at her with a slightly impish smile.

'I just wish it had happened to me sooner,' she said. 'I would have let John go. We were never right for each other. Why did I have to wait for so long?'

'Because I wasn't available,' he said, taking her arm. Other people were decanting from Land Rovers and starting to tramp towards the butts. 'Now, just remember, whatever you do, you'll be perfectly safe so long as you keep your head down.'

It felt colder in the butts, out of the sun, and Grace slipped on wool-lined leather gloves for warmth.

Everyone and everything went quiet. Then a cry went up. There was a fluttering in the heather. Birds rose like a fan opening in the sky above. The sound of gunfire cracked and whistled through the air. The winging birds fell back to earth.

'Good shot, Michael,' Arthur said to one of the party. Then everything fell silent again.

Grace felt something moving near her feet. Her eyes narrowed, her frown came down and she peered closely at the undergrowth. She heard a hiss. Then she saw a snake spiralling rapidly towards her.

She screamed and jumped up as gunfire rang out across the moor. Two bullets went straight into her spine and lower abdomen.

The last shot had been fired before Viscount Grampian saw that the woman he loved and hoped to marry was lying face-down on the rough ground.

＊   ＊   ＊

'Lady Brodie does not have long,' the surgeon-doctor said to John as they walked down the corridors in Inverness Royal Infirmary.

The best resources of the State in the shape of a helicopter from RAF Pitreavie had been put at his disposal to fly him north as soon as Viscount Grampian telephoned him with news of the accident on the moors.

He saw the greyness of death was already upon his wife as he entered the room where she lay supported by a mound of pillows and he sat on the edge of the bed and looked at her, with only minutes of her life left to run. She tried to lift her fingers but she had not got the strength.

He reached for her hand and held it between his own. It was already cold.

'Forgive me,' she whispered. 'Forgive me for what I did. I had nowhere else to go ... not even in the beginning ...'

Then she was gone and he realised that it was only her will, that proud defiant will with which she had always sought to fashion the world to her own ends, that had kept her alive until he got there.

He let her hand go and bowed his head, grateful for Arthur Grampian's decency in leaving him alone with her at the end.

Afterwards they went for a long walk along the banks of the River Ness, in silence, their heads bowed, their hands clasped behind their backs. As they retraced their steps along the river bank, their pace slowed until they stopped and gazed across the water to the castle, which looked like a giant pink chess piece. It was actually the Sheriff Court House and John had often appeared at sittings of the High Court circuit held within its sandstone walls.

'Grace was a very beautiful and brave woman,' said

Arthur Grampian. 'She was full of kindness and under-standing for what people suffer in this life — because she had suffered so much herself. Yet the face she showed to the world was always smiling. She was a very brave woman indeed.'

Their eyes held in a long, meaningful look. Arthur Grampian was talking about a woman John Brodie had never met, though he felt he had perhaps glimpsed her on her deathbed. A woman redeemed by love.

At that moment he wished with all his heart that it could have been different for them.

'We wasted each other's lives,' cried John in anguish. 'I should have stood up to her father and refused to marry her. But I didn't. Why? Because I was afraid he would destroy my career. I should have left her at the end of the war. But I didn't. Why? Because I was afraid it would damage my career. Grace should have left *me* at the end of the war. We had been apart all of it. But she didn't. Why? Because she was afraid she would be alone. We weren't happy and all we did was to prevent each other finding happiness with anyone else. Our lives were based on fear, not love. And now Grace is dead my life is nearly over and it's too late!'

Chapter Thirty-Four

London and the Scottish Borders – June, 1970

'It looks to me as if the Court of Appeal got it quite right,' said Lord Warrender, strumming his fingers on the arm of the big comfortable red leather armchair in which he was sitting in the library of the House of Lords.

As a peer and holder of high judicial office, he was sometimes invited to sit in judgment with the Law Lords, the team of nine full-time judicial peers who were the highest civil Appeal Court in the land. Though two of the permanent team were drawn from the Scottish Bench, Scottish criminal appeals did not get beyond Edinburgh.

Most of these final appeals were heard by five Law Lords and sometimes the Lord Chancellor, who was titular head of the team, presided over a case himself. But he was not among those sitting with Lord Warrender around a stone hearth, drinking coffee from fine white china cups decorated with the gold portcullis insignia of the Palace of Westminster.

'Oh, I'm not at all happy about how the Appeal Court argue several points,' said Lord Harvey, an English judge.

Monday mornings always begun in the same way for the Law Lords. Having read the judgments of all the courts below over the weekend, they met in the library on Monday mornings to discuss a case among themselves before the Court sat at eleven o'clock.

Unlike judges in the lower courts, the Law Lords did not dress-up in wigs and robes or sit at a higher level than the counsel who appeared before them. They wore lounge suits and sat around a semi-circular table in a room at one end of the Committee Corridor in the Palace of Westminster. Its high ceiling was decorated with an ornate cornice where it met walls covered in a red and gold flocked paper and lined with leather-bound legal volumes. Judges, counsel and solicitors all sat on upright red leather chairs, the backs of which were embellished with brass studs and the gold portcullis insignia, and each judge had by his side a small bookcase in which relevant legal reference books were placed. Sometimes a civil servant from the Lord Chancellor's Office sat by the carved wooden fireplace at the judges' backs and two attendants in tails sat or stood near the doors, ever-ready with a large glass jug to replenish the decanters of water placed beside each judge and counsel. The public seats were at the back of the room – two rows of wooden benches, each big enough for three people.

It was in this atmosphere of awesome informality (where the lower courts were simply referred to as 'below') that decisions which could affect everyone who lived or did business in the United Kingdom were made. Out of two million cases started in the courts each year only about a hundred got this far and only because the law was uncertain and needed to be settled.

'The Law Lords always have to be looking ahead,' Robert had once told Helen. 'They have to think of the effect their decisions could have. They have to consider if they are improving the law or if they might be making a mess of things.'

While a case was being heard the Law Lords discussed it over lunch and when a hearing was finished and they had cleared Committee Room One of lawyers and public they continued to sit around their semi-circular table discussing it. Starting with the most junior, each judge gave his opinion and if they all agreed the presiding judge asked one of them, usually an expert in the particular field, to write a first draft of the judgment, which was then circulated to the others for amendments. If they disagreed, they all wrote separate judgments in the first instance.

'They just keep talking after that,' Robert had told Helen, 'and having lots of discussions. Some of them change their minds as they go along and they listen to what others have to say, particularly if it is a knife-edge case.'

The Law Lords did not reconvene to deliver their judgments; one of them simply announced their decision at a sitting of the House of Lords and their judgments were made available afterwards to lawyers, Press and public.

The case of the Northumberland Housing Trust -v-Whitelaw Construction had been rumbling through the courts for years, and when he read the papers at the weekend Lord Warrender decided the English Appeal Court had been right in deciding that the builders had overcharged. But he had not felt well all weekend and it had taken him twice as long as usual to read the papers.

On Monday morning he left the flat in Hyde Park Gardens, where he and Helen made their London home, early to walk across Hyde Park and St James's Park to Westminster. But he could not shake off the persistent pains in his left arm.

Counsel were on their feet when they entered Committee Room One and, as they sat down, Lord Warrender raised his right hand to summon an attendant.

'It's a bit stuffy in here. I think we could use these for a bit,' he said, pointing to one of two three-prong fans suspended from the ceiling.

The fans began to spin around, but he felt no better and

400

now he had chest pains. Why did he have indigestion? He had hardly eaten any breakfast. Be still, he willed his stomach, and, concentrating hard, focused his eyes on Donald MacLeish QC, senior counsel for the Northumberland Housing Trust, who was already on his feet.

With Robert's encouragement, Donald had left Edinburgh and carved a successful career at the English Bar. And he was married and had a family now.

A hint of a smile played Robert's eyes as he recalled how he had fashioned Donald's career.

'Mr MacLeish,' the presiding Law Lord addressed Donald.

'My Lords . . .'

The words and Donald's face, dark and intense, were the last things Robert Warrender heard and saw before a fatal heart seizure engulfed him.

Lord Warrender was buried in the family vault beneath the chapel at Auchinvreck on a summer's day exactly like the one on which he had brought his second wife to his ancestral home twenty-four years ago.

Watching his coffin being lowered to his last resting place through her veil and her tears, Helen did not feel she was really saying goodbye to this strange, complex, fascinating man who had given her a new life and identity when she had been lost and alone, and the daughter she had longed for. Their great friendship had endured throughout their marriage. Death could not take it away. They were simply going their separate ways for a bit and one day they would meet up again . . . as they had always done . . .

Chapter Thirty-Five

Parliament House, Edinburgh – September, 1972

'Your daughter and my son make a fine professional team, don't you think?' said John Brodie.

He and Helen were standing in Parliament Hall watching Roseanna Warrender, who had been called to the Bar that morning, and Angus Brodie pacing the hall in the time-honoured style of lawyers discussing their cases.

'Roseanna certainly enjoyed devilling for him,' said Helen.

'A new generation preparing to take our place,' he said. 'But not yet. Not while we're still here. Time passes so quickly, don't you think?' Helen nodded, smiling. 'Forty-two years seems no time at all since you and I were their age and first met on that wonderful yacht. Of course, they've probably got another forty-two years to waste if they're as silly as we were.'

'We?' Helen raised her eyebrows.

'Correction. *I*,' he said. 'But you and I don't have that kind of time to waste any more. And it seems a pity to waste what we do have left . . .'

As their eyes met and held she knew that at last everything was possible for them now, as it had been in the beginning . . . and at last the time was right . . .

Author's Note

A conservative government under Winston Churchill was in power in 1952 when the Lord President of the Court of Session and Lord Justice-General was the late Lord Cooper of Culross and the Lord Advocate was the late Mr J. L. Clyde QC (later Lord Clyde).

The tradition of the Lord Advocate's automatic appointment to the top judicial posts in Scotland was not broken until 1972, when an Outer House judge, George Emslie, became Lord President and Lord Justice-General.